ALSO BY TONY BULL

TINKERS CREEK

FINAL

RECKONING

For Pat

with love from

Tony Bull

Tony Bull

This is a work of fiction.
Events described here are imaginary.
Some settings exist but characters are fictitious
and not intended to represent specific persons.

FINAL RECKONING

Paperback ISBN 978-0-9522661-8-1

Published and distributed by
Laburnum Books,
Furze Hill, Fordingbridge,
Hampshire, SP6 2PX

Printed and bound in Great Britain by
CPI Antony Rowe
Chippenham & Eastbourne

For Beryl

Acknowledgements

I would like to thank my friends Jan Deakin and Keith Coello for their help with editing, Mike Hallett for his help in preparing this book for the printer, and members of the Ringwood Writers' Circle for their helpful criticism and support.

PROLOGUE

Brackenslade Friday

The phone call from Dan taking him back more than thirty years came when Greg was a couple of miles out on the heath.

'Hi Greg. Dan here.'

'Hey, Dan! Hello!'

'Where are you? In the garden?'

'No, I'm out on the Forest with the dog as it happens, why?'

'I've been ringing the cottage since before lunch. Then it occurred to me you might just sometimes switch your mobile phone on! Listen, something weird has come up. Concerning you.'

'Me? How come?'

'Remember I told you my chaps found some bones when we started on the extension to the marina?'

Greg chuckled. 'Yes, and your bad temper when they turned out to be human and the police made you stop work!'

'Well, they have identified the bones.'

'Oh, right. So you can get on now then, can you?'

'Well, in a few days apparently. But the point is, the police are saying they are going to have to interview you. I thought I'd better let you know as soon as possible.'

'Interview me? What on earth for?'

'The remains were of somebody called Nigel Heapes.'

'Ah.' Greg's stomach gave a lurch.

He couldn't have said he had completely forgotten but it was many years since he'd given any thought to what had happened all that time ago. The body had never been found and no-one had ever known what really took place that day. No-one except him, that is, and he knew only part of the story. And Suzy, of course, although he'd never been quite sure how much she had actually seen.

Part One

—

In The Past

ONE

Seastone, Sunday,

It had never occurred to Greg to consider whether or not he was happy. Every now and then though, a sense of well-being would come over him and he just knew it was good to be alive.

He was always alone at such times, the way he was one warm evening, just after his eighteenth birthday, sitting back, relaxed, tiller in his right hand, making his way on a beam reach across Priory Bay towards the afterglow of the sunset. There was not much on the water, a big tanker on its way to the oil terminal, a few home-going yachts in the distance. It was peaceful, just the background hum from the direction of the naval base and the small sounds the boat made as it cut through the wavelets.

The sea was calm, low tide but coming in, and just enough off-shore breeze to keep the little boat steady on course to round the rocks at the Point. Once past the Point he would line up directly on the pier-head and after that it would be plain sailing indeed across to the slipway at the end of the High Street. It would be getting dark by then, but Pete and Frank should be there to help put the boat on its trailer and he'd have time for a coffee with them before going to work at the Pier Hotel.

He felt good.

As he was coming up to the Point, he could see someone climbing out over the rocks. There was not enough light to see clearly, but it looked as though he was carrying a fishing rod, which was strange because within half an hour the rocks would be under water.

Just then he began to notice the sound of a high-revving engine from somewhere astern, and glancing over his right shoulder, he saw a white speedboat about half a mile farther out racing on a course almost parallel to his, which he guessed would bring it in to the Yacht Club. He watched it for a while, wondering how it might feel to be rich enough to own a boat like that and go dashing here and there across the water. That was just the sort of thing that would impress Josie's mother. Then he realised it was in fact the boat that Nigel Heapes had been showing off in earlier in the day. Josie had been duly impressed with the boat, but it hadn't changed her mind about Nigel. 'Heapes gives me the creeps,' she'd said, as she slipped her arm through his and pulled him away.

He smiled at the thought and then had to turn his attention to altering course as he came past the rocks at the Point. He pushed the tiller away from him, pulled in the sail and lined the bow up on the pier-head.

He'd just settled back again when it occurred to him that the speedboat sounded surprisingly close. He looked back and saw twin bow waves like great, white wings a few lengths away, rushing directly at his stern. He leapt up, pulling the tiller hard over and got ready to jump.

The speeding boat missed by inches and a cascade of water struck the dinghy, tilting it and flinging him out. He smacked into the sea with a shock hard enough to knock all the breath out of him, and sank in gurgling, bubbling darkness until his shoulders hit the bottom. He straightened up and kicked hard towards the dim light high above. It was probably no more than fifteen feet but it seemed much too long before he came to the surface, spluttering and gasping.

He started to swim back to pull himself back on board, and the speedboat, having continued its circle, came drifting up close alongside, with the engine idling. Nigel Heapes grinned down from the cockpit.

Greg yelled up at him, 'You crazy bastard!'

'What's up? Fall in, did you?' said Heapes, grinning all over his fat face.

'What the hell d'you think you're doing?'

'I want that parcel you collected.'

'What?'

'That parcel you picked up at Foreland. I'll take it!'

Greg had no idea what he was talking about. 'Squire' Davis had paid him a few pounds to collect his dinghy from Foreland and sail it back to the slipway. Nothing had been said about a parcel. He swam back to the dinghy and grabbed hold.

'I haven't got any parcel!'

'You'd better have!'

'I haven't got a bloody parcel!' he said.

'Stop buggering about.' said Heapes. 'I know you've got it, so just get back in the boat and hand it over.'

'You're mad!'

Greg turned his back and started to pull himself into the dinghy, but Heapes swung the wheel, easing his boat forward so that its bow nudged the dinghy's side, rocking it and pitching Greg painfully, head first into the stern.

'Just do as you're told, you scruffy little oik!' Heapes yelled.

Greg had had enough. The Heapes family had been bullying them and pushing them around for as long as he could remember. Maybe Dad felt he had to put up with it - but Greg didn't.

He scrambled up, pulled himself on to the speedboat by the bow rails and leapt at Heapes, catching him with a solid punch right between the eyes. The boat surged forward - Heapes must have jerked the throttle open - and Greg fell towards him. Heapes, back-pedalling and flailing wildly with his fists, trying to keep his balance, caught him on the temple with a blow which sent him crashing down. His head smashed into the side of the cockpit, and he slid to the floor, stunned. He tried to get up immediately but fell over, dizzy, his head ringing from the blow. When eventually he managed to stagger upright, ready to defend himself the boat was pitching and rolling so much he had to grab hold with both hands to steady himself.

He looked around. Heapes had gone.

He lurched over to the other side of the cockpit and looked down, then clambered over to the stern. There was no sign of the fat man.

He stood up and looked all about. The two boats were drifting apart and he waited, expecting to see Heapes surface in the widening space between them. After a bit he went forward and looked down over the bow, then went all around the boat, peering down into the dark water. He called several times and listened. Nothing.

The daylight had almost gone and he began to get worried. He started the engine and eased the speedboat in a tight curve slowly back towards the dinghy, and then past it towards the shore. There was nothing to be seen. He continued to circle slowly, gradually widening the area of search, thinking Heapes might have tried to swim ashore but after several minutes, by which time it was quite dark, he was forced to conclude that he was in trouble.

Although he'd hit Heapes pretty hard, it was certainly not

enough to knock him overboard, but how was he going to explain what had happened?

He toyed with the idea of pointing the speedboat towards the shore, opening the throttle and jumping clear. He was almost sure it must have been too dark for anyone on land to have seen what had taken place. Then he could just take the dinghy to the slipway as planned. No need to mention the speedboat unless he was asked, and then he could merely say he had heard a boat in that area at that time.

But it was more than half a mile offshore, and there was no certainty that the boat would go directly to the land; it could end up anywhere, even drift into the main shipping channel. He just could not chance it.

He manoeuvred the speedboat carefully so that he could grab the painter from the bow of the dinghy and make it fast to the speedboat's stern. Then he got into the dinghy and furled its sail and strapped the tiller so that he could tow it to the slipway.

His friends Pete and Frank were waiting at the slipway. He gave them a rough outline of what had happened and they agreed to take the dinghy in, saying they would meet him in Sam's café later.

Then he took the speedboat to the Yacht Club, tied it up and went to find Commander Vanderling, who owned the club, and told him what had happened. When he came to the point where he'd hit Nigel, though, he missed that part out. The Commander listened carefully until he'd finished and then told him to go home and get changed into dry clothes, but to come back straightway because the police would want to see him. Meanwhile he would inform the authorities and start organising a search party.

oOo

Greg lived just across the road from the Yacht Club, in a couple of rooms above Sam's café. Sam was not only the village postmaster but he also owned the row of buildings opposite the Yacht Club. There was the post office, then the ship's chandlery-cum-general store, and the café on the corner by the bus depot. Behind the café was the hall also belonging to Sam where the Seastone Amateur Drama Society (known locally as the SADISTS) had their headquarters, and between this hall and the café a narrow alley led to an iron staircase which gave Greg a private entrance to his rooms. He usually went in through the café but in his present state he wanted to avoid comment.

He was towelling himself dry after a hot shower when Sam called from outside his door.

'Greg? Are you alright, son?'

Truth to tell Greg was feeling a bit shaky. It was the shock or stress or something like that he supposed, but he said, 'Yes, I'm okay, Sam. Come in.'

'Here's a hot cup of coffee,' Sam said as he came in. 'Frank Hawkins and the Grant boy - Peter is it? – are downstairs. They said there has been an accident. Nigel Heapes fell off his boat and you went in after him?'

Greg took the coffee, which he really needed, and gulped a mouthful. 'Thanks, Sam.'

'Are you sure you're alright?' The old man was looking closely at Greg's face. 'That's a nasty graze you've got on your forehead and there is quite a big bump coming up next to your left eye. I'll give you something for that.' He waited while Greg emptied the cup. 'Now then, what has happened?'

Greg told him all about it as he got dressed, not missing anything out.

'You will have to give a statement to the police,' said Sam, when Greg had finished. 'I'll come with you. You were wise to say nothing to the Commander about hitting Nigel. Don't tell anyone else about that and make sure you have a good reason ready to explain those bruises when the police speak to you.'

'What I don't understand,' said Greg, 'Is how Nigel could have disappeared so completely. I mean, if you fall off a boat you try to swim back, or at least call out for help. But there was no sign of him.'

'I'm afraid the police will think it's strange, too, Greg. If you can't account for it you can be sure they will come to the obvious conclusion – that you must have done something to prevent him from getting back onto his boat - so you'll have to stick rigidly to your story.' He paused, and then said with a sigh. 'Unfortunately it is well known that there is little love lost between the two of you and that won't help either. No, it is a mess. But we'll see it through, son, don't worry.'

'Thanks Sam. It's good to know someone believes me.'

'Well, let's hope they find Nigel and he's alright. But it doesn't sound too hopeful from what you've told me.'

'His father will take it very hard if he isn't found,'

'Yes, of course he will. But don't worry, he won't put any blame on you.'

'Well, I don't know. He might not want me to go and work for him after this.'

'Don't worry about that, Greg. Arthur may be many things but he is always fair.'

'But he thinks the world of Nigel.'

'Yes, he does. He's always had high hopes of him too, but, oh, I don't know, he's a good man is Arthur and he doesn't deserve all the trouble he's had with Nigel. And now this.'

Greg was not sure he agreed with Sam about Arthur Heapes being a good man and his doubt must have shown because Sam looked at him quite severely.

'Now then, Greg, I know you think Arthur's hard on your father but just remember this: he didn't have to go to London five years ago to look for the two of you when he heard you were down and out. It's a very sad thing, son, but your father is an alcoholic and can't look after himself. Arthur gives him a home where he can keep an eye on him. Ideally he would give you a home too but that didn't work out, did it.'

'OK, fair enough. Sorry. It's just I don't like the way he treats my Dad.'

'Well, it's a complicated story, son, and there is quite a bit of history that perhaps you should know more about. I'll tell you all about it one day. Meanwhile we'd better go down and see what's going on.'

Downstairs in the café PC Tindall, the village bobby, was telling Pete and Frank they would be wanted for the search party that was being organised to cover the shore-line looking for Nigel.

'Greg, I have to have a word with you,' he said.

'Let's go through into my sitting room,' said Sam, making it clear he was going to be present.

In fairness to PC Tindall in the light of what happened later, Greg had to admit that he was polite and considerate, even sympathetic. He told Greg to tell him exactly what had happened from when he first saw Nigel's boat until he arrived at the Yacht Club. Sam caught Greg's eye and nodded as if to say: 'don't forget what I told you.'

PC Tindall took notes and let Greg tell him the whole story, interrupting only when something was not quite clear. Then, when he had finished the policeman wanted him to go through it all again while he referred to his notes, and this time his questions were more probing. Greg stuck rigidly to his story, though.

At the end Tindall said, 'We might need to talk to you again, Greg, so please stay in the village for the next few days.'

'Has anyone told Mr Heapes?' Greg asked.

'Yes. He is over at the Yacht Club. They are organising the searches from there. He said he wanted to talk to you. Shall I tell him you'll come and see him?'

Sam said. 'Tell him Greg's a bit shaken up by it all, but he'll be here if wanted. Alright son?'

'No, I'd better go and see him, Sam. In any case, they'll need me to show them exactly where it happened.'

He went with PC Tindall across the road to the Yacht Club and they found Arthur Heapes. Then he had to go through the story once again and he noticed that PC Tindall was carefully checking his notes all the time. Arthur Heapes asked what had happened to make Greg fall into the dinghy; was he sure that Nigel had knocked it on purpose? Greg said he believed so and that's why he was angry, but added he didn't think Nigel had deliberately tipped him out in the first place, just misjudged his speed and come too close. Arthur nodded and gave Greg a sad little smile, saying he was not to blame himself for what had happened and thanking him for all he had done to try to find Nigel.

A uniformed policeman, Sergeant Attrill from Ryde, was organising search parties to cover the sea shore between the Point and the Yacht Club and there were several boats already setting out with torches to search the bay. Commander Vanderling asked Greg to go with his group in the Yacht Club's cabin cruiser, which had a powerful searchlight, and show them where it actually happened. It was quite dark by now, but Greg was fairly sure he could find the place.

They cruised along slowly, the searchlight covering an arc ahead of them, until they were about two hundred yards west from the end of the Point.

'This is more or less where I was when Nigel's boat tipped me out,' said Greg. 'And I circled all round here, almost up to the Point looking for him.'

11

Somebody said, 'Tide would have been about half in wouldn't it? If something fell off a boat here I reckon it would either drift up against the pier or finish up around about the Slipway.'

'Yes, probably' said Vanderling. 'Or it could miss altogether and eventually come ashore on the mainland.'

They searched the whole area between the bay and the Yacht Club several times.

After about an hour without success nobody was saying anything and eventually the Commander said, 'I think we've done all we can tonight, Arthur. Clearly there is no point in carrying on. If there's no news, we can bring the boat out again at first light if you like.'

When they got back to the Yacht Club, 'Squire' Davis and his son, Teddy, were waiting.

Teddy Davis was a couple of years older than Greg and one of Nigel's cronies. Quite unlike his father, who was a bluff, hearty Yorkshireman, known as 'Squire' because of his habit of riding around the village on a big horse, Teddy was generally surly, and his pale, spotty face seemed capable of bearing only one of two expressions, sly or sullen. He was wearing his sly face now.

'Nasty business, Greg,' said 'Squire', clapping him on the shoulder. 'Sorry you had to be involved in a thing like that, lad. What exactly happened, then?'

It had been a long day and the last thing Greg wanted was to go through it all again.

'All I know is Nigel Heapes fell off his boat after nearly capsizing me in your dinghy.'

'What, playing silly buggers was he?'

'Yes, well, you know Nigel - he came up too fast. He said he wanted a parcel I was supposed to have. I told him you never said anything to me about a parcel and he got mad and rammed the side of the dinghy. I don't think he damaged it though,'

'Then what happened?'

'I don't know. I fell head first into the bottom of the boat and when I got up he'd gone.'

'You didn't hear anything? Or see anything?'

'No, Mr Davis,' Greg said as patiently as he could, 'I banged my head when I fell in the boat. Look.' He showed him his bruises. 'I haven't the faintest idea what happened to Nigel.'

'Oh. Yes. Right,' said Davis. 'Well, it's a mystery, then.'

'Yes.'

'Well, as I say, I'm sorry I got you involved in it, lad.' He turned to leave. 'You coming, Teddy?'

'In a minute, Pop.' Teddy sidled up to Greg. 'What was all that about a parcel, mate?'

'Nigel thought I'd collected a parcel at Foreland.'

'Did he say why?'

'No.'

'Somebody must have told him you had a parcel though.'

'I suppose so. Look, Teddy, I've had enough questions for one day, alright?'

'Yeah, only it seems funny, that's all. He didn't say who it was who told him?'

'No he didn't, and I never asked him, okay? Now bugger off!'

'Yeah, alright mate, sure, Sorry.'

TWO

Suzy had waited all afternoon. It was now well into the evening and she'd finished her third, or was it the fourth, vodka, and she was feeling very sorry for herself. She realised she'd known all along that Bob was just using her. After all, she was well aware of his reputation. But at least he always made her feel wanted, and when she made him agree to see her just one more time she imagined, hoped anyway, that she could keep him interested. But he hadn't come, hadn't even phoned.

She knew she had everything a woman could ask for. She ought to be content. Roddy had told her when he first asked her to marry him that she could always have anything she wanted. He just wanted her to be happy. He kept telling her that, every time he proposed to her, and although she had eventually given in five years ago, he was still telling her. She knew it pleased him to give her things. She knew he really did want her to be happy. She wished she knew why she was not. And the vodkas weren't helping a bit.

But she took her empty glass to the bar and poured herself yet another generous measure, catching a glimpse of herself in the mirror. At least she still had her looks. The youthful freshness may have faded, but she was maturing well

She wandered out on to the terrace, and resting her elbows on the balustrade, she looked out over the lawns and the paddock and down to the bay. It was a pleasant evening, warm and still. Overhead a ridge of high cloud was mauve tinged with pink, and to her left the horizon was a strip of bright orange, above it a thin line of pale violet haze. Otherwise the sky was clear.

Out beyond the Point a small white motorboat was speeding in towards the shore. There was a dinghy sailing across the Bay and it seemed to her that the motorboat was heading directly for it. Suddenly attentive, she watched as the two boats came together.

She moved quickly to the telescope at the end of the terrace. Focussing on the dinghy, she was surprised to see that it had not capsized but its occupant must have been thrown out.

The motorboat was coming back towards it. Arthur Heapes's boy, Nigel, was in the cockpit and she saw that he was looking down at someone in the water but making no effort to help. Then, to her amazement, as the swimmer was trying to get back on board the dinghy Nigel Heapes seemed deliberately to drive the motorboat into the dinghy's side. She was horrified, believing that she was watching a deliberate attempt to sink the dinghy. She'd never liked Arthur's boy, finding him uncouth and ugly, but she'd never thought of him as dangerous.

As she watched, the man from the dinghy scrambled up on to the motorboat and attacked him. This was really exciting. They exchanged a few blows and the other man fell out of her sight into the cockpit. Nigel Heapes climbed forward and picking up a boathook, leant out from the bow as if to pull the dinghy alongside, but suddenly he threw up his arms, twisted round, and toppled over the rail on the far side of the boat. What had happened? She panned the telescope around the two boats but in the fading light she couldn't see clearly and there was no sign of Nigel.

Then she saw that the other man was now looking for him. He turned his face towards her and she could see it was that beautiful young man who lived in the Post Office, William Gregory. Later, she thought that the reason why she behaved as she did was because of the way Greg looked. He was so extraordinarily beautiful. And the wonderful thing was he seemed not to know it.

She watched as he searched for a long time, expecting him to find Nigel, of course. But eventually it was too dark and he must have had to give up. He tied the dinghy to the back of the motorboat and set off to the yacht club, or so she supposed.

Why did she not report what she had seen? Well, for one thing, she had told Roddy she was spending the evening with her sister in Ventnor and it would have been awkward explaining why she was still at home. Also she was not entirely sober, but she knew that is always a poor excuse. It might seem callous, but having seen what had happened, although she did not understand it, she knew it was not Greg's fault that Nigel fell overboard and she supposed she felt protective.

Of course, it was unforgivably irresponsible, but looking back, how could she say she had any regrets? If she had called the coastguard, or PC Tindall in the village she would have missed the most wonderful thing that could ever happen to her.

And the fact is, the incident itself was intriguing, the most exciting thing she had seen for months and she felt enlivened and invigorated, and violently attracted to Greg as she watched him go.

Then she remembered that Arthur had recently given him the chance to train as a barman and her immediate thought was to go to the Pier Hotel in the hope she might see him.

Her depression forgotten, she took the MG too fast down the drive and it skidded on the gravel, narrowly missing the left-hand gatepost as she braked to enter the lane. Realising she had had a good many vodkas, she took it very steadily down to the Pier Hotel.

The first person she saw as she entered was Arthur himself. He was facing her at the far end of the bar, chatting with Graham and Louise Wilson. He waved and beckoned her to join them. Her heart seemed to freeze as the true seriousness of what she had witnessed suddenly struck her, although she didn't know then, of course, that Nigel would never be seen again. But he was Arthur's son and she just couldn't see how she could tell him. She paused, and to give herself time to settle she took a tissue from her bag to remove a non-existent speck from her eye.

By the time she reached them, the barman was ready to hand her a vodka; Arthur knew her poison. She exchanged air kisses with all of them.

'Don't often see you in here on a Sunday, Suzy,' said Arthur.

'Oh, I was just feeling a bit bored and wanted company,' she said lightly. 'Roddy's got a crisis with the regatta committee. He'll be at the Yacht Club till midnight at least. I was going to Ventnor to see my sister but that fell through. So here I am.'

'Always nice to see you,' said Graham, with a sardonic smile.

They had been lovers for a short while when they were much younger and he still made the occasional pass at her. He often told her he married Louise on the rebound from her, which was nonsense as they both knew he married her for her father's money, just as she had married Roddy for his. To be fair to Graham, though, at least he had made good use of the money. He had turned Manor Farm into a thriving concern after his family had let it run down for years, and the estate agency he set up for Louise was doing very well, too.

Suzy noticed that Louise was putting on weight, looking quite matronly and middle-aged, although she was only four years older than herself.

As if on cue, Graham said, 'We were just talking to Arthur about an important event that's coming up soon.'

Louise sighed and rolled her eyes heavenwards. 'Important event! I'm going to be forty in a week or so, Suzy, and he seems to think it's important that everybody should know!'

'Life begins at forty,' said Arthur as if it was an original idea.

'We're going to celebrate here if Arthur will do the catering,' said Graham. 'You and Roddy are invited of course.'

The barman interrupted. 'Excuse me, Mr Heapes, you're wanted on the phone.'

'Who is it?'

'Commander Vanderling from the Yacht Club.'

Suzy jumped guiltily, knowing immediately what Roddy must be calling about. They all looked at her in surprise.

'Roddy checking up on you, Suzy?' Arthur smiled as he went behind the bar to take the call.

'Are you alright?' said Louise, 'You've gone all peeky.'

THREE

At about half past seven the next morning Greg was in the shop carrying out his usual Monday routine of checking and re-stocking the shelves with the various items Sam always liked to have in ready supply.

.Sam called through the open door from the café. 'How are you feeling this morning, son?'

'Oh, alright. I slept pretty well, considering.'

'No wonder. You were dog tired.'

The phone rang in the shop.

'Answer that will you? I'm busy. Tell them I'll ring right back.'

Greg picked up the phone. 'Chandlers.'

'Oh, hello. It's Suzy Vanderling here.'

'Good morning, Mrs Vanderling. I'm afraid Mr Morris is busy. Can he ring you back?"

'Is that William Gregory?'

'Yes.'

'Oh, hello! I'm so sorry to hear about your trouble last night, William. My husband told me all about it. It must have been horrible for you.'

'Yes, it was.'

'How are you this morning? You must feel awful.'

'Er, well, yes.'

'My husband says they are continuing the search this morning. Will you be going too?'

'I don't know. Nobody has said anything to me.'

'Well, look, I hope I'm not being a nuisance but I wonder if I could ask you to bring me a new gas bottle. Oh, and I'm completely out of Nescafé. Could you bring a large tin of decaf as well?'

'Yes, alright, Mrs Vanderling.'

'It's rather urgent. Say within the next hour?'

'One moment Mrs Vanderling.' He put his hand over the mouthpiece of the phone. 'Sam, it's Mrs Vanderling. She wants a new gas bottle and a large tin of decaf delivered, within the next hour, she says.'

'Ah. And I need the van. I'm off to the wholesalers in a minute.

Tell you what, get the old delivery bike out. You can put the gas bottle in the front pannier – she has the big Camping Gaz one.'

'OK.' Greg took his hand from the phone. 'That will be alright, Mrs Vanderling. I'll be there as soon as I can.'

'Thank you so much. Bye-ee.'

'You'll probably have to pump the tyres up,' said Sam, wiping his hands on a cloth as he came through from the café. 'When was the last time you used it?'

'Back in the winter some time. Mrs Vanderling says they are going to carry on searching. Should I offer to help?'

'If I were you, son, I'd keep a low profile unless they ask you particularly. Taking that gas bottle out to Abbots House will be a good excuse. I should go as soon as Sophie gets in, and don't hurry back.'

Sophie Hawkins was the older sister of Greg's friend Frank. She ran the Post Office counter very efficiently and also helped in the shop when necessary. Greg was somewhat in awe of her because she stood no nonsense, rarely smiled and did everything, as she liked to say, 'by the book'.

The old bike was right at the back of the store room. Greg pumped up the tyres and oiled the wheels, steering and chain, then found a piece of rag and gave it a good wipe over. It was a big, clumsy thing of nineteen-twenties vintage, with a wide metal basket fixed to the front of the frame, a battered old saddle and just the one gear. Even without a load it was hard work pedalling up hill.

After washing his hands Greg packed the coffee and gas bottle into a cardboard box and put it in the metal basket. Then after Sam left, he manned the shop until Sophie arrived at exactly half-past eight as usual.

'I hear you've been getting yourself into trouble, young Greg,' she said as she let herself into the Post Office counter.

'Mmm,' he replied. There was no point in trying to explain to Sophie that he hadn't exactly got himself into anything. He didn't know what Frank might have told her but she would have formed her own opinion regardless; as far as she was concerned her young brother and all his friends were irresponsible young ne'er-do-wells and whatever happened to them was their own fault.

He said, 'I'm going out. I've got to go over to Abbots House with a delivery.'

19

'Don't be too long, then. I don't want to be running this counter *and* the shop all morning.'

'You won't be. Sam will be back by eleven.'

'Eleven! For goodness' sake! It shouldn't take you more than half an hour, surely!' She was always easy to wind up.

He took the bike out the back way into Rope Walk and pedalled off to the Square. This was the longer way round but it was a more gradual climb and he didn't fancy standing on the pedals all the way up the High Street.

It was already a warm, sunny day and by the time he reached the top of Pier Road, he was breaking into a sweat, and glad of the long freewheel down to the pier. Then it was another hard slog up Priory Road until he came to the entrance to Abbots House. He dismounted here and pushed the bike all the way up the steep gravel drive to a flat parking space by the garages. The door of one of the garages was open so he lent it just inside against the wall and took out the box.

A flight of steps led up to a paved area around the front and one side of the house, which was a rambling single storey, built in the nineteen-thirties in an art deco style, the walls white and curved, with wide windows.

Greg went to an open door at the side, put the box down and rang the doorbell.

A woman's voice called, 'Who is it?'

'Chandlers, with the Gaz bottle and coffee.'

'Just one moment.'

After a minute or so, Suzy Vanderling appeared in the corridor in front of him. In the light from the morning sun streaming through a window behind her, her long, blonde hair was a bright golden halo and her flimsy clothing was almost transparent as she stood, slightly in profile so that he had a clear view of her perfect figure - a teenage boy's fantasy. He began to feel even warmer and embarrassed. He had never seen a woman's body so exposed before, except in pictures.

'Come in,' she said.

He picked up the box and walked towards her. She smiled warmly at him and didn't move. She was certainly a good-looking woman, he thought, not exactly pretty like Josie, but there was a kind of perfect ripeness about her.

'I'll take the coffee,' she said and reached forward to take it out of the box. Her dress fell open, as she must have known it would, revealing one bare breast.

She smiled at him again, adjusting her dress.

'If you will just bring the gas bottle through and leave it in the scullery, at the end on the right-hand side.' She moved aside, slightly. Her body gave off a musky fragrance and he felt nervous and excited as he passed her in the narrow space.

'Just leave it on the floor by the sink, would you, please.'

He went into the room, put the box down, stood up and turned to leave. She was standing just inside the door, staring intently at him, her lips slightly parted. There was something in her expression that he couldn't identify, as if she was struggling against an internal pressure. He felt even more uncomfortable.

'Do you have to hurry back?' she said, tilting her head and smiling up at him under one raised eyebrow, 'Or can you join me for coffee?'

'Er, no,' He stammered, 'I mean, I don't have to hurry back.' The words seemed to come out of their own accord and as soon as they were spoken he felt he ought to have said he had to get back to the shop, but she was being so pleasant and friendly he didn't want to seem rude.

'Come on through to the sun lounge then.'

Almost reluctantly, because somehow she had taken control and he didn't know what to do about it, Greg followed her into a long room with windows all along one wall, overlooking the sea. There were rush mats on the polished wooden floor. Chairs and sofas in light-coloured cane with patterned cushions were grouped around two low, glass-topped tables.

She motioned with her free hand at one of the sofas. 'Take a seat and I'll make us some coffee. What do people call you? William? Bill? Billy?'

'Greg usually.'

'Greg.' She paused. 'Yes, it suits you better – you don't actually look like a William.'

He sat on the edge of the sofa she had indicated and she stepped towards him, clutching the coffee tin close to her with one hand and with the other touching her fingers very gently on the bruise by his left eye.

'That looks painful.' She moved her fingers onto the graze on his forehead and away. 'Last night?'

'Yes.'

'Poor you. It must have been awful when you realised you couldn't find him.'

She shook her head, looking down at him sympathetically. She was standing very close.

Greg stared up at her. He noticed that her large eyes were a very deep blue and there were tiny creases at the corners. He wondered what was going to happen. The strange look came over her face again and for one moment he thought she was going to bend down and kiss him. Her mouth looked soft and inviting.

Then she moved away quickly. 'I'll go and see to the coffee.'

Greg sat there in confusion. She seemed almost to be enticing him, but that couldn't be so. Could it? Suppose she *had* kissed him, though, what would he have done? It looked as if she had nothing on under that flimsy robe. And she was very attractive, very sexy. He thought of Josie, sweet, pretty seventeen-year old Josie, who was the only girl he had ever really wanted to make love to, although so far they had never gone farther than intimate fondling. What would it be like to kiss someone so much older, a married woman, experienced in love-making? The idea excited him and although he was sure she was just having fun at his expense, he felt a flutter of anticipation as he waited to see what she would do.

She came back carrying a small tray which she put on the table by the sofa he was sitting on.

'I prefer decaffeinated coffee,' she said as she leant forward and poured from an earthenware jug. Again, her dress fell open in the front. This time Greg glimpsed both bare breasts before quickly lowering his eyes. 'Proper coffee seems to make me twitchy, but I really quite like Nescafé with plenty of milk or cream.' She passed him a mug of black coffee. 'Help yourself to milk and sugar.'

She readjusted her dress, picked up her own mug, moved quickly but gracefully around the table and sat demurely at the other end of the sofa.

Greg put milk and sugar in his coffee, stirred it and took a sip.

She said, looking at him over the rim of her mug, 'I believe you are friendly with Graham and Louise Wilson's daughter, Josie?'

'Yes.'

'Are you going steady, as they say?'

'Well, yes, I suppose so. I don't go out with anyone else, anyway.'

'Serious, then, is it?'

'Oh, well, I don't know about that. We just like each other's company.'

'I can't say I know her very well, but she seems a nice, quiet girl. Very pretty.'

'Yes.'

'And I can see what she might see in you. You really are an attractive young man.'

He knew that anything he said to that would sound gauche and inadequate so he stayed silent and waited.

'I'm sorry,' she said, laughing softly. 'I don't want to embarrass you. And I hope it didn't sound patronising because I meant it. Even though I *am* almost old enough to be your mother, I *do* find you attractive. Does that shock you, Greg?'

In fact, he was neither very embarrassed nor shocked, because he had been almost expecting her to make some kind of advance. He didn't know how seriously to take her though.

'No,' he said, 'I can't say it shocks me, Mrs Vanderling, but I don't really know what to say.'

'No, of course you don't.' She smiled. 'But I can see from your face that you are not too upset at the idea, are you?'

'N..no,' he said, somewhat grudgingly, because he still thought she was playing with him and he didn't know the rules of the game.

'And in any case after last night I'm sure you have enough on your mind at present without older women making passes at you. What do you think will happen about the Heapes boy?'

'I really don't know.'

'Are they holding you responsible? What do the police say?'

'Well, I told PC Tindall what happened and he just said I've got to make a proper statement about it sometime today.'

'Well, I'm sure it will all work out right for you. Would you like some more coffee?'

'No thanks, I ought to be getting back. Mr Morris is out and Sophie's having to mind the shop and the Post Office on her own. We get busy on Monday mornings at this time of year.' Greg put his mug on the tray and stood up. 'Thanks for the coffee.'

'And thank you for bringing it. And the Gaz bottle.' She stood up, pulling her flimsy dress around her. I've enjoyed meeting you, Greg. Will you come and have coffee with me again one day?'

'Yes, alright. Thankyou Mrs Vanderling.'

'Good, one day soon then. I'll think of something else for you to deliver.' She gave him her lovely warm smile again looking hard into his eyes. Then she walked quickly to the door. 'I'll just show you out.'

As he followed her through to the door he had come in by, Greg had the impression he just had passed a test.

In the doorway she lightly touched his wrist. 'I do hope everything works out alright for you.'

'Thankyou, Mrs Vanderling.'

'Suzy,' she said. 'Think of me as Suzy, Greg, Bye.'

He smiled goodbye and went back down the steps to the bike in a state of euphoria. This rich lady – considered by many to be the best-looking woman in the area, whose husband, Commander Roderick Vanderling, owned not only the Yacht Club, but also the very exclusive Quarterdeck Club and the Pier and its Amusement Arcade – fancied him! And on the way back to the shop he didn't mind admitting to himself that he was attracted to her too, even if she was quite a bit older, and he hoped it would not be too long before he had to make another trip to Abbots House.

By the time he was coasting the bike down from the Square into Rope Walk though, he had started to calm down. But his uneventful life had been remarkably transformed in the past twentyfour hours by two very significant events, and Sam always said important things tend to happen in threes. Greg didn't have long to wait before finding out what the third would be.

FOUR

Monday

Suzy stood back, one hand on the edge of the door, watching as Greg ran down the steps, collected the old bicycle and free-wheeled down the drive. She closed the door and leaned back on it with a sigh of pleasure. She had done it, met him and spoken to him and touched him, and although he was just a boy, a beautiful boy and she was double his age and he might think she was too old for him, she knew she had made him interested in her, willing to see her again.

When she had taken the can of coffee from him and then moved aside for him to pass her in the narrow passage, he had been so close she had wanted to reach out again and touch him, but her limbs had seemed to stiffen. Following him to the door of the utility room, and watching his lithe body move as he bent down to place the heavy gas bottle on the floor, she had been shaken by a flood of desire, feeling faint and breathless for a moment, wanting to gasp as she leaned back against the door frame.

And in the sun lounge she had run her fingers over the bruises on his face as he sat looking up at her, and her mouth had ached with the desire to be kissed.

It was strange, but exciting, an adventure, and she wondered if she could make him love her. Then she realised that she was thinking like the kind of man who uses a woman's love for him to get her into bed; did she really need to make Greg love her to gratify her lust? Because that's all it really was. It wasn't love and she knew it. No, all she had to do was find some way to get him to herself, in secret and on her own terms, and give him just enough encouragement.

She yawned suddenly. It had been well past midnight before Roddy had come home and then he had wanted to tell her all about the search. He had been unusually animated, saying repeatedly that he couldn't understand why they had not been able to find any trace of Arthur's boy, as he called him.

She had to pretend to be shocked at the news, of course, and listened patiently while Roddy described Greg to her, but he seemed very anxious to impress on her his belief that Greg was

25

in no way to blame and she wondered why.

Afterwards she had spent a restless night. On the one hand her conscience was troubling her because she had not said anything about what she had seen, but on the other she was planning a way to meet Greg and see if she could get to know him. Now, she thought ruefully, it was too late to be bothered by her conscience because her plans were working out.

She went to the bathroom, ran a bath and soaked in it. Lying there, she let her mind wander, thinking about the men she had known. None of them had stirred her as much as Greg did, and the thought of his closeness to her made her touch herself, just a little, then a little more until, if she hadn't reined herself in she would have climaxed. She could give herself an orgasm as powerful as the best anyone else had given her, but that wasn't what she needed.

She thought back to what Becky had said only a few days ago.

'Your biological clock is ticking, love. In not so many years time it will be too late and your body is telling you that, even if your mind doesn't recognise the fact.'

A child. That was what her sister was telling her she needed. But although Suzy dearly loved her neices, and had followed with delight their progress from infancy through to adolescence, she had never envied Becky, never having thought of herself as maternal.

She had asked Roddy, when they were first married, if he wanted children, thinking that that may have been one reason why he had so persistently asked.her to marry him. But he had merely said he wouldn't mind having a child, if that was what she wanted. She had stopped taking the pill, mainly because she couldn't see the need for it any more, but also out of a vague curiosity, wondering what might happen. After the first few weeks, however, their lovemaking had become infrequent and sporadic, only occuring on her initiative, because although he was so attentive to her well-being in every other respect, Roddy was quite unaware of her sensuality.

A child.

She wondered if Becky might be right. She tried to envisage a baby at her breast, miming the action of nursing, but she felt nothing at all, so if there was a maternal need in her it must be hidden in her subconscious.

The water was getting cold. She stood up and stepped out of the bath, and vigorously rubbed herself dry. Then without putting on her bathrobe, she walked through to the bedroom and opened the doors of her master wardrobe to pose before the full-length mirrors inside. Adjusting the doors so that she could view herself from various angles, she was pleased with what she saw and believed Greg would be too. There was no surplus fat, no sagging flesh; she looked fit and healthy, her due reward for the regime of exercise she had followed for many years.

She supposed she was lucky that she enjoyed physical exercise, especially swimming and running. Her day generally began with several lengths of the pool, followed by ten to fifteen minutes working with weights, although this morning had been an exception. Every Tuesday she drove over to Ventnor and ran with her sister for an hour on Boniface Down unless the weather was exceptionally poor, and once or twice every week she visited the Sports Club to use their up-to-date equipment, toning up the muscles that the other exercises missed.

Thinking of the Sports Club, reminded her of Bob Clarmont Brown, whose idea the club had been and who had persuaded Roddy to back him in setting it up a few years ago. He could at least have phoned on Sunday, instead of letting her wait in vain all evening. Well, compared with Greg he was nothing and she wanted no more to do with him. She would tell him so next time she saw him.

Meanwhile, she would put her mind to making arrangements for her next meeting with Greg.

FIVE

Monday

Greg went in the back way and left the bike in the storeroom, going on through to the Post Office to let Sophie know he was back. There were two large men standing to one side of the counter.

Sophie said, 'These two gentlemen have come to see you, Greg,' She looked even more serious than she did usually.

One of them stepped forward, a fat, middle-aged man whose large round face had features that seemed too small for it. When he spoke he had a hoarse, high-pitched voice, and a supercilious manner. Greg took an instant dislike to him.

'I am Inspector Salway and this is Sergeant West of the Hampshire and Isle of Wight Constabulary, sir. You are William James Gregory?'

'Yes.'

'I have to ask you to accompany us to Ryde, Mr Gregory,'

'To Ryde? What for?'

'To help us with our enquiries into the disappearance of Nigel Heapes.'

'But I told Mr Tindall all about it yesterday.'

'We would like more details, sir. And we shall have to have a signed statement, if you don't mind.'

'Can it wait until Mr Morris gets back,' he asked. 'He shouldn't be long.'

'I'm afraid not sir, We have already experienced some delay.'

'Oh, well, alright. Will you explain to Sam, Sophie, tell him what's happened?'

'Yes, of course, just as soon as he comes back.'

The inspector took Greg's arm to steer him towards the door. He shook him off.

'Just a minute,' he said, 'How long is this going to take?'

'I really couldn't say, sir.'

'Well, if I've got to go into Ryde I'll just pop upstairs and fetch a jacket and my wallet and stuff - if *you* don't mind!'

'Very well, sir. Sergeant West will accompany you.'

He began to feel very nervous. The sergeant followed him upstairs, peered through the doorway into the kitchen, opened the door to his little sitting room and had a brief look around, then came into the bedroom and watched while Greg changed his clothes and put wallet, keys etcetera in his pockets.

'Cosy little place, sir,' he said. 'Been here long have you?'

'Five years.'

He nodded, wandered over to the windowsill and picked up the book that Greg was currently reading, "Brighton Rock" by Graham Greene.

'Saw the film, sir, years ago,' he said, waving the book in the air. 'Dickie Attenborough, wasn't it?'

Greg said he didn't know and the sergeant followed him back downstairs.

There was a police car with a uniformed driver waiting outside. Greg was told to sit in the back and Sergeant West sat beside him. The inspector muttered something to the driver but apart from that nobody said anything on the short journey to Ryde. Only the occasional chirp from the radio broke the silence

At the police station they took him into a small room with a bare table and two hard, upright wooden chairs in it, told him to sit down and left him there on his own. He sat there getting more apprehensive by the minute. He tried to calm himself down by thinking back to his meeting with Suzy Vanderling, but that didn't help at all. He could hear the sound of voices in the corridor and occasionally footsteps passed the door, but nobody came in until, after about half an hour a uniformed constable put his head round the door.

He said, 'Would you come with me please, sir.'

He led the way to a much larger room where Sam was waiting, then left them together.

Sam said, 'Now, Greg. I've come along to see fair play and make sure they treat you alright. They have given us a few minutes before they question you.'

'Thanks Sam.'

'I asked the inspector if you're here as a witness or a suspect and he said as a witness, but just to make sure, tell me, have they arrested you?'

'Arrested me? No!'

'They didn't caution you?'

'No.'

'Have they told you that anything you may say may be given

in evidence?'

'No.'

'Good.' He smiled. 'Have you said anything to them already?'

'Well, no, except that I have already told PC Tindall what happened.'

'And have they said why they've asked you to come here?'

'Only that they want more details. And they want me to sign a statement.'

'Right, well, you stick rigidly to what you told Ray Tindall, no variation at all, you understand?'

'Yes, of course.'

'OK. Now, just so that you are clear on your rights at an interview, remember, you are here of your own free will, helping the police with their inquiries, so nothing you say can be held against you. But, if during the interview they decide to caution you, from then on the situation changes.'

Greg's confidence was steadily slipping away. 'I'm beginning to think they do suspect me. You know, of doing something to Nigel,' he said.

Sam looked solemn. 'Well, to be frank, Greg, they wouldn't have brought you here if they didn't think, rightly or wrongly, that you have information of some kind.'

'Well, I can't add anything to what I've already told them.'

'That's right, and remember, you don't have to answer any question you don't want to.'

'Won't that look bad though?'

'Doesn't matter how it looks, son. If there is any question you feel doubtful about, for whatever reason, don't answer it.'

Greg thought about this for a moment or two. 'What do I say if I don't want to answer?'

'Keep it simple. Let's put it this way, it's better to say you can't remember than to be vague or change your mind about something. And if you are simply not sure of something, say so, or that you don't remember.'

The same constable as before opened the door and asked if they were ready for the interview. Sam told him they were. They followed him along the corridor to a door marked 'Interview Room 1'. This room was similar to but slightly larger than the one Greg had been in earlier. The floor was covered in a kind of shiny beige vinyl, the chairs and table were of the same cheap wood,

30

and one of the two fluorescent lights flickered spasmodically. The air was stuffy and stank of stale tobacco smoke. Inspector Salway and Sergeant West came in behind them and the uniformed constable went away.

Sam and Greg sat on one side of the table, the two policemen on the other.

Sam asked the inspector what was the current state of his investigation.

Salway opened the folder he had brought in with him and after leafing through the documents quickly, he looked up at Sam and said in a flat voice, as if giving evidence in court: 'We are making extensive enquiries, but as yet there is no indication as to what may have happened to Mr Heapes. We are continuing with extensive searches of the sea and coastline in the immediate vicinity. We are in process of arranging for a recent photograph of Mr Heapes to be circulated and arrangements are being made to put him on the missing persons register. Local media are being kept informed and are co-operating.'

Then he muttered a few preliminaries in a monotone, thanking Greg for being willing to help them with their inquiries (as if he had any choice), saying that Sergeant West would take notes, and explaining that there were certain facts he wished to establish. Salway had a small mouth with thick, pouty lips in a pudgy face and the flabby build of a man who likes his beer. His little eyes were pale blue and deep-set, but Greg had the impression they would not miss much.

He asked first what was Greg's relationship with Nigel Heapes.

Sam asked if this was relevant and the inspector said it could be and would he bear with him.

Greg told him the bare outline of his connection to the Heapes family and he asked Greg if he liked Nigel.

'No,' he said.

'Why not?'

'Because he is a bully,' he replied.

Then he wanted Greg to tell him what had happened on the previous afternoon starting from when he arrived at Foreland to collect the dinghy.

Greg went through the whole story again and Salway listened without interrupting until the point where Greg had been flung out of the dinghy and was swimming back to it.

31

'The speedboat came back drifting up close alongside the dinghy, you said?' he asked.

'No. Close alongside me.'

'So he was looking down at you from the cockpit?'

'That's right.'

'How far away from the dinghy?'

'About twenty feet.'

'OK. What happened then?'

'I swore at Nigel for tipping me into the sea.'

'And?'

'He said he wanted a parcel.'

'He wanted a parcel. What were his exact words? Can you remember?'

'I'm pretty sure he said: "I want that parcel you collected." I didn't understand so I asked him what he'd said. He said: "That parcel you picked up at Foreland. I'll take it.".'

'OK. Go on.'

'I didn't know anything about a parcel. I just swam back to the dinghy and grabbed hold of the side and told him I didn't have any parcel. He didn't believe me and he swung his boat round and rammed the side of the dinghy just as I was climbing back into it. I was pitched head first into the stern. It knocked me a bit dizzy and when I managed to get up I was pretty angry so I pulled myself up onto the bow of the speedboat to have a go at Nigel.'

'You were going to attack him?'

'Yes, I was. Well, I'd had enough. First he tips me into the water then he gives me a nasty bang on the head. As I said, I was angry.'

'OK. Go on.'

'Well, he wasn't there. I mean, not on the boat.'

'He wasn't there. It's not a very big boat though, is it. Didn't you notice he wasn't there before you climbed onto it?'

'No.'

'Why not?'

This was a question Greg couldn't answer of course, so remembering Sam's advice he said he didn't know.

'Don't know? Didn't you look to see where he was?'

'I just pulled myself up onto his boat.'

'Even though it must have been obvious he wasn't there?'

32

He didn't answer and Salway stared at him for a full minute, eventually saying, 'Let's get this clear. Nigel Heapes in his speedboat rams the dinghy as you are getting back in and it tips up and you fall into it and bang your head hard enough to make you dizzy. Right?'

'Yes.'

'Banged it twice, did you? Bit of a black eye *and* a graze on your forehead.'

'Must have done.'

'Must have done. Hmm. Bruise easily, do you?'

Again Greg thought it best not to answer.

'Only, if you hadn't said otherwise, I would have thought that lump by your left eye was just the sort of bruise a right hook would make, say from a big fellow like that Nigel Heapes, who as you say, you didn't like because he was a bully.'

Sam could see Greg was more than irritated by the inspector's insinuations. He said mildly, 'Greg has already said Nigel wasn't there, Inspector.'

'Yes, he has, hasn't he. Okay, Mr Gregory, so you got on board the speedboat to have a go, I think was the expression, at someone who wasn't there. Then what?'

'Well, when I couldn't see him, I started to look for him.'

'Why?'

'Sorry?'

'Why? Why were you looking for him, still wanting to have a go at him, were you?'

'I don't know, I think I was more puzzled than anything else.'

'Puzzled. Hmm. Okay. Where did you look first?'

'In the cockpit I think.'

'Why there?'

'Well, he wasn't on the deck.'

'OK.'

'Then I shouted out, called him, and looked all around the boat, thinking he must have fallen off trying to get into the dinghy to get this parcel he thought I had. But there was no sign of him.'

'Must have fallen off. Hmm.' Salway pursed his fat lips, sucked in a long breath and exhaled noisily. 'How long did that take?'

'I don't know. A couple of minutes maybe. Anyway, it was soon obvious he wasn't anywhere near the boat, so I started the engine and drove around slowly looking for him.'

'And what were you going to do when you found him?'

'Well, get him back on his boat, I suppose.'

'And that's all, is it? You weren't angry with him any more then?'

'I was pissed off with him to be honest! Look, I was supposed to be taking the dinghy to the slipway and he'd made me late. It was getting dark and my mates were waiting for me. But I couldn't find him anyway and in the end it got too dark to see.'

'So you gave up.'

'No, I didn't just give up! I went to get help, and I couldn't leave the speedboat drifting around the bay so I took it back to the Yacht Club.'

Salway nodded, leant back, yawned as he stretched his arms above his head and said, 'OK. That all seems to tally pretty well with what you told PC Tindall last night.' Then he leant forward, elbows on the table, hands clasped under his double chin and looked steadily into Greg's eyes in silence. After a long moment he said slowly, 'Only there's the matter of the boathook, you see.'

'Boathook?'

He nodded. 'You haven't mentioned it.'

Greg looked at Sam, wondering what was coming next. Sam raised his eyebrows and shrugged.

'When they took the speedboat to its mooring last night,' said Salway, 'They noticed the boathook was missing.'

When Greg said nothing he continued, 'You didn't notice the boathook was missing?'

'No.'

'Not even when, as you say, you went to get hold of the dinghy to tie it behind the speedboat?'

'No.'

'Surely you would have looked for it at least?'

'I didn't think about it.'

'Didn't think about it. Hmm. Well, I'm not much of a boating man myself, but I've always understood that's what a boathook was for. Hooking boats. No?'

'As I said, I never even thought about the boathook.'

'Mind you, it would make quite a handy weapon if, say, you happened to be thumped on the side of the head by a bigger bloke and wanted to keep him away from you, wouldn't it?'

Again Greg could see that was a question he shouldn't answer.

'Anyway, it was found early this morning, floating by the pier. We've sent it to the boffins for examination, just in case there's any evidence on it, but it's probably been in the sea too long. Any fingerprints or blood on it would have been washed off, I expect.'

When Greg made no comment, he went on, 'Of course, there may not have been any blood on it at all. I mean, a good hard prod in the belly, in self-defence, perhaps, would be enough to knock the breath out of someone even of Nigel's size and make him fall into the water. Was that what happened, Mr Gregory?'

Sam stood up and said forcefully, 'You have no grounds whatsoever for making these insinuations, Inspector. We do not know yet that anything has happened to Nigel Heapes. It's been less than twentyfour hours after all, since he was last seen.'

'Quite so, sir,' said Salway, 'But Mr Gregory here was the last person to see him, apparently, and I'm afraid that in view of the fact that he has so far been unable to explain satisfactorily what did actually happen, I am going to have to detain him for further questioning.'

He stood up, and intoned formally, 'William James Gregory, I am arresting you on suspicion in connection with the disappearance of Nigel Heapes.'

Greg shook his head in disbelief.

'You do not have to say anything at this time but anything you do say may be given in evidence. You should be aware that if you do not mention when questioned, something which later you rely upon in court, your defence may be harmed. Do you understand?'

'This is ridiculous!' said Sam.

Salway ignored him. 'Do you understand what I have said to you, Mr Gregory?'

'Yes,' he said, 'Yes, I understand but you're wrong. I told you what happened.'

Salway picked up his folder and moved towards the door.

Sam asked if he could have a few minutes to speak to Greg in private. Inspector Salway readily agreed, rather to their surprise. He and Sergeant West picked up their papers and went out leaving Greg and Sam together.

Sam said, 'First of all, son, don't worry, arrest on suspicion is just a formality. It's not the same as being charged, but they can question you more thoroughly and record everything you say and use it in evidence if they do bring a charge against you.'

'How long will they keep me here?'

'I believe they can hold you for twentyfour hours without charge. Longer if they can prove good cause. I expect you'll have to spend a night in the cells.'

'But what can they charge me with, Sam?'

'Nothing at the moment, son. There's got to be evidence that a crime has been committed before a charge can be brought.'

'The evidence in this case being Nigel's dead body, I suppose,' said Greg. Then he had an awful thought: 'Suppose they do find him dead, will they charge me with murder?'

'No, son. Before they could do that there would have to be something clearly showing he was killed, and, something directly connecting his death with you, and we know that's not going to happen, don't we.'

'Yes.'

'Well, then. Now, you just stick to your story and we'll have you out of here tomorrow at the latest. In the meantime, just in case there's any hold-up, I'll have a word with one of my pals whose son is a solicitor and we'll see if he can help. I'll pop in again this evening. Is there anything you want me to bring?'

'Oh, I don't know. Something to read perhaps?'

'OK. Keep your chin up.'

Sam left and a little later the uniformed constable came and took Greg to a cell.

During the afternoon Sergeant West spent the best part of an hour with him in his cell going through all the questions he had answered in the morning and then after leaving him alone for another couple of hours, Salway came and went over the whole thing yet again. Greg was sticking tight to his story, however, and eventually it must have become obvious that they were not getting anywhere, so they produced a typewritten statement which Greg duly signed, but only after two or three re-drafts, and when Sam arrived at the police station with his friend's son, the solicitor, they made no objection to Greg going home.

Of course, word that he had been arrested had spread through the village and although he had been released without charge, the damage was done. Over the next few days it would become painfully clear to him what most people thought.

SIX

Tuesday

The next morning after breakfast Suzy phoned her sister Becky to confirm their usual Tuesday meeting. 'And there's something rather special that I need to talk to you about,' she added.

She had spent much of the previous day trying to think of ways by which she and Greg could get together without drawing attention to themselves, and she had come up with an idea which she thought would probably work. However, the more she thought about putting it into action, the more she worried about whether she would have the courage to see it though. After all, this would be an entirely new experience for her and she needed to confide in somebody who would give her moral support, although perhaps moral might not be quite the right word, she thought wryly. Becky had always been her only real confidante though, and she was never censorious.

She broke her journey to Ventnor to call in at Bob Clarmont Brown's boatyard, and found him immersed in paperwork in his office. He looked up as she let herself in. She shut the door behind her and stood leaning back against the frame, waiting for him to say something. He just looked at her, his face expressionless.

'I waited for you on Sunday until it got dark,' she said eventually.

'Ah, yes. Something came up, I'm afraid,' he said.

'You could have phoned.'

'Wasn't anywhere near a phone, and then it got late so....' He shrugged.

'So you didn't bother,' she said. 'Well, you needn't bother in future, either. You can find someone else to play with.'

'Okay, Suze,' he said.

'Is that all you've got to say?'

He shrugged again and raised his eyebrows. 'It's your choice.'

She shook her head, 'You really are a cold bastard, aren't you?'

Knowing he wouldn't deign to reply, she turned angrily, flung the door open and strode out.

He didn't even have the decency to apologise, and she was well rid of him she decided as she drove out of the village.

Becky was waiting as usual outside her house in Mitchell

Avenue when Suzy arrived. She got into the MG and they drove the short distance to the little lane leading up onto St Boniface Down and stopped in the car park at the viewpoint end. Their regular run was a little over 3 miles in a circular route along footpaths, starting roughly north from this car park for about a mile then left downhill and then left again through a farm and up the steep slope to rejoin the lane leading back to the car, thus completing the circuit. Occasionally, when the surface was not too wet and if they felt up to it, they would extend their route a further mile by turning off towards Wroxall before heading back through the farm.

Becky said, 'What do you want to do today, the short run or the long one?'

'I'd prefer short and sharp today, fast as we can, alright?'

'Yes, alright. Race you?'

'OK.'

The sisters were very much alike except that Becky, the older, was taller and beefier. Both were very fit and looked strong and healthy.

They set off at a fast pace, Suzy leading. By the time they had reached the farm and were starting up the steep slope, she was several yards ahead, but gradually Becky gained on her until they arrived together at the junction with the lane. Then it was a mad race to the car, Becky winning by about a second. They bent over the bonnet of the car, facing each other, laughing and gasping for breath.

'Oooh! Gosh! That's cleared all my cobwebs away,' said Becky, 'How about you?'

'Yes. Just what I needed.'

When they had got their breath back they got into the MG and Suzy drove them back down to Becky's house. As she was parking the car Becky said, 'On the phone you said there was something special you wanted to talk to me about.'

'Yes, that's right but it can wait 'til we have our coffee.'

Becky looked at her. 'Serious then, is it?'

'Sort of, but, you know, it would help to talk to somebody.'

'OK. You have first shower while I get the coffee.'

When they were seated in a shady spot behind the house, Becky passed a cup of coffee to her sister and said, 'Is it anything to do with your, um, arrangement on Sunday, by any chance?'

'Well, yes, I suppose it is, in a way. Did you hear about the boy who went missing in the bay on Sunday?'

'Yes, I did. From the Pier Hotel wasn't he? They haven't found him yet have they?'

'No.' Suzy paused. 'I saw it happen,' she said.

Becky stared at her. 'What do you mean, you saw him disappear?'

'I saw what actually happened.'

She told Becky all about what she had seen on Sunday evening and her subsequent meeting with Greg on Monday morning. 'Roddy says the police arrested him yesterday afternoon and took him to Ryde but then they let him go. Poor boy, he hasn't done anything wrong. And, oh, Becky, he's such a lovely boy!'

'A lovely boy?' Becky's eyebrows rose.

'Yes, he really is! He's beautiful!'

Becky smiled sympathetically. 'I haven't seen him, of course, but I accept that to you he is beautiful and so you cannot help feeling attracted to him.'

'But why do I feel like this? It doesn't make any sense.'

'It doesn't have to make sense, love, but it is a perfectly natural human reaction because we are all affected by beauty. It could be anything, a piece of jewelry, a view, or a person even. We all like beautiful things, we want to be near them, to hold them, to possess them. It's how we are.'

'It's certainly how I am with Greg. But it's such a strong physical attraction.'

'Yes, well, he's not only beautiful, he's male And perhaps you happen to be especially vulnerable.'

Suzy was silent for a moment. Becky's insights were usually right. If Greg did not look the way he looked, then he would be just another teen-aged boy, and would not be able to affect her in this way. But the fact was that he did. Then she realised what else her elder sister was saying, aware as she was of Roddy's limitations.

'So,' said Becky, breaking the short silence, 'What do you want me to say? And don't ask me for sympathy because I'm too envious.'

Suzy smiled. 'I want your advice, I suppose. Tell me what you think I should do.'

'Oh, that's easy. It's too late to tell you what you should have done at the time, but you know that already. As to what you should do now, you have a straightforward choice of action and you already know that too, really. One, try to make sure to never see him again. That could be painful and, later, you might have regrets but it would be safe. Or two, go for it, let yourself enjoy the chance to do something different. That could be exciting and risky, and it could also end up being painful because eventually you will have to lose him.'

'Lose him?'

'Of course. You don't imagine there can be any future in such a relationship?'

'I hadn't thought.'

'No, you are infatuated, intoxicated by this young man's beautiful body, aren't you? And you don't need my advice, you just think you need my approval. Well, I strongly disapprove.'

Suzy looked at her in dismay.

Becky gave her a broad smile and said. 'So come on, give us a hug!.'

SEVEN

That same morning Bob Clarmont Brown had come into Sam's shop and asked him if he could spare Greg for an hour.

Clarmont Brown ran a boat-building and repair business from a workshop in Rope Walk just behind Chandlers. A tall, lean, sun-browned man in his late twenties who rarely smiled, he was clean-shaven, usually immaculately dressed in tight-fitting flared jeans with a wide leather belt, open-necked white shirt, and a gold medallion on a chain around his neck. He wore his dark hair long, sometimes in a pony-tail and drove a souped-up pre-war Jaguar sports car around the Island roads and a powerful speedboat around its coastline. A champion sea angler, he ran fishing trips from the Yacht Club for wealthy visitors. He was also a first-class shot, and unbeatable locally at darts, billiards and snooker. It was said that he played a mean game of poker too, and that women were fascinated by him.

Greg's friend Frank, who was apprenticed to him, admired him immensely, as did other young men of the village, but although Greg could appreciate his versatility, he found him arrogant and self-absorbed, with little regard for the feelings or the needs of others. Sam was one of the few people for whom Clarmont Brown seemed to have any respect at all, but Greg suspected this was because he found Sam useful to him from time to time.

He often asked Greg to help out in his workshop when he needed an extra hand or some unskilled labour for the odd hour or two and Greg insisted he was always paid in cash. This morning he wanted Greg to clear the floor of the main workshop so that a catamaran that had just been repaired could be taken away at lunch time. He showed Greg what needed doing, telling him to salvage anything useful or re-usable and scrap the rest. Then he went into his office by the entrance, closing the door and leaving Greg to it.

Having cleared the floor all around the catamaran Greg was fetching the broom from the back of the workshop for a final sweep through when a red MG two-seater drew up at the entrance. Suzy Vanderling got out and went quickly into Bob's office without knocking. She was wearing a red track suit and running shoes, he noticed.

Before he had swept halfway the office door swung open suddenly and Suzy strode out, head up, with a tight smile, and eyes blazing. She didn't notice Greg and he watched as she flounced into her car and sped off. He glanced into the office through the open door. Bob was busy writing at his desk as if he had never been interrupted.

When Greg had finished and put the broom away he went to the office door.

Bob looked up. 'All done?'

'Yes.'

'Good.' He fished in his pocket and threw a few fifty pence coins at Greg. 'Catch! And shut the door, would you,' and he went back to his paperwork. Greg thought that was typical of the man.

He walked back to the shop thinking to himself that if he had not had coffee with Suzy the morning before he would have taken no notice of her brief visit to Bob's office. As it was he was intrigued, wondering about her relationship as a married woman with this single man, well known as a philanderer. Her husband, the Commander, was at least twenty years older than she was. Perhaps he was not able to satisfy her and she was looking for someone who could. Hence her behaviour yesterday towards him? She had said quite plainly that she thought he was attractive and she clearly meant physically. Greg found himself becoming aroused at the idea and realised that he wanted to play along with her, but what should he do?

She had said she would invite him for coffee again. Should he wait to hear from her or make contact first, show her he was interested? He didn't know. This was a new situation for him and he saw it as an opportunity that he didn't want to lose.

For the rest of the morning he was distracted. He couldn't get Suzy out of his mind. Sam must have noticed, although he misunderstood the reason for Greg's preoccupation and at lunch time he told him he felt sure the police would not bother him again, so he was not to worry.

He said, 'If you feel a sense of guilt over Nigel's disappearance, that's only natural. But you did everything you could to try to find him and it's really not sensible to blame yourself for a situation which Nigel brought on himself.'

Dear old Sam. He meant well, of course, but in fact he made Greg feel guilty for misleading him over the true cause for his distraction – lust after another man's wife. Not that Greg felt any guilt about the lust itself, far from it.

He took the van out in the afternoon to make some deliveries. Coming back he had to pass the entrance to Abbots House and he tried to pluck up courage to go in, but when it came to the point he drove on past, afraid of humiliating himself.

When he got back to Chandlers, his father was waiting for him in the café. He had made an effort to smarten himself up and was wearing a clean tee-shirt and jeans and had shaved. Greg had not seen him since the previous Saturday evening when he was in his most usual state, maudlin drunk, and now, seeing him leaning on the counter with a cup of coffee in his hand, chatting and laughing with Barbara, the day manageress, he was struck by how frail he had become, how old he looked. He was fiftyseven years old and looked more than seventy. Greg felt a sudden rush of love and sympathy as he went to join him.

'Hello Bill,' he said. He had always called him Bill. He had been Billy to his mother, but after he had come to live with Sam, five years before, they had decided that he would be known as Greg to everyone else.

His father took Greg's hand in both of his. 'Sorry about your trouble with Nigel. How are you coping with all the fuss?'

'Oh, I'm alright,' Greg said, disengaging his hand.

'Yes,' he said, blinking his watery eyes and smiling. 'You'll be alright. You're tough. You're a survivor, you are.'

Barbara poured Greg a cup of coffee. 'You want another, Steve?'

'No thanks, love,' he said. 'I'll be getting along in a minute. Just wanted a moment with my lad here.'

'How are you, then, Dad?'

'Oh, same as ever. Listen, I told Arthur I was coming to see you. He wants you to know he hasn't forgotten about the bar job, but he's going to leave the training for the time being.'

'I see.'

'It must be awkward for him, Bill.'

'Yes, of course.'

'He wants you to come in tomorrow night, though, about half-

43

eight to help as usual.'

'Alright.' During the peak holiday season Arthur employed Greg on a casual basis to do odd jobs like helping with washing up after dinner, collecting and washing used glasses, emptying ashtrays and cleaning tables in the bars.

Greg was not really surprised that Arthur had put off the training but he was disappointed. Sam had been trying to get him to decide what he wanted to do with his life but he had not yet come to any decision. Arthur had offered to train him in hotel management, starting with learning how to run the bar, and Greg had quite liked the idea. He knew that Nigel would not object because he wanted a career in the army and was not a bit interested in taking over from his father. That would be for his younger brother, Simon, who was only fifteen and with whom Greg got along very well. He had been looking forward to having a regular full-time job, though, and his disappointment must have shown.

'People make up their minds about things without knowing the facts,' his father said in a matter-of-fact voice. 'I know they do 'cos I do it myself. I mean, I don't know what happened out there in the bay, but I'm damn sure it couldn't have been your fault.'

'No, it wasn't, Dad.'

'No. . Well. .' He sniffed, patted Greg's shoulder and moved away from the counter. 'I'll let you get on.' He shuffled to the door, 'Bye Babs.'

'Bye, Steve. You take care now.'

'And you, love.' He turned, waving a hand vaguely at them and went out.

Barbara said, 'He feels badly that he can't be more help to you, Greg.'

'Yes, I know. I realised that some time ago. I think he knows I understand, though.'

'You were going to start that job yesterday, weren't you?'

'Yes.'

She gave him a measuring sort of look and then moved to the kitchen doorway. 'You and Nigel were fated, weren't you. Something like this was just bound to happen sooner or later.' She smiled sadly, shook her head and backed into the kitchen.

Greg's heart sank. Barbara, who had always been a kind of honorary aunt to him, and in whom he had sometimes confided when he was troubled, obviously believed he had done something to get rid of Nigel. He was deeply hurt that she should think him capable of such a thing. And she hadn't even bothered to ask him to tell her what had happened.

Was this a sign of what he could expect in the coming days he wondered?

It was. That evening, when he met his friends Frank and Pete, even they hinted that he could tell them what really happened out there in the bay - his secret would be safe with them, and later, when he rang Josie to arrange a date, she said that her parents thought it might be best if they did not see each other for a while, especially as they were going on holiday to Monaco at the end of the week. Greg didn't see what that had to do with anything but he got the message.

Nigel Heapes was generally unpopular and it was widely known that Greg intensely disliked him. 'No smoke without fire' was the suggestion that was coming across, and it was the consensus that as a confrontation was bound to happen eventually it was just unfortunate although understandable that Nigel had pushed him too far once too often.

'However', thought Greg, 'Apart from my poor old Dad, and Sam, who is being a tower of strength for me, there is one other person who believes in me - Suzy Vanderling.'

EIGHT

10.00pm, Tuesday

Greg was feeling very low-spirited at the thought that people whom he had taken to be his good friends – Barbara, Pete and Frank, and Josie - believed that he was capable of doing harm to anyone. He had always thought of himself as a good person. In all his eighteen years he had never made enemies, or been in a fight, or met anyone who showed they disliked him, (with the sole exception of Nigel Heapes, of course) and he could not even remember anyone else directing a harsh word at him. Now he was starting to have self-doubts. There must have been at the back of his mind, at least, the idea that if he had not climbed on board that speedboat, Nigel would still be around.

It was beginning to get dark as he walked out of the village, away from the sea with its unpleasant associations, and when he came to Sally Wilson's Gardens, a little triangle of land donated to the village by one of Josie's elderly aunts, he turned left onto the Priory Path which led past Josie's house and through fields and woods to the old ruined Priory, and from there on to St Helens.

He had no clear idea of where he was going or why, except that he wanted to be alone and try to come to terms with his new situation. He knew, somehow, that he had to make a decision of some kind and could not expect always to rely on Sam to tell him what to do.

After about half a mile the path passed behind the grounds of Abbots House. Greg wished he could just call in and see Suzy, the lovely lady who had been so unexpectedly friendly to him (was it only yesterday morning? So much seemed to have happened to him lately), just to tell her how much he appreciated her not accusing him like everybody else, and, he had to confess, to hope she might offer to comfort him, 'make it all better' as his mother used to say.

He wandered on., beyond the ruins, through St Helens and down into the wet lands along the River Yar, and found himself suddenly at the spot where Sam had taken him several times during the summer to teach him how to shoot a gun.

He'd been helping Sam sort out his attic when he'd come across a bundle of cloth strapped up with webbing. He'd commented that it seemed heavy when he pushed it to one side and Sam picked it up, unstrapped it and revealed a .38 semi-automatic pistol with a box of ammunition wrapped in an old army tunic. He didn't say anything about how he'd come by it, but he gave Greg a quizzical sort of look and asked if he'd like to learn to shoot.

There and then, up in the attic, Sam had demonstrated what he called the drill.

When it was Greg's turn to hold the gun he stood behind him giving instructions 'Feet apart, knees slightly bent. Right arm full length, straight out. Hold your left hand against the barrel, cupping it. And keep your eyes on the target!'

Then he made sure Greg understood the necessity of keeping a pistol clean and showed him how to do it.

Sam had chosen this place for practice because few people came here except wildfowlers and the sound of shots would be unlikely to be queried, even out of season. Greg was a willing pupil and Sam was pleased with his progress.

One day, after a particularly successful practice, shooting at targets they'd set up against a muddy bank, Greg remembered saying, 'This is good fun, Sam, but I won't ever be able to fire it, really, will I? I mean, you have to have a licence, don't you?'

'Greg,' said Sam, 'If you're ever in a situation where you really need to fire a gun, the question of a licence will be irrelevant. The point is, you'll be ready.'

Standing here now in the half-light, it occurred to him that he had really enjoyed those sessions, and perhaps the germ of the idea which grew into his eventual career was born at that moment.

Without having resolved anything, but feeling suddenly much less dejected, Greg turned back and retraced his footsteps.

It was nearly midnight when he arrived back at Chandlers. Sam was waiting up for him.

'Barbara told me about the job, son,' he said.

'Dad said it must be hard for Arthur,' said, Greg 'But it's a disappointment, Sam. Why did it have to happen?'

'Come and sit down for a few minutes, there's something I want to say,' he said, leading the way into his sitting room.

Greg sat in his usual chair and Sam went to his sideboard and took out his pipe and tobacco pouch.

When he had his pipe going satisfactorily, he said, 'The other

47

day when we were talking about Arthur I said there was a bit of history you ought to know. I don't know why it was never discussed and I'm sure it would have been easier for you and Nigel, for both of you, if the background had been explained when you first came to live here. But anyway....

'You know I served in the First World War. I was called up in 1917 and after a few weeks training I was posted with a lot of other eighteen-year olds to the trenches in Flanders. There was a big offensive going on when we arrived and the support lines were in complete chaos. Nobody seemed to know what to do with us new arrivals, but eventually some of us were attached to a small group of men who had just come back from leave in England. Their unit had been wiped out in the offensive so they were being sent to another company.

'Three of these men were from Seastone. They were close friends and they had joined up together - Henry Niton, the old gardener who gives you jobs from time to time, Arthur's father, Albert Heapes and your grandfather, Jack Gregory. Jack was engaged to be married to Albert's sister Lillian. They were all older than me and they took me under their wing. We were stuck in the reserve trenches for several weeks and I got to know the three of them quite well.

'Then another big offensive was launched and our company had to go up to the front line in support of the main infantry advance. It had been raining for days and we were charging forward through the mud when suddenly we came under machine gun fire and had to dive into shellholes for cover.

'Henry and I fell into a deep hole half full of water, and above the terrible noise of the guns and men shouting and screaming we heard Jack call out from not far away, 'Albert's been hit.' Henry lifted me up to the rim of the hole and I saw Jack scuttle fast across the mud to where Albert was trying to crawl along several yards away. Jack lifted him onto his back and staggered back through the enemy fire towards our hole. He had reached us and was lowering Albert into the hole when the machine guns got him too. We dragged him in with us but he was very badly hurt.

'All four of us were trapped in that shellhole for twentyfour hours. Henry and I managed to keep Albert and Jack above the water level and we did what we could with our field dressings for their wounds, but just before we were rescued, Jack died.

'Albert was taken back to hospital in England. He recovered but he was considered unfit for further service and was discharged.

'Back on the Island he discovered that he was about to become a father; and that his sister Lillian was expecting Jack's child. Sadly, a few days after his son, Arthur, was born, Lillian died giving birth to your father, Stephen.

'Now then, remember that Jack and Lillian were not married, so Stephen was not only an orphan but also illegitimate. This was much more of a stigma in those days, but Albert felt obliged to take responsibility for the boy, who was in any event his nephew, reasoning that he might well have died in the Flanders mud if Jack had not gone to rescue him, and Jack could have survived. So he registered the baby as Stephen Gregory, giving him Jack's surname, you see. Then he adopted him and brought him up with Arthur.

'I was not around in those early days. I wrote to Albert and Henry at first, but Henry was badly affected by the trenches and wanted to forget those years and everything to do with them. That's why to this day he still lives in that old caravan on his own.

'Albert kept in touch, though. We exchanged long letters every Christmas, and it was him who encouraged me to come and live here in nineteen fortynine. After that, of course, we saw each other often until he died in nineteen sixtyseven, so I think I know quite a bit of the history of Arthur and your father.

'Stephen was a delicate child, whereas Arthur was big and strong, but they were treated exactly the same. Both were expected to help in the daily chores of the hotel and I rather think your father always found it more difficult. I certainly got the impression he felt some resentment that no allowance was made for him being smaller. But the two cousins grew up together happily enough and I don't think there was any bad blood between them.

'When the second World War broke out they were both twentyone, and they volunteered to join the army together, just as their fathers had done. Ironically, though, Stephen, who had been the delicate child, was accepted, but Arthur was rejected on health grounds – he had a heart murmur.

'After about a year Stephen came home on leave and Arthur introduced him to his fiancée, Rose. Stephen and Rose promptly fell in love with each other and before his leave was up they went off together to London. Arthur was upset, of course, but Albert, his father, was furious with Stephen, who he thought had repaid all the years that the family had cared for him by betraying his cousin.

'Several months later Stephen and Rose wrote to say that they were married. But, as you know, they never came back to the village together.

'Albert never forgave your father and mother, but Arthur kept in touch with them, and it wasn't not long before he met and married his Doris, so obviously he was not too upset.

'When Albert died in nineteen sixtyseven Arthur took over the hotel and he wrote to invite you all to visit but your mother was not well enough. Sadly she never got better and then, of course, after she died everything fell apart for your father and you know the rest.'

Sam paused and re-lit his pipe. He exhaled and looked across at Greg with a smile. 'So there you have it. Arthur's a good man, Greg. I know he's always wanted to do what was best.'

Greg sat quietly thinking about what he had just learned. He realised that he had been doing an injustice to Arthur these past years, and felt regret that he had not known the truth before.

NINE

7.30am, Wednesday

Greg and Sam had just finished their breakfast when there was a knock on the closed door of the café and Roddy Vanderling smiled a greeting to them through the glass.

The Commander, as he liked to be called, had taken over Seastone Yacht Club on leaving the Royal Navy in nineteen fortynine. He was a thickset man in his mid-fifties, a little below average height, with a florid complexion, square-shaped head and very short sandy-grey hair. He wore steel-rimmed spectacles and as often as not had a cigar in his mouth. He was generally respected in the village with his pleasant, friendly manner, and in spite of retaining his navy title, always seemed to get his own way by never imagining it could be questioned rather than by a commanding attitude.

'I'll go,' said Sam, folding his Daily Telegraph as he stood up. 'Wonder what he wants, this early in the day.'

They never normally saw the Yacht Club people in the café because the club had its own catering facilities, and Greg assumed the Commander must need something urgently from the chandlery.

He cleared their breakfast things from the table and went into the kitchen to wash them up before starting to set up for the day's business, getting everything ready for when Barbara came in at nine o'clock. This was a routine that he and Sam usually went though together and today he worked as if on automatic pilot – seeing the Commander had inevitably set him thinking about his wife, Suzy.

She had not contacted him since inviting him to coffee and in the cold light of morning, two days after the event, the idea of a relationship between a simple village lad like himself and a beautiful, rich lady like her seemed so fanciful as to be foolish. She was clearly a sensual woman, even he, inexperienced as he was, could see that, and it occurred to him that perhaps he just happened to be lucky on Monday morning to catch her at a time when she was feeling bored or neglected and frustrated and needing a young man to show off to and to flirt with.

Of course, he was flattered that she had showed an interest in him, but although he felt himself more than eligible for a Roedean-educated girl like Josie Wilson, despite her mother's snobbery, he was well aware that he lacked the charm, sophistication and probably even the masculinity that might qualify him as the prospective lover of a woman such as Suzy Vanderling.

So he was amazed at what Sam had to say when he joined him at the sink.

'The Commander's got a little job for you,' he said. 'Apparently Mrs V. has to go to her optician in Newport and he wants you to go with her in case she has to have drops in her eyes and can't see to drive back. Her appointment's at eleven o'clock and she'll pick you up here between ten and half past. I told him I could spare you if you can get the deliveries done before you go. Okay?'

'Er, yes, right, okay,' he stammered.

'It'll make a bit of a change for you, son, get you out of the village for a few hours. She's got an MG sports car, have you seen it?'

'Yes. A red one.'

'Fun to drive, I'll bet. She's a nice lady, is Suzy Vanderling. We don't see as much of her as we used to before she married the Commander.'

'Right, well I'd better get the orders packed, then,' said Greg, much more calmly than he felt.

For the next hour or more he was back on automatic pilot as he packed and then delivered the orders for customers in the outlying areas, but now his fantasies did not seem at all far-fetched. She had kept her word about seeing him again – he had no doubt it had been her idea for him to accompany her – and the prospect of being with her occupied his mind completely.

By ten o'clock he had finished the deliveries and was upstairs in his flat, showered and changed into clean shirt and jeans. As he combed his hair he examined himself in the mirror to check for unsightly stubble, and was glad that his skin looked fresh and clear of acne these days, not that he had ever suffered unduly but it had been an occasional nuisance until a few months ago. And his bruises were beginning to fade, although his left eye was still colourful.

He waited by his bedroom window, looking across to the Yacht Club car park opposite and his heart gave a jump when Suzy's car arrived. The morning was warm and sunny and she had folded back the top of the little two-seater. She got out and walked gracefully over to the shop. She was wearing dark glasses, a short sleeved, light summer dress, sandals on her feet, and her long blonde hair was covered by a bright red headscarf, matching the colour of the MG.

The sight of her had a disturbing effect on him. It was not so much erotic as significant, as though she was bringing news of a special event about to happen.

Greg went down the stairs shakily, knees trembling, heart beating fast and he paused before going through the café into the shop, trying to get himself under control.

'You're only going to Newport in a car with a woman who is twice your age and is only interested in a teenager like you as someone to drive her home if necessary,' he told himself. He didn't believe a word of it though. He was as excited as he ever had been, but he made himself relax and walk casually into the shop.

There was a small queue at the Post Office counter and he didn't see Suzy at first. She was standing at the back of the shop talking to Sam.

Sam said, 'Here's Greg now. Greg, this is Mrs Vanderling.'

Suzy stepped forward, taking off her dark glasses with her left hand and holding the other out for Greg to shake. 'We met the other morning didn't we, Greg, when you brought those things for me', and she winked at him as she gave his hand an extra hard squeeze.

'Hello Mrs Vanderling,' he said.

'Thankyou so much for agreeing to come along with me at such short notice.'

'It's a pleasure,' he said, amazed at his self-assurance. He was beginning to enjoy the game.

'Well, we had better be going. I mustn't be late.' She turned to Sam. 'Thanks for lending me this lovely young man, Sam. Do you need him back in a hurry? Only I might not want to come straight back from the opticians.'

'No, you can have him as long as you like, Suzy. He could do with a bit of a break after all he's had to go through lately. And I'm sure he's dying to try out your MG.'

Suzy put her dark glasses back on and Greg preceded her to the door and opened it for her. There was a slight smile on her face as she passed him and crossed the road to her car. He followed, enjoying the way the light material of her dress revealed the movement of her hips.

They got into the car. She turned in her seat and gave him one of her lovely smiles, then she started the car and reversed onto the road.

As they drove off she said. 'It's all working out very well so far, isn't it?'

'Is it?'

'Oh, come on! You must have guessed.' She shouted over the noise of the engine as she accelerated down the road out of the village. 'This is a perfect opportunity for us to get to know each other. You don't think it happened by accident, do you?'

'Well, I didn't think it was the Commander's idea for me to come with you.'

'Of course it wasn't.'

'What's wrong with your eyes, anyway?'

'Not a thing. But I am due for my annual eye test and after you left on Monday I made an appointment and invented the idea of the eye drops for Roddy's benefit. It occurred to me that it would be an ideal way of seeing you again without attracting unwelcome attention and if it didn't work out between us no harm would be done.'

Greg was amazed at her frankness and he didn't know what to say. He looked across at her. She had told him she was nearly old enough to be his mother, but she didn't look old at all, not like Barbara who he knew was thirty-six, or Josie's mother who must have been about the same.

Suzy was lovely. The lightly-tanned skin of her face, neck and arms looked soft snd delicate. She had kicked off her sandals when she sat in the car and her legs were bare from her painted toe-nails to the hem of her dress which had ridden halfway up her thighs. He wanted to reach out and stroke her.

She sensed him staring at her. 'How have you been getting on these last two days?'

She sounded genuinely concerned and the gentleness in her voice touched him and brought him back to earth.

'Well,' he said, 'I think I've learnt who my friends are.'

'Really? What do you mean?'

'Everybody seems to be convinced I bumped old Nigel off,

everybody that is except Sam and my father.'

'And me, Greg. I don't think so either.' She reached across and patted his thigh.

'Thankyou, Suzy,' he said. He took her hand and held it for a moment.

'I was in the Pier Hotel last night,' she said, disengaging her hand to change gear. 'And, of course, everybody is concerned for Arthur, but he is taking it very well and I didn't hear him accusing you at all. I asked him if he was still going to give you a job and all he said was that it might be as well to let things settle down for a while.'

'Yes, that's what my father told me.'

'You are related to Arthur, aren't you?'

'Yes, he and my father are cousins.'

'I thought there was some relationship.' She paused and gave him a sidelong glance. 'Your girl-friend's parents were in the bar last night, too.'

'Ex-girl-friend,' he said.

'Yes, so I gathered. In fact that was what finally made up my mind about today. It seemed unfair that people had turned against you for no good reason. I knew you hadn't done anything wrong and I thought at least I might show you some support. And Roddy agreed, bless him.'

'The Commander doesn't think I did away with Nigel, then?'

'No. He believes what you told them. He said when you went out with the search party on Sunday night you certainly didn't act as if you had done anything wrong. Mind you, Roddy never has had much time for Nigel. He might even back you up if you *had* got rid of him.'

They were silent for a while. Suzy had decided to by-pass Ryde, taking a longer route to Newport via the country lanes. Greg was enjoying the ride in the open-topped car and they had passed through East Ashey and were heading up towards Mersley Down before she spoke again.

'I hear they arrested you at one point.'

'Yes.'

'What happened?

'It's funny,' he said, laughing. 'After I left you I realised that in less than twentyfour hours my ordinary life had suddenly been changed by two very important events: Nigel disappearing and

55

then meeting you. Well, Sam always says important things come in threes. The arrest was the third one.'

'Meeting me was important to you?'

'Oh yes.'

She slowed down and turned the car off the road into a small layby. She switched off the engine, took off her sunglasses and said, looking straight ahead, 'It was important to me, too, Greg.'

She moved her hand towards him and he covered it with his. Then she turned and clasped his hand in both of hers, and looking straight into his eyes, she said, 'I saw what happened on the boat.'

'You did?'

'Yes, that's how I know it wasn't your fault.'

'But how could you have seen?'

'I was looking out to sea and I noticed a speedboat heading straight towards a dinghy in the bay as if to ram it, so I went to look through the telescope and..... I saw what happened.'

Oh Lord, he thought, this is going to be very awkward.

'Did you see everything that happened, Suzy?'

'The first thing I saw clearly was that the person in the dinghy - I didn't know it was you then – had been knocked into the water. Then I recognised Nigel in the speedboat and saw him drive it into the dinghy as you were getting in. You got up onto Nigel's boat and hit him and you both fell down into the cockpit. Nigel got up and went towards the bow and picked up his boathook, and then, suddenly he fell overboard on the far side from me. After a short while you stood up in the cockpit and that's when I recognised you.'

'So you saw me hit him.'

'Yes.'

Greg realised he was going to have to take the risk of trusting Suzy.

'Have you told anybody else about this?'

'No.'

'Please don't then,' he said, 'You see, the only other person who knows I hit Nigel is Sam and he will never tell. If the police knew they might feel they could charge me with causing Nigel's death.'

'Your secret is safe with me, Greg,' she said, with a little smile.

'No, seriously, Suzy, I could be in real trouble if you told anyone.'

'Rest assured Greg, I won't tell a soul.'

She withdrew her hands from his and faced the front. From their position on the hillside there was a beautiful long view over the upper valley of the river Yar and they both stared without really appreciating it for a long moment.

Then Suzy said, 'Greg, we must be on our way soon if I am to keep my appointment, but before we go I have to tell you something and I want you to try to understand. The reason why I cannot tell anyone what I saw is that I was not supposed to be at home last Sunday evening.'

She paused, rested her forehead on the steering wheel and suddenly banged both hands down hard on the dash board. 'Oh, God! This is so humiliating! But if we are going to be friends I have to be honest with you.' She took a deep breath and went on. 'I knew Roddy was going to be out all day until very late and I told him I was going to Ventnor to see my sister, but in actual fact I had arranged for someone to visit me. A man. He didn't turn up.'

'I see,' he said.

'I wonder if you do.'

He had a sudden insight. 'Was it Bob Clarmont Brown?'

She was astonished. 'How on earth did you know?'

'It was just a guess. I was in his workshop when you called on him yesterday morning.'

She stared at him, her eyes wide and shook her head. 'You are an extraordinary boy!'

He laughed. 'I beginning to think I must be or I wouldn't be sitting here with you having this conversation.' As he said it he realised that his feelings for Suzy were not exclusively sexual. This exchange, following on from their previous meeting, had extended him in a way he had not known before. He felt more mature, more self-confident and he supposed, more of a match for Suzy.

'So we can still be friends?' she said.

'I think we'll have to be if we both want our secrets kept. Agreed?'

She laughed as if in relief, leant across, took his face in her hands and kissed him hard on the lips. 'SWALK,' she said, her eyes sparkling happily.

'Pardon?'

'SWALK – Sealed With A Loving Kiss.'

Then she put her sunglasses back on, switched on the ignition and pulled out onto the road.

They arrived at Newport in good time for Suzy's eye test. She found a space in a car park in the centre of town and Greg helped her put up the hood.

'I have to pop in to see a friend after my appointment,' she said. 'I expect you can find something to do for an hour or so, can't you? Meet me here at twelve o'clock and I'll take you somewhere nice for lunch.'

'Okay'

'Get yourself a cup of coffee or something. Oh, I didn't think, have you got any money with you? Here,' she rummaged in her handbag and came out with a handful of coins which she thrust at him. 'Expenses.'

'No, no, that's alright,' he said, backing away.

'I insist. I don't want you to be out of pocket, Greg.' She reached forward, dumping the coins into his shirt pocket, and kissed him on the cheek. 'Come on, walk me to the optician.' And she threaded her arm through his and drew him along with her.

TEN

It was a few minutes before twelve when Greg got back to the car. Suzy was already sitting in the driver's seat and she reached across to open the passenger door as he approached.

'I love the way you walk,' she said as he settled into his seat, 'Striding out, head up, shoulders back as if you know exactly where you are going.'

He laughed. 'Ah, well, I can't say I know exactly where I'm going at the moment, but I do know you said you'd take me to lunch.'

'I hope you like French food,' she said as she drove out of the car park.

'You're taking me to *France* for lunch?'

'Fool, I'm taking you to a French restaurant in Cowes. Roddy took some friends there for lunch during Cowes Week and he was very impressed so I thought I'd try it and compare notes.'

'I've never been to a French restaurant,' he said. 'Is it posh? I'm not dressed for posh.'

'No, it's quite casual. And don't worry, I'll order for you.'

'Frogs' legs? Snails?'

'If you like.'

They chatted about foreign food, not that Greg knew much about it, and what they each liked to eat. He was surprised that Suzy had an enthusiasm for good food. He had thought that most women of her age were constantly on strict diets to try to keep their figures, and that she was sure to be with a such a lovely figure as hers.

'You noticed, then,' she said, with a sly smile.

'You made sure I did.'

'Touché. But I did want to make an impression. Being that much older, you see, I have to try harder. Incidently, Greg, exactly how old are you?'

'I was eighteen three weeks ago, on the fifth.'

'Gosh, what a cradle snatcher I am! But you look so mature. You could easily pass for early twenties.' She sighed dramatically. 'I shall be thirtysix on the third of next month, twice your age.'

'Seriously, Suzy, you don't seem that much older than me. You certainly don't look it.'

'Well, thankyou kind sir' she said, bowing her head and fluttering her eyes at him. 'But I have always done plenty of exercise, especially swimming. We have a lovely big pool, and I try to swim several lengths every day, summer and winter. And I run and I do weights too.'

They had reached the outskirts of Cowes and Suzy drove through the town and down to the Marine Parade, parking at a place overlooking the harbour mouth.

Taking Greg's arm again she directed him into the High Street, where after a short walk she stopped in front of a plain door set back a pace or two from the pavement. An illuminated sign above it read "chez henri" in small letters. Suzy pushed open the door and they heard a bell tinkle nearby. They entered a small vestibule and a waiter appeared immediately. He approached looking directly at Greg.

'Good afternoon, monsieur, madame,' he said with a French accent.

Suzy said something to him in rapid French.

He replied and led them through the restaurant, which was as unpretentious as its entrance and dimly lit but nevertheless quite full. He indicated a small reserved table at the back, next to a window overlooking the water and asked Greg if they would like the wine list. Suzy said they would. The waiter fetched one and passed it to Greg.

When he had left Suzy took it, glanced at it, put it aside and picked up the menu. 'Is there anything you particularly don't like? I gather you're not vegetarian and not allergic to fish or anything?'

'No, I usually eat anything that's put before me.'

'Good. That makes it easy. As I said before, I shall order for you. I'm sure you won't be disappointed with my choices.'

Then she seemed to stop and think for a moment. She put the menu down and looked at him with a serious expression. Reaching across the table she took his hand in hers and said, 'Greg, you are like a breath of fresh air to me after the men I usually have to put up with and I enjoy your company very much and I want to share something with you.

'All my life I've been "looked after". There has always been some man who will do things for me, as if I am quite incapable of doing things for myself, making my own choices, my own decisions. Today I thought I would like to find out what it feels like to take the man's part.

'I have already chosen who I want to be with: you. And I booked a table for two in this French restaurant because it will be a new experience for you and I can show you how to enjoy it. I shall order the wine and the food and generally do all the things a man would do for me.'

'OK,' he said. Sitting in this strange, intimate little restaurant miles from home with her hand in his he was too excited to care very much what she wanted to do.

She went on, looking down at their hands and linking her fingers in his, 'I've made arrangements for the rest of the day as well.' She paused, then looked up at him, gazing into his eyes and smiling. 'Please don't think it is any reflection on you. It isn't. To me it's the same as if I were the older man and you were the young woman. Do you understand?'

'I think so,' he said, hardly daring to hope that she meant what he thought she meant. 'It's what they call "role reversal", isn't it? We did that at school once. I don't know. I suppose it makes me feel...sort of uncomfortable. No, not uncomfortable. I can't explain it. It's just that the idea takes a bit of getting used to that's all.'

'Yes, of course it does, because it's different. But it's fun, isn't it!'

'Just being with you is fun, Suzy.'

Suddenly Greg felt shy and looked down, in his turn, at their hands still linked upon the table. He hoped he had not grossly misunderstood and was not about to make a fool of himself, but nobody had ever been as frank with him as she had just been so he risked it and said, 'I've thought about you a lot since Monday morning, hoping you meant it when you said we could meet again, and this morning, before the Commander came, I had almost given up. I mean, it's pretty unlikely isn't it, a rich, married lady like you and an ordinary young chap like me?'

'Oh, but you are so wrong, Greg! You are not ordinary. When I saw you and what happened to you on the boat, my heart went out to you. That's why I rang the shop first thing the next day. I had to see if you were alright. And then, to meet you and talk to you, was wonderful.'

61

'But I still say it's unlikely, Suzy.'

'Yes it is, but it is happening to us, so let's make the most of it if we can. Listen, I've known since I was sixteen years old that men find me attractive. And I could choose from any number of ordinary young men if I wanted to. But none of them affect me like you do.'

It was probably at this moment that Greg finally accepted that Suzy was not just playing with him but genuinely wanted them to be close. For the past seven years, since his mother had died, there had been no adult woman in his life, with the exception, as he had mistakenly thought, of Barbara. Now this lovely lady was making it quite clear that he meant something to her, and he felt immensely happy.

The waiter returned and Suzy ordered in French from the menu and the wine list. Greg was very impressed, and amused by the waiter's initial confusion; obviously he was not used to the lady taking charge. In Greg's limited experience nor was he of course, but he decided to do as Suzy had suggested and make the most of it.

He must have enjoyed the meal and being cosseted by Suzy, but all through it he was thinking about what she had said, that to her it was as if she was the older man and Greg was the young woman. Gradually he became convinced it could mean only one thing.

At one point, fishing for confirmation, he asked her what she had meant when she said she had made arrangements for the rest of the day.

'You heard Sam say I can have you for as long as I like,' she said with a little smile.

'Yes, but I don't think he meant all day.'

'As long as I like means until the end of the afternoon at least. Unless you insist on going home earlier, Greg, in which case I would be terribly disappointed.' She made a sad face at him.

'So what are we going to do this afternoon?' he persisted.

'Sam said you are dying to try out my MG. Are you really?'

'Well,' he said carefully, 'I wouldn't mind, if it doesn't interfere with your arrangements.'

That made her laugh. 'We'll have to see,' she said. 'Did you enjoy your crevettes?'

She clearly didn't want to say what her plans were and he

wondered if she perhaps was not so sure of herself as she wanted him to think. It gave a certain satisfaction to his male ego, he supposed, but there was no way he was going to play hard to get.

By the time the meal was over they had drunk a full bottle of wine between them. Greg was not at all used to alcohol, but he was already floating on air over the idea she had put into his head, so it probably made no difference to how he felt.

When the time came to pay, he was intrigued to see "Seastone Yacht Club" printed on the cheque she presented.

She saw that he noticed. 'Business lunch, Greg,' she said. 'I shall compare notes with Roddy and I'm sure we will agree to recommend this place to our members. It was very pleasant wasn't it.'

'Yes, it was. Thankyou.'

They walked back to the car with her arm linked through his again, unconsciously altering their strides so that they matched. It felt comfortable and right for him to be with her, although a moment's reflection should have told him otherwise.

Back in the MG Suzy said, 'We're not going far, just up the hill into Baring Road. We have a little job to do for the friend I went to see in the Tourist Office in Newport. There is a big house which has just been turned into holiday apartments and she needs to know if they are up to standard and ready for occupation. I said I would have a look at one of them for her.' She passed him a set of keys and they set off.

Suzy seemed to know her way around Cowes and after a very short journey they turned into Baring Road.

'The house is called "Eaglehurst", and it's not far along on the right,' she said.

They soon found it, a large Edwardian-style house set well back from the road, with plenty of space to park in a semi-circular driveway. It had recently been redecorated and looked very smart.

Suzy led the way to the front door. 'The whole place is empty at the moment,' she said as Greg found the right key. 'What's the betting it smells of paint and new carpets inside?'

The front door opened into a hallway with three doors leading off it, numbered one to three and in fact there was only the faint odour of cleaning materials together with the stale smell of a house which has been closed up for a while. It was not too unpleasant.

'Number three is ours. It's the top flat.'

The key for number three opened the door to a lift, which took them up slowly and silently. They stood very close, facing each other. Greg was longing to kiss her and he put his hands on her hips to draw her to him, but she put both palms on his chest and gently pushed him away, then took one hand in hers as the lift stopped and the door came open.

'Let's explore the apartment,' she said, pulling him out into the corridor.

There were doors on each side, all open and she wanted to examine every room, opening windows to let in fresh air, turning on taps and switches to test that everything worked properly. There were three en suite bedrooms, a separate bathroom, a modern kitchen with a dining area, and at the end of the corridor, a sitting room stretched across the entire width of the house. Its end wall was mostly glass, facing north, and a settee and chairs were positioned to take in the view. It was all very modern and new.

Suzy went to the window and stood as if admiring the long view over the rooftops to the yachts in the Solent. They had hardly spoken since entering the apartment except to comment on the rooms as they went through them. Now she said, 'Well, everything seems to be in good order.'

She turned and walked towards him, put both hands on his shoulders and looked up into his eyes.

'So what do you think of my arrangements for the rest of the day?'

His heart leapt. He had been right then, to believe that what he had wanted since first seeing her two days ago was not a fantasy. It was going to happen. She wanted it to happen.

Greg drew her gently to him. 'Perfect,' he said.

His experience so far when kissing a girl for the first time had been that they all reacted in the same way, closing their eyes and exerting a gentle pressure with their lips, and then withdrawing after a few seconds.

Suzy was something quite different. She relaxed her whole body, seeming to melt into him, and opened her mouth, searching for his tongue with hers. Her thighs pressed against him provocatively and she soon showed she was aware of the effect she was producing, swaying her hips very slowly from side to side.

She began to undo the buttons of his shirt with both hands. He used his to pull the zip of her dress all the way down, and then to unfasten the clasp of her brassiere.

When she reached the belt on his jeans she unbuckled it and then stepped back, shrugged off her dress and bra, kicked off her sandals and stepped out of her skimpy panties. She held out both hands to lead him to the settee facing the window. She was beautiful. His body seemed to burn, his mouth went dry at the sight of her naked.

'Oh God, Suzy, you're lovely,' He said. He tore his own clothes off and stepped towards her. She took his hands and pulled him gently down on top of her on the settee. He was uncertain and clumsy, over-eager. 'Just relax and let it happen,' she said softly, and she guided him gently with her hands. He could feel the tension give way into a natural rhythm as his entire being became concentrated on her eyes, open very wide, just below him, and he lost any sense of contact with reality for a while.

Only it was such a very short while.

Suzy whispered, nibbling his ear, 'Never mind sweetie, it was your first time. You just need to practise.' And her body shook as she giggled silently.

He started to say something, but she stopped him with a finger to his lips, 'No, don't say anything, just hold me tight.'

They must have stayed in each others' arms like that for several minutes, neither of them saying a word. Greg dearly wanted to apologise for his inexperience and clumsiness, but eventually he realised she had taken this for granted, and he was so grateful to her that a lump rose in his throat and tears came to his eyes. He released her and sat back, and looking down at her lovely smiling face he told her she was the most wonderful thing that had ever happened to him.

'Oh, Greg.' she said, 'I don't know how it is for men, but a woman never forgets her first man, and I'm so happy to be your first woman.'

'I shall never forget this day, Suzy.' He leant forward and kissed her softly on the lips, and then disentangled himself and sat back on the settee. She moved too, curling herself around him.

It was pleasantly warm in the room and neither of them felt like putting clothes back on. Greg was happy just to be with her, stroking her, enjoying the softness of her skin, the femaleness of her.

'Greg,' she murmured, 'I want you to know that this is the first time I've been with a man for a long time. It isn't that I haven't wanted to – I've already told you about last Sunday, haven't I – but I was beginning to believe I was no longer able to attract a man. You have just shown that I still can. But I have a confession to make. When I saw you on that boat, I wanted you in an intensely physical way, and then again when you arrived the next morning, I felt the same. At first, that is.'

She ran her hand over the hairs on his chest, pulling gently. 'But somehow, the attraction started to become more than mere lust and I wanted to know you as a person as well. Do you understand what I'm trying to say?'

'Yes, I think so,' he said, 'Because it was a bit like that for me too. At first I just wanted you because you're very sexy. I thought "Wow! This sexy lady fancies me!" and it really turned me on. But today I enjoyed your company in the car. And then in the restaurant, this role reversal thing and your feelings about it, well, you're interesting.' He paused while he tried to get his thoughts together. It seemed important to tell her how he felt. 'What I'm trying to say is, I'd still want to make love to you but I know I'd just enjoy being with you anyway, even if I couldn't.'

'You are sweet,' she said and reached up to kiss him.

She was quiet for a minute or so. Then she said, 'I suppose it goes without saying that I don't want Roddy to know about us.'

'Won't he wonder though, about you buying me lunch and us staying out all day?'

'It just won't occur to him, Greg. If he should ask, and I doubt if he will, I shall tell him you came with me in the car, we tried out the French restaurant and I agree with his opinion of it, and we went to check out an apartment for Sandy at the Tourist Office. And, if anyone asks you, I'd like you to say the same, please. Otherwise, the less said, the better. Agreed?'

'Yes, alright then.'

They sat quietly again. Suzy had closed her eyes and she was so still he thought she had fallen asleep.

From the moment at his bedroom window when he had seen her car arrive at the Yacht Club, he had felt keyed up and nervous, anxious about how he might measure up to her expectations, if indeed she had any. But she had been tolerant and kind and he felt more calm and at peace, sitting there with her in his arms than he would have thought it was possible to be. He also realised then that a genuine affection was growing between them and he wondered at the strangeness of it.

Suzy roused herself and sat up, using one arm as a prop.

'I don't mean to be unkind to Roddy,' she said, looking at him with a very serious expression. 'He is very good to me in so many ways, but not in the one way that's important to me as a woman. I've always tried to remain faithful, but it's just not in my nature to stay celibate. You see, he has a very low sex drive and he is one of those men who cannot understand that a woman can feel desire for a man's body just as a man feels for a woman's. In fact, I think if he ever did come to believe that it would put him off completely. So you see, it's difficult for me to get him interested in bed.'

Greg was not sure that he wanted to know intimate details of Suzy's married life, but he was soon shown that she was not going to reveal any.

'I'm only telling you this in case you might think I make a habit of this kind of thing. Athough,' she said, letting herself fall back again and pulling his face down to be kissed, 'You might be able to persuade me to, if you really felt like it.'

He was quite unable to answer and the second time, with skilful guidance from Suzy, they were very much more successful.

Afterwards she said as she lifted herself off him, 'You are a very quick learner, sweetie. With enough practice I'm quite sure you would not take long to become expert.'

Matching her playful mood he said, 'But only if I have access to a skilled tutor, I think.'

'As the senior partner in this enterprise,' she said, tapping him lightly on the nose, 'I shall continue to be available for guidance as and when required. But for the moment I think we should see if the showers work because it's time we got ready to go home.'

ELEVEN

At a quarter past eight that evening, Greg was still in a state of euphoria as he set out from Chandlers to walk along the sea wall path to his job at the Pier Hotel.

Suzy had asked him as they were leaving the apartment in Cowes, if he would like to try out the MG, and he had driven them all the way back to Seastone with the hood down, enjoying the feeling of the wind in his hair. Neither of them had said much during the journey, both being preoccupied with their own thoughts about the afternoon's experience.

In the Yacht Club car park he had taken the key out of the ignition, and lent across to pass it to Suzy. Gripping his hand as she took the key, and pulling him towards her, she had kissed him quickly on the lips. From the corner of his eye, Greg had noticed Sophie Hawkins leaving to go home from the Post Office and realised that, glancing across the road, she had seen the kiss. Suzy, however, was unaware and, opening the car door, she had stood up, smoothed her dress, and smiled at Greg, saying 'I'll be in touch. Not tomorrow, but soon. Take care,' and she went quickly into the Yacht Club.

Now, as he approached the hotel, he wondered what Sophie would make of what she had seen.

He found Fat Lena, the ageing, pseudo-Italian chief cook and supervisor of the Pier Hotel kitchens, leaning against the back door, smoking a cigarette. She usually greeted him with a smile and a mocking reference to his good looks, telling him to remind her that he was not a girl, more's the pity. She made no secret of her sexual preferences, but for some unknown reason she liked people to believe she was Italian, called Lena Malone. She was certainly swarthy enough to be mistaken for southern European but Greg knew from his work in the Post Office that she was actually Irish, real name Colleen Molony,

There was no joking this evening, however.

She merely said, 'Ah, good. You got the message then. We didn't know if you would come.'

Greg said, 'Why shouldn't I come?'

She concentrated on her cigarette, took a final hard drag on it,

68

blew out a long plume of smoke, dropped the butt-end and looked down as she put her foot on it. Then she looked back up at him, shrugged, and moved back inside indicating the unwashed cooking utensils.

'Start on those, would you,' she said as she turned away.

Greg knew most of the hotel staff and he was often included in the good-natured banter between kitchen workers and the waiters hurrying to and from the dining rooms, but now he sensed a difference in the atmosphere and nobody said a word to him as he scrubbed and rinsed the pots and pans before stacking them in the big washing machine. Later, as the waiters began bringing him the dirty dishes to be washed, they started, one by one, exchanging the odd word or two, mostly in a respectful, sympathetic tone, and it became clear to him once again that people were now regarding him in a quite different way.

After about two hours, by which time he had done all that Fat Lena wanted him to do in the kitchens, she told him he should go and see what help the head barman needed.

There were three bars in the Pier Hotel: the public, a small room at the side of the building, with a dart board and bar-billiard table, patronised mainly by locals, the saloon, which was usually the busiest and favoured by holidaymakers, and the lounge, expensively furnished and primarily for the use of the hotel residents.

Greg was told to start in the residents bar, collecting all used glasses for washing, emptying ash-trays and cleaning tables. When he had finished there, he did the same in the saloon bar and finally came to the public bar just before closing time.

Bob Clarmont Brown was there, neatly dressed in the trousers and waistcoat of a dark blue suit, pale blue tie, and white shirt with the sleeves tidily rolled up; he was playing darts, 501 up, at a pound a game, with Jeremy Marlow, a crony of Nigel Heapes.

Marlow was a silly, affected young man from a wealthy family who lived just outside the village. Like Heapes, he was a subaltern and he, too, managed to get frequent home leaves. He liked to be seen playing darts with Clarmont Brown because he believed it showed he was one of the boys, but he always lost heavily. This evening not only was he losing, he was also drinking too much.

Clarmont Brown muttered to him as Greg was passing them with a tray of empties. Marlow turned from the dartboard, eyes

69

blazing, 'Hey! You!' he yelled, 'What are you doing in here? You should be in jail!' and he lunged, punching Greg heavily on the shoulder. Greg, off-balance, staggered into a table and fell, the tray and glasses scattering over the floor. Before he could pick himself up, Marlow had charged at him and swung a foot into his body. Fortunately Greg had seen it coming and rolled away so that he only caught a glancing blow on his ribs, and by the time he had started to regain his feet the barman and a couple of customers were pulling Marlow away.

Shocked and angry, Greg looked up to see Clarmont Brown leaning against the wall and holding a thin cigar in one hand and a glass of whiskey in the other, the only expression on his face being one raised eyebrow and a slight curve of the lips, while Marlow, shouting obscenities at his pal's 'murderer', was frog-marched off the premises by the barman.

Arthur had been summoned as soon as the trouble began and he arrived just as Greg had set about picking up the debris.

'What's the trouble, Greg?' he said.

'Oh, Jeremy Marlow. Must have had a bit too much tonight. He pushed me over. Mind those bits of broken glass.'

Arthur looked across at Clarmont Brown. 'He was with you wasn't he, Bob?'

Clarmont Brown nodded. 'Can't hold his liquor. Went for Greg. Upset about Nigel.'

'Yes, well, we're all upset about Nigel, but we don't have to take it out on everybody else.'

The barman came back in, saw Arthur and said, 'Bloody idiot! Greg had a tray full of empty glasses, and he knocked him flying. Leave that broken glass, Greg. I'll get the dust pan and brush.'

Greg was rubbing his bruised ribs.

'You all right, Greg?' said Arthur.

'Yes, a bit of a bruise that's all.'

'Well, look, you just pop off home now. I'll need you tomorrow night, and Friday and Saturday, if that's okay?'

'Yes, sure.'

Arthur seemed about to say something else but he was distracted by a customer wanting service at the bar. 'See you tomorrow, then.'

Greg walked home with his emotions in a muddle. On the one hand, his day with Suzy had been the most exciting one of his life so far, but on the other his treatment by the hotel staff during the evening had made him feel like some kind of freak, or at best like an outsider.

TWELVE

From the moment he woke up, Greg's mind was filled with thoughts of Suzy: Suzy's body, Suzy's lovely smile and the ecstasy of knowing Suzy wanted him as her lover. He had no sense of guilt. There were no thoughts about the future, about the impracticality of their relationship, about where this involvement would lead them.

What would she be doing this morning? He wanted to see her. She had said she would contact him soon – not today, but soon. How soon, though? How long before he would see her again?

Sam brought him back down to earth at breakfast. He said, 'You're working with Henry this morning, aren't you?'

'Yes. He wants me to help him clear the ground under an old orchard at the back of Chiverton's Place.'

'Oh yes, I heard old Annie Chiverton had passed away at last. She always said she would never sell it. Have you ever been in there?'

'No, it's always been locked up ever since I can remember.'

'It's a big house in about fourteen acres. It was the original grand house of the village, you know, although there wasn't much of a village in those days. Annie's grandfather built it apparently, and paid for it, so they say, from the profits he made out of the Crimean War. It must be in a terrible state now though. It's been empty for years.'

'Wasn't there a hippie commune there at one time?'

'That's right. They squatted there and stayed for about five years I suppose, before they were moved on. There was a big fuss because they grew a lot of their own food and reckoned they were entitled to stay to harvest it.' Sam paused and then smiled at a memory. 'Henry was the Chivertons' gardener, you know, until the Navy took the place over in nineteen forty. There was a bit of gossip about him and Annie at one time too, - but don't you dare let him know I told you.'

'Hard to imagine that about Mr Niton,' said Greg.

'Yes, well, I suppose it would be for someone of your age. What time have you got to be there?'

'Start at eight o'clock, he said.'

'You'd better buck up then.'

'Is there anything you need doing before I go?'

'No, nothing I can't see to.' Sam got up to pour them another cup of coffee. 'I haven't had a chance to ask you before,' he said, 'How did your day go yesterday?'

'Oh, it was great.' Greg smiled at Sam, wishing he could tell him all about it.

'Did you get to drive the MG?'

'Yes. Suzy - Mrs Vanderling, took me to lunch at a French restaurant in Cowes and I drove all the way back here.'

'A bit different from driving the van, eh?'

'Yes. For one thing you're a lot lower down, and it seemed very light and nippy at first, but I soon got used to it.'

Sam smiled. 'I had an MG once, in the nineteen thirties. I had a lot of fun in it, but that was in the days before the roads got too busy. And talking of busy, you'd better get on – I'll clear up here.'

It was a grey, overcast morning, quite warm but with a threat of rain. Old Henry Niton, the gardener, was waiting outside his caravan when Greg arrived at the Salterns just before eight o'clock.

'Morning,' said Greg.

Henry nodded. He was a lean, wiry old man, clean shaven with a tanned and lined face, and a mop of wavy white hair, and still very much alert and strong at eighty. He handed Greg shears, a rip-hook, a pair of thick gauntlets, a rake, a bow saw and a long-handled lopper.

Then he picked up a haversack and a similar set of tools for himself, saying over his shoulder as he set off, 'You staying all day?'

'If you want me to,' said Greg.

'Got your nammut?'

'No. I'll go home.'

Greg had worked with Henry before and knew that he only spoke when necessary. They walked side by side in silence the short distance along Salterns Walk to where it became the Salterns Path and Salterns Road joined at a right angle. The entrance to Chivertons Place faced straight up the centre of Salterns Road towards the Square.

A heavy chain holding the wrought iron double gates together was secured by a padlock. Henry unlocked it and pushed one side open. It swung easily on newly greased hinges.

The drive, which curved round to the front of the house, was rutted and full of weeds. It was edged with rhododendrons, some of which, having grown unchecked for many years, had recently been hacked back to allow access.

The house itself was a large, redbrick building with tall arched windows which could have given it an ecclesiastical look if they had not been shuttered with cracked and buckled sheets of plywood. Ivy and other climbing plants clung to much of the façade, weeds were growing out of the guttering and the roof tiles were covered with moss.

Henry led the way around the house, and followed an overgrown path through what had once been a walled kitchen garden to a wooden door at the far end. The door had been painted red at one time but was now a faded pink and warped by sun and rain.

He lifted the rusted iron latch and pushed but the door would not budge.

'Give us a hand,' he said, putting down his tools and his haversack.

After several hard shoves the door was open enough for Greg to wriggle through. He found that a garden roller had been left against the door many years before and had sunk into the ground. The handle had rotted away but Greg managed to heave the lump of rusty iron out of the way so that the door would open.

Henry joined him and looked around. Where there had once been an orchard was now a wilderness of brambles, nettles and thorn trees. Some of the hundred-year-old fruit trees were still standing, but many had fallen into the tangle of undergrowth.

Henry shook his head, 'Thought so. Too far gone. Job for a bulldozer.'

He stood for a moment, considering. Then he said, 'We'll see if we can get through to the lane. Bring your rip-hook.'

'This backs on to Pond Lane then, does it?'

'Right. Used to be a field gate there.' He started forcing his way through a clump of chest-high nettles and brambles, then stood back. He was, after all, eighty years old.

He said, 'Here, you go ahead.'

It took about half an hour for Greg to clear a track for them to get through to the gate.

Henry said, 'If they want this lot cleared they can get a tractor in.' He turned and retraced his steps. By the time they got back to the door in the wall, it had started to rain

'What are we going to do now then?' asked Greg

'Potting shed.'

Greg followed him back through the faded red door to a small brick lean-to built against the north facing wall in the old kitchen garden and they went inside. Apart from a great many dusty cobwebs and a few wooden crates the place was empty but dry and it appeared to be quite sound.

Henry dumped his tools on the floor and used his rake to brush away the cobwebs. He put his haversack on one crate and up-ended another to sit on near the door.

'When this lot eases off,' he said, 'We'll make a start on the drive.'

Greg found a crate and joined him. They sat in silence staring out at the pouring rain, Greg thinking of Suzy and wishing he was with her. After a while he shook off those thoughts and said, 'Sam told me you used to work here, Mr Niton.'

Henry nodded. 'Ten years I was here. Till the navy took it over in the War.'

'I bet it was a bit different when you were here?'

Henry looked at him and chuckled, 'Yes, lad, you could bet on that alright.'

They were silent again for several minutes, then Greg said, 'Sam told me something else, too, about you being in the army together in the first war.'

'Sam likes to talk.'

'He said you knew my grandfather.'

Henry gave him a long, hard look. Then he said, 'You're a lot like him to look at.'

'Am I?'

'Good-looking bloke, was Jack.' He paused. 'And one of the best.'

There was another long silence, broken at last by Henry. He said, 'He was my best mate. We joined up together right at the start, Jack and me, and Albert Heapes and a couple of his mates, and the two lads that lived here in this house, Walt and Alf Chiverton. It was their idea.' He sniffed. 'And when it was all over, Albert was a cripple, I was a nervous wreck and the others were all gone.'

He stood up and leant one hand against the door frame, gazing out into the rain in the direction of the house.

'Coming back here must bring back memories then, I suppose,' said Greg.

'No, lad. No. They never go away.'

After another long silence, Greg said. 'This place is coming up for sale now then, is it?'

'You going to keep on chattering all day?' said Henry, still looking straight out at the rain,

'Sorry.'

'Alright.'

They sat and watched the rain until at last it began to slacken.

Henry turned back in and picked up his tools and haversack. 'We'll get on back to the drive.'

The rain had stopped by the time they got there.

Henry said, 'You clear this side. I'll do the other. Cut back about three foot from the edge and rake all the litter up into heaps at the side.'

They worked in silence for more than an hour, getting wet from the effects of the rain, then Henry needed Greg's help to cut through a particularly thick rhododendron branch. When they had succeeded in moving it out of the way, Henry opened his haversack and took out a flask of coffee.

'Only got the one cup, but you're welcome to share,' he said, pouring the cup full and passing it to Greg.

Greg thanked him and took a sip. It was black, strong and very sweet. He drank half and passed the cup back. Henry drank the rest and put the flask away. He said, 'We'll finish this lot, collect up all the litter for burning, then stop for nammut. Then I'll go up to Wilson's and tell 'em I'm not doing the orchard and see what else is wanted. You be back here at two.'

They finished, just as Henry had forecast, and Greg went back to the café for lunch. When he returned at two o'clock he took with him a flask of tea and some plain chocolate biscuits, which Sam had told him Henry was fond of.

Louise Wilson had told Henry to use his judgement in clearing away everything that might prevent easy access to the house and main parts of the grounds and they worked steadily through the afternoon, starting around the outside of the house. Greg was impressed with the old man's stamina.

They stopped for a break at four o'clock and he offered Henry his flask. When he saw the chocolate biscuits Henry said with one of his rare smiles, 'You can read a man's character, young Gregory. You'll go a long way in life.'

Then, as they went back to work, he said, 'Place is going up for auction, so now you know.'

At five o'clock, Henry said he'd had enough for one day and it was agreed that Greg would give him a hand in the morning to finish off the job. For Greg it had been another day away from what he had begun to feel as the village's criticism

Later, at his job in the Pier Hotel, however, he felt the same restrained atmosphere from the staff as he had experienced the evening before, but the bars were quiet and the evening passed uneventfully.

THIRTEEN

It seemed to Suzy that she always woke up early these days. She lay in bed thinking about Greg, wishing she had him here with her. Then at a quarter to seven she went into Roddy's room as usual to wake him, but for once he was up before her. The clothes he had worn the day before were neatly folded as always on the chair at the foot of his bed and his slippers were gone so she assumed he had not dressed yet. She looked into his bathroom and then went downstairs in her nightdress to find him. He was not in the house. The back door was open and she called his name. No answer. This was puzzling. Roddy was a creature of habit and hated any change in his daily routine.

It was a bright, clear morning and as she walked past the swimming pool to the summerhouse, the sun felt warm on her back. From here the grounds sloped down towards the sea in the southeast. It was an interesting garden, secluded on all sides except to the sea. Created between the two world wars, terraced and landscaped with lawns and paths among flower beds, each dedicated to a different plant species, it had given her much pleasure, but lately she had been too restless to enjoy it fully.

She went into the summerhouse. It was empty. Oh, well. Now that she was here she might as well have her morning swim. Deciding not to bother to go back for her bikini, she took off her nightdress and dropped it on the floor, but as she stood naked on the cool tiles, a movement in the full-length mirror on the wall at her side caught her eye. Roddy, still in his pyjamas was standing by the door, watching her, a cigar in his hand and a solemn, almost woebegone expression on his face.

She turned and went quickly to him. 'What is it, Roddy? What's wrong?'

She put her hands on his shoulders. He was only about an inch taller than her and he looked straight into her eyes.

He said, 'You really are a beautiful woman, my love. I don't deserve you.'

'Oh, Roddy, what a thing to say!'

'But it's true.'

'Of course it isn't! What on earth makes you say a thing like that? What's wrong?'

He shook his head slowly. 'I can't tell you, Suzy.'

'But you look so sad.'

'I've been very silly, my love,' he said, looking away. 'And now I'm afraid I'm going to have to pay for it.'

'What do you mean, you've been very silly?'

'I can't talk about it. I'm sorry.'

'Why? Are you in some sort of trouble?'

'Trouble? Yes, I suppose I am.'

'Then why can't you tell me about it?'

'I just can't, that's all. I'm sorry.'

'Is it a business thing? The Yacht Club? The regatta? Or what?'

'No, no, it's nothing to do with any of that.'

Suzy wondered for a moment if he had found out about Greg. With her heart in her mouth she knew she had to ask him. 'Is it anything I've done?'

'Oh, Suzy, how could that be?'

'What then?'

'I'm not going to talk about it, so please don't ask any more.' He leant forward to kiss her on the forehead and stepped back. 'Whatever happens, you know I always want you to be happy, and I would never want to do anything to upset you. And that's all I'm going to say.'

He started to turn away. 'I'd better go and get showered and dressed. I've got a very busy three days ahead, getting everything set up for the regatta.'

'Is there anything I can help with?' she said.

He smiled at her. 'No thanks. You just do your usual thing for me at the ball tomorrow. That's worth your weight in gold to me. Do you need a new dress or anything?'

'No, I've already seen to that.'

'Yes. Of course. Silly of me.'

She watched him as he squared his shoulders and marched off. He paused to stub out his cigar in a tall ashtray by the back door, turned and looked back at her. 'Go and have your swim,' he called, 'Then come and have breakfast with me.'

She wondered what had happened to upset him so much. It was obviously not her new relationship with Greg - Roddy could not be so devious as to ignore that if he was aware of it. But she knew him well enough to accept that if he had made up his mind

79

not to tell her, then he would not.

She realised, suddenly, that she was really very fond of him, but that she loved him in the way she would have loved a kind and gentle older brother if she'd had one, and that she was worrying about him in that same kind of way, as if she had the right to sympathise but it was none of her business to interfere.

She sighed, turned back to the pool and dived in.

She swam her customary twenty lengths as fast as she could, emptying her mind so that she was thinking only about completing each length.

She emerged dripping and gasping and found a towel in the summerhouse to dry off most of the water, then, with her nightdress over her shoulder she strode back indoors to shower and dress and join Roddy in the breakfast room.

Nothing more was said about Roddy's 'trouble' and over breakfast he seemed back to normal as he chatted to her about the various minor problems involved in the forthcoming Seastone Regatta, including an amusing anecdote concerning the two rival fireworks manufacturers, both of whom happened to have holiday homes in the village, each wanting exclusive rights to organise the display on the final night.

Later, when he was leaving for his day at the Yacht Club, Suzy went with him to his car and as he prepared to drive off she said, bending down to his open window, 'I just want you to know that I want you to be happy too, and you can always talk to me about anything. I don't like to see you unhappy, Roddy.'

He smiled and put his hand to cover hers on the sill of the window and squeezed gently.'Thank you.'

After he had driven away, she remained in the driveway for some moments, feeling sad that there should always be this constraint between them. Roddy's attitude toward her was never going to change, she could see that now. He would never see her as an equal. He seemed to see himself either as her custodian as if she was some sort of goddess to be propitiated, or as her protector, with the responsibility of doing his very best to care for her, as if she was some superior kind of domestic pet. But she was not so much angry with him as disappointed that her life had come to this state where it had no focus.

She wandered around the house to the terrace, and paused by the telescope which was still pointing towards the spot in the bay where she had first seen Greg. Thinking about him, about making love to him, made her pulse beat faster and she felt a surge of warm, happy desire. When was she going see him again? Where could they meet? It would have to be somewhere private where they could not be overlooked, and not too far away because it would not do for her to be seen taking him out in her MG twice in a couple of days.

Then it came to her. Of course! She was looking straight at the ideal location – the sea. The Yacht Club boat was hardly ever used and she would take it out and he would join her and they would be alone together and nobody would ever know.

FOURTEEN

Friday

Greg spent the morning as arranged working with Henry. They finished the work that the estate agent wanted done and Henry paid Greg out of his own pocket.

He said, 'You can work with me any time, lad. And I told the Wilson woman that.'

Greg thanked him, knowing what he meant and grateful for his goodwill. He guessed what Louise Wilson must have said, he felt bitter and angry for a moment. Then he reminded himself of the people who mattered to him, his father, Sam and Suzy. Yes, especially Suzy. He wondered if he would hear from her today.

After lunch he had a few odd jobs to do for Sam and he kept himself busy in the shop. Then at about three o'clock the phone rang.. He went to answer it.

'Oh good it *is* you!' His heart leapt. It was Suzy. 'I hoped it wouldn't be that prim and proper Post Office girl,' she said, 'Or Sam - I hate making excuses to him. I'm in Roddy's office and I can just see you through the window. You can't see me because I'm behind the curtain but turn around and give me a smile.'

Greg moved towards the window and looked over to the Yacht Club. He couldn't help the grin that spread over his face.

'Ooh, that's lovely. I'm almost tempted to come over and grab you! Listen. sweetie, it's such a lovely afternoon, why don't we go out in the boat? I'll bring a picnic and we can anchor somewhere quiet and go for a swim before tea.'

He was puzzled. 'How can we do that?' he said.

'Oh, easily. You wait for me at the far end of Priory Bay and I'll bring the boat and you can swim out. Or I could pick you up in the dinghy if you'd rather save your energy.' She giggled. 'Perhaps that will be best, hmm?'

'Are you sure it will be alright?'

'Greg, it will be wonderful!'

'You know what I mean.'

'Yes, and you know what I mean too, don't you? But, seriously, you let me worry about whether it's alright or not. You just get yourself over to Priory Bay. I'll be there as soon as you are.'

She rang off, taking it for granted that Greg would have no

plans of his own. He saw Sophie giving him a quizzical look from behind the Post Office counter, but so what? Suddenly life seemed wonderful and exciting again and he ran up the stairs to change into shorts and tee-shirt, and grab his bathing trunks and a towel.

He went out the back way, along Rope Walk, through the Square, up Seastone Lane and joined the Priory Path at Sally Wilson's Gardens. When he came to the Wilsons' gate he glanced over into their garden, feeling a slight pang of regret that Josie had proved to be such a fairweather friend. She was sun-bathing on the lawn and happened to look up as he passed. He paused.

'Hello Josie.'

She flushed a deep pink from her face to the top of her bikini and she murmured something he couldn't hear.

'Getting a nice tan ready for Monaco, then?'

She stood up a walked slowly over to the gate.

'I'm sorry, Greg,' she said. She looked up at him, her eyes big and sad. He thought how very young and pretty she was, and compared with Suzy, how untouchable.

'I was sorry, too,' he said

'They insisted,' she said, 'Perhaps you could call me after the holidays when all the fuss about Nigel has died down?'

'Perhaps,' he said. 'But let's face it, your mother has never approved of me.'

'She has never said anything before.'

'No, but she's had no excuse before, has she!'

'She will have forgotten all about it by the time we come back.'

'Possibly,' said Greg, looking directly into her eyes, 'But I won't.'

He nodded to her and walked on, knowing it would be impossible, after Suzy, to renew that good and innocent friendship which he and Josie had shared. It was over.

oOo

As he came down the steps through the woods into Priory Bay he could see the Yacht Club boat out beyond The Point. The beach was crowded at the sandy end nearest the rocks but almost deserted as usual farther on where it was mostly pebbles and a steep bank.

By the time he reached the end of the little promontory, Suzy had dropped anchor about halfway to the old fort and was getting into a pram dinghy. She handled it expertly in the calm sea, soon bringing it close enough for him to wade out and get aboard. He didn't offer to row, knowing she would refuse.

She was wearing just a bikini bottom and a shirt, unbuttoned in front. He sat in the stern facing her with a big grin on his face, admiring the effect her rowing technique had on her bare breasts as she pulled hard back to the boat.

She brought the little dinghy up against the boarding ladder on the seaward side of the boat, shipped oars and grabbed the painter, which she tied to the rail, then climbed easily aboard.

Greg followed her. She took his hand and led him through the open-backed wheelhouse, and down a short ladder into the forward cabin.

The only time Greg had been on this boat had been in the dark on the previous Sunday during the search for Nigel. Then he had stood on the foredeck and had not noticed anything about the boat's accomodation. Now he saw that the cabin was open-plan and spacious, but he had little time to admire it, for, without a word, Suzy took him straight through the galley area, forward past the dinette and the settees on either side to the space under the foredeck where she had converted the two large single berths into a double bed. There she turned and faced him, putting her arms around his neck, and pressed herself against him, smiling up into his eyes.

'Are you happy?' she said.
'Yes.'
'Good.'
'Are you?'
'Yes.'
'Good.'
'We're going to make love.'
'Are we?'
'Yes.'
'Good.'
They both laughed.
She said, 'And it will be.'

Greg put his arms around her and kissed her and immediately the intensity of her desire for him transmitted itself to him. He felt tension in her limbs and heat from her body, and when their

84

kiss ended she spoke breathlessly, in a broken voice, 'Oh, I want you. Now.'

He kissed her again, holding her as close against himself as he could. At that moment, for him nothing in the world existed except the two of them.

They sank down onto the bed. The initiative had been hers, but Greg soon matched her excitement and enthusiasm and they made love frantically, almost violently.

Later, as they lay side by side, getting their breath back in the heat of the cabin, Greg gently brushed a strand of her hair away from her face with his fingertips and said, 'Suzy, meeting you has been the most wonderful thing that could ever happen to me.'

She shook her head, smiling into his eyes. 'No. I'm sure lots of much more wonderful things will happen to you, but it's nice that you think I may be one of them.'

They were quiet for several minutes.

Then Suzy said, 'I know there has been no woman in your life for a long time. It's been all men, hasn't it? And men have to show each other that they are strong and manly, and hard, and not afraid, don't they?. So for you, there has been no softness, no love.'

'Oh, no, that's not true,' he said, surprised that she should say such a thing. 'My father loves me. And I know Sam does, too.'

'Yes, I'm sure they do, but in a manly way, not like a woman would. You see, a man doesn't have to pretend to a woman who loves him.'

He was puzzled. 'Alright,' he said. 'But why do you say that?'

She said, because she was remembering her exchange with Roddy that morning, 'I just want you to know that when a woman loves you, it's alright to tell her when you are anxious or uncertain, or when things go wrong for you.'

'Oh. Okay.'

'You can even be afraid,' she said. 'In fact, you can always be whoever you really are.'

Greg smiled at her. 'I don't think I know who I really am, Suzy. I think I know who I used to be before I met you, but now, I don't know, I think I may be somebody else.'

She laughed happily, her serious mood broken. 'Oh, you are sweet! And I do love you!' and she pulled his face to her to kiss him. Then she slid off the bunk, jumped up and said, 'Come on!

Let's cool off in the water!'

She ran through the cabin, dived straight off the boat into the sea and swam quickly away. He followed her and although he was a powerful swimmer, they were more than a hundred yards from the boat when he caught up with her. She rolled over and dived down letting her long hair trail like a mermaid and he followed, chasing her. He almost caught her, but she turned as quick as a fish, twisting away with a mocking smile, and kicked back up to the surface. They played around splashing at each other like a couple of children for several minutes, until she shouted, 'Race you back!' and set off at speed towards the 'Serena'.

She won and was pulling herself up on the boarding ladder when Greg, close behind, noticed a small motorboat not far away heading towards them. The people in the cockpit were looking in their direction.

'Suzy!' he yelled to her.

She turned, saw the approaching onlookers for the first time and dropped straight back into the water. Coming up next to him she said, 'Do you think they saw me?'

'If they did they saw every little bit of you.'

'Whoops!' she said.

Treading water, they watched the other boat as it continued slowly on its way past them.

Suzy said, 'I don't recognise the boat. Probably just trippers.'

When it was far enough away they both climbed back on board.

'We'd better make ourselves decent,' said Suzy. 'Just in case anybody else comes by. Though why that lot needed to come so close, I can't imagine.'

As they were getting dressed, she said, 'I don't know about you, but all that exercise has given me an appetite. I've brought some cold meat and salad and rolls and some fruit, but I'd love a cup of tea first. Or would you sooner have coffee? Or a cold drink? We've got practically everything.'

'Tea would be nice,' he said. He noticed that she was now dressing conventionally in underwear, jeans and a white tee-shirt, in contrast to what she was wearing when she picked him up. He smiled to himself, acknowledging what she had done. But he said nothing

Suzy went through to the galley. Greg followed. He was very

impressed with the style of the cabin cruiser and the quality of its fittings and he watched as she took a kettle from a locker under the units and filled it from the tap over the stainless steel sink before lighting one of the burners on the gas cooker. Then she slid back a perspex panel and reached into a cupboard for cups, saucers, and plates.

'What kind of boat is this, Suzy?' he asked, as she moved him aside so that she could get their food from the refrigerator.

'A Fairey Swordsman,' she said. 'Roddy bought her new about four years ago.'

'I bet she goes pretty fast.'

'Yes, she's pretty quick. She's got two big powerful engines. Turbo diesels,' she said with her head in the fridge, 'And Roddy says they're very thirsty. I know it takes two hundred gallons to fill her up, anyway.'

Greg was in the way again and she had to sidestep around him. 'Why don't you go up and have a look in the wheelhouse while I'm getting the tea ready,' she said.

He went up the steps and sat on the seat in the helm position. In front of him was an instrument panel full of switches and dials, some of which were a mystery to him but he identified an echo sounder and the autopilot, and recognised the radio, the steering compass, the horn, the speed and distance log, and the clock and barometer.

'This is an ocean-going boat, I suppose, isn't it?' he called down to Suzy.

'Yes,' she said, as she reached up the steps to pass him a cup of tea.'But she isn't used all that much really, mostly around the Island or along the coast. Roddy uses her on business trips to the continent from time to time, though. I went with him to Spain a couple of times and last year he took me to Venice. That was fun.'

'You don't get to use her much then, yourself?"

'No, not much. I go to Southsea, sometimes. Otherwise when Roddy wants to take out small parties for the day, to Lymington, or Beaulieu, or Poole Harbour, places like that, I go along because he likes me to share the driving.'

Less than a week ago, thought Greg, seeing Nigel in his little speedboat had set me wondering about different lifestyles. But that now seems nothing compared to a way of life that goes with a boat like 'Serena'.

Looking again at the clock he was surprised to see how much time had passed. He went back down the steps.

'I'm supposed to be working this evening Suzy,' he said.

'Oh, are you? In the Pier Hotel?'

'Yes, at eight o'clock.'

'Well, it's only half-past six. How long will it take you to walk home? Half an hour?'

'More or less.'

'Plenty of time, then. Come and have your tea and then I'll row you back to the beach.'

They sat and had their meal in the dinette.

Suzy said, 'We won't be able to meet at all tomorrow. It's my busiest day in the Yacht Club, the day before the regatta starts, and I've got lots of things to see to and people to talk to, and in the evening there's the annual dinner and dance. I suppose you'll be working at the hotel?'

'Yes, in the kitchens I expect.'

'So we won't be far apart then, will we, and I'll think of you slaving away while I'm being the gracious hostess. I'll keep an eye out for you in case you get a chance to take a look in the ballroom. If you do, you won't recognise me, I'm sure, because I shall be all dolled up and prettified.'

Greg smiled. 'And I'm sure I would, but I expect it would be better if I didn't, eh?'

'Under the circumstances,' she grinned at him. 'But on Sunday you must come and have tea at Abbots House.'

Greg looked at her in surprise.

'Roddy will be out all day,' she explained. 'He won't be back before midnight and I'm not expecting any visitors so we'll have the place to ourselves. Come at five o'clock.'

'Alright. Thankyou.'

'And now we'd better get you ashore.'

FIFTEEN

'It's exactly one week ago, almost to the minute since I stood here and told 'Squire' I'd collect his dinghy from Foreland.,' thought Greg, walking past 'Squire' Davis's shop in Pier Road.

It was hard to believe that so much had happened to him in such a short time. Last Sunday, Suzy Vanderling had just been "that good-looking, rich lady married to the Commander"; this Sunday he was on his way to make love to her at Abbots House. Last Sunday, he had not a care in the world and Nigel had still been alive; this Sunday Greg knew that the village was blaming him for the fact that Nigel was still missing and the authorities had announced that it was now unlikely he would be found alive.

Arthur had said as much to him late last night when they were working together, clearing up the debris after the Yacht Club Annual Ball.

'If he's still alive he would have made contact by now,' he said. 'No, he's gone, I'm afraid. I only wish we knew what happened to him, that's all.' He stopped and put his hand on Greg's shoulder. 'And I appreciate it must be difficult for you, too, Greg. I know what some people are saying, but you must try not to let it upset you too much. Have you thought about getting away for a while perhaps?'

'Where?' said Greg

'I don't know. Would Sam have an idea?'

'It's a thought, I suppose.'

But Greg had no thoughts whatsoever of going anywhere far from Suzy.

He had managed to take a peep into the ballroom during the evening and had spotted her immediately, looking spectacular in a backless, low-cut, scarlet ballgown and dancing with Josie's father. Josie was on the dance floor too, clinging to Bob Clarmont Brown, he noticed. Then, Suzy came closer to where Greg was standing and she caught sight of him. Her face lit up and she gave him one of her lovely smiles and a wink over Graham Wilson's shoulder before being whisked away. He felt such a surge of love of her that he thought his heart would burst.

He was becoming obsessed with her, he knew.

Today had seemed particularly long because he had to wait until five o'clock to see her. His watch now said half-past four and he was dawdling so that he would not arrive too early at Abbots House. He wondered if the watch was slow. Five more minutes passed and he had already reached the Pier Hotel. In another five he would be at the end of the drive to Abbots House. He went down the steps onto the beach and sat in the sun amongst the holiday makers, trying to calm his racing heartbeat, until he could wait no longer.

He presented himself ten minutes early at the same open door whose bell he had rung on Monday morning, and the memory of that first fantastic view of Suzy's body, together with the anticipation of being with her again, aroused him, so that when she came in answer to his ring on the doorbell, he immediately enfolded her in a fierce embrace and kissed her hungrily.

She responded happily, and when she broke free eventually she said, breathlessly, 'Oh, my, sweetie, you are pleased to see me! I was going to suggest we had a swim first and then perhaps, something to eat.'

'I want you,' he said.

'Yes,' she said, and led him into her bedroom.

They made love as they had on the boat, wildly and passionately, but this time it was Greg who was the initiator. Afterwards they lay spent in each others' arms, getting their breath back.

After several moments she clasped his head and held it away from her. Her flushed breasts were rising and falling with each shallow pant of her breathing and she smiled happily up at him.

She said, 'We're getting good at this, aren't we.'

'Mmm.'

'You don't seem very convinced.'

'Oh, well, yes, I mean, I think it's marvellous.'

She laughed and pushed him gently away from her.

'We're a strange couple aren't we? You know, when I saw you last night, I couldn't help thinking how different you are from all the others in that room. And I was just like them, except for one thing, one very important thing – I had you and they never would!'

Greg smiled at her, not understanding, and not even trying to guess what she might mean.

'When we were on the boat,' she went on, 'You said you knew who you used to be before you met me but now you think you may be somebody else, do you remember? Well, that's just what I think about myself. I know who I used to be and I was playing at being her yesterday, but when I am with you I am somebody else - myself, the person I think I really am.'

Greg said, 'I know I'm only really happy when I'm with you.'

'Yes,' she said, 'That's exactly it, isn't it.'

'When I saw Arthur last night,' he said, 'He suggested perhaps I should go away somewhere to avoid all the snide comments about Nigel. I couldn't do that, Suzy.'

'Good, because you have given me a reason for living. I would hate it if you went away.'

They lay together for a few minutes longer, happy to be holding each other. Then Suzy sat up and said, 'I was getting together a little barbecue by the pool when you came and swept me into my bed. You could have a swim while I'm seeing to it, if you like.'

It was warm and peaceful by the pool and when they had eaten they stretched out on sun-loungers in the evening sunshine.

Suzy asked him what he had been doing since they parted on Friday.

He told her he had worked in the shop all Saturday morning, then gone to St Helens with Pete and Frank to play cricket in the village team They lost for once. He described the match and was delighted that she seemed to understand the game quite well. In the evening he had worked until one a.m. at the Pier Hotel. Then this morning he had gone back there to finish off, and the rest of the time had dragged until he could see her again.

She amused him with comments about various members of her social set, most of them also Yacht Club members. He realised that she was very observant and at times could show a caustic wit, and he began to understand that she felt justifiably undervalued in her role as rich man's plaything.

At about eight thirty the sun dropped over the top of the hill behind them and the temperature started to fall.

'Let's go back to bed, shall we?' she said, taking his hand and leading him indoors.

This time they spent time exploring each other's bodies, and their love-making was easy and unhurried, and Greg felt, the best yet.

When it was over Suzy snuggled up against him, her head on his shoulder, her hair a golden fan on his chest.

'Greg?' she murmured.

'Hmm?'

'I want to tell you something,. Something I think you ought to know about yourself.'

'OK,' he said, happy that she always seemed to like to talk after they had made love.

'I'm sure you are not aware of it but there is something special about you, for women I mean, or at least the kind of woman I am. You seem to have an understanding that most men never get.'

He was happy to know that she was pleased with him but he had no idea what she meant and said so.

'It just seems to me,' she said, 'That to have an older, married woman as a lover would have gone to most boys' heads.'

'Well, it has gone to my head.'

'No, not in the conceited way that I mean. You don't swagger about believing yourself to be God's gift to women.'

'OK.'

'And when we make love you are happy to be guided and you don't gloat the moment it is over as if you are the most virile male ever.'

Greg could have told her that it was because he was always so grateful. In truth he knew he was extremely lucky to have access to such a lovely woman and he was perfectly content to be guided by her, and in any case their differences in age, experience and social background would have made it difficult for him to be otherwise. But he said nothing. Besides, he was in love with her.

After a while she went on, 'I suppose what I'm really trying to say is that your attitude to my body is not dominant or arrogant, as if expecting submission, but you are respectful, and that is quite rare and romantic I think. And I'm sure it's not just because you are young and have little experience, but it's part of your nature.'

Greg saw that she meant this as a compliment and he took it as such and loved her the more for it. But he did wonder if past experiences had made her vulnerable to what she saw as his humility and perhaps she was moved that he had chosen not to display feelings of male triumph at possessing her physically, even though he did have such feelings every time.

They lay together quietly for a few minutes.

Then Suzy sat up and said, smiling down at him, 'It's time for you to go, sweetie. I wish you could stay with me all night but it isn't possible. I'm sorry.'

'When can I see you again?' he said.

She slid out of the bed and stood up. 'I'll phone the shop tomorrow after lunch and we'll arrange something.'

'OK.'

She padded softly across the room, naked. Greg watched her fascinated. She was not in any way self-conscious about her body, but then again, he thought, she had no reason to be.

She slid back a wardrobe door, took out a towelling dressing gown and slipped it on, then came back, took his hands and pulled him off the bed.

'Come on now, up you get.'

When he was dressed, Suzy said it would be best if he left by the back garden.

The evening was still warm and there was no moon. She took his hand to lead him past the swimming pool and around to the back of the summerhouse where a narrow path of crazy paving with shallow steps every few yards led up through shrubs and trees to a gate in the hedge.

They kissed goodbye and he walked home along the Priory Path as quickly as he could in the starlight, recalling what she had said about his attitude towards her, and realising that she was right, and that was the way it should be. For the first time, though, he began to wonder about their future. He could not see how it would be possible for them to go on for ever in the way they had been, but on the other hand he could not face the idea that they might have to stop seeing each other, and by the time he had reached the little alleyway leading to the iron staircase up to his rooms, he had decided there was nothing he could do about it anyway, so he would just have to take each day as it came.

As he put his foot on the first step of the staircase, a shadow moved suddenly in front of him and a boot caught him a solid blow in the ribs. He fell backwards, all the breath knocked from his body. Someone grabbed his arms from behind and held him upright. A bright torchlight shone in his face and a voice from above him said, 'Yeah. It's him.'

The torch went out. The man behind him freed his arms, spun

him around and hit him hard in the belly doubling him over, so that he caught the full force of the man's knee as it came up in his face. He felt his nose break. He fell to the ground dazed and before he could do anything to protect himself, both men were kicking him savagely about the head and body and he blacked out. Apart from identifying him, neither of his attackers had said a word.

When consciousness started to come back to him he was being dragged by his feet along the road with the back of his head bouncing dully on the rough surface. He had a faint sensation of being lifted up and then of falling, before another tremendous blow to his head sent him into oblivion.

Part Two

—

Twentyone Years later

SIXTEEN

A split second before the explosion, Luke had yelled something and hurled himself at Greg, throwing them both to the ground. Greg had a vivid flash of déja vu, as he was lifted up and then dropped, crashing into unconsciousness.

That had been in early March. He came round on April the first, and when they told him the date and that he had lost three weeks of his life, they assured him they were not fooling.

At least he still had the rest of it to look forward to though, eventually, when all his wounds had healed, but Luke had never regained consciousness, and in June their Officer Commanding, Major Nick Southwell, had come personally to tell Greg that Luke's medical team had finally had to decide to switch off his life-support system.

Nick Southwell had regularly come to see them both in hospital, sometimes accompanied by Luke's sister, Zillah., whom Greg had met many times over the years.

Now, she stepped forward to his bedside and bent down to embrace him. She didn't say anything, but her tears mingled with his as they held each other silently.

After Nick and Zillah left, Greg lay in his bed staring up at the ceiling, trying to come to terms with the fact of Luke's death. He was quite unprepared for the intensity of the grief he felt. It had simply not occurred to him that Luke would not recover. They had been a team, on and off, for fifteen years, since they first met in 'The Det', and he could not imagine life in the Regiment without Luke.

Nick Southwell had said he would take him to Luke's funeral and bring him back to the hospital, if the medical authorities would allow Greg to travel. The doctors were pleased with the progress his battered body was making towards full recovery – he could now walk a short distance unaided - and so they would probably agree he could go.

They were not so hopeful about his mental condition, however. Even before the news of Luke's death, Greg had shown no sign of pulling out of the depression he had remained in since regaining consciousness.

At the funeral service in the little church of Luke's home village in Dorset, he was ushered into the seat next to Zillah, and afterwards as they stood together at the graveside, she said, 'I know you will miss him even more than I do, Greg. Would it help if I come to visit sometimes? Perhaps we might exchange memories.'

Just at the moment Greg could not see how anything could help. He said nothing.

'I think I would find it comforting, anyway,' she added.

'Yes, alright,' he said, not really caring, but he liked Zillah and did not want to hurt her feelings.

On their return journey neither Greg nor Nick felt like speaking, but when they arrived back in the hospital car park, Nick switched off the ignition and turned in his seat to look directly at Greg.

'Greg,' he said, 'I'm being transferred. To CRW Wing. As from the beginning of next month. So I won't be around when you come back.'

'D'you think I will get back?'

'Depends entirely on you. The medics say you're making good progress now. Physically you should be as good as ever. Well, give or take a year or two – what are you now, thirtynine? Past your 'best before', perhaps, but there's still a place for you. You've got to *want* to get back, though.'

'Yeah. Just at the moment I don't know.'

'Give it time. But in any case, what I wanted to say is this - if there is ever anything you need, at any time, and I mean *anything, at any time*, don't hesitate to get in touch. Please. Because I never forget that I wouldn't be here if it hadn't been for you and Luke.'

Greg looked away.

'No, look at me, Greg. I mean it. You never know, you might just be able to use a bit of help one day, and then you'll be giving me a chance to do something. To justify what you two did for me, I mean.'

Greg looked back at him and nodded. 'Thanks,' he said.

Nick opened his door and came round the car to help him get out. They made their way slowly back to Greg's room where Nick took his hand and gripped it firmly.

'Remember basic training?' he said, with a smile, 'Running for miles across the hills with a full pack and arriving at the truck absolutely knackered, and then being told you have to run all the way back again? You think you can't do it and you find out that you can because stopping is not an option. Right? Be seeing you, Greg'

They shook hands and Nick left.

Greg sat alone in the armchair by his bedside. He was already depressed at the knowledge that he would never again be working with Luke. Theirs had been a unique partnership, each being able to rely one hundred percent on the other, and Greg knew that he would not find that level of trust in anyone else. Now, the news that Nick was leaving the Squadron as well, was making him feel that there could be little point in going back and he just had to accept that his career was coming to an end.

He thought about what all the years in the army had done to him. He had seen and taken part in many actions, the results of some of which could disturb the peace of mind of even hardened veterans like himself, but until now he had always been able to cope with what he was required to do. He had not switched his emotions off, but when the feeling was there he had allowed himself to feel it and then get on with the job in hand, even in Bosnia, where he had seen atrocities which he would not have believed could take place in the Europe of the last decade of the twentieth century.

It was in Bosnia that he and Luke had spent two days and nights looking for Nick Southwell who had been leading a team of Bosniak saboteurs trying to get out of Goradze. They eventually found him, alone and wounded, trapped on a hillside by a force of Montenegrans. He and Luke had dealt with the Montenegrans and taken Nick all the way back to comparative safety in Sarajevo. On the way they had passed through deserted villages. In one, Christians had been crucified and left there by their Moslem neighbours, and in another the entire population had been herded into their mosque by Christian militiamen and burnt to death.

Even then he had not allowed himself to get wound too tight by it all. But now it all seemed pointless.

The next morning he phoned Suzy.

Although they had always kept in touch, seeing each other whenever possible in the early years, they had communicated mainly by letter since Sam had died in nineteen eightysix. Greg had received a letter from her a few days before he was injured but he had not replied to it, wanting to keep quiet about his injuries until he had fully recovered. Now, though, he felt the need to talk to her.

It had been several years since they had actually spoken and he hoped she would be at home and answer the phone herself. He listened anxiously while the phone rang and rang, and when it was eventually picked up, she just said, 'Hello?'

He said, 'Suzy?'

'Greg!' she said immediately.

'Amazing! How did you know?'

'I know your voice, of course, silly!'

'It's been a long time.'

'Yes, it has. I've been worrying. You didn't answer my last two letters. And you missed Dan's birthday. Is everything alright?'

'No,' he said, 'I'm afraid it's not.'

'Why? What's wrong?' He heard the concern in her voice. 'Have you been hurt?'

'Yes, but I'm okay now. But the thing is, Luke's dead.'

'Oh, Greg!'

'Yes. We both caught it, but he got the worst of it.'

'Oh, Greg, I am sorry. But how are *you*?'

'I'm alright - making good progress, as they say.'

'Were you badly hurt? Where are you? Can I come and see you?'

'Well, at the moment, I'm at a place called New Hall, just outside Salisbury, but I'm being sent back to Haslar tomorrow for a week of tests, so you could come and see me there.'

'Haslar, that's the navy hospital just across the water at Gosport isn't it?'

'That's right. How are you, anyway, Suzy? And Dan?'

'Oh we're fine. But...did you get my last letter?'

'All about skiing in Switzerland?'

'Oh.' Suzy paused for a few moments. 'Well. There have been some changes, Greg. I wrote and told you a couple of weeks ago. You obviously didn't get the letter. I'll tell you all about it when I see you. Will they let me see you tomorrow, d'you think?'

'I don't see why not. I'm supposed to be going there first thing in the morning so you could ring up about lunchtime and see.'

'Alright. So what are these tests you're having, then? Were you badly hurt?'

'Broken bones. Cuts. Burns. Internal damage. We were blown up, Suzy.'

'Oh my god. When *was* this?'

'In March.'

'*March!* Three months ago! Why didn't you let me know before?'

'Well, I wasn't much good for a couple of months, only came out of plaster last week, and well… I've been a bit low, to tell the truth, Suzy, and it was Luke's funeral yesterday, and this morning I just felt I had to talk to you. But, yes, I should have got someone to contact you. Sorry.'

'No, no, it's me that should say sorry. I didn't think. It's a shock hearing about it now, that's all.'

'So you'll try and come tomorrow, then?'

'Yes. Is there anything you want me to bring, anything you need?'

'No thanks. But it'll be good to see you. How's Dan? Sorry I haven't got around to a birthday present yet, but I thought about him on the twentyeighth. Twenty years old, eh?"

'Yes. It doesn't seem possible. Next thing I know, I'll be a grandmother.'

'Oh, come on! Give the lad a chance!'

She laughed. Then she said, 'He thinks the world of you, you know and he was disappointed not to hear from you on his birthday. It's the only time you've ever missed. But he'll understand now.'

'How is he getting on at uni?"

'Well, that's one of the changes I've got to tell you about when I see you.'

'Oh?'

'It's all right, nothing to worry about, but it's too much to talk about on the phone.'

'Now you've got me intrigued,' he said.

She said, changing the subject, 'I know you said you're alright now, but you are still in hospital so does that mean you're bed-ridden?'

'No, I can get about, but I can't manage for long without crutches and I can't go any distance without getting tired. They tell me it's just a matter of time, though, and I'll soon be back to normal.'

'And you said you were burnt. Not on your face?'

'No, just the backs of my legs, and that's all healing up nicely. I still look much the same, Suzy.'

'I wish I could say that. You won't expect me to look much the same, will you? Ten years have gone by since you last saw me and it shows.' She gave a little laugh. 'But I am trying to grow old gracefully.'

Greg told her that he just wanted to see her, and whatever she thought she looked like she would always look lovely to him anyway, and after chatting a little longer, mostly about Greg's injuries and his current state of recovery, they said goodbye until tomorrow.

SEVENTEEN

Cheered by the expectation of seeing Suzy, Greg's thoughts turned to memories of their occasional meetings over the years. These had always been arranged discreetly through Sam, and then one day in nineteen eightysix when Greg was in Northern Ireland, a letter had come from Suzy, telling him that Sam had died in his sleep in his room at the Pier Hotel. Greg had obtained compassionate leave to attend the funeral and that was the last time he and Suzy had met.

Sam had retired eight years before that, persuaded by Arthur, the son of his old friend Albert Heapes, to go and live with him at the Pier Hotel. Sam had sold his properties in Seastone to Roddy Vanderling, who had long coveted the chandlery, and at the suggestion of estate agent Louise Wilson, he had invested much of the proceeds in a property development company which she and her husband Graham were involved with on the mainland. One of the projects this company undertook was the conversion of a terrace consisting mainly of run-down hotels overlooking South Parade Pier in Southsea and as a result Sam eventually became the owner of a pair of high-class apartments.

In his will Sam had left them to Greg, together with a small sum of money and the old .38 semi-automatic pistol with which he had taught Greg to shoot. After the funeral, Greg had arranged through Louise Wilson's agency for both apartments to be let on short-term leases, the nett income being lodged in his Hereford bank account.

Now, with the possibility that he would no longer have a career in the army, and therefore would need somewhere to live, came the idea of moving into one of them and he wondered how he would adapt to living alone in his own space after twenty years of rarely staying long in one place and always having to share his living quarters with others.

The thought lowered his spirit once more and he was still feeling gloomy late the next afternoon, when, his tests for the day completed, he had not yet heard anything from Suzy.

He put on his best uniform and made his way slowly, without his crutches – he didn't want her to see him on crutches - to the front of the hospital, in the hope that he might see her arriving,, and there she was getting out of a cab.

She saw him immediately and came towards him in her quick, light stepping way.

'Hello, Sweetie,' she said, and smiling her lovely smile she reached up, lightly resting her hands on his shoulders, and kissed him on the lips.

She took his hands and stepped back a pace. They looked at each other for a few moments.

She was very smartly dressed in a light summer suit in her favourite colour, red. Her hair was now ash-blonde, shorter and neatly styled, and to him she looked as lovely as ever. Older, of course, but exactly as he had imagined she would look. He felt a warmth in his chest that he had not felt since Luke died.

She said, 'Can we go somewhere quiet, where we can talk in private?'

'I don't know,' he said. 'The Airing Grounds would be best, I suppose.'

'The what?'

'Airing Grounds, sort of gardens. For convalescent patients, like me, to walk and "take the air". But I should warn you, I can't walk too far yet.'

'You're not on crutches any more?"

'No. Well, not all the time.'

'Well, we needn't go far. I just didn't want to talk in a crowded ward, that's all.'

'OK, come on then.' Greg tucked her arm under his. 'I'm in the Sick Officers Block, actually, four beds per ward. Only they used to call them "decks" here, apparently,' he added as they set off.

'What?'

'The wards. This being Royal Naval Hospital, Haslar, they used shipboard terms. They called the loos "heads", for instance.'

'How quaint,' she said. 'And if it's Royal Navy, how come you're here?'

'Defence cuts. They've closed military hospitals like Aldershot and Netley, so we're all sharing now – we've got light-blue jobbies here too, staff as well as patients.'

'I see,' she said. 'I've never understood about defence cuts. Is this rationalisation, or whatever, likely to affect your job at all?'

103

'Don't know,' he said. 'Don't really care much, to be honest.'

'What?' She looked at him sharply. 'You aren't thinking of leaving the Regiment, surely?'

Greg told her how he felt now that neither Luke nor Nick would be in the Squadron, and even as he spoke the words, he knew his feelings were not logical. But it did not change how he felt.

Suzy was quiet for several paces. Then she said, 'Shall we find somewhere to sit.?'

They made their way to a bench set near the high wall.

'So what are all these changes, then,' said Greg as they settled themselves. 'And why isn't Dan getting on at university? I thought he was doing very well.'

'Yes, he was, but Roddy died just before Easter and that changed things.'

'Oh. I see. I'm sorry, Suzy.' He squeezed her hand.

'Yes. It was very sudden. He was drowned. In the sea by the jetty. Our jetty at the Yacht Club. Dan found him.'

'Dan?'

'Yes. He was home for the Easter holidays.'

'Poor kid!'

'We don't know how it happened,' said Suzy. 'At first we thought he must have had a heart attack and fallen. He'd had a heart attack a few weeks before, so that would have made sense. But it appears it wasn't his heart at all. Just death by drowning.'

Greg could think of nothing to say. From the tone of her voice Suzy appeared reluctant to accept that Roddy would have fallen into the sea from the Yacht Club jetty, and on the face of it, it did seem unlikely, after all he had known the place intimately for forty years. But on the other hand Roddy was an old man; he must have been well over seventy.

'That afternoon,' continued Suzy, 'Dan had taken the Mercedes and gone to Freshwater to see one of his friends He was back by six o'clock as promised, to collect Roddy and bring him home, but at first he couldn't find him. He wasn't in his office, he wasn't in the bar, in fact it seems that nobody had seen him for a while. Dan said he wasn't too worried though, because he thought Roddy must be out looking at a mooring or something, so he went outside to see if he could see him and there he was alongside the jetty, face down in the water. They tried to bring him round but it was too late.'

They were quiet for a while, then Suzy said, 'I'll never understand it. Roddy was always a good swimmer. He could still swim two or three lengths of our pool quite comfortably. It doesn't make sense that he should go like that.'

Greg said, 'How has Dan taken it?'

'He was very upset at first. He would have been upset at his father's death anyway, of course, - they always had a good relationship - but it was a dreadful shock, finding him like that.'

'Yes. And I know from your letters that they were close. It must be hard for him.'

'Well, as I said, it was at first. But Roddy left the club to him in his will, so after the funeral Dan said he owed it to his Dad to take over directly. He didn't see any point in going back to university. Roddy wanted him to take over eventually anyway, so it just brought things forward a bit and that has helped him get over it.'

'Good. And how is he managing?"

'Very well. Roddy always involved him in the club, right from when he first showed an interest as a little boy; he couldn't have been more than ten years old. They had this private joke: when Roddy gave him a job to do he'd say, "Carry on, Number One!" and Dan would reply, "Aye, Aye, Skipper!" and salute. It was rather sweet.'

Greg said, 'I've always been grateful that Roddy turned out to be such a good father for the boy. We were very lucky, weren't we.'

Suzy squeezed his hand. 'Do you know,' she said, 'In all the years Roddy never once even hinted that he had any doubts about Dan being his.'

Greg smiled at her. 'I suppose that does rather go to prove the point you always made - that it couldn't have been him that had me beaten up.'

'Of course it wasn't. He never knew about us, I'm absolutely sure.'

'Well, if that's so I'm glad,' said Greg. 'I always envied him, you know, having you and Dan, but he did a damn good job of looking after you both, much better than I could ever have done. But how about you? You must miss him too.'

'Yes, of course I do. After all, we were married for twentysix years and he was always very kind to me and gentle and undemanding, and I was very fond of him. But I never really got to know him properly in all that time. I think Dan got closer to him than I ever did. I do miss him, yes, but rather in the way one might miss a favourite uncle, I suppose.'

'He left you well provided for, though?'

'Oh yes, although there was not as much as we would have thought. But I have the house and a good income for life from money in trust that goes to Dan when I die. Roddy left me his shares in the Sports Club and the Quarterdeck Club, too, as well as his majority shareholding in the Pier and Amusement Arcade, but Bob Clarmont Brown made me an offer I couldn't refuse for all that. I didn't want the bother anyway, and I've invested the money in something rather more solid.'

'Bob Clarmont Brown, eh?'

'Yes, he's quite a figure in the area these days. In line for a knighthood now, so they say.'

'Good Lord.'

'He was very keen to get my shares. With his usual finesse he approached me immediately after the funeral, told me what the shares were worth and offered me double so I doubled it again. He quibbled a bit, but I realised he particularly wanted the Quarterdeck Club shares, which give him a half-share with the Wilsons, so he had to pay up. He now has complete control of the Sports Club and the Pier complex, too, so we'll see a few changes there soon, I expect.'

Greg said, 'I suppose Dan inherited my old home as part of the Yacht Club?'

'That's right. The café has been neglected lately and we're thinking of doing it up and putting a new manager in, but the chandlery has always been worth its keep.'

'You're helping him, I take it?'

'Well, just until he finds his feet. He's doing very well so far. He's got all kinds of ideas for the future. You must come and see. When you're well enough, I mean.'

'OK.'

After a short silence Suzy turned to him and clasped his hand in both of hers. She said, looking directly into his eyes, 'If you did decide not to go back to the Regiment, what would you do?'

Greg shrugged. 'No idea. Depends, I suppose.'

'On what?'

'How fit I am, for one thing.'

'How about coming in with us? Helping Dan run the club?' She smiled expectantly, lifting up his hand and squeezing hard.

Greg stared at her, taken completely by surprise.

EIGHTEEN

Greg had only ever had three close friends in whom he knew he could confide completely: Sam, Suzy and Luke. Sam and Luke were both gone now, but he still had Suzy, his first and only love. When, at this low point in his life, he had decided to telephone her, he had known she would do whatever she could to give him support. She would listen and sympathise and he would feel better for telling her about his unhappiness, and perhaps just talking about his fears for the future might make him feel more like taking some positive action. She had always been able to make him feel valued and that was probably all he really needed. After her visit he would do his best to get on with his life and she would return to her life with Roddy. From time to time she would write to him, her amusing letters always including news of Dan, and maybe they would arrange see each other again some time.

But now, suddenly, she was presenting him with the possibility of a whole new future and in his current state of mind the unexpectedness of the idea overwhelmed him.

He continued to stare at her, unable to relate to what she had said. He could see the feasibility of it, of course, now that she had lost Roddy, but of necessity, he had long ago abandoned the notion that the two of them might ever have a life together. Also, trying to picture the Yacht Club after all these years, he could not imagine any circumstance in which he would fit in there either. Suzy clearly hoped he would be attracted to the idea, though, and he did not know what to say to her.

She said, still clasping his hand and smiling, 'The idea came to me bit by bit on the ferry, on the way over. It just seemed to me that it would be wonderful if you could come and stay with us while you were getting better and I could look after you, and then I thought, when you were better, perhaps you might not want to stay in the army any more, and then you could live with us all the time and you could help Dan with his plans for the Yacht Club.' She paused, finally registering his blank expression. 'If you wanted to. You see?'

'Yes,' he said. He took a deep breath. 'It's all rather a lot to take in, Suzy.'

'Yes, well, it's something to think about, anyway, if you're thinking of leaving the Regiment.'

She released his hand and sat still, looking away from him towards the hospital buildings.

He watched her face, side on, for a moment and he saw that she was cross with herself for taking for granted that he would immediately accept her idea. And perhaps she was a little embarrassed, too, about sounding so eager.

He felt a wave of tenderness flow over him. Could he still be in love with this woman after all this time? Certainly, she had always been the yardstick by which he measured his feelings for any woman he was attracted to; nobody had ever quite compared to her. That, he'd always supposed, was because what had happened between them had occurred when his life was still at a formative stage.

Perhaps now there might be a chance that they could be together after all. It seemed as though she thought so anyway. But was that what he wanted? He wasn't sure that it was.

'What about Dan?' he said. 'I mean, he'll have his own views, surely.'

'Oh, Dan would love to have you with us, I know. He would have come with me today, but I wanted to see you on my own this time.'

'But, me living with you – wouldn't he wonder at that?'

'Perhaps,' she said.

'You haven't thought about telling him?' he said, 'Now that Roddy's gone?'

'No. I don't think I could ever do that, Greg.' She turned towards him with a faint smile.

'No.' He sighed and looked away. 'Life's a bastard isn't it.'

'But that *is* what we agreed.' She sounded concerned. 'Have you changed your mind? You want him to know?'

'Oh, I don't know. I do and I don't. Sort of evenly balanced. But I expect it's best to leave things as they are.'

Suzy leant back against the wall. After a while she said, 'I can understand that you want Dan to know you are his real, his biological father, of course I can, but don't you see? It would mean admitting to him that for twenty years you and I have deceived not only him, but the man he loved as his father as well, and I can't face that.'

Greg said, 'It would be a hard secret to keep if we all lived together.'

'For you, perhaps,' she said, 'But I've lived with it for a long time, and I can't tell you how many times I have wished we could all three have been together with no need for secrets.'

'Me too,' said Greg. 'But it's too late now.'

'Not too late for us to be together, surely?' she said. 'You don't believe that, do you?'

'I meant that twenty years have gone by, and I've met my son only once in all that time. Okay, we've become very good pen-pals through the years and I'm very grateful for that at least, but, well, you know...' Greg tailed off unhappily.

Suzy suddenly realised that the explosion which had killed his friend Luke had not only badly injured Greg's body, but had left him mentally depressed as well, and her vague hope of taking him home and helping him get better now became an urgent desire. She vowed to herself that she would get him out of the hospital and into her care as soon as she possibly could; he needed her and she would not fail him.

But she could see that he had yet to be persuaded, and besides, he was looking anxious and tired now. It was time for her to go.

Promising to come and see him again the next day and bring Dan with her, she walked slowly with him back to the Sick Officers' Block.

Greg sat quietly alone in the ward after she had gone, thinking about her visit. It had not had the effect he had anticipated. He had hoped she would simplify his thoughts, removing his doubts about being able to continue his career in the Regiment, but just at the moment he was feeling more confused than ever.

He was attracted to the notion of being with Suzy and Dan, but he had never wanted to go back to Seastone. The feeling that he had been rejected by the villagers after the incident with Nigel Heapes, and then the savage beating which had almost killed him, had turned him against the place, and on the one occasion he had returned ten years ago, to attend Sam's funeral and to meet Dan, he had been glad to leave as soon as decently possible.

Over the next few days he underwent the remaining medical checks at Haslar.

Suzy came to see him every day. She brought Dan with her as promised on her second visit, and Greg was almost overcome at meeting his grown-up son. The tall, handsome young man, very much a masculine version of his blonde mother, was clearly delighted to see him, although distressed at the circumstances, and after an initial nervousness on both sides, they very soon re-established the rapport which they had developed in their letters over recent years.

By the time Greg went to sleep that night he was thinking seriously about Suzy's invitation to spend some time with her and Dan during his convalescence, if that could somehow be made to fit in with the army's plans for him.

Just before dawn he woke, confused and sweating out of a nightmare. His anxiety about leaving the Regiment hit him again, and his stomach clenched, his heartbeat raced frantically and his throat and mouth felt tight and dry. Twenty years in the cocoon of service life could be coming to an end. For the first time ever he might have to take responsibility for directing his own affairs, and, not knowing whether he would eventually regain complete physical fitness, he had no confidence about deciding the direction in which the next phase of his life should start.

With part of his mind he was disgusted at his weakness, dreading to think what Luke or Nick would think of him in his present state. He lay on his back, trying to calm himself, and staring towards the window, where the faint glow from the security lights outside slowly changed and mellowed to pale grey as the dawn came up, while his pulse-rate eased and his stomach and throat muscles gradually relaxed.

When Suzy arrived later that day his attempts to explain his feelings to her made her more than ever determined that she must take him home and nurse him back to health herself.

'Have they told you how long you are staying here?' she asked.

'Oh, I'm only here for the tests, I think,' he said. 'I don't know. I've just had the last lot so I assume they'll send me back to Salisbury once they've got the results.'

'Let's hope they'll show you're well enough to come and stay with us for a few days. Do you think they'd let you?'

'I don't know. I suppose it's possible.' He smiled. 'You know, being cooped up in bed for the best part of three months, I've had time to think about things, and one thing that *has* sunk in is that I don't have anywhere outside the army to go, so the idea of home leave never occurs to me. Other blokes go home to parents, or

111

wives and kids, but I've never had that. Not that it's bothered me. I've stayed at friends' places, or gone on leave with a couple of mates, and always had a good time.'

'Well, you do have somewhere now, so what do you think?'

'Yes, why not. Thanks,' he said, 'I'll see the MO about it as soon as I get back.'

'The MO?"

'Doctor in charge of my case. Been pretty good to me, actually.'

'Will you say anything about leaving the Regiment?'

'I could ask him what he thinks, I suppose.'

'You still aren't sure, are you?'

'No, I told you, I don't know if I'm ready to cope with civvy street yet.'

NINETEEN

The next day, before she went to meet Greg, Suzy made enquiries of the hospital staff about the outlook for him. She was dismayed to be told that although the results of the tests confirmed that he was well on the way to complete physical recovery, his mental condition was giving cause for concern and he was being referred to a specialist unit in the Midlands where he would receive appropriate treatment. She asked if it was possible for Greg to convalesce privately and was told that if he had any leave entitlement he could spend it wherever he liked, provided his medical officer sanctioned it, otherwise he was subject to normal military discipline. On her way to meet Greg she decided to persuade him to apply for leave straightway.

He had not yet been informed about his impending transfer and was understandably indignant, not only about learning about it from Suzy but mainly because he did not believe he had what they called 'a mental condition'.

'OK, so I'm a bit fed up with not being fit,' he said, 'And maybe I've been feeling a bit too sorry for myself, but there's no way I'm going to the loony bin.'

'Is there anything you can do to avoid it?' she said.

'Short of telling them I want out altogether? Probably not.'

'Look, have you got any holiday due?'

'Must have.'

'Well, remember what we were saying yesterday? Why don't you see if you can talk them into letting you come and stay with us? Before they send you to the loony bin, as you call it.'

As a result of this conversation Greg confronted the medical officer in charge of his case and over the next two days, with Suzy's active intervention, it was agreed that he could spend the next month at Abbots House with Suzy, returning to Haslar for weekly check-ups.

Greg spent that month resting and being mollycoddled by Suzy. He rapidly rebuilt his physical strength and when the month was up he believed his condition had so far improved that he was fit enough to return to his normal duties. He was told, however, that he was being transferred for treatment at the specialist psychiatric unit.

He appealed to Nick as his former CO to intervene but the medical authorities were adamant.

Greg could not accept this. He could see no way that he could return to the Regiment and carry on as before with what he saw as the stigma of 'a spell in the loony bin', and encouraged by Suzy, he decided to leave the army.

The next few months at Abbots House were difficult.

On the one hand Greg revelled in the opportunities to get to know his son. They spent much of their time together. As Greg's physical fitness improved, Dan, who was a skillful sailor, enjoyed taking him out in various boats and teaching him all he knew about yacht racing. At the end of October, Greg took Dan to the Brecon Beacons. For three weeks they lived rough, Greg, familiar with the terrain, using his experience to give Dan in his turn, as good an idea as was possible about survival techniques. There was no doubt that the two of them were establishing a strong bond.

On the other hand, Greg gradually found Suzy's mothering of him becoming irksome. She was genuinely anxious that he should not over-exert himself and they almost quarrelled about the trip to the Beacons.

Added to this was the fact that the Yacht Club did not run itself and while Dan and Greg were out enjoying themselves, Suzy had to manage the club on her own, a task she found increasingly burdensome.

By early December it had become clear to Greg that coming to live at Abbots House had been a mistake. He felt guilty about not always conforming to Suzy's plans for him, and spending much of his time with Dan at her expense. He liked the idea of helping Dan, but he found the minutiae of the day-to-day affairs of the Yacht Club and the petty concerns of its members tedious, and although he quite enjoyed messing about in boats, he could not raise any lasting enthusiasm for it.

In the week before Christmas he rang Nick Southwell to ask his advice and see if there was a chance of rejoining the Regiment. Nick invited him to spend the weekend with him at Hereford.

Over the two days they discussed a variety of options for Greg's future and eventually agreed that as there was no real possibility of him rejoining the Regiment it would be best if he left Abbots House and got a job not far away so that he could remain in contact with Dan and Suzy.

Nick then obtained an interview for Greg with Safeguard Security, a firm based in Portsmouth and run by. an ex-colleague who owed him a favour, and thus it was that on his way back to the Island on the following Monday, Greg went to Safeguard's office where he was told that if he wanted to, he could start on the first Monday of the new year. This was his first real experience of the influence of the 'old boy network'.

He then made arrangements through Louise Wilson's estate agency, who still controlled the lettings, to move into one of his apartments in Southsea. After this all that remained to be done was tell Suzy he was moving out. He decided to leave this difficult task until after the Christmas holiday.

In the event it was not too painful. Suzy had been well aware of his discontent and although clearly upset when he told her of his decision on the morning of New Year's Day, she accepted it without any fuss, especially after Greg asked her to help him settle into his flat.

The move was simple and straightforward. He had few personal possessions and they were easily contained within two large suitcases.

Greg's two apartments were situated one above the other in a modernised Victorian-style building on Southsea's seafront. In the ten years since he had inherited them from Sam he had only ever been inside either of them once, having been happy for Wilsons Estate Agents to make all arrangements on his behalf, and the income from the lettings had grown to a considerable sum deposited in his bank account in Hereford. Nick Southwell had commented on this at the weekend, suggesting that Greg should get advice on investing it more profitably. It was another new thing for him to learn about, he realised.

Both flats were let on short-term leases and the penthouse flat had conveniently become vacant on New Year's Day. Wilsons had arranged for it to be thoroughly cleaned and when Suzy came with him on the following Saturday, there was still a faint smell of cleaning materials as they came out of the lift which led directly into the apartment's hallway.

She sniffed the air and said, 'This reminds me of a certain afternoon a good many years ago when it all began for us. How strange that it should come to an end in the same way.'

Greg put down his two suitcases and turned to her. He put his hands on her shoulders and looked into her eyes. 'Nothing's coming to an end, Suzy. You are still the most important woman in the world for me. But it wasn't working out, was it, and it will be better like this.'

She said nothing but put her arms around his waist and rested her head on his chest.

He kissed the top of her head and gently pushed her away. 'Come on,' he said, taking her hand in his, 'Let me show you around and then you can tell me what you think.'

None of the rooms in the apartment were very large, but they were certainly of an adequate size for a small family or a man like Greg living alone. There were two double bedrooms, a good-sized bathroom, a fully fitted kitchen with a breakfast area, a lounge with a space near the kitchen furnished as a dining area, and at the other end an attractive spiral staircase leading up to a private roof terrace. The gas central heating had been switched on and the flat was pleasantly warm.

They examined every room, even going up onto the terrace to admire the panoramic views of the city and over the Solent to the Island.

Suzy expressed herself as satisfied that Greg could live comfortably enough here, but considered that the flat contained only the minimum amount of furniture to justify describing as furnished and all of it, though of good quality, was too old and, like the fitted carpets, showed signs of much wear and should be replaced.

Greg would have been quite happy to accept it just as it was but he did not argue.

'Would you see to that for me, then?' he said.

'Yes, if you want me to,' she said, her face lighting up, as Greg had known it would, at the idea of designing his living space for him. 'Now, then, let's go and find where the local shops are and stock you up with basics.'

This was another lesson Greg was going to have to learn. He was more than capable of cooking himself simple meals, but shopping of any kind was outside of his experience. Suddenly, and to his surprise, he found himself enjoying the prospect of providing for himself, and he listened with genuine interest at Suzy's suggestions and hints about what was worth buying and what was a waste of time and effort, as he pushed a trolley around his local supermarket.

They returned to the flat and Greg watched while Suzy packed away his purchases.

When she had finished she said, 'I did all this for Dan when he first went away to the university, but I didn't expect I'd ever be doing it for anyone else. Especially not you. It's like having an extra son.' Then she realised what she had said and a strange expression spread over her face.

Greg smiled and said, carefully, 'Well, if it's any consolation I never did think of you as a mother-figure, and I still don't.' He stepped towards her and kissed her on the lips. Then he stood back and said, 'Let me make you a cup of tea as the first guest in my new home. Then it'll be time for you to go or you'll miss the last ferry.'

When they had had their tea, Greg walked with her to her car. He bent down to her window to kiss her goodbye and she said, 'I'll ring tomorrow. I'll give you a week to settle in. and I'll come and start measuring for curtains and things. Alright?'

'Thanks.'

He watched as she drove off, feeling a surge of relief that they had parted as close friends and not as he had feared, with recriminations.

Back in the hallway of the apartment, he picked up his suitcases and took them into the blue bedroom. He had chosen this one because it was safer, the other being on the corner of the building and therefore vulnerable from two sides. Then it occurred to him that he was still thinking as if he was on assignment in the Regiment. He chided himself as he unpacked and put his clothes away, wondering how long it took to accept normality.

When he had finished, he walked around the apartment once more, trying to get the feel of the place and glad to be on his own at last. He ended up in the lounge and poured himself a large whisky, which he took up the spiral staircase to the roof terrace.

It was almost dark now and a cold breeze was coming off the sea as he gazed out over the Solent. A cluster of lights slowly moving against the dark background of the Island resolved itself into an oil tanker on its way from the refinery at Fawley. Much nearer, just across Southsea Common towards the harbour mouth, he could hear the diesel engine of a small boat straining to make

117

progress against the outpouring tide.

He looked at his watch. Suzy's ferry would be leaving in a few minutes.

He sipped his whisky, watching the oil tanker. By his reckoning it must be about mid-way in a direct line between him and Seastone Yacht Club.

Should he have tried harder to settle down with Suzy and Dan? Perhaps. Who could tell? But living with them had been too much of a strain.

One thing he did have to admit to himself: he should not have left hospital so soon. His depression was still hanging around. They had known he was not ready to go and they had tried hard to keep him in, but, as he was now willing to accept, he was becoming afraid of returning to the Regiment, unsure that he would be able to function any more, and he had taken the easy way out. Perhaps he should have left it to them to decide his future for him. They would probably have made a better job of it than he was doing so far.

Suzy had been so sure, though, that all he needed was for her to look after him and help him back to life and she had helped to persuade them. She had tried very hard for him too, but eventually she had to accept that there was not very much left in him of the boy she had known and loved, just as, for him, there was the hard fact of having to recognise that the powerful attraction that that eighteen-year-old had felt towards her had been almost entirely physical and just wasn't there any more.

He fully appreciated what she had tried to do for him though, and he was deeply saddened that she had been so hurt when he had told her he was moving out. He knew he would always be very fond of her, and he fully intended to maintain the good relationship they had had for the last twenty years if he could.

He shivered. It was far too cold to be standing up here without a coat. Suzy was not expecting him to watch her go home alone, and as he took his whisky back down to the warmth of his lounge he reflected gratefully that the one good thing, the wonderful thing, to have come out of those last six months had been the bond forged with Dan. They had formed a close friendship, and for that reason alone he would move heaven and earth to ensure that the three of them always remained close.

TWENTY

Greg had been with Safeguard Security for two-and-a-half years when they finally told him he had to go. It was a Friday morning, the day after his fortysecond birthday and a year since Suzy had told him she had only six months to live. It was also the fifth consecutive day he'd arrived at the office just before noon, reeking of whisky.

He didn't argue or plead with them to let him have another chance. He couldn't care less about them or their job. He couldn't even summon up the effort to refuse to take the dog, a young German Shepherd, which they said would not work with anyone else because it was devoted to him. He didn't want it, but he couldn't deny that it would be a shame to have it destroyed.

He used his office phone for the last time and called a taxi. Then he emptied his desk, packing his few personal possessions into a cardboard box, and took the box and the dog home in the taxi to his flat in Southsea. Then he went down the road to the off-licence for another bottle of scotch. He took the dog with him and walked it across the Common on his way home. He spent the rest of the day drinking the bottle of scotch.

Late in the evening he awoke to a terrible noise, interspersed with the sound of gunshots, or so it seemed to his fuddled senses.

Somebody was banging on his door and the dog was barking furiously

He struggled out of the armchair he had passed out in, and the room whirled around him. He staggered woozily in the darkened room and fell over the dog. Somehow he summoned the presence of mind to quieten the dog, before regaining his feet and reaching for the light switch. The room was now undulating and he felt violently sick.

'Hang on!' he yelled at the door, and rushed into his bathroom, reaching the toilet bowl just in time to empty his stomach. He had not eaten since the night before so he had little to bring up.

A voice called, 'Greg, it's me, Southwell,' and the dog started to bark again.

Greg lurched to the sink, turned on the cold tap and held his hands under. After a long, cold drink he splashed the water over his face and head several times.

Feeling only slightly better, he grabbed the dog, went to the door and let Nick in.

Nick walked past him into the living room and looked around. It was a mess. 'Not so good, Greg,' he said, picking up the empty whisky bottle from the floor and putting it on a table.

Greg said nothing. He knew Nick must be upset about him losing the job.

'You know what drink did to your father.'

'Yeah, right.'

'So cut it down, man. You don't need it.'

He recognised what Nick was saying and thought perhaps he ought to resent the interference but he really didn't care enough to bother. He flopped back into his armchair and sat with one hand over his eyes.

Nick sat on the sofa facing him.

Neither of them said anything for a while. Then Nick said, 'Look, I know you'll think it's none of my business, but it started after you left the Island, didn't it.'

Greg didn't care whether it was any of Nick's business or not, but he didn't say so.

'The long drinking sessions? Because you were lonely? Depressed after we lost Luke. And then you left the Regiment and it didn't work out right with Suzy. But drinking didn't do any good then, did it? And you cut it down, right?'

Still Greg stayed silent. He felt awful. He didn't need this.

'But now Suzy's gone, so it's started up again.'

He knew Nick felt he had a right to be concerned but it didn't seem to matter.

'No good telling you to go to the medics, I suppose?'

Greg wanted to tell him it would be pointless. The whole of his life just seemed pointless. Okay, so supposing he stopped drinking, so what? Whar difference would it make? He didn't want the job back. He didn't need a job anyway. He didn't know what he did want, except another drink, but whatever it was he couldn't say it and they sat in silence for another long while.

Eventually, Nick said, 'Why didn't you tell me how bad it was? I've told you, any time. You want a chat, someone to listen. Or whatever. But you've always been so much of a loner. You try to get by on your own, so now you don't think there's anybody you can go to. But I'm still here, Greg.'

There was another long silence.

Nick stood up to leave. He put his hand on Greg's shoulder.

'Why don't you go and see Zillah,' he said.

Greg moved his hand away from his eyes and looked up, surprised.

'We chat on the phone from time to time,' Nick said. 'She still misses Luke of course, and she asks about you, knowing how close you two were. She'd be glad to see you.' He squeezed Greg's shoulder and went out.

In the three years since Luke had died there had rarely been a day when something had not happened to make Greg think of him. The idea of talking about him with his sister was not unappealing, he supposed. It was something to do, anyway, and he quite liked Zillah. She was big and practical, straightforward, like Luke had been.

He thought of Suzy then, her loving smile, her patience even after he'd moved out of Abbots House, and her continuing concern for him which had lasted right up until the day the leuchemia took her away. It was only then, too late, that he realised she had truly loved him.

He sighed. All the people who mattered to him died – first his mother, then Sam, then Luke and now Suzy. He wondered if it was worth ever getting close to anyone.

The dog came and stood staring fixedly at him.

'What do you want, then?'

Head on one side, tail slowly moving, the German Shepherd gave a sharp bark.

'Oh, right, okay.' Greg roused himself and made the effort to stand up. There was a dull ache in his head and he went to his medicine cabinet, shook out a half dozen aspirin tablets and swallowed them in a long drink of cold water. The dog had gone into the hallway, waiting by the lift until Greg fetched the lead to take him out.

The walk across the Common in the fresh air and the company of the dog, together made him feel a bit better, and as he got ready for bed he decided, yes, he'd go and see Zillah.

oOo

The next morning after plenty of strong, black coffee and a

cold shower, he shook off his hangover, put the dog in the back of his Citroen ZX and set off to travel along the length of the M27 and on into the New Forest. Leaving the A31 at Ringwood, he pulled into the Furlong car park.

Feeling a little apprehensive about getting back in touch with Zillah, he sat in the car for several minutes wondering what to say to her. Eventually he left it to chance and rang her home number on his mobile phone.

She answered brusquely, 'Leave a message and I'll ring you back,' and rang off.

His problem solved, he dialled again and left his name and number.

After about ten minutes his phone rang. 'Hello?' he said.

'Hello Greg. How are you?'

'I'm fine, thanks. And you?"

'Busy.'

'Oh. I see. Um, I was hoping to come and see you, but if it's inconvenient ...'

'No, I'm not that busy - it's nice to hear from you. Where are you calling from?'

'Ringwood.'

'Alright. So let me tell you how to get here.'

Zillah gave him detailed directions to her out-of-the-way smallholding. 'See you in about fifteen minutes, then,' she said.

As he arrived there were two cars just leaving and he had to pull over onto the edge of the narrow lane to let them go by.

Zillah was standing at her gate and she indicated he should drive in.

He got out of his car and they greeted each other with a kiss on each cheek. Zillah put her hands on his shoulders and held him away from her. She looked at him severely.

'You look awful. What have you been doing to yourself?'

'Drinking too much, apparently.'

'Yes,' she said, 'It *is* apparent.'

She left him and walked towards the car. 'And what have we here?'

The dog barked aggressively as she approached.

Greg shrugged. 'It belonged to Safeguard Security. Guard dog. They sacked me yesterday and I got saddled with it.'

'I see. One man dog, eh?'

'Guess so.'

'Well, leave him there for now and come on in,' she said. 'Those two cars you met as you came in, one brought an injured badger and the other was the vet. Badger's sedated, but it's no place for a guard dog at the moment.'

Greg followed her around the cottage to the back door, and she ushered him inside, past the sleeping badger in a kennel, and into her kitchen.

'Nick Southwell rang yesterday,' she said. 'Didn't say much, except that you lost another old friend recently and might get in touch. I told him you'd be welcome.'

'Thanks,' he said, and, unaccountably, a lump rose in his throat at her unquestioned acceptance of him, and of Nick's continuing concern for him, in spite of everything. He realised then that Nick must have dropped everything yesterday and come straight to Southsea as soon as Safeguard told him. He felt tears coming and hurriedly moved away, blinking them back. 'Christ!' he thought, 'I am in a bad way!'

He took a deep breath and tried to steady himself. He hoped Zillah hadn't noticed.

She had turned away and was filling a kettle at the sink. 'I usually stop for coffee about now,' she said, 'And I happen to have the remains of a rather good dundee cake that somebody gave me the other day. If you fancy elevenses you can help me finish it.'

'That sounds good,' he said, realising that he was hungry.

Zillah put plates on the kitchen table and invited him to sit. She cut thick slices from the cake. 'I gather your friend was not with the Regiment. Nick would have said if he had been.'

'No. The friend he meant was a woman. She died a few weeks ago, actually. I'd known her a long time. But it wasn't ...' he tailed off, not wishing to explain.

She poured their coffee and waited while they each added milk and sugar. Then she said, 'Nick seemed to be suggesting you might want to talk about your time with Luke.'

He took a slice of cake and nibbled at it. 'Well,' he said. 'That's what I thought too. I don't know. I still miss him, of course. And the whole way of life, I suppose, but...'

'But that's not all that's troubling you.'

'I don't really know what it is. But I've no right to come and

123

bother you with it, anyway.'

Zillah said, 'But if you were bothering me with it, what do you think my advice would be?'

Greg shrugged. 'Stop feeling guilty?'

'About what?'

'Luke dying and me still being here?'

'And?'

'Suzy?'

'And?'

'I don't know. What?'

'About drinking too much and losing your job, and not being able to cope with civilian life, and generally, not being who you think everybody thinks you should be.'

Greg looked at Zillah who looked straight back at him while he thought about that for a whole minute. Then she said, 'You and Luke.' She shook her head. 'I always admired both of you for the same reason – you knew who you were. You never needed to impress anybody by being who they might think you ought to be.'

Greg smiled. 'You're like that yourself,' he said.

'Well, if I am it's because I had two good examples to follow.' She paused, then said, slowly, 'It seems to me that among all the other damage, that explosion made you forget to be who you are.'

Zillah took his hand and stared into his eyes. 'Do you know what I think, Greg,' she said seriously. 'You should go a long way away for a while. Break contact with your ghosts.'

He smiled ruefully. 'I can't do that. What about the dog? I couldn't take him with me.'

'Don't worry about the dog. You can leave him with me.'

'He doesn't take to strangers.'

'Then he'll have to learn to adapt,' she said, as if the matter was easily settled.

The more they talked about the possibility of Greg leaving everything behind him for an indefinite period, the more the idea seemed to make sense to him. Zillah was quite certain it would be the best thing for him to do.

'Nobody,' she said, 'Can survive being blown up and losing his best friend, nearly dying himself and spending weeks in intensive care without being affected. Both emotionally and mentally, I mean. You are intelligent enough to realise that Greg; it's just hard for you to accept it.'

'OK.'

Zillah smiled. 'All you need is a spot of "R & R", rest and recreation,' she said. 'I'm sure of it. Then you can start again, something new, somewhere new, someone new. Or perhaps all three. Why not?'

She persuaded him to stay for lunch, a simple meal of salad and vegetables from her own kitchen garden, with her home-made bread and preserves. Afterwards she told him to take the dog for a long walk across the Forest and think about what they had discussed.

He did, and by the time he had found his way back to the little track leading to Zillah's cottage he had decided that it did make sense to have a complete break, get away from everything he knew for a while at least.

Later, on his way home it occurred to him that she had not asked why he'd been sacked, nor had she said anything at all about his heavy drinking, as if taking it for granted that that wasn't in itself a problem. He was grateful to her for her apparent belief in him and he resolved there and then that he would not let alcohol take over his life as it had taken over his father's.

TWENTYONE

Los Angeles seemed far enough away and as good a place to start from as any, and he had never been to the States, so he bought a one-way ticket. But after a couple of days of sight-seeing, confirming that Hollywood and Sunset Boulevard were just as he had expected them to be, he found that LA wasn't doing him any good at all, and he needed to move on.

Sam had told him once that he had been in Hollywood in July 1936 when the Spanish Civil War broke out. He said the film he'd been involved with had just been completed and one of his fellow technicians had turned out to be a sympathiser of the Spanish Republicans. This fellow had taken him on a fund-raising mission which included visiting a horse ranch owned by an uncle in New Mexico a few miles from Stanley, south of Santa Fe. The ranch had been called Rancho La Ventura and the name had intrigued him as it could mean anything from happiness, through chance and fortune to danger and he wondered what might have become of it.

Greg decided he would follow Sam's footsteps and go there to find out.

Before moving on he phoned Zillah to enquire about the dog and tell her what his plans were. She approved whole-heartedly, told him not to worry about the dog which had settled in well, and reminded him that she had asked him to send her a weekly postcard.

Sam had spoken of travelling from Pasadena on the Santa Fe express and then going on by car, but Greg couldn't face the idea of being cooped up with any number of people on a train for over seven hundred miles so it was back to LAX.

In Santa Fe he hired a cab to take him around the used car lots until he found a small second-hand camper van that took his fancy. Then he bought a map and drove out of Santa Fe on Route 285, branching off on to the 41 to Stanley, where he spent the night in a small commercial hotel. In the morning he went out to stock up on groceries and other essentials for his traveling home and made enquiries about the Rancho La Ventura. Nobody seemed to have heard of it but eventually Greg was directed to the home of a retired policeman who lived some distance out of town and who, he was told, knew everything that had happened locally since World War Two.

Greg found the old man dozing in a hammock in his back yard. He was delighted to meet an Englishman, telling him he had been stationed in 'Dorsetshire' as a young airman in nineteen fortyfive and had always longed to go back but it was too late now.

Yes, he said, La Ventura turned out to have been appropriately named whichever way you looked at it. By all accounts it had been a happy and prosperous place in the early years, but there had been less and less demand for horses after the coming of the automobile and the ranch had slowly fallen into decay until by the nineteen sixties there were no horses there at all and it had been taken over by a commune. Then in nineteen seventy there had been a disastrous fire and nothing of the ranch now remained. So much for La Ventura.

But, having no other clear objective in mind, Greg decided he'd carry on following in Sam's footsteps as far as he could remember them so he headed south through El Paso into Mexico and after a week or two wandering around in the Sierra Madre with very little human contact, he eventually came to Mazatán on the old Coronado Trail. Sam had stayed here in a small hotel before heading back to the States and then on to the war in Spain.

It didn't take Greg long to find the same small hotel, but now that he had come to the end of Sam's journey he was not sure what to do next. He knew he was not ready to go home yet so, feeling the need of a bath and laundry facilities he decided to take a room there for the night.

That evening he was just finishing his meal in the dining room when a young American woman approached his table. She was quite good looking and dressed like a hippie, colourful but clean.

'Hi,' she said, smiling a greeting, 'You're Mr Gregory?'

'That's right.'

'I'm Mary Sue.' She offered him her hand.

He stood up and took it briefly.

'You came in today in that old trailer, yeah?'

'Yes.'

'You moving on soon?'

'I haven't decided yet what I'm going to do,' he said, puzzled by her interest. 'Why?'

'I'm heading south and I guess I'm hoping you might be too. I could use a lift.'

'I see.' He was amused by her cheek and waited to see what she would say next.

'You're English, yeah?'

He nodded.

'And you're traveling alone?'

He nodded again.

She just stood there smiling at him, not in any way fazed by his continuing silence.

'So what brings you all the way from England to this one-horse pueblo?'

Greg raised his eyebrows. 'You are a very inquisitive young lady,' he said.

She grinned at him. 'Well, see, I been stuck here for a week and I figure there's any chance you might be moving on I maybe could talk you into going my way. If you ain't got other plans. Mind if I sit down?'

Greg waved a hand at the empty seat and they sat facing each other.

'Case you're wondering, I been working here. Dishes and floors. Nothing special, but it gets me bed and board. But I'm sure wishful to be on my way soon as ever I can.'

It had been several days since Greg had had any real conversation with anyone, having restricted his contact with people to the minimum necessary for day-to-day living. Now he found himself intrigued by this perky young woman.

'So where exactly in the south are you heading for?'

'Place called Vascos. It's just a little old village on the coast. A bunch of us from college agreed to meet up there and just hang out for a while.'

The way she described it, it sounded to Greg as good place as any to do nothing in so he soon found himself agreeing to take her there next day.

They left early in the morning and arrived at the picturesque little village late in the afternoon. He drove around until she found her friends, about a dozen hippie-types, gentle souls like herself. They insisted that Greg stayed and shared a meal with them, and he enjoyed their company and their conversation. Later, he wondered if he could ever drop out of modern Western society just like they seemed to be doing. He wished he could, but didn't think it was likely.

He liked the atmosphere of the sleepy little village, though. He could see why Mary Sue and her friends had chosen it as a place to, as she'd said 'just hang out for a while'. He went into a little café-bar and enquired about renting a room somewhere. The proprietor said he had a room above the bar, if Greg would like to look at it. It was clean and comfortable so he took it.

The second night he was there Mary Sue called in to thank him for bringing her, and because, she said, she preferred older men. He didn't think of turning her away.

After that she spent every third or fourth night with him. She was fascinated by the scars on his body and made him tell her how he acquired them. This encouraged him to tell her things about his life in the Regiment and gradually, on subsequent nights when they were lying together in the dark, he unburdened himself to her, speaking to her more freely than he had ever done to anyone, because she was a stranger, because he was a long way from home and because she was interested and listened uncritically and without any kind of judgement. Her only consistent comment was that we all need times to relax and appreciate the here-and-now rather than dwell on the dead-and-gone or worry about the still-to-come.

For over a month he enjoyed a quiet, simple life.

Every morning he ran for half an hour on the cool beach, went back to the little café-bar for *huevos rancheros*, then returned to the beach to cultivate a tan. Sometimes Mary Sue and her friends might pass by, stopping briefly to say hello, but mostly he just sat alone, mulling over his midnight talks with Mary Sue, or composing notes for his weekly postcards to Zillah and Dan. He spent hours soothed by the distant sound of the big waves breaking over the sand-bar beyond the entrance to the little bay, and when the tide was out, watching the birds pecking and probing along the shoreline, until the day became too hot and it was time for *siesta*. In the evenings he would sit for an hour or two with his friendly landlord in the café-bar, drinking coffee, smoking a Mexican *cigarillo* but refusing any offer of alcohol, and brushing up his Spanish as they exchanged views of the world situation and agreed on the futility of nearly everything in modern life.

Then one night Mary Sue asked him if he would run her up to the border at Nogales. It was time to go home, she said

Greg realised then that he was feeling about ready to try again to find some purpose in his life. He had proved to himself that he could survive on his own without having to reach for a drink, and his comfortable daily routine for the past few weeks had put him well on the way back to real physical and mental fitness.

This, he reflected, had come about directly as a result of Mary Sue coming to his table at Mazatán, and to acknowledge his gratitude to her for her help in his recovery he decided he would take her all the way back to her home in San Jose.

Early the next morning, while Mary Sue phoned her parents to warn them of her impending return, Greg said goodbye to his landlord, thanking him for his companionship during the past month, and they set off on their long journey in the camper van.

They decided not to drive north to Nogales but take a more westerly route and head for San Diego. They spent their last night in Mexico in the mountains north of Magdalena, and crossed into the USA late the next afternoon. By early evening they were still some way south of Los Angeles and Greg was feeling tired after two long days of driving, so he turned off the coast road up into the hills and eventually found a track leading to a quiet place to park for the night.

Mary Sue clung to him in the narrow little bed in the van that night and cried a little at the prospect of their parting the next day, saying that Greg had been a really good friend and she would never forget him. Greg told her that she had helped him through a difficult phase of his life and he would always remember her for that.

When they arrived at Mary Sue's home the next evening, her parents were pleased to have their daughter home and grateful to Greg for bringing her. They invited him to stay for a day or so, and Mary Sue's father went out of his way to find a buyer for the trailer at a price that paid for Greg's return flight.

So Greg sent his final weekly postcard to Zillah, telling her that he was coming back to the UK and would phone her in the next few days to arrange to collect his dog.

TWENTYTWO

Early on his first morning back in Southsea, Greg rang Zillah and they agreed that he would collect the dog in the evening. She invited him to stay for an evening meal. Then he rang Nick Southwell, who suggested Greg should come to Hereford for 'debriefing' over lunch in a pub just outside the city where they knew from past lunches that the food was simple, tasty and plentiful.

Nick was waiting in the pub car park when Greg arrived and he took his hand, shaking it vigorously, and saying he was glad to see him in such good shape.

'And how's the drinking?' he added pointedly, as they headed towards the pub entrance.

'Haven't touched a drop since you came to sort me out last month,' said Greg, 'What's that – seven weeks now.'

'Well done.'

'It wasn't easy at first but it doesn't bother me now. I don't think I will take after my Dad after all. He was definitely an alcoholic, couldn't help himself.'

'So what are you having?' asked Nick when they reached the bar.

'Mineral water, please, fizzy. I'm still taking it one day at a time, as they say.'

They ordered their steak and kidney pies and took their drinks to the table Nick had reserved in the corner of the lounge bar. While they waited for their food, Greg gave Nick a summary of all that had happened to him since they last met.

Nick nodded appreciatively, 'Well, that's good,' he said. 'That Zillah, she's really something, eh? Must run in the family.'

Greg paused. Then he said, 'I still miss Luke, you know, Nick.'

'Yes, of course. He was a good man. You were something special, you two. Doesn't happen often but when it does… What is it they say about the whole being greater than the sum of its parts? That's what it was with you two.'

They were quiet for a minute or so and then their table number was called and they went to collect their meals at the serving area.

For some minutes they ate in silence. Then Nick said, 'Any idea what you're going to do?'

'No. Haven't a clue. Don't have to do anything, really.'

'No, I dare say you can live comfortably enough on your pension and the income from your other flat. And you've got the money Suzy left you, too, haven't you?'

'That's right.' Greg looked at him quizzically. 'I could always write my memoirs, I suppose. What do you think?'

Nick shook his head. 'I think you ought to try and keep at least a few of the skills we taught you. Would you be up for a job if there was something suitable?'

One of the things Greg had realised during the past month while ruminating on the beach at Vascos was that his self-confidence had been badly damaged by the depression which followed his injuries, and he knew he was not ready just yet to subject himself to any kind of unnecessary stress.

'What sort of a job?' he said warily. 'The Regiment wouldn't want me back, surely?'

'You're still on the Reserve, aren't you?'

'Well, yes, but ...'

'We might well want you back one day then,' said Nick with a smile. 'But that's not it. There's a firm in Poole that needs someone to carry out surveillances and security surveys, and help them with field evaluation of new technology as it comes along. It could be a nice little part-time job, no stress, no hassle. Would you be interested?'

'Not if it's another Safeguard. The only good thing about that job was training the dog. The rest of it was for morons only. Even part-time it would drive me to drink. Again.'

'No,' said Nick. 'No, I wouldn't wish that on you. This firm is a lot more versatile than Safeguard; they cover a much wider range. It's quite a go-ahead set-up, actually.'

Greg said he would think about it.

'They're sure to take you on if I say the word. It could be just the thing for you.'

'Sounds as though you're telling me to take it. Are you doing this for me or for them?'

'For you and for them, but let's face it, it's not going to do you a bit of good to be completely idle, is it?' Nick paused. Then he said, 'Heck, I might as well be straight with you. I'm leaving in a few months time, and I'm hoping to take the firm over'

'Really?' Greg was surprised. He had always assumed Nick would go on rising through the Regiment to the very top.

'Yes.' Nick was obviously excited at the prospect. 'There's still a lot to be sorted out yet, but it's looking good so far.'

'So I'd be working for you, then?'

'Well, yes. Look, I know there's no need to tell you to keep this under your hat, but I'm aiming to set up a European-wide operation. I've started talks with a fellow I know in Munich - he used to be with the BND. And I've got a couple of Frenchmen interested too. They've got contacts in the DST and DGSE, so we should have quite a bit of background between us.'

'Let's get this clear,' said Greg. 'We're talking about a security organisation, are we?'

'That's right, corporate security. Basically offering support and training in risk management and the protection of people, property, information, products, operations,' he shrugged, 'Whatever.'

'Sounds like a pretty wide field.'

'It is, and there's an increasing demand for the sort of thing people with our background can do, so if this gets off the ground I could certainly use your experience. What do you think?'

This sounded to Greg like the start of the sort of project he might have expected from Nick and he could not help feeling curious about it.

'Part-time, you said?'

'Yes. To start with, anyway. You may feel like getting fully involved later, perhaps.'

'OK, When do I start?'

Nick laughed. 'Good! That's more like the old Greg! But there's no rush. I can't do anything positive until I've left the Service, and that's not until the end of February. In the meantime, though, it would be helpful if you could have a look at the Poole set-up from the inside for me. From what I've learnt so far it seems pretty good. I know they've got one or two useful chaps, but there has been an increase in their workload lately, and they're a bit short-handed at the moment.'

'Right. Okay. So, if it's a part-time job, what sort of hours are we talking about?'

'What I have in mind, and I'll suggest this to them, is they pay you a small retainer, say a couple of thou a year, and call you in as required for specific projects. That way you're on their payroll and you'll get the going rate per hour when you're actually working.'

'OK. So I wouldn't have to move or commute from Southsea every day?'

'That's right.'

'But you would want me to start pretty soon?'

'As I said there's no rush, but could you manage it by Monday, the first of November?'

'That's what, five weeks? Oh yes, I don't see why not.'

'Good. One of the things that's been bugging them, if you'll pardon the pun, is the so-called Millenium Bug, and they've got some new gear on order that's supposed to be guaranteed bug-free. First of November would give you a couple of months to get it all tested.'

'And that would give me time to check on the way they do things there, too.'

'Yes. Now, they've got two locations. One is just off the High Street, near the Dolphin Centre. That's where all the run-of-the-mill detective agency work comes in, missing persons, family history research and so on, and, of course, routine domestics – you know, wifey wants to know why hubby is so often late home from the office, and when she's told the reason, how much money can she get out of him in the divorce settlement. There is a receptionist-cum-secretary, who is pretty sharp I gather, two middle-aged ex-coppers and two youngish women part-time investigators. I intend to keep that side of it going, for a while at least. But the other place is the interesting one. That's in a smallish unit in an industrial estate at Hamworthy, outside the town itself.'

'And that's the one you want me to look at.'

'Right.'

'So what do they do there?'

'All kinds of different aspects of economic intelligence. Corporate investigations such as anti-fraud work, the protection of intellectual property like copyright, trade marks, anti-piracy. Computer forensics. Locating and dealing with electronic surveillance, like a bugged boardroom, for example. In fact any kind of industrial espionage. As I say, they're versatile.'

'How many staff there?'

'Only six at present, four men and two women. Both of the women are computing experts. One spends most of her time on computer searches. Apparently her expertise is knowing where to look for absolutely anything. The other one is a software whizz-kid. One of the men used to be with us, Hamish Petrie. You may have come across him?'

'Don't remember a Hamish.'

'Good man, you'll like him. One of the others is American, used to be a journalist and is said to be a good investigator. Big fellow - he's also handy for anything from bouncer to bodyguard. The other two are office johnnies, auditors, working on finance, accounting, commercial credit, and insurance, that sort of thing.'

'As you say, versatile.'

'Yes, and a good base to start from, I believe. The firm already provides security guards and security training on an ad hoc basis to businesses all over the south and west. I want to build on this to include other protection services as well and go on to cover the whole of the EU and possibly elsewhere eventually. It's an expanding market, Greg.'

Greg could not help being impressed. 'But who would your customers be, Nick?'

'Anyone who needs something protected. Could be anything - an individual, an MP, say, or an archbishop, or a group like a football team, or a place - oil refinery, railway station, embassy, anything that may be thought to be vulnerable.'

Nick paused for a moment and looked hard at Greg as if wondering how far he should confide in him. Having decided he went on, 'And I'm convinced there's a place for a firm that can supply a security task force to protect humanitarian organisations like aid agencies. Nowadays, wherever there's a breakdown in law and order, civilian agencies are becoming more and more liable to attack. We saw it in Bosnia and Kosovo, didn't we? And it's happened in other places, too, the Congo, East Timor, south Sudan and so on. So I'd be looking to recruit people with operations experience in those places. People like yourself, in fact.'

'Sounds a bit like a private army, or what do they call 'em these days, a PMC.'

'No, it would not be a private military company, more a commercial security company.'

'If it's an armed force, Nick, and it would have to be wouldn't it, what's the difference?'

'Well, PMCs are set up to help in military actions, like the taking and holding of ground. A commercial security company would definitely not be involved in anything like that. If they were, I can't see that many businesses, or any of the humanitarian agencies, would want anything to do with them.'

'But they would be armed?'

'Oh, yes, most definitely.'

'So when would they use their weapons?'

'When attacked, obviously, but otherwise the main use of weapons would be as deterrent.'

'Well, it sounds like a very ambitious undertaking, Nick,' said Greg. 'But I must say I've always had reservations about private armies of any kind. Fighting for Queen and country, okay, but for a commercial business, I don't know. I've never fancied being a mercenary.'

Nick looked disappointed. 'You wouldn't be interested in joining me, then?' he said.

'Well, I didn't mean that, exactly. It's just that I reckon I've had enough actual combat experience. It's part of the reason I left the Regiment in the first place. This part-time job in Poole sounds alright, though. And I wouldn't mind a job helping in training, if there was one going.'

'Good. Well, look, I wasn't sure how much you'd want to get involved at the moment, anyway. That's why I suggested the part-time approach. But you will take that on?'

'Sure. Thanks.'

'Good. I'll ring you during the week and we'll fix a time to take you around the place.'

TWENTYTHREE

Greg had a lot on his mind as he drove back to Hampshire later that afternoon.

He had asked Nick what had made him want to give up his career in the Regiment

'A combination of things, really,' Nick had said. 'There's been a lot of irritating changes in the way we're expected to work, for one thing. I won't go into details, but there is too much of a PC attitude these days, it seems to me. Too many petty restrictions. I was beginning to resent having to double-check everything. But when this move from Stirling Lines to Credenhill came up, it involved some other changes as well and it meant there was a chance to rethink. I took the chance to have a look around and opted to leave instead.'

'Well, at least you've prepared yourself for life outside the Regiment,' Greg had said. 'When I left I had no idea how hard I'd find it and I just felt irrelevant in civvy street. Okay, I was not properly fit, but looking back, the worst thing was the feeling of not belonging anywhere, you know? Until then I'd thought I belonged in the Regiment.'

Nick had nodded understandingly. 'It quite often happens, I believe, when a chap has been in the Service for a long time and suddenly has to leave. And don't forget you had been very seriously injured. That took a hell of a lot out of you.' He paused. 'I hate to have to say it, Greg, but perhaps it would have been better if you'd stayed in until you were properly recovered.'

'Yes, you're probably right.'

'Never mind, I'm sure it's just a matter of time. I think you should take it easy for a little bit longer. Ease your way back into things.'

But now, as he headed towards Ross-on-Wye on the A49, Greg was doubting that he would ever get back to the person that Nick had known. That person would always have felt irrelevant in civilian life. He'd been highly trained in just about everything, but his skills were not needed in the civilian world and there could be nothing to motivate him there.

These thoughts were mainly the result of his time in Vascos, where, partly through talking with Mary Sue, and partly from reflecting on his experiences in the Regiment, he had slowly come to see life from a different perspective, no longer thinking exclusively in terms of Queen and Country.

He had spoken honestly when he had told Nick he had reservations about serving with a private army, and although he had no doubt of Nick's integrity, he wondered if he himself would ever want to participate actively in an organisation such as the one Nick intended to set up.

He wished there was somebody he could share these thoughts with, as he would have done in the old days with Luke. The only remaining person he felt really close to was Dan, but Dan was far too young to share such confidences.

The perception of his continuing loneliness made him melancholy, but then he thought of his dog, utterly loyal and devoted to him, and that cheered him a little. The big, brindled German Shepherd was wary of other people, tending to growl and snarl if a stranger came too near, and Greg wondered how Zillah had been able to cope with it.

Thinking of Zillah made him feel less lonely and he chided himself for momentarily overlooking her friendship. He may not know her well enough to confide in, but they had always been friends, as her recent kindness in taking care of the dog for him showed. Then he realised, guiltily, that there had been no discussion about how he should pay her for looking after it all this time; she had just taken the dog from him on the day he left and wished him on his way. When he had spoken to her on the phone from Los Angeles, though, he'd got the impression that it had given her no trouble and she seemed to be enjoying having it with her.

She was a strange woman, he thought, living alone in such an out-of-the-way spot. He knew that she had been married at one time to a much older man who had died and left her a small amount of capital from which she had, presumably, bought her little holding in the Forest.

Much of her life, that part that was not given over to self-sufficiency, was devoted to the welfare of wild animals and birds, with which she seemed to have an affinity. Her world was so different from anything that Greg had experienced that he could not begin to comprehend it. But she had a certainty and a serenity which he envied, and which, he assumed, came from her way of life.

About five miles south of Salisbury on the A338 he noticed a roadside flower stall, so he stopped and bought a large bunch to take to Zillah. They had not fixed a time for him to arrive and it was only a few miles from here to the turning which would take him eventually to the little lane at the end of which was Zillah's cottage. He was early, but he knew it wouldn't matter.

Part Three

—

In The Present

TWENTYFOUR

'Greg? You alright?'

Greg had left Dan on the other end of the phone while the memories had come flooding back

'Yes. Sorry Dan. It's a bit of a surprise, that's all.'

'The name does mean something then?'

'Yes, I'm afraid it does.'

'Weird...I mean, is this serious, Greg?'

'Well, it was at the time, but...' He was struggling to adjust to Dan's news. That encounter with Nigel Heapes had changed his life. He had been a normal, happy-go-lucky adolescent, well-liked in the village, with plenty of friends and no enemies that he knew of. Afterwards everyone treated him differently. Even old Sam, his guardian and dearest friend changed towards him, treating him more as an equal, as if he had suddenly become an adult, a man of the world like Sam himself. And then, when he'd had to leave the Island following that savage, unexplained beating, he had decided to keep that part of his life secret and he had never spoken about it since.

'Did the police say why they want to see me?'

There was a pause. Then Dan said, 'Well, look, when they came this morning the inspector told me they were treating the case as a suspicious death, and they would have to interview anybody still around who knew the fellow. Then he said the last person to see him alive was an eighteen-year-old called William James Gregory. According to their records he had moved away to the mainland shortly afterwards and current enquiries indicated he was now living in the New Forest.'

'Right. So what did you say?'

'I didn't say anything. Well, it didn't sink in straight away, and when it did I couldn't believe it would be you'

'No, of course.'

'It's true then, you really were the last person to see him alive?'

'Apparently. But I don't see how I'm supposed to help the police after all this time.'

'Well, I thought I'd better let you know straight away.'

'Yes, and thanks. At least I'm forewarned.'

'But what a weird coincidence!'

'Coincidence is putting it mildly. And it's come as a bit of a shock. That business was all over and done with years ago. Now I suppose it's all going to be dug up and raked over again. Oh, Hell! I'm sorry you've become involved, Dan.'

'Well, it's just a damn nuisance for me, holding up the work I mean, but what about you? Are you going to be alright?'

'Oh yes. As I said, I can't tell the police any more about it now than I did at the time. But I suppose I'll have to go through the motions.'

'Look, do you want to come over and stay for a few days. I mean, would it be easier for you?' It sounded as though Dan was offering to help but not wanting to seem too curious. 'It would be good to see you anyway,' he finished rather lamely.

Greg smiled, wondering for the hundredth time why everything in his early life had gone wrong except the one thing that mattered, his son Dan. Also for the hundredth time he wished he could show him how much he loved him.

'Yes, yes, I'd like that, Dan, if it won't put you out too much.'

'Great! I'll pick you up at Yarmouth in the morning then. Nine o'clock. Okay?'

'Nine o'clock, right.'

Dan rang off and Greg put his phone back in his jacket pocket. The news had put him on edge. His mouth felt dry and he stood still for a moment, closing his eyes and taking a few deep breaths while he tried to relax. It's a damn nuisance but that's all it is, he told himself.

The dog had wandered off while Greg was talking, but it came bounding into sight as soon as he whistled.

'Come on boy! Let's go and see your Auntie!' He set off at a fast trot, the dog running close behind his heels.

He'd been to the Royal Oak at Fritham for lunch, just a ploughman's and a half of bitter, and was heading for home by an indirect route, passing Hasley Hill when Dan rang. Now he turned off the main path onto one of the many little tracks, often no more than a foot wide, which criss-cross the open heather. These tracks have been made over countless generations by the ponies and cattle which roam freely across the forest, and they usually lead to favoured grazing areas, or to water or places of shelter -

from the flies in summer or from driving wind and rain in winter. Greg had come to know all these little tracks in this part of the forest; this one would lead him eventually to Zillah's cottage.

The dog knew that too, and as they came near it bounded past him and raced ahead.

Zillah's cottage nestled on a slope facing the sun in a picturesque setting of about two acres fenced off from the forest. The whole of her northern boundary was a thick holly hedge nearly a hundred yards long. Directly behind the house was her kitchen garden where she grew all of the more common vegetables and soft fruit, and a wide range of herbs. There were two paddocks, one on either side of the house, which was three hundred years old with walls of cob and a thatched roof. A brick extension had been added at the back in Victorian times, and several lean-to wooden outbuildings tacked on since then. One of these was the garage where she kept the Toyota 4x4 pickup which she was just backing out as Greg came over the hill.

The dog was standing at her gate, tail slowly waving as it watched. It could easily jump over the wide cattle grid, but she had trained it to wait until invited in – some of her patients, as she called them, would become very nervous with a boisterous German Shepherd bouncing around.

She parked the vehicle, got out and called the dog to her. It raced up to her and she bent over to greet it. Its kennel name had been Shep, but she had decided to call it 'Rocky'. When Greg had left it with her before his trip to America, she had said, rocking her hand backwards and forwards, 'He thinks he's hard but he's just a wobbly. See the way he behaves? One minute he thinks he might tear me apart straightaway, the next he thinks perhaps I'm not afraid of him after all, so maybe he should wait a bit.'

It had taken her less than a day to tame the dog and now he was as faithful a companion to her as he was to Greg, although he always went to him in preference.

Zillah stood up and looked around. Tall, only about an inch shorter than Greg's five foot eleven, and strongly built, she had a broad, happy face, with laugh-lines at the corners of her mouth and around her bright blue eyes. Her skin was very pale and her long, dark auburn hair was usually in a plait wound around turban fashion. Most of the time she wore men's jeans and a large floppy sweater or in warm weather, a loose, flowing, long-sleeved chemise buttoned well up to the neck, and she always wore a wide-brimmed hat out-of-doors. An eccentric animal-loving widow in her mid-forties, she was one of the very few people that Greg, and for that matter, the dog, felt could be trusted absolutely.

Greg called and waved. Zillah waved back, walking down to her gate to wait for him as he trotted down the long slope.

Pleased with himself for being only slightly out of breath after his long run, he told her that Dan had called and invited him to stay with him on the Island.

'He's going to meet me at Yarmouth nine o'clock tomorrow morning,' he said.

'That's rather sudden isn't it?' she said. 'You didn't mention that when we spoke yesterday. Is he in trouble or something?'

Zillah knew something of his relationship with Dan, but she had never met him.

'No, no,' he said, his mind confused by the news from Dan. Although Zillah knew more about him than any other living person Greg had never told her about his reason for leaving the Island and he didn't feel ready to discuss it with her yet.

'It's a long story.'

She sensed his confusion, nodded in an understanding sort of way, and looked down at the dog. 'You want to leave his lordship with me, I take it.'

'Yes please. I don't know how long I shall be away though. It rather depends on what happens when I get over there.'

'Sounds intriguing,' she said, 'Tell you what, come and have dinner with me this evening and you can tell me about it if you like. I'm just going out to the Village Stores to get a few things. I'll call in at the farm and get a piece of beef.'

Despite her love of animals, Zillah was no vegetarian, but she was careful about where she bought her meat. Their local farm had a deserved reputation for the way it treated its stock and for the quality of its meat.

'That will be nice,' said Greg, 'And I've got one bottle left of that Merlot you liked. I'll bring it with me.'

Zillah turned to go back to her vehicle, then looked over her shoulder and smiled. 'Do your packing and bring your toothbrush as well. I'll run you to the ferry in the morning.'

Greg and Zillah had a comfortable easy-going relationship.

They both liked to think they were free spirits, independent and not committed in any way. If they were honest enough to admit it to themselves, however, they actually relied upon each other to the same extent that they would have expected to if they had been a married couple. As a result each probably had much more respect for the other than many married couples have.

Their closeness had developed over the eight years since he had followed her advice to take a complete break from his past. When he had come to her house to collect the dog on his return from America, he had told her over dinner, about the job that Nick had offered him in Poole with the new security company he was about to set up. Zillah had realised that Greg had misgivings, but she had convinced him he should at least give it a try.

Before he'd left she'd asked him to let her know how he got on, but after a month had gone by and she had not heard, Zillah had called him, ostensibly to enquire about the dog, but also because she cared about him and was anxious in case he might regress into the depressed state which had led him to drink too much.

Greg had reassured her, however.

'In the end I decided I didn't want to join the firm,' he'd said. 'Nick and I agreed that I'll work for him on a self-employed basis, as a consultant. That way I can be more independent and choose the type of work I want to do. I've already started as a matter of fact, in the Hamworthy office.'

'And how are you getting on?' Zillah had asked.

'It's pretty good so far. Commuting from Southsea every day is a bit of a bind though.'

Although Zillah had asked him to keep her informed, Greg had been uncertain about bothering her with his personal affairs, but he'd been pleased that she'd rung him and after this he'd begun phoning her at least once every week. Gradually an affection had grown between them.

On the Monday before Christmas, Greg rang her from the agency's office in Hamworthy to tell her he had finished the work Nick wanted him to do there.

'I've got to come in tomorrow morning to tidy up a few loose ends,' he'd said, 'Then I'm free until the New Year. Can we meet somewhere for lunch?'

'Yes,' she'd said immediately. 'You could come here.'

'No, I was thinking perhaps I might treat you to a meal in your favourite restaurant.'

'Well, that's very kind, and thankyou. But I was going to call you anyway. There's something I'd like you to see. We could go to the local pub, if you like. They do quite a decent lunch.'

'Alright. What time would suit you?'

'Come as soon as you're free.'

Greg had arrived in time for morning coffee and as they sat opposite each other at her kitchen table Zillah had said, looking at him speculatively over the rim of her mug, 'You mentioned that you were getting fed up with commuting all the way from Southsea. Have you thought about moving closer?'

'Yes, I have. I had a look at a flat in Parkstone the other day as a matter of fact.'

'Would you be interested in moving out this way?'

'I don't know. Why?'

'The old lady who lives in the cottage next door has had to be taken into care, and I think the owners will want to put it on the market.'

'I see.'

'It's not very big and it probably needs some work done on it, but I wondered if you would be interested.'

Greg's ideal living quarters had always been an apartment with all mod cons and within convenient reach of shops and other services. He had never given any thought to living out of town so the idea of buying an old cottage in the New Forest was entirely new to him and he said so.

'So what's wrong with a new idea?' she'd said.

'Nothing, I suppose, but it does need a bit of time to register.'

'Alright. Meanwhile, there's nobody living there at the moment and I've got a key. Come and have a look at it.'

Greg had allowed himself to be shown around the old cottage.

It was still full of the old lady's possessions, and in the cold, damp December weather it smelt musty and unwelcoming. Nevertheless, Greg had found himself agreeing with Zillah's opinion about its potential as a comfortable little home.

Before saying so, however, he had asked her why she was suggesting he should live there, half hoping perhaps, that it was because she wanted him to be near her, but her reply had deflated him; accustomed to having a quiet old lady living next door, Zillah was concerned mainly about the potential disturbance a new neighbour might cause to her peaceful environment.

'Better the devil you know,' she had said, and then, as if as an additional inducement to Greg, 'It will be so much nicer for Rocky, too. He'll have a garden to run in and not have to stay cooped up in a flat for hours on end.'

They had discussed the pros and cons of living in the New Forest over their lunch in the pub, Zillah trying hard to show Greg how the advantages outweighed any inconveniences, and Greg had been encouraged when she had pointed out that living next door would give them the chance of seeing each other more often.

Before driving back to Southsea, Greg had accepted Zillah's invitation to lunch with her on Christmas Day. She had said it would be just the two of them, and told him to bring the dog, saying that she had a spare bedroom and he was welcome to stay overnight, if he wished.

On the New Year's Eve, Nick had rung him to wish him all the best for the year two thousand, and to tell him that he wanted Greg's help in interviewing staff for the expansion of the Hamworthy office.

They arranged a date to meet to discuss this, then Nick said, 'How's the drinking?'

'I don't drink now.'

'Not at all?'

'Not like that.'

'Alright. How long since you had a drink?

'Saturday. Zillah and I drank a bottle of Merlot between us in the evening. And I'd had a brandy too, Alright?'

'What happened to "one day at a time"?'

'Yes, that was when you convinced me I needed to stop drinking. That's when I reckoned it had to be one day at a time for me, that I would not, must not, ever have that first drink. But things happen, circumstances change the way you are, I suppose. I don't drink now, Nick.'

'You think you're cured?'

'I never was a real alcoholic.'

'You seem pretty sure.'

'I am.'

'What happened?'

'To make me sure, you mean? It's a long story. Zillah suggesting I should get away from everything I was used to was a good start. As you know, I went to the States and then on to Mexico and whenever I felt thirsty I had a soft drink. Have you any idea how many different soft drinks there are over there? Must be thousands. But I didn't dare go into a bar.

'Then, the week before Christmas, Zillah and I went to her local for lunch. I had an orange juice and watched while she drank a twelve-year-old malt. I don't suppose that would be generally recommended, but it didn't feel dangerous to me, or inappropriate and somehow she knew it wouldn't. So, on Christmas Day, when she asked if I was ready to risk it, I accepted a glass of brandy at her house. Just the one drink. No after effects. That's how I knew it would be okay to share the bottle of Merlot with her in the evening.'

'So you spent Chistmas with Zillah?'

'That's right.'

'Good for you. And you think you won't feel like going on a binge at all now then?'

'No. I shall never drink to excess again, Nick.'

'Well, that's great news.'

Greg had then told Nick about his decision to buy the house next door to Zillah.

'You two getting together, then?'

Greg laughed, 'No, not literally, Nick. We're both too independent I think. But we've always been friends and maybe we're getting a bit closer. We'll have to see how it goes.'

And eight years later their relationship had matured to its present comfortable state.

Greg called the dog to him and stood out of the way as Zillah manoeuvred the 4x4 out of her drive and onto the track.

'Seven o'clock!' she called as she went by.

Rocky lolloped after her as she eased the vehicle slowly down the gravel track, then he waited by Greg's front gate. Greg knew the dog would be perfectly happy no matter how long he had to stay with Zillah, but she was the only person he could trust him with.

The phone was ringing as Greg unlocked his door but it stopped before he could reach it. He checked for messages. There was one from Dan timed at before he had reached Greg on his mobile phone and one from Ringwood police, wanting to know when it would be convenient for an officer to call. They were not wasting any time he thought, and smiled at a mental picture of himself contacting them in all innocence, thinking it would be in connection with a job involving the agency, as had happened occasionally. He had not done any work for the agency recently though, so he would have been taken completely by surprise. Thank God Dan had the foresight to warn him, giving him time to think back and try to recall everything he could about that encounter with Nigel Heapes.

But as he accepted that his involvement with Nigel's death would soon become public knowledge again, he felt a faint echo of that awful 'butterflies in the belly' feeling that had started in his final days with the Regiment, after Luke had been killed, and developed into a full-blown depression when Suzy died three years later. Zillah's help then had kept him sane and he knew he had to talk to her. Besides, it was important to him that she should hear his side of the story, so this evening after dinner he would take her up on her offer to listen and he'd tell her all about it. Remembering the details would also help clarify his thoughts and then, but not before, he would be prepared to speak to the police.

He decided to spend the rest of the afternoon on domestic chores. His army training ensured that he never let his living quarters become scruffy, and taking the vacuum cleaner out of its little cupboard and shutting Rocky out of the way in the garden, he started by going methodically over each room in the house.

It was only a small cottage, a typical eighteenth century forester's home with cob walls and thatched roof. He had never regretted buying it, although by the time all the repairs and renovations were done, it had cost him almost the complete sum he had received from selling his two flats.

There were three rooms downstairs, a good-sized kitchen with up-to-date equipment and a serving hatch to a small dining room, and a sitting room with views on three sides and from which a narrow staircase led up to a landing with two bedrooms and bathroom opening off it.

The one thing he did let slide occasionally was his ironing, and as he searched his wardrobe for clean clothes to pack for the weekend, he realised that he had a week's backlog to clear, so that was his next job. Then he stripped his bed and put duvet and pillowcases in the washing machine together with the week's wash, and the clothes he was wearing, set the machine going and ran himself a hot bath.

As he lay back in the bath, soaking in the heat from the water, he let his mind wander, thinking about his meeting with Dan in the morning.

Dan had married Zoë, a beautiful American yachtswoman when he was twenty-five and they had been very happy together for two years. But then Zoë had been taken ill suddenly and had died within a few months. That was four years ago and Dan had only recently started dating again. Greg knew he had been seeing a lady from Ventnor lately and he was hoping Dan could become happily settled with a partner again. He smiled at the thought and then, for the first time, the possibility occured to him that he might become a grandfather in the not too distant future.

The shock of the revelation made him sit up suddenly, splashing a little water over the side of the bath. 'Christ!' he thought, 'I'm getting old.'

Stepping out of the bath, he stood for a moment examining his reflection in the full-length mirror and felt reassured at what he saw. Yes, he was definitely looking fitter these days, damn good for his age, and there was still that extra something there, something cool and hard, forged during his training and tempered by his experiences. From the back of his mind where it had been deeply buried for many years he dragged forward the memory of those awesome early days in training, days of the ultimate testing, day after day in solitary, in silence, hunger and squalor, when his spirit had not been broken and he had learned more about himself than most people can ever learn.

In the Regiment he had found friendship, brotherhood, and camaraderie. He thought especially of Luke. He still felt the loss of his best friend and he knew he always would, for in dying, Luke had not only saved Greg's life, he had also led him ultimately to Zillah.

TWENTYFIVE

At seven o'clock Greg was carrying a bottle of wine, a bunch of flowers, and a small suitcase, and Rocky was holding a plastic bag full of frozen raw meat in his jaws when they presented themselves at Zillah's back door. This led into a wooden summer house built onto the rear of the Victorian part of her home and was what she called her reception area for sick and injured animals. It was also where Rocky would remain during his stay.

Zillah greeted them wearing a large red apron bearing the stencilled legend 'End Of The Food Chain'. She accepted the flowers with a smile and took the plastic bag from Rocky, pointing him to a large bean-bag in a corner of the room and telling him to stay.

Greg followed her into her small, modern kitchen where she put the dog's meat in a freezer.

'Go on through to the sitting room,' she said. 'I've almost finished here. Help yourself to a drink and pour me one too. I'll join you when I've put these lovely flowers in a vase.'

Zillah's sitting room was part of the Victorian extension to her house, about five metres square, with tall windows in opposite walls overlooking each of the paddocks. The furniture was oddly assorted, not modern, mostly large and well-used. A deep red, eastern style carpet covered the floor with a large thrown rug in front of the brick fireplace. There were six overstuffed armchairs, all with different but complementary loose covers and footstools. A thick elm-wood mantle-piece held a brass carriage clock in the centre between brass candlesticks, a picture of her parents on one side and one of her brother on the other, and at each end, a very realistic carved wooden model of a cat. The wide recess by the fireplace was shelved and full of books. Small side tables between pairs of armchairs also had books and magazines piled on them. The overall feeling was one of ease and comfort.

Greg poured the drinks, a dry sherry for Zillah and a whiskey and soda for himself, and found a space for them on one of the small tables next to his favourite of the armchairs.

Zillah had removed her red apron when she joined him. 'Dinner will be about ten minutes,' she said.

He saw with surprise that she was wearing a stylish black dress that he had never seen before. He had known her now for more than twelve years but had rarely seen her in such feminine clothes.

'You are very elegant this evening,' he said. 'I'm sorry to say that sometimes I forget how attractive you really are under your thick sweaters and jeans.'

She made a face at him and picked up her glass, 'Cheers! Here's to the Isle of Wight!'

Zillah was rarely subtle and he took that as her way of indicating that she thought she ought to be told why he suddenly needed to go there,

He smiled, 'OK, I'll tell you all about it after dinner, but it's a long and rather painful story, I'm afraid.'

'Oh dear. Does it concern Dan?'

'Yes, it does. But it is difficult to explain so please be patient with me.'

'Now you really have got me intrigued,' she said. 'But I won't pester you. I know you'll tell me all about it in your own good time. Did I tell you about my latest success?'

That afternoon she had released a raven that had been brought to her with a broken wing about a month ago, and she went on to talk with her usual enthusiasm about how effective many of the old herbal treatments were, especially the herb 'knitbone' which she had used on the rescued raven.

This topic continued through dinner, which was a delicious beef stroganoff followed by a fruit pie, most of the ingredients coming from her garden, and by the time they adjourned to the sitting room Greg was feeling relaxed and quite ready to tell his story.

'You were saying earlier that this trip tomorrow concerns Dan,' she prompted as she poured him a large brandy.

'Yes, in two ways actually, one immediately and the other, well, fundamentally.' He paused for a moment wondering how to explain, where to start.

'I've never told you about my upbringing, have I?

'I was born in London in 1957. My parents both came from Seastone but they married in London during World War Two. My father was an orphan and was brought up by his mother's brother, a publican who, it seems, used him more or less as a bond-servant. When the War broke out in 1939 he left the Island and joined the army. About a year later he went back to Seastone on leave and ran off to London with my mother, Rose. She had been the girlfriend of the cousin he had grown up with, Arthur Heapes, and not unnaturally, there was bad feeling afterwards and they didn't go back to the Island.

'After the War they took over the licence of a pub in London – it was what my father knew about. They were very happy together and I had a very happy childhood until I was eleven years old. Then my mother died. My father was distraught. He took to drink (see, it runs in the family!) and we lost everything over the next two years. That was a bad time. Then somehow, I don't know how, Arthur Heapes came to hear about us and took us back with him to Seastone. He owns a big hotel there. By this time my father was an alcoholic and quite hopeless, but Arthur gave him odd jobs to do about the hotel and looked after him right up until he died in 1988.

'I was a bit of a problem. I didn't get on with Arthur's eldest boy, Nigel, who was a few years older than me and a bully, and I don't know what would have happened if the local postmaster hadn't taken me under his wing. His name was Sam Morris. He adopted me and really kept me on the straight and narrow. I lived with him for five years earning my keep by helping in his shop and café, and making myself available for stray jobs around the village, like window cleaning, or garden work, such as rough digging, weeding, trimming hedges, creosoting fences, and so on.

'I had some good pals of my own age and a very nice girlfriend, and I always found it easy to get along with people in the village, most of whom seemed to like me, so I'd never given serious thought to leaving the place, although Sam was beginning to hint that there was a wider world out there which I should take a look at fairly soon.'

Greg paused for a moment, remembering.

Then he went on. 'When he died, Sam left me the apartments in Southsea and a letter full of advice and wisdom which I wish I'd had the sense to take notice of. He also left me a diary kept by my grandfather in the First World War. Sam had been with him and Arthur's father in the trenches.

'Sam was a wonderful old man. He gave me a home and I lived with him until I left the Island for good when I was eighteen, which is really what I am leading up to.'

TWENTYSIX

It was nearly midnight by the time Greg had brought the story of his last week on the Island to the point where he had been attacked on the iron staircase leading to his rooms above the café.

'It seems,' he continued, 'That very early the next morning, a holiday-maker, jogging along Quay Lane, happened to glance over the seawall and see a body stretched out on the rocks ten feet below. She ran across to the Quay Hotel, and roused the staff who called police and ambulance.

'By the time PC Tindall arrived on the scene at six a.m., thinking Nigel Heapes's body had turned up, the ambulance was on its way with me, still unconscious and unidentified, to St Mary's Hospital in Newport. He followed the ambulance, identified me at the hospital and phoned Sam.

'Sam came immediately, but I was in intensive care and they wouldn't let him see me. They told him I was seriously ill, with fractured skull, several broken ribs and suspected internal injuries. Then, after three days, still unconscious, I was taken to Southampton General Hospital Neurology Unit, where they brought me round.

'The police came to see me but all I could remember was being kicked in the ribs and the man with the torch saying, "Yeah, that's him". They thought that showed it was not just a random attack and they kept on at me to give them some idea who it could have been, but all I could think was that Roddy must have found out about Suzy and me, and I didn't want to say anything about that. The police, though, seemed convinced it was linked to Nigel's disappearance, so I didn't argue.

'The news soon spread through the village, of course.

'Sophie Hawkins put two and two together and told Sam she believed I had been seeing Suzy Vanderling. Sam didn't believe her at first but then Suzy came to see him, having heard about the attack from the Commander. She was very upset. She told Sam everything, saying her affair with me was entirely her doing and that she had led me along. Sam brought her to see me in hospital and told both of us that we had been foolish and had to stop seeing each other.

'Suzy said she honestly did not believe Roddy would have been responsible for me being beaten up. I couldn't think of any other reason for it, though, so it remained a mystery.

'But whatever, it convinced Sam to persuade me not to go back to the Island when I was eventually discharged from hospital. He arranged for me to convalesce in Ross-on-Wye instead, at the home of an old friend of his that he'd known in the Regiment. Bear in mind, I hadn't known until then that Sam had ever been in the Regiment.

'So there you have it.

'I suppose it was inevitable that I should go on from there and end up as I did. You see, the beating I had from those two bastards made me want to make sure that in future I would always be prepared to look after myself, so I didn't need much persuading to join up and work for the opportunity to be trained to do just that.'

Greg paused and looked down at the drink in his hand.

'When you look back at your life,' he said, 'It's easy to see how one thing leads to another, isn't it? In my case you can see how that incident in the boat all those years ago set off the long series of events that, among other things, led me to Luke and from there on to you.'

He looked up and smiled at her.

'And it seems that it still hasn't finished with you,' she said. 'Because you have to go to Seastone tomorrow.' She raised her eyebrows. 'So what has happened?'

Greg told her what Dan had told him on the phone.

'I see. What a nuisance for you, ' she said, leaning back in her chair. She gave him a quizzical look. 'But there is one thing you have been very careful to avoid telling me, isn't there?'

Greg was puzzled. 'I don't think so.'

'When I asked you if your trip tomorrow concerned Dan, you said it did in two ways, if I remember, one immediately, and the other, I think you said, fundamentally. I can see how it affects him immediately, by delaying his work on the extension. But... "fundamentally", Greg?'

'Ah.' Greg took a deep breath. 'Suzy and I promised each other that we would never tell him I am his father,' he said, 'And he still doesn't know,' he added.

157

'So that's it,' said Zillah. She leant towards him and took his hand. 'You were obviously very fond of each other, all three of you, and from what little you have revealed about your relationship over the years, I guessed some time ago that that must have been the case.'

TWENTYSEVEN

Saturday

Greg was awake when Zillah's alarm went off at six a.m.

He had been reflecting upon the previous evening, when he had told her all that he could remember about the events leading up to his departure from Seastone in nineteen seventy-five

Now, propping himself up on one arm he looked across at her. She smiled sleepily, her face framed in the mass of her auburn hair spread over the pillow. He leant across her to switch off the alarm and touched his lips to hers. 'Hello, lovely lady.'

'Hello, lovely man,' she said. 'How are you this morning?'

'Oh, I'm fine.'

'You slept alright? Not worrying about your trip today?'

'No.' He shook his head. 'Talking about what happened, telling you all about it seems to have eased my mind. I slept like a log until a few minutes ago.'

'Good.' She pulled his head down and kissed him fully. They held each other tight for a long moment. Then she said, 'You'd better get up or we'll never get you to that ferry.'

Greg moved away reluctantly. 'Cup of tea while I'm shaving and showering?'

'Silly question.'

He did not often stay all night with Zillah, but on the first occasion, some time ago, he had taken her a cup of tea in bed the next morning.

She had said then, 'There isn't any point in getting up to make oneself a cup of tea and then coming back to bed to drink it on your own, but this is a really enjoyable way to start a new day, just sitting here like this and listening to the sound of you in the shower.'

So now Greg indulged her whenever he did stay over.

He put on the old dressing gown she kept for him and went downstairs. Rocky was as usual delighted to see him and ran to the door to be let out.

While Greg waited for the kettle to boil he started an abbreviated version of his morning exercise routine. At fifty he was proud that he could still do that number of press-ups before getting a little out of breath. At home he had built a chin-up bar in his loft and he would follow his press-ups with twentyfive pull-ups, and a range of stretching and strengthening exercises, touching toes and lifting weights.

In Zillah's kitchen he followed his press-ups by touching toes and stride jumping until he had raised a slight sweat and the kettle had boiled.

By the time Greg had made a pot of tea and found some biscuits to put on the tray, Rocky had completed his inspection of the premises and, having taken note of nocturnal visitors, he was back at the door waving his tail. Greg let him back in and they played his favourite game for a minute or so, where Greg pretended to try and hit him and he caught the sleeve of the dressing gown, pulling hard and growling fiercely. It always amazed him how careful the dog was not to bite his arm.

When Zillah was settled with her tea tray, Greg had a hot shower, and as he dried himself off he wondered, not for the first time, how long it would be before they agreed that it would make sense for them to live together. Perhaps when they were a few years older they might feel it would be more practical if he sold his place and came to live here with her. It would certainly ease matters for them financially. Neither of them was well off and Greg's little cottage had appreciated considerably in value since she had encouraged him to buy it at the turn of the century. He didn't think either of them was ready for that yet though and he was not going to propose it. But the idea was not unattractive.

TWENTYEIGHT

As the ferry came in at Yarmouth Greg could see Dan waiting at the quayside.

Tall and blonde with his mother's good looks and Greg's build, he looked fit and strong, standing ramrod straight with an old-fashioned military bearing, and Greg felt a surge of pride, quite unjustified of course - he'd had no hand in Dan's upbringing.

Dan walked forward with a big smile as Greg came off the boat, took his overnight bag from him, dropped it at his feet and gave him a big hug. 'Welcome home, Greg.' That was always his greeting when Greg went back to the Island. Then he picked up the bag and hustled Greg over to his Range Rover in the car park.

'I thought we'd take the scenic route this morning,' he said as they put on their seatbelts. 'I rather fancy a drive along the Military Road, okay?'

'Yes, I haven't been that way for years.'

'It hasn't changed much – except for the traffic. That gets worse every year. Shouldn't be too bad at this time of day though.'

On the journey across the Island to Dan's house at Bembridge they talked about anything but the bones of Nigel Heapes. Dan wanted all Greg's news, such as it was now that his life had more or less settled into a comfortable routine (at least it had until that 'phone call interrupted it), and Greg was particularly keen to know about any developments in Dan's home life.

Dan gave him a broad smile in answer to his question. 'Oh yes,' he said, 'We see each other two or three times a week. She's away for the week-end, I'm afraid, otherwise we could have all got together. Then the week after next we're going on holiday for a fortnight. Borrowing a boat from a friend of hers in France. The plan is to sail along the coast of the Med and around Corsica. It'll be a first for both of us.'

'Sounds great. Just the two of you?'

'That's right. It'll be the longest time we've had together on our own. A sort of test.'

'Ah ha! Getting serious, eh?'

'Well, you know, Lucy's still recovering from a nasty divorce and I suppose I must be getting pretty set in my bachelor ways. It wouldn't be easy for either of us to settle down again.'

'Yes,' said Greg, speaking from heartfelt experience. 'When you've been on your own for a while it isn't easy to adjust to sharing everything with someone else.'

'What about you and your neighbour. No chance of you two getting together?'

'What we have suits us both very well as it is, Dan.'

'Well, you're looking pretty fit, so you must have got it about right.'

They followed the coast road all the way round to Sandown and then instead of carrying on through Yaverland and on to Bembridge, Dan decided to detour to Seastone to show Greg the work being done on the marina extension.

He parked the Range Rover in his reserved space at the Yacht Club, and they walked back along Quay Lane, passing Chandlers, Greg's old home, which Sam had sold to Roderick Vanderling when he retired. Dan had inherited it and had kept the shop but sold the café.

Dan led the way to the marina development and pointed out progress so far. Greg was duly impressed and said so, and then they walked along to the place where the bones had been found. Police 'keep out' tape stretched from the west side of the slipway to the wall at the end of Quay Lane. Looking out from there, beyond the pier, to where the boats had been that day, Greg reckoned that it was not much more than half a mile in a direct line, and remembering how thoroughly they had searched the area for Nigel at the time, he was at a loss to understand how they had missed him.

He was commenting on this when Dan's phone rang. After a brief conversation, he rang off and said, 'Sorry, Greg, something's come up. I'll have to leave you to your own devices for a bit, I'm afraid. Shouldn't take much more than an hour though. See you in the café, say, some time about half eleven?' He hurried off back to the Yacht Club.

Greg was feeling unsettled and perhaps a little apprehensive about the outcome of his inevitable interview with the police. He hadn't been back to Seastone since Suzy died, and then it had been only to attend the funeral at St Peters Church. Three years before that, when he had lived with Suzy and Dan at Abbots House for a few months, he had not spent any time in the village, merely passing through to and from the Yacht Club.

Now, with an hour or more to spend he thought he might as well have a walk along the sea shore and perhaps come back along the path through the fields behind the village. The idea of seeing the familiar places made him start recalling his life as it had been when he was eighteen years of age, just an ordinary lad, not very worldly-wise, and with no special skills or physical strengths, or particularly useful knowledge. Although, he supposed, looking back, his life until then had led him to become adaptable, and yes, he had been very happy in those long, slow days, until everything changed for him, and from being a rather naïve, carefree adolescent he started to become a hard, uncompromising adult.

On a Saturday morning at this time of the year there would not be not many people about and he hoped he would not meet anyone he would recognise. The only people he had really cared about in the village, his father, Sam and Suzy, had all gone and he had no wish to talk about the old days with anyone else, so it was with mixed feelings that, noting the tide was well out but coming in, he walked to the end of Quay Lane, crossed the upper end of the slipway and set off along the sea-wall path in the direction of the pier. With the sun straight ahead of him and the heat already reflecting off the stone wall to his right, the day promised to be fine and warm.

At about every thirty yards flights of steps led down about ten feet to the beach, which was drifts of shingle and rocks set among coarse sand. Blackheaded gulls called as they sailed overhead and the old familiar smell of warm seaweed wafted up from the rocks. He felt his spirit rising.

He went down the next set of steps onto shingle and headed diagonally towards the tide line in the direction of the pier, picking his way around weed-covered rocks and small pools before reaching the firm sand.

A small flock of oyster catchers at the water's edge suddenly took off, disturbed by a little dog which came racing out from under the pier.

Then the dog saw Greg and came bounding up, dropped a small rubber ball at his feet and stood looking up, wagging its stubby tail frantically. Greg looked around for its owner and saw an elderly woman near the pier with a walking stick in one hand

and a dog lead in the other so he threw the ball in her direction. The dog tore after it, picked it up and came racing back to him, so he threw the ball again. Of course the dog immediately recognised a soft touch and by the time they had repeated the performance three or four times Greg had approached close enough to the woman for her to speak.

'Hello Greg,' she said, with a hesitant smile.

He stared and eventually recognised Barbara Black, the day manager of Sam's café. She had been a big, vigorous woman, always bouncing with energy, but now, leaning with both hands on her stick before him was this stooped, shrivelled version of her, whose features had all drawn inwards towards each other, leaving a shrunken form of the face he remembered. Of the very few people in Seastone that he would not mind meeting, Barbara Black was not one. She had run Sam's café during all the time Greg had lived there and he had thought of her as a good friend, almost 'one of the family' as it were. But he had been mistaken; she had shown she was just as ready to blame him for Nigel's disappearance as any of the others were. Even so he was sorry to see how badly she had aged.

'Hello Barbara.'

'He often brings me company,' she said, indicating the dog which was still eager to play. 'But I didn't expect to see *you* when I left home this morning. What brings you back again after all this time?'

'Nigel Heapes,' said Greg.

'What?' She looked startled. 'Nigel Heapes? But we all thought he was dead, years ago!'

'I know,' he said, 'And you all thought I'd done away with him, too, didn't you.'

'But, do you mean to say he's not dead? Has he turned up again then?'

'Oh, he's dead alright. They found what was left of him in the sand near the slipway.'

'Oh, those bones they dug up! That was him then?'

'So I'm told.'

'Oh.' She gave him a puzzled look, 'So, there's going to be an enquiry, is there? Is that why you're here?'

'There is bound to be an inquest, isn't there, and the police say they want to interview me.'

'Oh dear. You've got to go through all that again have you?'

'No, Barbara. No, I haven't. What I went through before, when this village made a pariah out of me, won't happen again. This time it's just a damn nuisance, bringing back bad memories.'

He started to move on. The dog wanted to follow, so Greg took the ball and threw it as far as he could back in the direction he had come from. Then he quickened his pace and strode off towards the pier, irritated by the chance meeting with someone he would sooner have avoided.

By the time he reached the pier, though, he had shaken off the bad feeling. He went up the steps to the little esplanade and looked across to the Pier Hotel. The brick and stone façade of the big Edwardian building had been cleaned recently, and between the second and third floors the four-foot high golden letters of the name shone brightly in the morning sunlight. It looked prosperous and Greg tried to picture himself as the manager of such an enterprise, which he might well have been by now if he had followed the hotel trade as intended, but the idea seemed absurd and made him smile.

He ought to go in and see old Arthur, he thought, but now was not the time. He would, though, after he'd seen the police.

Back down on the beach he walked across the corrugated sand to the edge of the sea and followed it round the bay to the rocks at The Point. The sea-wall path ended here but it was possible at low tide to find a way through into Priory Bay. He was tempted to try it but he didn't trust his shoes on the wet seaweed. Then he noticed that where the path ended with steps down to the beach, an easy way to get over into Priory Bay had been built by concreting some of the rocks into wide ledges, so he climbed up and stood watching the incoming tide breaking in small waves over the rocks at the far end. The picture prompted something at the back of his mind but he couldn't quite grasp what memory it may have been.

A hundred yards or so along the bay he came to the Priory path and started to climb the wooden steps winding up the steep hillside among trees to the ruined Priory. He turned round at one point and looked out to sea as his memory went back to the Friday of that fateful week more than thirty years ago, when coming down these steps he had looked for and seen the Yacht Club's boat heading towards the end of the bay, and known that in a few minutes time he would be making love to Suzy in its cabin.

Continuing along the path, he noted that the little gate into the garden of Abbots House was still there. Suzy had kissed him goodnight at that gate two nights later, and he had set out to walk home along this path in the dark.

'How naïve I was,' he thought. 'And what a rude awakening I was in for.'

He felt angry suddenly, on behalf of that innocent eighteen-year-old, who had done nothing that would justify such a savage beating and he wondered yet again, if Roddy hadn't ordered it, who had, and why?

A little further along he came to another gate with memories. He wondered what had become of Josie, his teenage sweetheart. Her mother had not approved of their friendship, thinking, of course, that a daughter educated at Roedean deserved more than a common lad such as him. All he remembered of her father, Graham Wilson, was that he was a prosperous farmer, owning Manor Farm whose fields this path went through, as well as other farms on the Island and that he had set up her mother, Louise, as an estate agent and she had made a success of the business. Sam had been happy to use her office to let his flats in Southsea, and Greg had seen no reason not to continue the arrangement right up until they had sold the flats for him when he moved to the Forest.

He left the path at the little park called Sally Wilson's Gardens and made his way down Seastone Lane into the Square and via Rope Walk back to the Yacht Club, passing on the way the iron staircase up to the entrance to his former home.

All in all this walk was reviving plenty of memories.

TWENTYNINE

Greg was still too early to meet Dan, but he fancied a cup of coffee anyway after his walk so he went into the café

It had been altered, modernised of course, since Greg's day, and seemed much smaller with the door to the shop sealed off, but from where he sat at a table by the window the view across the road to the Yacht Club was just the same.

A large, heavily-built man, about sixty by the look of him, brought Greg's coffee and sat himself down opposite him. His face seemed vaguely familiar.

'Remember me, Mr. Gregory? Ray Tindall?'

They stared at each other for several seconds.

Yes, Greg remembered him alright and his mouth suddenly felt dry. He took a sip of coffee.

'You were the village bobby,' he said.

'That's right, I was. But I ended up in Hampshire CID. Chief Inspector.'

'Really? You'll be retired now though, surely?'

'Right.'

'So what brings you to Seastone?'

'I live here. This place I mean.' He made a gesture with his arm. 'It's mine.'

'Oh, I see.'

'Married a local girl. Sophie Hawkins. When I retired eight years ago she wanted to move back here and the café was up for sale so I bought it. You'll remember Sophie I'm sure, seeing as she worked next door when it was the Post Office.'

'Yes, of course I remember her. And Frank, her brother, of course.'

'They remember you too. And they often used to wonder what happened to you. Never kept in contact with any of your old mates, did you. Except the lovely Mrs Vanderling, of course.' He smiled, raising his eyebrows in a suggestive way. 'Coffee alright is it?'

'What do you want, Mr. Tindall?'

'You're here because the Nigel Heapes case has been reopened.'

He was stating it as a fact and when Greg did not deny it, he smiled in a patronising way and said, 'I'm curious to see if anything new will turn up.'

'Oh, you are, are you? Why?'

Still smiling, he leaned back in his chair.

'I'll be honest with you, Mr Gregory, I was never happy about that statement you gave. There was something not quite right about the way you put it over. But you stuck rigidly to it all the way through the investigation, so we had to let you go.'

'You had to let me go, as you put it, because I hadn't done anything wrong.'

'Ah, but I reckon there was more to your involvement than you let on, you see.'

'Such as?'

'That parcel Nigel Heapes was supposed to have been looking for, for instance.'

'There was no parcel.'

'According to your statement he was pretty sure you had picked up a parcel at Foreland.'

'Yes, he was. But he was wrong. I didn't know anything about a parcel.'

'So why would Nigel think there was one? Perhaps he knew you were in the habit of collecting parcels for the Vanderling associates – outside your normal Post Office duties, that is.'

Greg was puzzled at this suggestion. What was Tindall getting at?

'What do you mean, "the Vanderling associates"?'

'I didn't know anything about it at the time of course, but it so happens that Hampshire CID had recently opened a file on Mr Roderick Vanderling and, later, when I joined them they gave it to me as one of my first jobs, having been the local man as it were.'

'You've lost me, I'm afraid.'

'Bear with me. That file stayed with me for over twenty years. Nothing definite ever turned up, either while Vanderling was alive or afterwards when his associates took over, but over the years there were plenty of indications pointing to some queer goings-on. We could never prove anything, though, and that still niggles me.'

'But, I don't see what it's got to do with me, or Nigel's disappearance.'

168

'Well, this is where it gets interesting. See, when they found those bones and identified them as Nigel Heapes I dug out my old notes on the case.'

Greg looked at him in surprise. 'But it was more than thirty years ago! And you've still got your village bobby's notebook?'

'Kept all my old notebooks, got quite a stash of them. There's some interesting stuff in there. Thought I might write my memoirs one day. Anyway, I thought it was curious that the chap whose dinghy you were in, Freddie Davis, was one of Vanderling's lot, as was your girlfriend's father, Graham Wilson. And another of them, Clarmont Brown, was someone you were always doing odd jobs for. See where I'm coming from?'.

Greg couldn't believe it. To start with he was surprised to hear that Hants CID would have had a file on Roddy Vanderling. As far as Greg had known, Roddy had always been a respectable and respected local businessman. Certainly Suzy had never even hinted about anything underhand. But now this ex-copper with time on his hands and a conscience about not clearing the file was making weird assumptions and connections.

'Mr Tindall,' he said. 'Josie Wilson was my girlfriend, yes, but all I knew about her parents was that her dad was a farmer and her mum was an estate agent. I wouldn't have known whether they had anything to do with the Vanderlings. As for 'Squire' Davis, to me he was just the local newsagent. Okay, I know he had an old MTB and did a bit of dodgy fishing on the side, but so what? I don't know about Bob Clarmont Brown. He was into all sorts of things.'

'Take it from me they were all involved together. Still are for all I know.'

'Involved in what?'

'You name it, they were in it.'

'So you think they had something to do with Nigel's disappearance, do you?'

'I think it's quite likely, yes.'

'And I was part of the plot, was I?'

'Well, your close association with Mrs Vanderling at the time and your continuing acquaintance with Mr Vanderling Junior, would indicate more than a remote connection.'

'Mr Tindall,' said Greg, as patiently as he could, 'I'm sorry, but I'm afraid you are way off beam here. You're making a

169

connection that never existed.'

'Is that right?'

'I had never even spoken to the Vanderlings before that night.'

'Really? Well, you certainly made up for it after, by all accounts.'

Greg was becoming more and more irritated by the man's attitude which seemed to him impertinent and quite unjustified. 'Listen, my close association with Mrs Vanderling, as you put it, didn't start until after Nigel disappeared. She was good to me, stood by me all the way, when everybody else, except old Sam Morris, and including you, made it pretty clear they thought I'd bumped him off.'

'And why would she 'stand by you', then?'

'Well, for one thing, she knew I was innocent.'

'Really? How? How could she know that?'

'Because she actually saw what happened that night.'

'What? Don't tell me she was on the boat as well!'

'She was at home and just happened to be looking through her telescope.'

Tindall shook his head in amazed disbelief. 'OK, so why didn't she come forward then?'

'Because she wasn't supposed to be at home that evening. She'd told her husband she was going to Ventnor to see her sister but in actual fact she was expecting somebody to visit her. She didn't want to have to explain why she had stayed home.'

He raised his eyes towards the ceiling. 'Jesus wept!'

Suddenly Greg saw how unlikely it would sound to a mind already predisposed to suspect anything to do with the so-called "Vanderling Associates", and he felt himself becoming angry because he really did not need to justify himself to this retired policeman.

Tindall must have sensed how he felt.

'Look,' he said, in a conciliatory tone, 'If she genuinely was an innocent witness she should have come forward, shouldn't she. That would have saved us all a lot of trouble - you especially. Just happened to be looking through her telescope, you said. Now why would she be doing that, at exactly the right moment, eh? See what I mean? There's just too many funny questions to be answered.'

'Alright then,' said Greg 'I've got another one for you. Why would these "Vanderling Associates" of yours want to get rid of Nigel, anyway?'

'Why indeed. I'll tell you what I think though, shall I? It was to do with the parcel-that-never-was. I reckon Nigel had found out something and they had to shut him up.'

'So they left it to me, did they?' Now it was Greg's turn to ridicule. 'Bear in mind I was only a teenager, no experience with weapons, no training in any sort of combat, out in the bay on my own in a little dinghy and this big army second-lieutenant comes along in his power boat. Right? So what did I do, hand over a parcel to him that just happened to have a bomb in it?'

'Well it's an interesting idea but that wasn't how it was done.'

'But you know how it *was* done, do you?'

'Yes. At least I know how he died.'

'You do?'

'I may be retired but I still have a few useful contacts. According to one of them, Nigel Heapes was hit in the head by a bullet from a high-powered rifle.'

Greg just stared at him.

Tindall gave a little smile and nodded. 'Yes... I must admit I was a bit surprised, too, because there was never any reference to a shot being heard. There seems to be no doubt about it, though. Apparently there's a neat entry hole about eight millimetres across on the left hand side of the skull and a somewhat bigger exit on the right. As an ex-military man, you'll know what that adds up to.'

'Yes,' said Greg, 'A high-velocity round would do that. But it doesn't make sense.'

He tried to think back to what had actually happened on the speedboat. How could Heapes have been shot without Greg either seeing it or at least hearing the report? Then it occurred to him that Tindall had been playing him along, deliberately holding back about the head wound, hoping that Greg would say something incriminating, like, for example, letting slip that he had boarded the speedboat *before* Nigel disappeared. Greg hadn't let anything slip, though, and his original story still held.

But now Greg saw that that did not matter any more. If Nigel had been shot there was no way he could be held responsible for his death, and the guilt which had forced him to leave the Island all those years ago, and which he had carried with him ever since, buried deeply it's true, suddenly lifted as the significance struck home; he was in the clear.

Tindall's voice brought him back to earth.

'Sorry?' he said. He had missed whatever Tindall had said

'I said, when are you seeing the investigation team?'

'I don't know. They haven't been in contact.'

'Oh, I thought…..Oh., of course!. Danny Boy! He'll have told you what was going on, and you've come over to get your story straight!' He gave Greg a knowing look. 'That's smart.'

'And now that you've told me about the head wound,' said Greg, 'I'm sure I can think up a story that will be really convincing.'

He stood up, bored with the man's fixation with his "Vanderling Associates". 'What do I owe for the coffee.'

'Oh, forget it. Look, hang on a sec. Give us another minute or two, will you? Please?'

He got up and put his hand lightly on Greg's shoulder, urging him back down into his seat. He looked so serious that Greg sat down again out of curiosity.

'I reckon I owe you the benefit of the doubt at least,' said Tindall. 'See, I know your life hasn't been all sweetness and light but there's never been any suggestion of anything criminal, so for all I know your connection with the Vanderlings may have nothing to do with their business activities.'

Greg interrupted him. 'Before you go on, let me make one thing quite clear. Whatever ideas you may have about the past, Dan Vanderling is as straight as a die, so be very careful what you say.'

'Right,' he said, 'OK. No problem there. But getting back to Nigel Heapes. I reckon you were set up.'

'Oh yes? Who by?'

'Well, there were four of them in those days: Roderick Vanderling, Graham Wilson, Frederick Davis and Robert Clarmont Brown. I used to think Vanderling was the main man, but now I'm not so sure. They were into contraband of all kinds, alcohol, tobacco, currency, you name it, even drugs, though in the early days it was just soft stuff, marijuana and amphetamines. Nothing could ever be proved though. They were damn clever! My theory is that Nigel Heapes found out something and had to be silenced.'

'They went about it in a peculiar way then.'

'Well, whatever, it worked.'

'I just can't see how it could be done,' said Greg.

'No, well, that's why I wonder about that statement you signed. See, if it was all true there's no way you couldn't have either seen what happened or heard the shot, is there?'

Greg thought about a high-velocity bullet hole in a skull found near the old slipway. On the search boat that night, when they reached the spot where Nigel disappeared somebody had said anything falling off a boat there could end up by the slipway. So, accepting the fact that Nigel had been shot before he fell off, it would have happened after he knocked Greg down into the cockpit and Greg had not heard it because he must have been knocked out for longer than he had thought. But, of course, that bit was not in the statement.

'The gun could have been silenced,' he said.

Tindall gave him a hard look. 'The way it looks to me, you were lucky not to be silenced too, if you were not in league with them.'

'Didn't you just say you owe me the benefit of the doubt? Look, I can assure you that I was definitely not in league with them, or with anybody else to get rid of Nigel Heapes.'

'Yeah, okay, but, see, in that case if you were there when somebody shot Heapes, why didn't they shoot you too?'

He had a point there, thought Greg.

Tindall went on, 'See, going from your statement, which I've got a copy of by the way, I can't see how you wouldn't have seen or heard something, even if the gun was silenced, I mean, at the very least he would have made a pretty big splash when he fell in.'

Greg was saved from having to answer that as Dan arrived and strode across to their table.

'Good,' Dan said with a smile. 'At least you've had company, Greg, sorry about leaving you so long. Hello Ray.'

Tindall stood up. 'You stopping for coffee, Dan?'

'No thanks. We'll get along home, if that's okay with you, Greg?'

'Sure.' Greg got to his feet.

Tindall put out his hand to delay him. 'Before you dash off, I wonder if we can meet again? I mean, this case is very important

173

to me. See, I've got a hunch that if we can find out what really happened that night it will give us a good lead into that old file. You're the only one who can help.'

'You're still giving me the benefit of the doubt, then?'

Dan was looking from one to the other of them with a puzzled expression.

Tindall was almost pleading. 'I need you to tell me the whole story in detail as close to the real facts as you can remember.'

'But you're retired, man. Why not leave it to the investigating team?'

'Because they don't know the background! And even if they did they wouldn't be interested in a past they had no part in.'

This was exactly what Greg was hoping would be the case, of course, in fact he was rather expecting it to be, judging by the type of policeman he'd had dealings with in the recent past, but he was surprised that an ex-DCI would take this attitude.

'I don't know,' he said. 'That part of my life has been buried deep for over thirty years and besides, it's complicated and may involve others whose feelings are very important to me.'

'But I'm sure that together we could crack this. I just need your help.'

'No. It can't be done.'

'What do you mean? We can't crack it or you can't help?'.

'Both.'

'Well, we could give it a try.'

'You keep saying *we*.'

'See, from where I stand you're the ideal bloke. You're tough, you know all the background and you've got just the kind of experience I need.'

'And from where I stand I couldn't care less,' said Greg, irritably.

'Look,' said Tindall, 'I know you had an interesting career in the army, and that you've done some useful work since, with Safeguard and especially with this Poole set-up but that's only part-time isn't it, so I know you're not too busy. Come on! What have you got to lose? Surely it's important to you to vindicate yourself at least, after all the aggro you had at the time? I mean, you damn near died, didn't you?'

Dan couldn't restrain himself any longer. 'Am I right in assuming you are talking about those bones?'

Greg felt an awful premonition. Unless he was very careful this was going to lead to a situation he had been avoiding for years.

'That's right,' said Tindall. 'Nigel Heapes. He disappeared on my watch as the local bobby and I am still curious to know what actually happened. I'm rather hoping that Greg here can fill in some details for me.'

Greg noted that Tindall tactfully refrained from mentioning his obsession with the "Vanderling Associates" and the CID file. Whether this was out of consideration for Dan's feelings, or just the caution which would come with long experience, he was not sure, but he was grateful for the way he put it.

'Well, it all sounds very intriguing, Greg,' said Dan.

'Look,' said Greg to Tindall, 'I came over to the Island because Dan rang me yesterday and told me the inspector in charge of the investigation said he wanted to interview me. Dan very kindly offered to give me bed and board, and he picked me up this morning at the ferry but I haven't had time yet to tell him what it's all about. Bear with me, will you, and when I've seen this inspector, perhaps we can have another chat. Alright?'

'Yes, fair enough. Thanks. Ring me on my mobile phone.' He wrote the number on the back of one of the café menu cards. 'I'll look forward to hearing from you then.'

Greg put the card in his pocket and walked with Dan across the road to the Yacht Club car park.

THIRTY

Dan said, 'I gather Ray Tindall doesn't like being retired. He told me that a few years ago he was called in to help as a sort of consultant on a couple of old cases. Apparently, there was a special team set up to review what they called "Cold Cases" where past investigations had ground to a halt for lack of evidence or something, and he helped to solve those two. The team has been disbanded now though, much to his disappointment.'

'Well,' said Greg, 'He is certainly keen to know everything I can tell him about Nigel's disappearance, but I think he may know more about it than I do. Anyway, I can fill you in on what I do know.'

Dan started the Range Rover and during the short drive to Bembridge Greg told him the story starting from Nigel's boat tipping him into the sea.

On the ferry from Lymington he had decided to tell Dan the truth about what happened in the encounter with Nigel, including the lie he had told to the police. He felt the same way about being entirely honest about it with Dan as he had done with Sam at the time.

Now, thanks to Ray Tindall, he could also tell him how Nigel had been killed, but he was at a loss to know how to explain Tindall's urgent request for him to help him discover the truth, because the truth as Tindall saw it was primarily to do with revealing the criminal activities of his "Vanderling Associates". The last thing Greg wanted was for Dan to think he was involved with anything that would taint the memory of Roddy. The two of them had been close; Dan had always looked up to Roddy and as far as Greg knew, still held him in high respect. He would just have to play it by ear and hope for the best.

By the time Dan was parking the car in front of the garage behind his house Greg had reached the point where he had been released by the police without charge, and he decided to stop there.

Dan had listened quietly, interrupting only to have the occasional detail clarified. Now, having grabbed Greg's case from the rear of the vehicle he ushered him towards the back door and said, 'You say you hit the fellow hard – 'a solid punch' I think you said – and yet you are quite certain that you didn't knock him overboard?'

'Oh yes,' said Greg. 'He fell back into the cockpit. I almost fell on top of him. He would have had to climb up again to go overboard.'

The back door opened as they approached and Mrs. Wade, Dan's daily help stepped out. A plump, middle-aged lady, who had been looking after him for several years, she stood facing them, both hands clutching the handle of a holdall against her ample stomach.

She nodded and smiled a greeting to Greg. 'Hello. Mr. Gregory. It's all ready for you, Mr Vanderling.'

'Thanks very much, Mrs Wade,' said Dan, 'It's much appreciated.'

'That's quite alright. You have a nice weekend.' She turned to leave. 'I'll be in at the usual time on Monday, then.' She bustled off down the footpath to the gate

They went into the kitchen where a buffet lunch, a selection of cheeses, biscuits, dips and bowls of salad, more than enough for the two of them, had been set on the table in the dining area.

'Look at that!' said Dan, 'I asked Mrs Wade to fix lunch for us. Thought you might like to settle in a bit before you got in touch with the police.' He passed Greg's bag to him. 'You're in your usual room.'

Greg went upstairs to the comfortable little room at the back of the house looking down over the nature reserve and unpacked his bag. Then he had a quick wash and brush up before joining Dan at the kitchen table where he was opening a bottle of red wine.

Dan looked up at him. 'Is this okay? I've got plenty of mineral water if you'd prefer.'

'Yes, that's fine,'

'I was thinking,' said Dan, continuing the conversation where they had left off, 'You were only eighteen. You must have been scared stiff. I know I would have been.'

'Yes. At one time I thought they were going to charge me with Nigel's murder but in the end they had to take my word for it. I think old Sam had a lot to do with that, too.'

'It was just as well you didn't tell them you hit him or they might well have made a convincing case against you.'

'Yes. And I could have gone to gaol for something I didn't do. Ray Tindall told me just now that in fact Nigel had been shot.'

'Shot?' Dan paused halfway through pouring a glass of wine.

'So he says, according to one of his police contacts. A bullet wound in the skull, from a high-powered rifle, it seems. I don't understand how I never heard the shot though, unless I was knocked out for longer than I thought.'

'But it was right out in the bay and you said it was getting dark, so how could anyone shoot him?'

'I haven't a clue. When we didn't find him that night I assumed he must have swum ashore. He was a good swimmer and I thought he'd turn up later.'

'Perhaps he did swim ashore and was shot somewhere else and his body dumped by the slipway. What do you think?' He poured a second glass.

'Could be,' Greg shrugged, not wanting to explore the possibilities any further with Dan. 'The thing is, from my point of view, the fact that we now know he was shot means I'm off the hook. There's no way this new investigation can link me to a shooting, so I'm a lot more relaxed about the whole affair than I was when you rang me yesterday.'

'Well, that's good. Now, what I suggest is, you give the inspector a call when we've eaten and get him to come here if we can, on neutral ground as it were. What do you think?'

'Yes, that will be great.'

'OK.' He passed Greg a glass of wine. 'Let's tuck in then. I don't know about you but I'm starving. Cheers!'

Between them they set about doing justice to the spread Mrs Wade had left. Greg was hungry too; breakfast with Zillah at six a.m. seemed a long time ago.

They ate in silence for a while. Then Dan started talking about a friend of his who had been wounded in action in Iraq and was now at home on leave before returning to Basrah next week. That led into a discussion about the decision to go to war and its inevitable aftermath, and the kind of problems the army was facing from the various factions. Dan wondered why they didn't seem to want to use the special forces out there, where the situation was not that different from what it had been in Northern Ireland, surely?

All Greg could say was that 'didn't seem to' was possibly the operative phrase, and left it at that. There was no way he was going to get involved in that kind of conversation with Dan. A few years may have passed but the memories were still there and best left to themselves.

When they had finished Dan said. 'I'll make a pot of coffee while you're phoning the cop shop. Use the phone in the study. The number to call is on yesterday's page of my desk diary.'

Greg dialled the number and it rang and rang until he was about to put the phone down, thinking they had all gone home for the weekend, but then a woman's voice answered. He gave his name and said why he was calling.

The woman thanked him for getting in touch and identified herself as Detective Sergeant Nash. After a brief conversation in which she asked if Ringwood Police had spoken to him and Greg told her they had not and he was spending the weekend at Bembridge with Dan, she asked when it would be convenient for him to go to Newport to make a statement.

'It would not be convenient at all,' he said. 'But if you really need a statement from me I shall be at Mr Vanderling's house for the whole weekend and you could come here.'

'Would that be Mr Daniel Vanderling, sir, of Seastone Yacht Club?'

'That's right. It was him who told me you wanted to see me.'

'I see, sir, and would this afternoon be convenient?'

'Yes it would.'

'And you are at Mr Vanderling's Bembridge residence at the moment, are you, sir?"

'I am, yes.'

'Then I should be with you in about an hour, Mr Gregory.'

She was. Dan brought her into the sitting room where Greg was watching TV.

Detective Sergeant Nash turned out to be a heavily-built woman in her late twenties, dressed in a blue jacket and skirt over a cream blouse open at the neck, and shiny black 'sensible' shoes. Her dark hair was pulled back and tied with a blue ribbon in a short pony-tail which, together with very thin eyebrows, accentuated the fleshiness of her face. Her only make-up was a very pale pink lipstick which made her mouth look too small and thin-lipped under a long, straight nose. Her pale blue eyes were large and protuberant; Greg wondered if she was wearing contact lenses.

He used the remote to switch off the TV and stood up as she came in. She showed him her proof of identity, and he just had time to register the words 'Detective Sergeant Tracey Nash' before she put it in her jacket pocket and took out a notebook.

Dan invited her to sit on the sofa, and he sat next to her. Greg moved to the window seat facing her, with the afternoon sun behind him.

She asked Greg to tell her everything he could remember about what happened on that August Sunday.

He explained that he doubted if he could remember in detail, but went through the story for the third time – not counting his conversation with Ray Tindall - in less than twenty-four hours.

DS Nash listened in silence, referring to her notebook and jotting down a note occasionally until Greg came to where Salway and West had taken him to Ryde police station.

'The rest of it you know,' he said.

'Thankyou,' she said. 'That's very helpful. Now,' She flipped through the pages of the notebook. 'Going back to the time when you were knocked into the bottom of the dinghy, and before you climbed onto the speedboat to confront Mr Heapes, did you hear anything unusual?'

Greg realised she must be referring to the rifle shot.

'In what way?' he said.

'Like a shout or a loud bang, for instance?'

'No. Not that I remember. Though to be honest, I don't expect I would have taken much notice if I had. I was pretty angry. Besides if I had heard anything unusual, I'm sure I would have mentioned it at the time.'

'Yes. Do you remember if you were asked at the time?'

'No, I don't think I was,' he said. She was staring at him with those bulging eyes, which made her look permanently astonished, as if she would never be able to believe anything anyone told her.

'Whereabouts was Mr Heapes positioned on the boat, do you remember?' she said.

'Well, in the cockpit I suppose. I had my back to him as I was getting in the dinghy, so I don't know.'

'Yes, I see.' Her cell-phone rang. 'Excuse me,' she said. She stood up, closed her notebook and put it in one pocket, took the phone from another and left the room.

They heard her say, 'DS Nash…Yes…Yes...Yes, just about... Alright, yes, straightaway.'

She came back in. 'Sorry about the interruption, but I think we had more or less finished, hadn't we? Thankyou for your co-operation, Mr Gregory. If there are any further questions after the weekend, we will be in touch with you at your home, via our colleagues at Ringwood.'

Well, thought Greg, that was easy. It looks as though Ray Tindall was right in thinking the police want to file away this thirty-two-year-old case with as little fuss as possible. He realised how stupid he had been to have worried about it, but it was a reminder that his self-confidence had still not yet fully recovered and he thought back ruefully to the time when he had been able to withstand even the most intense interrogation.

Dan showed DS Nash to the door and Greg heard them having a short conversation. Dan came back in with a big smile. 'Was that it, then?'

'Seems like it.'

'I liked the way you dealt with the "loud bang"'.

'She didn't actually say anything about the shot though, did she?'

'No.' Dan, flopped back onto the sofa and stretched out, linking his hands behind his head. 'You know, I think she was just going through the motions, Greg. She told me, off the record, they'll be taking the tape away in the next day or so, and I can arrange to go ahead with the extension work.'

'Ah, that's good news! And it seems to confirm what Ray Tindall was saying.'

'What was that?'

'He thinks as they have no obvious leads to follow up they'll probably file the case back in the old "Unsolved" folder. They won't take too much interest in something that happened long before their time.'

'He seems to be taking it very seriously though.'

'It's probably, as you said earlier, he doesn't like being retired and it gives him something to think about.'

'He seems very keen for you to help him.'

'Oh, it's just that he's seen through the statement I made at the time. He knows it can't be quite right. Anyway, now I know about the shooting and it's put me in the clear. I thought I'd tell him what actually happened That might set his mind at rest. I'll give him a ring in a minute, if I may.'

'Sure. I got the impression it was more than that, though.'

'Well, maybe. But I think if the police are willing to let sleeping dogs lie, so should the rest of us.'

'Suppose the media were to take an interest though.'

'They haven't so far, have they?'

'No, just a paragraph in the local paper when the bones were first discovered. But now the bones have been identified, and when the news gets out that he was shot they are sure to make a story out of it.'

'Are you suggesting Ray Tindall will tip them off, then?'

'No, no, all I'm saying is if the media do make a story out of it the police won't be able to just file it away.'

Greg could see that Dan was right and he wondered for a moment if Ray Tindall would pass on to them his ideas about the link with his "Vanderling Associates" file. Greg doubted it somehow. It was his own baby and he would be more likely to guard it jealously. He shrugged off the thought.

'Oh, well, it's not our problem anyway, is it?' he said.

'You don't feel the need to, what was it Ray said, "vindicate yourself" then?'

'No. I would have done if the people who stood by me were still around to share it with me, - Sam, your mother and my father. But they've all gone and nobody else matters that much.' He paused and corrected himself. 'Except old Arthur, perhaps, because I never really thought he blamed me.'

'You obviously still feel very strongly about it all though, Greg.'

'No. What I feel strongly about is having it all raked over again. It was painful at the time and through no fault of my own it changed the direction of my life, or at least, it completely altered my outlook on life because it made me see for the first time that life wasn't always fair. And I admit that, rightly or wrongly I have tended to blame it for everything that went wrong afterwards. But it's all very well looking back and saying "if only". It's been my life and I've lived it. And, after all, not everything that came out of it has been bad.'

'Do you know what I find strange, though?' said Dan. 'I don't remember anyone ever talking about a fellow disappearing. I mean, I grew up in this village, at least I spent most of my school holidays here, and since university I've worked here as well, but nobody has ever mentioned it, before the bones were found that is, so it must have been no more than a nine-day wonder to everyone here.'

'Except Nigel's family, of course,' said Greg. 'I was thinking earlier, I'd like to call in and see old Arthur while I'm over here. He always did what he thought was best for my Dad and me, and I've never contacted him directly since I left all those years ago. It's time I put that right.'

'Right. I'll drop you off there in the morning if you like. About elevenish be alright?'

'Thanks. And I did say I'd ring Ray Tindall after I'd spoken to the police.'

'Oh, well, look, perhaps it would be better if you just took the car. I don't need it. Then you can please yourself. And by the way, that phone call I had earlier was from the firm supplying the decking for the extension. There's a problem, apparently and I've got to go down to Plymouth to sort it out. If I go on Monday I can run you back home on the way.'

'Oh, you don't have to go to all that trouble, Dan. Just run me to the ferry. Zillah will come and collect me.'

'It isn't any trouble, is it, if I'm going through Lymington, anyway. And I've wanted an excuse for ages to come and see where you live.'

Greg had always felt awkward about inviting Dan to visit him in case Dan might consider it presumptuous, so in fact he was delighted at this opportunity and readily agreed.

'And I might even get a chance to meet your friend Zillah at last,' added Dan.

THIRTYONE

Sunday morning

Greg drove the Range Rover into the Pier Hotel car park just before eleven o'clock.

He was thinking, as he walked towards the main entrance, that the discovery of Nigel's remains would have brought to an end the uncertainty which must have persisted to some extent all down the years and at least make it possible for Arthur and his family to have what nowadays is called 'closure'.

In Greg's time the hotel reception area had been practically identical to that of 'Fawlty Towers', so that when Greg had first seen the TV comedy programme, he had almost expected Arthur to appear instead of John Cleese, but now he saw that it had been changed out of recognition. The main entrance had been widened and the interior gutted so that guests were now received in the space that had been the Lounge Bar, where he was to have started his training.

A neatly dressed young man behind the desk stood up as Greg approached. 'Good morning sir,' he said with a welcoming smile.

'Hello,' said Greg, 'Would it be possible for me to speak to Mr. Arthur Heapes, please?'

'Just one moment, sir. I'll enquire. What name shall I give?'

'William Gregory.'

The young man's eyes widened, and Greg immediately saw the family resemblance. This must be Arthur's grandson, Simon's son and he clearly knew who Greg was.

'Would you excuse me, sir,' He turned and went out of the door behind him, leaving it open. After a few moments, a burly middle-aged man came quickly through and strode over to Greg with a broad smile and his hand outstretched. 'Greg!' he said and shook his hand vigorously.

'Hello Simon.'

'It's good to see you! Come on through!' He lifted the flap at the end of the counter, opened the half-door and beckoned Greg to follow him. 'Dad's sunning himself out the back. He'll be so pleased to see you. He's eighty-eight years old, you know, but still bright as a button, losing his hearing and his sight's none too

184

good, but he keeps us on our toes.' He laughed, then became serious. 'You know they found old Nigel, don't you?'

'Yes, that's really why I'm here.'

'Ah, right. This is Jason, my youngest,' he said, indicating the young man who had followed him in.

Jason smiled nervously as they shook hands. 'I'm your third cousin, once removed,' he said.

Simon laughed. 'Jason is into family history. Traced us back to seventeenth century France, would you believe. Huguenots, you know. Bore you to tears if you're not careful.'

Greg said, 'I only know the bit about the twentieth century.'

'Grandad told me about how your grandfather died rescuing my Great-Grandad in the trenches in World War One.'

Greg smiled. 'I was a bit younger than you are when I was told about that and it seemed ancient history to me then so it must seem even more so to you.'

Simon led him through the hotel to the patio at the back. They had built a swimming pool since Greg's day and Arthur was sitting by it at a table, reading a Sunday paper with the aid of a magnifier on a stand. He was wearing a white floppy hat which was partly obscuring his face and he was half-turned away from them so he did not notice their approach.

Simon touched him lightly on the shoulder: 'Dad?'

Arthur looked up at him, glanced at Greg, and looked back at Simon.

'We've got a visitor.'

Arthur peered closely, and gradually recognition registered on his face.

'It's Stephen's boy, Greg, isn't it?'

'Hello Arthur,'

He got to his feet, with some help from Simon, and held out his hand. Greg took it and Arthur pulled him close in a warm embrace, then stood back and looked at him, beaming all over his face.

'I knew you'd come when the news about Nigel came out!' he said. 'It's good to see you, Greg. How are you, boy?'

'I'm fine Arthur, and it's good to see you too. It's been too long.'

'Yes, it has, and the fault's all yours, boy. You always knew you'd be welcome here. Isn't that right Simon?'

'Yes, Dad, but he's here now, that's what matters.'

'Yes, that's right. Come and sit down by me and tell me all about yourself.'

As Greg was pulling out a chair, Arthur said, 'Simon, fetch us a drop of something, there's a good man.'

'Not for me thanks Arthur,' said Greg.

'How about a cup of coffee, then? I'm ready for one anyway, and a plate of those chocolate biscuits, Simon.'

Simon smiled at them and said he would see to it.

Arthur said. 'I've heard a bit about you from time to time. I did rather hope we might have had a bit of a chat after Suzy's funeral but you didn't stay around, did you? Still, never mind. So what are you doing with yourself these days?'

'I'm more or less retired I suppose. I have a kind of part-time job with an agency in Poole, a security firm. It's more of a retainer really. They call me in for the odd job now and then. Otherwise I walk the New Forest with my dog, help my neighbour with her smallholding, and generally idle my days away.'

'You had a busy life for a while though, I believe. Twenty-odd years, wasn't it, in the Special Forces? Then you were wounded and invalided out.'

'Well, more or less. I asked to leave, actually.'

'Yes, I heard all about it from Suzy.'

'You did?'

'Yes.' Arthur nodded to himself and looked at Greg with a wistful smile. 'She was a lovely lady, wasn't she.'

'Yes, she was. I was very fond of her.'

'I know. So was I. She used me as a sort of Father Confessor, you know. She brought Dan to me just after he was born. I'd never seen her so happy. She was so proud of him. Then she told me about her love affair with you and that the baby was yours, but nobody else should know.' He put his hand on Greg's and squeezed. 'And nobody else does know, Greg.'

Greg said, 'After I left, we used to write to each other via Sam, but she didn't tell me about Dan until a week before he was born. By then, of course, she would have made sure Roddy would believe the baby was his, so there would have been nothing I could do about it and, after all, I was still only eighteen. Anyway, I agreed to keep the secret.'

'And it's all turned out for the best as far as Dan is concerned.

He's a fine young fellow, isn't he? You can be proud of him, Greg.'

'I am, of course, but it's no real credit to me, is it. It's all down to Suzy, and to Roddy as well, because he always did his best for Dan.'

Arthur said, 'Yes, he did.' He paused, looking across at Greg with his head on one side. 'That wasn't all that Suzy told me, Greg. She told me she'd seen what happened on the boat when we lost Nigel, so that I would know for certain you had not been responsible. I was glad to know that. And I did my best to assure her I could understand why she hadn't said anything at the time.'

'I've sometimes wondered,' said Greg, 'What might have happened if she had reported it immediately. There would be no Dan, and I would have started working here and probably ended up married with kids, running a hotel somewhere.'

'We'll never know,' said Arthur, 'Ah, here's our coffee.'

A very young waitress brought a loaded tray, and carefully set the table for coffee and biscuits. She asked Greg if he wanted cream and sugar and they watched as she served Greg first then poured a cup of black coffee for Arthur.

'Well done,' said Arthur. 'You're Katy, the new girl aren't you?'

She smiled at the old man and said 'Yes, sir. Will there be anything else?'

He smiled back. 'No thanks, Katy.'

When she had left them Arthur said, 'There still are a few pleasant youngsters around, but it's a devil of a job to find them on the Island. If they're any good at all, most of them seem to want to go to Australia or New Zealand, or to the mainland at least. Help yourself to biscuits. Where were we?'

'We were talking about Suzy, said Greg.

'Ah yes. Through the years we had a number of heart-to-heart chats, Suzy and I. She was not as happy as she deserved to be, you know. She should never have married the Commander. He was just not capable of appreciating her. I'm sure that's why she fell so heavily for you, you know.'

Arthur paused, gathering his memories.

'A few weeks before he died,' he continued, 'Roddy had a heart attack and while he was recovering, Suzy came to me with what I thought was a strange story. She said that when Roddy

187

had thought he was about to die, he had told her he had done things he shouldn't have. He'd said something like that a good many years before, she said, but she'd never known what he'd meant. He said he hoped she would be able to find it in her heart to forgive him if she ever found out what he'd done. That was all he'd say. Then, later, when he was fit enough to go back to work in the Yacht Club, she came to see me again. This time she said Roddy had told her he was being threatened. What had happened to Nigel, he said, could happen to him, or to Dan. He told her she was being watched and swore her to secrecy, but she was worried and came to see me.'

Greg said, 'If he said "what had happened to Nigel could happen to him", that sounds as though he knew what did happen to Nigel, doesn't it?'

'That's just what Suzy said. We didn't know what to make of it. I was tempted to have it out with him, but that would have put Suzy in an awkward spot.'

'So you never followed it up?'

'Well, no, I didn't. At the time it all seemed a bit far-fetched, you know, and besides, it wouldn't bring Nigel back. More than twenty years too late for that, wasn't it? I couldn't see that any good purpose would be served by bringing it all up again.'

'No, I see. Did Suzy give you any idea who was supposed to be threatening him?'

'Roddy never told her, but she seemed to have the impression from other things he'd been saying that Bob Clarmont Brown was putting him under a lot of pressure.'

'Clarmont Brown? In what way?'

'She didn't say. She didn't like Bob at all, you know. She told me she'd had a bit of a fling with him at one time, but she'd got fed up with him and then she met up with you. Apparently, he took that badly when he found out and told her to stop seeing you, or so she said.'

'He told her to stop seeing me?' said Greg. 'Really? What did it have to do with him?'

'Well, there we are,' Arthur shrugged. 'Bob's never liked losing. Anyway,' he went on, 'When Roddy died, it was assumed he'd had another heart attack and fallen into the sea off the Yacht Club jetty, but Suzy asked for a proper post mortem examination to find out how he actually died. The result showed it wasn't a heart attack and there was nothing to say it was anything other than drowning. Suzy told me she wondered if he'd been pushed and she was worried for her own safety and Dan's. I tried to reassure her. I told her that whatever the trouble may have been it had almost certainly died with Roddy.'

'But what sort of pressure would the high-flying Sir Robert Clarmont Brown want to put Roddy under,' said Greg. 'And why?'

'Yes, that would have been just about the time he was knighted, wouldn't it?' Arthur nodded thoughtfully. 'As to why he would be putting pressure on Roddy, I couldn't say. Anyway, it turned out I was right. Apart from persuading her to sell him her shares in the Pier and the Quarterdeck Club, which she didn't want to keep anyway, he left her alone.'

'What did he do that he got a knighthood for, do you know?' asked Greg.

'Services to industry, or something,' said Arthur. 'He was always a big supporter of the Tory government and they were quite free with their so-called honours for successful businessmen, weren't they. And he was certainly successful, businesses all over the place. The leisure industry was booming right through the nineties, remember? While our manufacturing industry was still being wound down? Well he took advantage of it. He bought up disused warehouses in Southampton, Bristol, Liverpool and Birmingham, among other places, and turned them into really posh nightspots. He called them all Cockaigne. You heard of them?'

'Yes, I think so. Gambling clubs, aren't they?'

'Yes. Very restricted entry. Exclusive, in fact. He even set up a special company to supply doormen and control their security. I'm told they're very much the fashionable scene for the sophisticated set.'

'Talking about the sophisticated set, what are the Wilsons doing these days?'

'Ah, yes, you were fond of young Josie, at one time, weren't you? Did you know she married Clarmont Brown and then divorced him after two or three years?'

'Yes, Sam told me about that.'

'Well, the divorce was quite nasty and she split from her parents afterwards. Went to New Zealand. Married a farmer, apparently.'

'And what are her parents doing these days? I expect you know

189

that Sam left me a couple of flats in Southsea, and Wilsons estate agents dealt with the lettings until they sold them for me, but I never heard any news of Louise.'

'Well, Graham and Louise are retired, I suppose. Anyway, they spend most of their time abroad. They've got a place in Monte Carlo and another in Barbados. They come back occasionally and stay at the Seastone Hotel. They bought that some years ago, too.'

'They've not done so badly, then'

'No. Graham set up a property development firm, you know, and built on his land at Manor Farm. They specialise in converting farm buildings now. And, of course, they're part owners of the Quarterdeck Club with Bob Clarmont Brown, and that was the prototype for the Cockaigne clubs.'

'Oh yes?'

'Yes. After Bob got hold of Suzy's shares he persuaded me to sell him mine and then he and the Wilsons turned it into an exclusive gambling club.'

'So they're probably involved in the Cockaigne business as well, then?'

'Yes, I believe so. We don't see much of them these days, as I said, but Bob's the major property owner in the village now. Lives in the biggest house too. Do you remember the old Chiverton's Place at the end of Salterns Road?'

'Yes, I do. I did a couple of days work there once, with Henry Niton, after the old lady died. And I seem to remember Sam telling me Bob had bought it when it came up for auction.'

'Surprised everybody, that did. Wondering where he got the money. And he's spent a small fortune on it over the years, too. But it's "Clarmont House" now, of course.' Arthur gave a wry smile. 'I remember when he first came to the village, you know. He was plain Bobby Brown then, just out of apprenticeship with a firm in Cowes. His grandmother had left him some money and he bought that old yard at the back of Chandlers, stuck "Clarmont" on the front of his name, (no hyphen, he insisted on that), and set up as a boat-builder. Now he's Sir Robert Clarmont Brown of Clarmont House.'

'Posh,' said Greg. 'And what about 'Squire' Davis?'

'Well, he's retired to his villa in Spain. We never see him. Teddy still runs the shop, though.'

'I see.' Greg paused for a moment, wondering how much to tell Arthur about Tindall's intention to investigate Nigel's death. He decided to be as open as he could with the old man.

He said, 'I saw Ray Tindall yesterday, Arthur. He is keen to find out what actually did happen to Nigel. He has a bee in his bonnet about an old CID file on what he calls the "Vanderling Associates" and he thinks it's connected in some way.'

'"Vanderling Associates?" What's that then?'

'According to Tindall, the Commander, Bob Clarmont Brown, the Wilsons and 'Squire' Davis, were or are, involved in some sort of underhand activity, but there has never been enough evidence to prove any wrong-doing.'

Arthur grunted. 'Sounds a bit far-fetched to me, Greg.'

'Yes, to me too, but he wants me to help him.'

'Hmmn. Are you going to?'

'No, I don't think so, but I've said I'll see him this afternoon to tell him what I can remember.'

'I see. Well, for what it's worth, I don't think he'll get very far, especially after all these years. The police didn't get anywhere with it at the time and I employed a private detective to look into it too, you know, but there was never anything to go on.'

'A private detective?' said Greg. 'I see. Do you think he'd still be around?'

'Why, you are thinking about following it up then, are you?'

'As I said, I don't think so, but Ray Tindall is very keen. Would it bother you to have it raked up again?'

'It's already been raked up, hasn't it?'

'Yes, I suppose it has. So do you happen to remember the name of that detective?'

'I remember he wasn't any good,' said Arthur, 'But it'll be in the old records somewhere. I'll get young Jason to look it out for you. He loves poking around in the archives. Now, listen, you must stop and have lunch with us. I'll get Simon to show you around first, so you can see what we've been up to here, keeping up with the times.'

THIRTYTWO

Sunday afternoon

When he left the Pier Hotel Greg was feeling much easier in his mind than he had felt for a long time. Arthur's family had made him very welcome in their home and had been at pains to make him realise and accept that he was one of them.

In the years following his mother's death Greg had come to think of himself as not having any family, and that belief had stayed with him since. Now, largely due to the enthusiasm with which they had all supported young Jason's emphasis on their blood relationship, he was at last aware of kinship. It felt unexpectedly comforting to him and he promised to keep in touch from now on.

He had arranged with Ray Tindall to be at the café by three o'clock, and having a few minutes to spare, he left Dan's car in the hotel car park and walked slowly along the sea-wall path, thinking about what Arthur had said about Roddy's death.

It seemed to tally with what he remembered Suzy saying when she had visited him at Haslar, when it had been clear that she was troubled by the way Roddy had died. She had never said anything to him about threats to Roddy, though, or about Roddy saying he had done things he shouldn't have, and now Greg was beginning to wonder if there may, after all, be some substance to what Tindall was claiming, especially as there appeared to be a connection to Clarmont Brown, one of the so-called 'Associates'.

Tindall was leaning over the sea-wall diagonally opposite the café, looking down, watching the high tide lapping gently at its base when Greg arrived and stood next to him.

Tindall didn't look round. With a jerk of his head, he said, 'That's where they found you, did you know? Tide was coming in but hadn't quite reached you. You were lucky to survive the drop, let alone probable drowning.'

Greg said nothing.

Tindall turned his shoulders and looking past Greg, indicated the police tape by the slipway. 'Ironic, isn't it, Nigel turning up, just a few yards away.'

Greg said, 'Yesterday morning I stood there and looked back to where he fell off the boat. I still can't see how we missed him.

We searched thoroughly between here and there several times.'

Tindall grunted, 'Yeah, and there's a lot more we still can't see, too.' He straightened up and offered Greg his hand. 'Thanks for coming,' he said.

Greg took his hand briefly. 'OK, but I can't see how I can be much use after all this time.'

'As I said, if you can tell me the whole story in detail as close to the facts as you remember them, something may click.' He led the way back towards the café. 'I thought we'd sit in my den, if it's alright with you. It's in what I believe was your bedroom, so you might feel at home.'

Tindall had fitted out the small room overlooking the yacht club as a neat and tidy office. There was an executive desk and on it a desk lamp, laptop computer and peripherals and a small stack of folders, and next to it a two-drawer filing cabinet. One wall was lined with shelves holding brightly coloured box files and ring-binders. A large leather-effect armchair on castors was positioned in front of the desk. Tindall indicated the visitor's chair in matching trim and invited Greg to sit.

Greg sat. He said, 'I'm sorry, but I just don't see what you expect to find out now that wasn't covered thirty-two years ago.'

Tindall sat himself at the desk. 'I'm not in the police force now, see, so I don't have to go by the book. I can have a go at doing some real detective work at last.'

Greg laughed. 'What were you doing as a Detective Chief Inspector, then?'

'There's a difference between police work and detective work,' said Tindall. ' See, police work is not much more than a matter of carrying out certain procedures, which, to be fair, if carried out correctly, can lead to criminals being caught. But that is not their main purpose. Their main purpose is to make sure nobody can point a finger if things go wrong., what the Americans call c.y.a., 'cover your ass', and a good copper makes sure that his bosses can show he went by the book. Most of my time and effort always seemed to go into going by the book, and there wasn't not much scope for individuality, following hunches, if you like.

'Detective work, on the other hand, is more a matter of seeing the situation as unique and looking for and then following a trail. There are no set procedures. I've got a hunch that our trail here starts with what happened on that boat.'

'But it was all so long ago,' said Greg. 'Any trail there may have been is too cold now, surely?'

'It's certainly not fresh and that's a problem, but somebody told me once that whenever something happens, the things around it are disturbed in some way and if you look close enough you can usually see some of those things. So then you try and find out what disturbed them, and follow the trail of disturbance until it leads you to what happened.'

'Well, it all sounds nice and straightforward when you say it like that,' said Greg, 'And I wish you the best of luck. What are you going to do about the investigation team, by the way?'

'How do you mean?'

'Are you going to be liaising with them?'

'No, I'm not. I offered my services as a consultant as soon as the bones were identified – I've left my name on the database of retired officers so I can be called in from time to time and they know I can still cut it 'cos I've helped them clear up three cold cases since I retired.' He shrugged. 'They didn't want to know. See, that's what made me think they'll just want to brush it under the carpet.'

'But if you do find out anything, who will you report it to, then?'

'Well, not the locals, that's for sure. No, I've got a couple of mates in Hants CID. I'll pass it on to them if and when we get anything definite.'

'Well, where do you want to start, then?' said Greg.

Tindall leant back in his chair. 'I told you, didn't I, that when I took over the Vanderling investigation back in the early eighties, I wondered if the unsolved disappearance of Nigel Heapes could be connected to it, so I got a copy of the 1975 file.' He waved his hand at the stack of folders on his desk. 'There's not much in it. Interviews with people who took part in the search, and a chunk on you as the only suspect. Your statement seemed to be the only probable line of enquiry. It didn't ring true to me. Still doesn't. But I couldn't re-open that case, so I've had to live with it.'

He picked two folders off the stack and passed one of them to Greg.

'This is your statement,' he said. 'I thought you could read it through, to refresh your memory, and then we'd go through it together. Okay?'

Greg took the file and opened it. The statement was the first page. He read it through.

"My name is William James Gregory. I am eighteen years of age and I live at Chandlers, Quay Lane, Seastone, Isle of Wight.

"On the evening of Sunday August the twentyfourth 1978, Mr. Fred Davis gave me five pounds to go to Foreland and collect a dinghy and sail it back to Seastone. Frank Hawkins took me over to Foreland on his motor bike and helped me get the dinghy in the water. I got in to sail it back, and Frank said he and Pete Grant would get Mr Davis's trailer and wait for me at the slipway in Seastone.

"Just after I had sailed round The Point, Nigel Heapes came up very fast in his speedboat and came so close I was tipped out.

"I swam back to the dinghy and Nigel brought his boat alongside. I yelled at him. I said 'you crazy bastard' or something like that. He just laughed. He said he wanted a parcel. I told him I didn't have a parcel. He said he knew I'd picked a parcel up at Foreland and told me to give it to him. I told him I didn't know anything about a parcel and started to pull myself back on board. He must have made his boat nudge the dinghy as I was getting in because it rocked suddenly and I fell into it head first, knocking me a bit dizzy. When I got up I was pretty angry and I pulled myself up onto the speedboat to have a go at Nigel, but he wasn't there. I called out several times and looked all round the boat, thinking he must have fallen in the water trying to get into the dinghy, but I couldn't see or hear any sign of him.

"After a bit I started the engine and went round in circles looking for him until it was too dark to see properly. Then I went back to the dinghy, tied it to the stern of Nigel's boat and towed it back to the slipway. Frank and Pete took the dinghy and I brought Nigel's boat back to the Yacht Club.

"Mr Vanderling was there and I told him what had happened. He said he would inform the Coastguard and the police. He told me to go home and get changed into dry clothes and be ready to talk to the police.

signed   W.J.Gregory 25th August 1975."

'OK?' asked Tindall when Greg had finished reading.
'Yes.'
Tindall looked at one of the documents he had taken from the

other folder 'Right, Let's go through it, then, from when you started to pull yourself on board.'

'Alright,' said Greg, 'There's no reason now why I can't tell you what actually happened. But it won't be any help,' and he told Tindall everything he had not told the police.

Tindall regarded Greg silently for a few seconds. Then he said, 'And you still say you didn't hear a shot? Or any other noise?'

'Right.'

'So Nigel must have been shot and fallen into the sea while you were down in the cockpit. How long were you out for do you think?'

'I've really no idea. It didn't seem very long at the time.'

'Nigel was in the cockpit when he knocked you down, though.'

'Yes.'

'So he must have gone onto the deck, otherwise he would have fallen back into the cockpit.'

'Yes, he would have, wouldn't he.' Greg had not thought about that.

'Now, we know there wasn't anybody else on either your boat or Nigel's, so whoever shot him must either have been on another boat or on land somewhere. Was there another boat nearby?'

'No. Earlier on, I'd seen a few boats going the other way, but there was nothing nearby.'

'So the shot must have come from the land. We don't know the direction of the shot, so we've got to try and work out possible places it could have come from.' Tindall thought for a moment. 'OK. Let's go back a bit. When did you first see the speedboat?'

'I heard it as I was coming up to The Point. It was behind me and further out, and when I looked I saw it was the boat Nigel had been messing around in that morning. I thought it was heading for the Yacht Club but the next thing I knew it was right behind me.'

'No, no, just a minute. Where you said you got swamped was *this* side of The Point.'

'Yes, that's right. Sorry.'

'Try to picture in your mind everything you can between when you first heard the speedboat and when you saw it coming at you.'

'It's too long ago, Ray. I can't remember every detail that far back.'

'No. Fair enough.' Tindall frowned and nodded in agreement. 'OK, let's try this - how did you know the boat was Nigel's?'

'It was white and it looked the same as the one I'd seen him in that morning.'

'So if you were able to recognise it, bearing in mind it was late in the evening and getting dark, it couldn't have been all that far away. How long did you go on watching it?'

'I don't know. Not very long.'

'OK, now, picture it. You're in Priory Bay, sailing a boat to the slipway here and you recognise Nigel's speedboat. How far out are you?'

Greg thought for a moment. 'The tide was out, and it's pretty shallow there, so to miss the rocks under the water at the end of The Point, I would guess roughly half a mile from the shore.'

'Alright, let's see what we've got so far. The tide is out, but it's coming in. The sun has set and the light is fading.' Tindall traced a finger over the document on his desk. Greg saw that it was a rough sketchmap of the scene of the incident. 'You are about half a mile from the shore, coming up to the end of The Point. The speedboat is white. It can't be very far away from you because you've easily recognised it. It must have changed course just after you spotted it and it catches up with you pretty soon after you've rounded The Point. About here,' His finger stopped on the place circled on the sketchmap where Nigel disappeared. 'It's getting dark, so whoever fires the shot must be close enough to see his target.' He nodded as if coming to a conclusion. 'Yes, I reckon the shot could have come from the rocks at the end of The Point.' He looked up at Greg. 'What do you think? Possible?'

Greg tried to envisage the situation. He would have come round The Point and lined up on the end of the pier, so he would still be fairly close to the rocks. But he would have noticed anyone on the rocks, wouldn't he? Then it came to him – the fellow with the fishing rod!

His surprise at the memory must have shown and Tindall leaned towards him expectantly.

'You've remembered something, haven't you?'

'Yes. I seem to remember somebody with a fishing rod climbing out over the rocks as I was coming towards The Point. I thought it was funny because he wouldn't have time to catch much before the tide came in.'

197

'A fishing rod?' Tindall raised his eyebrows.

'Yes. I know what you're thinking,' said Greg, 'And I'm with you.'

THIRTYTHREE

'If there was somebody on the rocks who might have had a rifle,' said Tindall, 'It would support my theory of where the shot may have come from, wouldn't it?'

'Doesn't get us anywhere, though, does it?' said Greg.

'Yes, it does. It reinforces the argument that Nigel was shot on the boat and fell into the water. See, he could have been shot somewhere else and his body dumped at the slipway. That seems less likely now.'

'Well, alright,' said Greg, 'But how would anyone know Nigel was going to be just there at that precise time?'

'Good point.' Tindall frowned and stroked his chin with thumb and forefinger. 'I still think there's got to be something in this parcel idea,' he said after a while, 'See, suppose, for the sake of argument, somebody told Nigel you were collecting a parcel when you picked up the dinghy, and Nigel wanted whatever he thought was in it, and he went there to get it, but you got there first.'

'OK.'

'So then he chases after you.'

'And?'

'Someone with a rifle is waiting on The Point to ambush him.'

'Bit far-fetched, isn't it? Too hit-and-miss, surely. There's no guarantee I would have sailed within range, is there? And there's the timing factor, too.'

'Yes, I agree, it's not a very likely scenario, but I'm not going to drop it altogether just yet.'

'It just seems to me,' said Greg, 'That if someone was planning to bump Nigel off they would have tried to be a bit more certain of getting him.'

'Perhaps they didn't have much time.'

'OK, but why involve me in it anyway?' said Greg.

'Ah! Yes, that's a point. Why did Davis ask you to collect the dinghy in the first place? Why couldn't Teddy have sailed it back for his dad?'

'I don't know. Never thought about that.'

'Do you remember how you came to be asked to do it?'

Greg thought for a moment 'If I remember rightly, we were

outside Davis's shop, Pete, Frank and me, and 'Squire' asked if one of us would go to Foreland and fetch his dinghy for him for a fiver. I said I'd do it. He gave me the five pounds out of the till there and then, I remember.'

'Hmmn. Did he say when?'

'Yes. Straightaway.'

'Well, that would fit with my hypothesis, wouldn't it.'

'I suppose so, but that's all any of it can be, supposition, after all this time.'

'Yes,' said Tindall, 'But it feels like progress.' He smiled at Greg. 'See, I knew there was something wrong with that statement of yours. Nice to be proved right. I can see why you withheld that bit about hitting Nigel, though. Salway would have latched on to that and almost certainly charged you. And he might have got a conviction, too. There were quite a lot of people willing to testify that you and Nigel Heapes were sworn enemies.'

'Sworn enemies? We didn't like each other, that's true, but everything else was just gossip.'

'Hmm, well, gossip can be a very useful resource, you know' said Tindall. 'If people kept their opinions to themselves the police would never solve half the crimes.'

Greg laughed. 'What? You're joking!! They don't solve half the crimes anyway!'

Tindall grinned amiably at him. 'Alright then, wouldn't solve half the crimes they do solve, that better?' He stood up. 'Fancy a cup of tea?'

'Yes, alright, thanks.'

'And Sophie said she'd like to say hello.'

'OK. Have we finished here, then?'

'Well, we've cleared up the query with your statement. Thanks for that.'

'You're welcome, but there's something else you might like to know,' said Greg. 'I went to see Arthur Heapes this morning and I told him you were keen to find out what really happened to Nigel.'

'Oh.' Tindall looked at him sharply. 'I didn't really want it generally known, you know. What did he say?'

'He doesn't think you'll get very far. But he did tell me he was so unimpressed with the progress the police were making at the time that he employed a private detective. I thought you might be interested.'

Greg took out his wallet and removed a piece of paper with the details Jason had written down for him. He passed it to Tindall. 'It might be worth having a word with him.'

'Thanks,' said Tindall. He glanced at the name on the paper. 'Cyril Ritter, eh? Yes, I've heard of him. I think he's still around. I'll pop in and see him. You never know, might give us a lead.'

He led the way downstairs and into what had been Sam's sitting room. Sophie had been sitting reading the Sunday Times magazine and she stood up, folding the paper neatly as her husband ushered Greg into the room. Greg smiled at her. He was amused at her expression. He thought she looked relieved, as if expected trouble had gone away.

'Hello, Greg,' she said, smiling in return and offering her hand. 'It's nice to see you.'

The Sophie Watkins he had known had been a thin, rather plain, hard-faced young woman, whose lips had seemed permanently pursed in disapproval. As Sophie Tindall, she had matured into a comfortably stout matron with a pleasant smile, whose eyes twinkling behind thick-lensed glasses, were genuinely pleased to see him.

'Hello Sophie,' he said, taking her hand. 'Nice to see you, too.'

Tindall said from the doorway, 'We're going to have a cup of tea, love. Shall I bring one for you too?'

'Yes, please. And perhaps Greg would like a slice of cake, or a pastry?'

'Oh, no thanks very much,' said Greg. 'I had a late and rather splendid lunch at the Pier Hotel. Haven't room for anything else.'

Sophie invited Greg to sit down on the sofa. and seated herself in an armchair facing him. While they waited for Tindall to return with the tea, she regaled him with news of his old friend Frank, who, it transpired, was happily settled in Australia where he ran his own very successful boat-hire business. She and Ray visited him every Christmas, she said, and were always very well looked after. She told him this with more than a trace of family pride, quite unlike her former attitude to her younger brother.

Then they fell to reminiscing about Sam. Sophie had been very fond of the old man, too, and had stayed working for him until he retired. Then Ray had asked her to marry him, she said, and soon after that they moved to the mainland when he transferred to CID.

She said, 'Mr Morris was very fond of you, wasn't he?'

'It was mutual,' said Greg.

'He was terribly upset when you were hurt and taken to hospital,' she said. 'He couldn't understand why anyone would do that to you.' She looked straight at him almost as if challenging him. 'I knew you had been seeing Mrs Vanderling and I wondered if it was to do with that.'

When Greg didn't say anything, she averted her eyes. 'Mr Morris just told me that if I did think I knew anything I was to keep it to myself, in the same way he always expected me to when I found out things about people through my work in the Post Office.' She looked up at him again. 'Well, the only person I ever said anything to about that was Ray, and that was a good many years later. But ... you were seeing her, weren't you?"

Greg said carefully, 'I told Ray she saw what happened that night on Nigel's boat and that's why she was on my side. And, apart from my dad and Sam, she was the only one in the whole of the village who stood by me at the time.'

Tindall came back through from the café bearing a loaded tea tray and Sophie positioned a small table so that he could place it between them. She said, as she started to pour the tea, 'How did you two get on, then, up there?'

'Greg's cleared up my query on his statement,' said Tindall. 'And he's given me a lead to follow up tomorrow.'

Sophie smiled at Greg. 'I told Ray you'd help him if you could,' she said. 'Help yourself to milk and sugar, won't you.'

As they sat drinking their tea Tindall gave his wife a neat and accurate summary of their conversation. Greg was surprised and impressed that he should do so.

'Did you discuss cases with Sophie when you were in the Force, Ray?' he asked.

'Sometimes,' he said. 'If it wasn't too sensitive. You'd be surprised how often she would see something we'd all missed, too.' He gave her a fond look, adding, 'I'd be a fool if I said I didn't miss those days.'

'That's why he won't let this Vanderling business rest, Greg,' she said. 'It keeps nagging at him since they found those bones. He's convinced there's a connection, and he's usually right.'

Greg shrugged. He could respect the ex-copper's reasoning about where the shot which killed Nigel had been fired from, but despite what he had heard that morning from Arthur, he was still dubious about Roddy having been involved in anything illegal. He had made this point to Tindall before though, and did not feel it needed repeating. He looked at his watch and stood up.

Tindall said, 'Before you go, could I have your mobile number? Might want to run something by you.'

'Alright.' Greg wrote it down on the notepad Tindall offered him. 'But I think we've covered everything, really.'

He turned to Sophie and thanked her for the tea, asking her to send his regards to her brother in Australia when she next contacted him.

On his way back to Dan's house, Greg reflected upon his conversation with Arthur. He had toyed with the idea of telling Tindall what Suzy had said about her feeling that Clarmont Brown might have been threatening Roddy. That had been more than ten years ago, however, and nothing had apparently come of it. It was all too vague, he decided, so he'd said nothing about it.

 He had to admit to himself, though, that Ray Tindall was an interesting fellow and his 'Vanderling Associates' theory was certainly intriguing.

In Greg's experience, policemen tended to fall into one of two types, the instinctive copper or the hardened one. Either could be a good policeman.

From what Ray Tindall had said he was not at all like the type who made sure to follow procedure, the hardened copper doggedly pursuing the rational path of evidence and who would not recognise a hunch if he had one. Greg reckoned he must have been more of an instinctive copper, which may have been why he never rose above DCI. Although on reflection, instinctive was probably not the right word, because the ability to form a hunch, let alone follow one, is not instinctive but has to be learned.

Greg had served with a similar division of types in the Regiment. Some became so hardened that nothing could deflect them. Others learned from their experiences and developed the skills which led them to have a feel for a situation, or a sense about a person, and although such people could learn to desensitise themselves to a degree, they could never become hardened, because even when their hunches were right, they were liable to bouts of conscience, and when they were wrong, they had to cope with embarrassment at least, or guilt at worst. He knew because he was one; he never learned how to become desensitised enough.

oOo

A new black Mercedes SUV with tinted windows was parked in Dan's driveway when Greg returned. He parked beside it, got out and went round to the back door of the house. He tapped lightly on the glass as he entered and called 'Hello?' He heard voices which stopped abruptly. Dan appeared in the doorway of the sitting room, looking irritated, then his expression changed to a relieved smile.

'Am I interrupting?' said Greg.

'No. No, come on in, Greg.' Dan stepped back to let Greg precede him into the sitting room.

Dan's visitor was standing looking out of the window. He turned as Greg came into the room. A strongly-built man in his early sixties Greg guessed, with a tanned, ruggedly handsome face and a fine head of iron-grey hair, wearing a light brown safari jacket and matching trousers, he reminded Greg of pictures he'd seen of the typical white hunter from the nineteen thirties, home on leave from the colonies. Greg had a sense of recognition but could not place him immediately.

Dan said vaguely from behind him, 'I expect you remember. . .'

The man reached out a hand, 'Clarmont Brown.'

Yes, of course, the lean, athletic young man that Greg remembered had filled out. He had worn well and had obviously looked after himself but, then, he would have, wouldn't he. As ever, he was immaculately turned out, his clothes well tailored and expensive. Greg shook his hand briefly, noting the diamond Rolex on the other wrist 'Hello Bob.'

Clarmont Brown's expression was guarded. 'It's been a long time,' he said. He took a pace towards the door, 'I'll wait to hear from you, then Dan.'

Greg had never seen Dan look so antagonistic and it took him by surprise.

Clarmont Brown nodded to Greg, his eyes still wary, and went out.

As soon as he had gone Greg said, 'Everything alright?'

'Yes. Yes, fine.' Dan turned his head away.

'But he has upset you, hasn't he?' said Greg, giving him back his car keys.

'Oh, it's nothing. It'll pass.'

'You sure?'

'Honestly, Greg, it's okay.' Dan smiled as if to reassure him. 'How did your day go?'

Just for a moment, because he was disturbed by Dan's reaction to Clarmont Brown, Greg was tempted to tell him what Arthur had said about Suzy's suspicions, but he decided not to because that might lead to difficult questions. He still felt the least said about the past the better.

Instead, he gave Dan a brief account of his day, saying how much he had enjoyed meeting the Heapes family and that he wanted to keep in touch with them from now on.

As for his talk with Ray Tindall, Greg said merely that they had had an interesting chat and he wished Ray well in his efforts to find out what did actually happen to Nigel, but he did not want to get involved himself in what, after all this time, could only prove to be a wild goose chase.

THIRTYFOUR

Monday

When Greg had phoned Zillah the previous evening to tell her that Dan would be bringing him home in the morning, her immediate response had been to invite them both to lunch.

Meanwhile Dan had called an old friend in Devon to suggest a meeting while he was in the area and the friend had invited him to stay for a few days. Dan had accepted, so before they could leave, he needed to organise the start of the week's work at the Yacht Club. That had taken longer than expected and it was almost one o'clock before they crossed the cattle grid into the forest.

Greg said, 'We'd better not stop at my place, if you don't mind, but go straight on to Zillah's. I wouldn't want to be late for lunch.'

He directed Dan along the narrow forest lanes and after a couple of miles he pointed out a house on their left. 'There we are. That's my place.'

'Hey, what a pretty little house,' said Dan, bringing the Range Rover to a halt. 'The way you've always spoken of it, I imagined it as just an ordinary old thatched cottage, but this is really pretty.'

'You don't think it's a bit "chocolate-boxy"?'

Dan considered for a moment. 'Well, yes, I suppose it is,' he said. 'But so what? It's still a lovely place to live. I like the way the roofline comes down over the garage. What was that in the old days, a stable, cowshed?'

Greg smiled. 'No, it wasn't, though it looks as though it might have been, doesn't it?. Actually, it was an ugly old concrete-block garage detached about six feet from the cottage. I'd been intending to smarten it up, and then, when I had the cottage roof done, the thatcher suggested extending the roof line down to cover it. It needed some repairs anyway, so I told him to go ahead. It cost a bit, of course, but it was worth it. It gave me a bit of extra storage space and I can get into and out of the garage without getting wet when it rains.'

They drove on and were greeted by Rocky at Zillah's gate, delighted to see Greg but when Dan got out of the car and approached, the dog stood still and stared. He didn't growl, but he didn't wag his tail either.

Dan said, 'He doesn't like me.'

'He doesn't dislike you either. He would growl if he did,' said Greg. 'But don't try to make a fuss of him; he only lets Zillah and me do that.'

He led the way around the house, Rocky walking possessively between him and Dan.

Zillah met them at her back door.

Greg made the introductions and Zillah invited them into her small dining room where lunch was ready to be served. Rocky went to his bean bag and sat down.

Dan apologised for their time of arrival, explaining what had delayed them and that he had not known, when arranging to be away for a few days, that Greg had accepted her invitation to lunch.

'But I didn't want to miss the opportunity of meeting you at last,' he said.

Zillah laughed. 'In all honesty,' she said, 'I wouldn't have minded what time you arrived. When he told me last night you were bringing him home, my first thought was, "now's my chance to meet Dan – I'll invite them both to lunch!". Greg has told me all about your friendship over the years. You're the nearest thing to family that he has, after all.'

Greg looked at her in alarm, wondering where this was going.

'Actually, Zillah,' he said, as she indicated that they should sit at the table, 'Although what you say is true, I do have real live family, you know,' and he told her how the Heapes family had welcomed him as one of their own.

'It's been a really good week-end,' said Dan, 'It's all worked out really well. Greg's back in touch with his relations. The police seem happy to accept what he told them, so that's got that out of the way, and I can go ahead now with the extension. And we've had some really good chats, haven't we Greg, catching up on things?'

'So this business with the bones is all cleared up, is it?' asked Zillah.

'Well, not exactly.' Greg explained about the bullet hole in the skull, and Ray Tindall's intention to investigate, despite the apparent lack of police interest.

'He wanted Greg to help him,' said Dan.

'And you said no, I take it?' said Zillah.

'I spent an hour or so with him on Sunday afternoon, clearing up a few queries.'

'But aren't you at all curious to find out why Nigel was shot?' said Zillah. 'I would be.'

'Yes, of course I'm curious. I think it's very strange. I just don't want to get personally involved, that's all.'

Dan changed the subject, much to Greg's relief, asking Zillah about her animal rescue activities. This topic dominated their conversation for the rest of the meal, Dan being able to contribute from his experience with oiled sea-birds, which still turned up from time to time on the beaches at Seastone.

Greg was very pleased that Dan and Zillah, the two people most dear to him, were getting along so well. He was disappointed when all too soon, the time came for Dan to leave.

Zillah and Greg, with Rocky at his heels, walked with Dan to his Range Rover where Greg retrieved his overnight bag, and Dan and Zillah said how pleased they were to have met each other.

After Dan had driven away, Zillah said, 'He's so much like you! Oh, I know he's taller and fairer, and I expect he favours his mother's features, but his mannerisms, the way he moves, and his general demeanour, is so exactly you! Anyone could see it!'

'Well,' said Greg, 'The only other person who knows for sure is Arthur. He said Suzy told him just after Dan was born.'

'He's a lovely young man. Too young for me, though. I'll have to make do with his father.'

Greg pulled her to him and kissed her gently, and released her 'I'm glad you two have met at last. Thanks for the lunch. Can I help clear up?'

'No, you get along home. And take your hound. He's been very good, but he needs more exercise than I can spare the time for.'

Greg walked down the lane and let himself into his cottage feeling all was well with his world.

When he had unpacked, he noticed he had a message on his answer phone and was surprised to hear a familiar voice with an Eton and Sandhurst accent.

'Southwell, Greg. Haven't heard from you for a while. Give me a call. Some time soon, eh? Usual number.'

That was all, but Greg knew that Nick would not phone without good reason. He called him directly.

They exchanged pleasantries, then Nick said, 'Your name came up on my message board over the weekend.'

'Oh?'

'Yes. When I looked into it I found CID had put out a search and my system flagged it. What's it all about?'

Greg knew that Nick's system kept tabs on all his associates and former associates.

'It's something that happened ages ago when I was a kid,' he said. 'I thought it was all over and done with.'

'You in trouble?'

'No, no. What it was, I had a bit of an argument with a cousin of mine and he fell off a boat and disappeared. It wasn't actually my fault but I was arrested on suspicion. Nigel was never found though, and I was never charged with anything. This was thirtytwo years ago, when I was eighteen.'

'Ah, yes, I seem to recall a note about that business on your initial screening.'

'Really? I didn't know that. I've never spoken about it, but I'm not too surprised. Anyway, a couple of weeks ago some bones were found when Dan was extending his marina and they've been identified as Nigel's, so the police wanted to interview me as the last person known to have seen him. I went over to the Island on Saturday and gave a statement to a plain-clothes sergeant. She seemed quite happy to leave it at that.'

'So that's it, is it?"

'I hope so.'

'Only hope so?'

'Well, the funny thing is, the thing that lets me off is that Nigel died from a shot in the head. High velocity round, apparently.'

'Hmmn. So he didn't just fall off a boat, then.'

'Apparently not, but there's no way I can be blamed for it.'

'No. It sounds serious though, Greg, high velocity round.'

'Yes,' said Greg, 'And it opens up a whole new aspect of the case, too. There's a retired DCI locally who has ideas of his own. He seems to think there's a link with an old case of his that never got resolved and he wants me to help him look into it.'

'And?'

'I told him no.'

'Not interested in finding out what happened to your cousin?'

Greg hesitated, 'Well, it's a long time ago and I don't really want to drag it all up again.'

'Can of worms?'

'Could be. He thinks Roddy Vanderling, Suzy's husband, was involved.'

'Ah. Yes, I see. But this ex-DCI is going to look into it anyway, is he?'

'I think so, yes.'

'So it could all be dragged up again whether you help him or not.'

'I suppose so, yes.'

'Hmmn. How's Dan?'

'Oh, he's fine. He's just left, as a matter of fact. I spent the weekend with him and he brought me home. He's on his way to Plymouth for a few days.'

'And Zillah?'

'Still Zillah, I'm glad to say.'

'That's great. Listen, if this business turns nasty and you need anything let me know.'

'OK Thanks.'

'Don't forget. Keep in touch' Nick rang off.

Greg sat for a moment wondering about Ray Tindall's investigation, what it might reveal if it ever went ahead. Perhaps there really wasn't any need to worry about his affair with Suzy becoming public knowledge, because unless it led to Dan asking outright, which was unlikely, their secret could still be safe. The thought cheered him and he felt more relaxed about Tindall's investigation.

He spent the rest of the afternoon doing odd jobs about his house and garden. Then he went to the village shop to replenish his larder. He bought milk and groceries, onions, carrots, tomatoes, mushrooms, a hand of five bananas, two red apples, and a bag of loose dog biscuits, Spillers Shapes, for Rocky.

After his evening meal he was sitting at his kitchen table reading the New Forest Journal and Rocky was sitting next to him with his head resting on Greg's thigh. After a while the dog stood up, stretched and yawned, then sat down again and stared at the refrigerator. Every so often he would turn his head for a moment and check the door of the cupboard where his biscuits were kept

Greg finally noticed and got up and fed him, and opened a can of beer and took it over to the window and looked out across Zillah's paddock. It was about an hour until sunset and the grass and the tall hedge along the side of the lane were bathed in a warm golden glow. Zillah's New Forest mare and foal were grazing side by side close to Greg's fence. A rabbit hopped out of the hedge a few feet away from the ponies, hesitated, head up and looked around, then moved a little further into the field and started grazing. All was peaceful and quiet as usual.

It wasn't so quiet in the kitchen though; Rocky's name-tag was clanging rhythmically against the rim of his stainless steel bowl as he ate his supper.

Greg took a long swig of beer from the can and stared out at nothing for several minutes. Rocky's name-tag took on a different note as he washed his food down with a drink from his water bowl. Greg took another long swig and went on staring out at nothing.

His visit to Seastone had released some buried emotions. He was thinking again of his conversation with Arthur, and wishing that he had been mature enough, or at least, sensitive enough at the time to have properly appreciated what he had tried to do for him and his father. And he was grateful for the knowledge that Suzy had found comfort from her talks with Arthur in her final illness

He was glad that he had gone to see him. It was right that Arthur should be happy in his old age, in the heart of his family with a son and grandson to care for him and carry on, now that he was becoming infirm.

Mentally addressing his own reflection in the dark window, he asked himself what he could look forward to if he reached Arthur's age, but he could think of no satisfactory answer, so he looked in the glass a little longer, then he toasted himself and emptied the can of beer.

Rocky came and nudged his hand.

'Walks time.'

211

THIRTYFIVE

Tuesday morning

Greg woke up at dawn, Suzy on his mind, how she looked as she was dying of leuchaemia.

He switched on his bedside lamp. Next to it was the photograph she had sent him when he first went to Northern Ireland, more than a quarter of a century ago. It had been taken aboard 'Serena', the Yacht Club boat, on her fortieth birthday, the sun on her face, her blonde hair streaming out behind her, and she looked young and beautiful and full of life.

Tucked behind the picture in its frame was another photo, taken on the same day, Dan aged three years and four months. Greg took it out and stared at both pictures for a long moment, thinking of what might have been.

He put the photo of Dan back, got out of bed, stretched, yawned, and went through to his bathroom, had a pee and sluiced his face and hands in cold water. Then up the ladder to the mini-gym in his loft, where he began his morning exercise routine. These days he no longer noticed from various parts of his body the aches and pains with which for years his exercises had rewarded him after his injuries had apparently healed.

When he had finished and dressed in jeans, tee-shirt and trainers, he ambled downstairs to be greeted enthusiastically as usual by Rocky. He opened the back door to let the dog out into the garden, then took a carton of orange juice from the fridge and poured himself a couple of inches in a tall glass, drinking it down in two swallows.

It was misty outside, a damp silence across the Forest. Greg and Rocky jogged down the stony lane, along the narrow road at the bottom and turned off at the bridle-way which crossed the brook and led steeply up to Gorley Common. While Greg did a fast circuit of the Common - about a mile by his reckoning, mostly flat but with a few dips and rises – Rocky tagged faithfully behind, ever alert for the unwary rabbit.

By the time they got back to the cottage, the sun was well over the horizon and the mist was clearing, promising another fine day, and as he showered and shaved Greg decided that after breakfast he would start on the fencing work that Zillah needed to make her northern boundary deer-proof.

But this was not to be.

The first phone call came just before eight o'clock as he was washing up his breakfast plates.

Puzzled and slightly irritated because nobody phoned him this early, he dried his hands, went into his sitting room and picked up the phone.

'Gregory.'

'Hello Greg, Simon here,' said a voice he did not recognise at first.

'Who?'

'Simon Heapes, Pier Hotel.'

'Oh ... Hello Simon.'

'Sorry to bother you this early in the morning, but we've just had a nasty shock. Tell me, when you saw the police last Saturday, did they tell you how Nigel died?'

Greg had been glad that while he was with the Heapes family on Sunday, Nigel had hardly been mentioned at all, and, as it happened, the manner of his death had not even been considered.

'No, they didn't,' he said, adding carefully, 'But when I saw Ray Tindall, he said he'd been told Nigel was shot.'

'Ha! *He* knew, then! And *we've* just read about it in the bloody paper!' Simon was clearly very angry. 'Dad likes to have a look at the headlines with his cup of tea before he gets up, and you can imagine how he felt when he saw that! We've had to get the doctor to him. I've been on to the police and given them a piece of my mind. Bloody hell, Greg, what sort of people are they, to let an old man find out from the bloody paper that his son died from a bullet in his head?'

There was no answer to that, thought Greg. He said, 'Is your Dad alright, Simon? What did the doctor say?'

'He's had some sort of seizure, they think. We're waiting for an ambulance to take him off to Newport. Oh, God, I don't know, Greg, I'm so bloody angry!'

'Yes, of course.'

'They must have known when they found Nigel. Why couldn't they tell us then instead of letting us go on believing he'd drowned? They told Ray Tindall, for God's sake!'

Greg said, 'I must admit, when he told me what he'd heard, I was a bit shocked, too. In fact, I found it very hard to believe, as

213

I expect you can imagine.'

'Yes, well, we're all a bit shattered here. Poor old Dad. He doesn't need this kind of thing.'

'No, that's right.' Greg had a thought: it was very unlikely that Ray Tindall would have told the press, so the news had probably come from the police themselves. He said, 'I'm surprised the press didn't say anything to you beforehand, Simon.'

'No. Well, some reporter rang up for an interview yesterday morning, on what she called the current developments, but they were such a damn nuisance when Nigel was first found, I said no.'

'Fair enough. And when you spoke to the police, did they say what they were doing about finding out what happened to Nigel?'

'To be honest, Greg, I didn't give them much of a chance. I was too bloody angry. You know, over the years you accept the fact that your brother must have fallen off a boat and drowned, and when his body eventually turns up, it feels like: that's it then, now we know. But to suddenly find out he was shot and the police kept you in the dark about it! I mean …'

'Yes, I agree, it's inexcusable. You'll keep me in the picture, will you, Simon, about your Dad? I'll ring you later to see how he is, if I may?'

'Yes, of course. Let's just hope it isn't too serious. Oh, hang on!' There was a pause. 'Sounds as though the ambulance is here. I've got to go.'

'OK, Simon. Give Arthur my love. I'll speak to you later.'

Greg put the phone down, wondering at the crassitude within the police force these days. Surely they could have given the facts about Nigel to his family? Told them to keep the details to themselves if necessary? He could see why Ray Tindall had taken the attitude he had towards the local force.

He finished his washing up and as he tidied everything away, he noticed his mobile phone where he had left it on charge the previous evening. He unplugged it and saw he had a message.

It was Sophie Tindall. She sounded upset. 'Oh, Greg, I was hoping to speak to you. Well, it's Ray, really. Um, can you ring back? It's urgent.' That was all.

Now what? thought Greg.

He found the café menu card with the mobile number Tindall had given him in his wallet. He rang the number but the mobile

214

must have been switched off, so he tried the number for the café printed on the front of the card. It rang several times before Sophie eventually answered:

'Quayside Café.'

'Hello Sophie, Greg.'

'Oh, Greg, thanks for ringing back! I tried to get you last night. Ray's been beaten up!'

'Sorry? Did you say beaten up?'

'Last night ... Two men came in through the back door. We were just going to bed. They came in, grabbed hold of him and pulled him outside and punched him and knocked him down and kicked him and ... Oh, Greg ...' her voice broke. 'He didn't stand a chance!' She tried to stifle a sob.

Greg waited while she got herself under control. 'Was he very badly hurt?' he said.

'Great big bruises all over him, and a cracked rib,' she said. 'But nothing really serious, thank the Lord. I've just brought him back from the hospital. They kept him in because they were worried about concussion, but he's alright. I was just putting him into bed. He wants to speak to you. Can he ring you on his mobile?'

'Yes, of course. But how about you? Did they hurt you at all?'

'One of them knocked me down when I tried to stop them, but I'm alright.'

'What were they after, the money from the till? Did they take much?'

'No, Greg, that wasn't what it was about. They said it was a warning for him to keep away from things that are none of his business. He went to see that detective yesterday.'

'Good Lord! What on earth did he say to him to get a reaction like that?'

'Well I gather all he did was ask the detective if he would look up his file on the work he did for Mr Heapes after his son disappeared thirty-odd years ago.'

Somebody must be very worried, then, thought Greg, and whoever it was had been pretty quick off the mark. 'You told the police about that, I suppose?' he said, 'When they came?'

'Well, no.' She hesitated. 'Ray wanted to talk to you first.'

'What for? It's a police matter, surely. I mean, he of all people should see that.'

'Yes, but he wants to talk to you, Greg.'

'I don't know Sophie, if I'd thought anything like this would happen I'd never have told him about that detective.'

'Oh, don't worry about that! This hasn't put him off, far from it! He's determined he's really on to something now, and he knows the locals won't take it seriously. But you know all the background and he's sure you can help him. I'll tell him he can ring you then, shall I? Please?'

Greg could well believe that Ray would be encouraged by what had happened. He would not be put off by such crude tactics. The attack would only tend towards confirming his belief that Nigel had been killed because he had known something, and that 'something' was connected with the 'Vanderling Associates'. Well, whatever, thought Greg, clearly it still matters quite a lot to somebody, and that 'somebody' is connected to the detective I sent Ray to.

He said, 'Yes, alright, Sophie, if he's feeling up to it.'

'Thanks, Greg. He'll ring you straight back.'

She put the phone down, and Greg sat for a moment, thinking.

Until four days ago his life had been settled in a comfortable rut. Then Dan had rung to tell him that the police wanted to see him, and he had been irritated at the intrusion into, what he could now see, had become a decidedly tame existence. He had resented the resurrection of his deeply buried memories of what had happened on the boat, mainly because it revived uncomfortable feelings of guilt, not only about Nigel but also about the secret he had to keep from Dan. But now that it was obvious he not been responsible for Nigel's death, he had no reason to feel guilty about that, at least.

Ray Tindall, Dan, Zillah and Nick had all implied that they expected him to show more interest in finding out who shot Nigel, and he had to admit to himself that he supposed he should because he knew that if he allowed himself to sink back into the rut, he would wonder for the rest of his life what possible motive anyone could have had to shoot Nigel.

So, although he was still uneasy about Tindall's theory that Roddy may have been involved in some way, when his mobile phone rang, he knew he was going to agree to go back to Seastone.

THIRTY SIX

Greg's phone conversation with Ray Tindall was short and to the point. Having decided that he would become involved, he saw little merit in talking at length about it from a distance.

'You take it easy this morning, Ray,' he said. 'And I'll be with you by lunch time. You can fill me in on the details then.'

He looked at his watch. It was not yet eight thirty. Zillah would still be on her morning rounds. He knew she would be unlikely to object to having Rocky back again, but before asking her, he would give her time to finish seeing to the needs of her livestock - ponies, goats, and poultry - and checking the progress of any recovering wildlife "patients", of which she usually had at least one on the premises.

Meanwhile he rang Nick Southwell to let him know his decision.

'If it's all going to be dragged up again anyway, Greg,' said Nick, 'You may as well be a part of the action, and from what you say it looks as if there could be some. With any luck there might even be enough to get your adrenal glands working again. You've been tucked away in your cosy little nest there far too long!'

Greg laughed, 'Point taken,' he said.

'And you could do worse than join up with this ex-copper. A tough old bird by the sound of him. Anyway, keep in touch.' Nick rang off.

Greg knew that Nick felt frustrated at having been unable to persuade him to take on any but the simplest assignments since he had joined the agency in Poole.

The fact was that, Zillah having persuaded him to buy the old cottage, he had soon found that the cost of refurbishing it was much greater than he had expected, so he had decided to do as much as he could himself. This had meant not only that that he'd had to acquire some new skills, but also that he'd become engrossed in the work and reluctant to spend much time away. By the time it was eventually finished to his satisfaction, he'd settled into a lifestyle completely different from anything he'd known before and from then on he'd been quite happy just to sit back and enjoy the fruits of his labour.

Now however, as he started to make preparations for another short stay in Seastone, he felt something inside him rekindle and he could not help contrasting this feeling of expectation with the mild anxiety he had felt when he'd packed this same bag just four days earlier.

Ray Tindall had invited him to stay with them, but Greg felt he would rather have an independent base. For the same reason, reinforced by the earlier phone call from Simon, he had decided against taking a room at the Pier Hotel. Dan's house would be empty for the next few days, however, and when Greg rang him explaining the current situation, Dan readily agreed to him moving back in.

'Ring Mrs Wade and get her to let you in,' he said. 'And after that you can use the spare keys.' He gave Greg the phone number. 'D'you think you'll still be there when I get back on Friday?'

'Don't know. Probably.'

'OK. Good. And I'm off again on Saturday, don't forget, so the place will be yours for as long as it takes.'

Greg laughed. 'That sounds like an open-ended commitment if ever there was one! But seriously, I've no idea how far Ray Tindall will want to take this business. The sooner we can find something to pass on to the coppers, the better, of course, – if there is anything to find, that is.'

'Well, there must be something or Ray wouldn't have been beaten up. Tell him I hope he soon feels better. I've got to go now. See you on Friday. Good luck!'

Greg took Rocky up the lane to Zillah and told her why he was going back to Seastone.

She gave him a long, hard look.

'I know you can look after yourself,' she said, 'But take care, won't you - I don't want to have to become this hound's permanent foster mother.'

He smiled and put his hands on her shoulders, then leant forward and kissed her gently on the lips. 'I'll ring you,' he said.

Back at his own cottage, he fetched his bag and was locking up when he caught a faint memory of how he used to feel when checking over his equipment at the start of a new mission. He paused. It was more than ten years since he'd had that feeling and he realised what was wrong. He had no weapons.

He went back indoors and up the ladder to his loft to retrieve the old thirtyeight semi-automatic pistol that Sam had bequeathed to him. He had not fired it since those far-off days when Sam had given him lessons, but he had cleaned it from time to time and he smiled to himself as he checked it once again. Compared with his former exploits, it seemed somewhat absurd to be arming himself before going to the aid of a retired policeman on the Isle of Wight. But whoever had shot Nigel and beaten up Ray deserved a certain amount of respect.

He put the pistol in its holster and selected a box of ammunition, trusting that it would still be in good order, but in all honesty not expecting to have to find out.

oOo

It was just after eleven o'clock when he parked in Dan's reserved spot at Seastone Yacht Club. He locked his car and walked across the road to the café, which, to his surprise, was open for business. Sophie greeted him at the door and ushered him through into her sitting room.

'I thought you'd be closed,' he said.

'I had to keep opening up for people asking after Ray, so I thought I might as well stay open.'

'How is he?'

'Well, he's in very good spirits. He must be sore, but I think the painkillers are helping. What hurts most, though, is that he didn't get a chance to hit them back. But go on up. He's in his study, he wouldn't stay in bed. I'll bring you up a cup of coffee in a minute.'

Ray Tindall was sitting at his desk, two folders open before him. His face was bruised and swollen, one eye almost closed. He gave a lopsided grin and offered his hand without getting up as Greg came in.

'Take a seat,' he said, indicating the chair next to him.

Greg said, 'Took you by surprise, then.'

'Completely. Didn't stand a chance. Bastards.'

'Would you recognise them if you saw them again?'

'They had balaclavas on, but the one that gave me the message had blonde hair sticking out the back.'

'They were pretty quick off the mark, weren't they?'

Ray said, 'Well, see, I saw Ritter in the morning. He wasn't any help. Told me he couldn't remember the case at all at first, but eventually he said he'd look up his files and let me know. I came home for lunch and gave him a ring in the afternoon, but his secretary woman said he was out. Anyway, I told her I was serious about wanting to know anything he might have found out at the time.' He paused. 'They came for me just after ten o'clock. So whoever it is I've upset, can organise a bit of muscle within half a day.'

'Which suggests,' said Greg, 'They must be very worried. So what's our first step, then?'

'Well, as I told you the other day, I've always hated loose ends, and especially the idea of anyone getting away with murder, so I've started going all through the Vanderling file.'

'You're convinced there's a connection, aren't you?'

Ray frowned and shook his dead slowly from side to side. 'Convinced is too strong. I just think it's very likely, so I'm looking for anything that might support the idea, or for that matter, contradict it. It's a long shot, but it's worth doing.'

'When was this file first opened?'

'Hang on,' Ray flicked through a pile of papers and picked out one sheet. 'In the May, just a few months before Nigel Heapes was shot.' He indicated a pair of box files on the shelf in front of them. 'That's the rest of it, up to when I retired, but not much was added after ninetyeight.'

Ninetyeight, thought Greg, that was the year Roddy died. He said, 'So the file was open for twenty years and nothing came of it?'

'Right, nothing that could be acted upon.'

Sophie came in with a tray of coffee and biscuits. Greg moved some papers from the top of the two-drawer filing cabinet by Ray's side, so that she could put it down. When she had left them they sat in silence for a minute or two while they drank their coffee.

Then Greg said, 'What's in the file that could be of use to us now, then, all these years later?'

'Names to be followed up, locations to be visited,' Ray put his cup down and turned towards Greg, wincing slightly as he did so.

'See, first of all,' he went on, 'When you open up an old case you mustn't assume the original work was all done properly. Most of it probably was but you don't know which bit may not have been. Some of the recorded facts, so-called, may be useless, may even lead you astray if you accept them as gospel. Perhaps at the time I had some preconceived ideas. And, of course, it's always possible I overlooked something relevant.' He picked up his coffee cup and drained it. 'Anyway, I'll be stuck here for the next few days, so that's what I'll be doing, sifting through it, while you are out and about. Okay?'

'Yes, sure, so where do I start?'

'How about going to see Ritter again?'

'Okay,' said Greg. 'See if he has bothered to open up his old case notes? And when I tell him you've been beaten up it will be interesting to see what his reaction is.'

'Exactly.'

'I want to go to Bembridge first, though. Dan's away but I'll be staying at his place.'

'Before you go,' said Ray, 'Have a look at this and see if you think it might be useful.' He took a small black box from his desk drawer and passed to him.

Greg opened it. Inside was a little black automatic. It was intended to look as if it was made of plastic and it was small enough to be mistaken for a toy.

'Point two two,' said Ray, 'Good for up to maybe five metres. There's no spare shells, but the clip that's in it has seven. Hopefully you'll never need to reload it. The thing is, it's light enough to go in your coat pocket and not be noticed.'

Greg examined the little gun. There were no maker's marks or identifiers on it that he could see. 'Where did it come from?'

'Had it for years. The man who showed it to me had no further use for it. I thought it might come in handy one day. Probably needs cleaning though. Put it in your pocket, just in case, eh?'

THIRTYSEVEN

Greg had phoned Mrs Wade while he was on the ferry from Lymington, and arranged to meet her at Dan's house at half past twelve. She had suggested that if he was staying for any length of time, she could go to the shops and get whatever items of food he might need.

She was waiting at the gate when he arrived and led the way around the house to the little porch by the back door and into Dan's kitchen, where she unpacked her shopping bags, identifying each item whilst putting it away where she knew it would belong.

When Greg had paid her, she said, 'If you're staying for a while Mr Gregory, I was wondering about my hours? Only I usually do Mondays, Wednesdays and Fridays, but I was going to leave it tomorrow as Mr Vanderling wouldn't have been here, you see.'

Greg asked her to keep to her usual weekly routine and she agreed.

After she had gone, he went out to the garage and hunted through Dan's toolbox so that he could take Ray's little gun to pieces. Judging by the skill with which it had been put together from such light materials, he guessed it had been made in Eastern Europe, probably in the former Czechoslovakia, but despite his best efforts he could find no identifying marks on it whatsoever. He cleaned it thoroughly, using the only light oil he could find, re-assembled it and checked the action, confirming that it worked perfectly. He put it back in his pocket.

He unpacked his bag in his usual room, and then he phoned the Pier Hotel for news of Arthur. Jason answered, saying that his grandfather had had a minor stroke and was being kept in hospital for observation. At present it seemed there was no obvious lasting damage, but Simon was still furious and had written to the Chief Constable. Greg rang off after telling Jason that he was back on the Island for the next few days and would call in and see them sometime soon.

It was lunch time. He made himself a couple of ham sandwiches and a pot of tea, and while he ate, he thought about Ray Tindall's Vanderling file. What useful information, if any, might it contain? Ray had suggested there would be names to follow up. Who would still be around, he wondered, whom he had known at all well in those days?

He went through them one by one in his mind.

Josie? – no, according to Arthur she was in New Zealand, married to a farmer, and her parents lived abroad most of the time. Frank? – no, Sophie had said he was in Australia. Pete? – possibly, he would enquire. Barbara Black he had seen. And Bob Clarmont Brown. Teddy Davis still ran his father's shop.

He could not think of any more offhand. It did not seem very useful. Well, perhaps something might come out of his visit to the detective, Cyril Ritter.

Ray had told him that Ritter's office was on the first floor above a video rental shop in Ryde High Street. Greg parked in the centre of the town and found the video shop at the top of the hill: At the side, an open door revealed stairs. He went up. From the landing he saw a half-open door with the one word, "Ritter", in black letters on the frame above it. He tapped on the door and entered a reception area. An attractive woman possibly a few years older than himself, was sitting at a desk and operating a word-processor. He smiled at her and she smiled back. She was still pretty, he thought, but her prettiest moment had been a few years ago.

She said, 'Be with you in a minute.'

'I'd like a word with Mr Cyril Ritter, if possible' he said.

A short, non-descript man of about retirement age came to the door of the inner office.

'That's me.'

'I'm William Gregory.'

The word-processor woman looked up sharply. Ritter just raised his eyebrows.

'Ray Tindall came to see you yesterday,' said Greg, 'About an old case involving the death of a young man who fell off a boat at Seastone and disappeared.'

Ritter scowled in irritation. 'The retired copper. Yes, he did.'

'I believe you did some investigating for the young man's father, Mr Arthur Heapes.'

'As I told Mr Tindall, I don't remember all my cases from that long ago.'

'I see. But I gather you told him you were going to see if you

223

could find your case notes.'

Ritter half turned back into his office. 'Yes, well, there wasn't anything to find really. As I remember, the fellow disappeared from a boat in Seastone Bay and no trace of him was ever found.'

He shrugged. 'End of story.'

'But the boy's father paid you for at least a month to look into his son's death. Presumably you did something to earn the money?'

'Presumably I did, but I don't remember what it was after all this time. Besides, I was very busy in those days.'

Greg said, 'Ray Tindall was beaten up shortly after speaking to you about the case.'

Ritter raised his eyebrows again. 'Really?'

'Yes. He was warned to lay off it, and you see, apart from me, you are the only one he has spoken to about it. So who did you speak to about it?'

Ritter looked at him with a blank expression. 'Why should I speak to anyone about it?'

'Exactly.'

'Anyway,' said Ritter, maintaining his deadpan look, 'How do you know I was the only one he spoke to? He could have told anyone.'

Greg could see it would be a waste of time to pursue the matter. He picked up a business card from a pile on the desk by the word-processor and wrote the number of his mobile on it.

'If you should happen to think of anything that might help, perhaps you would be good enough to contact me on this number.' He dropped the card next to the pile on the desk.

Ritter shook his head. 'Shouldn't think it's likely,' he said, 'Too long ago.' He turned and went back into his office.

Greg noticed that the woman was staring at him. She raised a finger to her lips and showed him an envelope with 'WAIT IN THE BOOKSHOP' printed on it.

He nodded to her. 'Well, thanks anyway,' he said to the office door.

He went back downstairs and walked along the street to the bookshop two doors away. A few minutes later the woman came in and went to the far corner. She looked very excited.

Greg went to stand at her side.

'I'm Molly Ritter,' she whispered, 'I recognised you as soon as you said your name. You won't know me, but you were the other boy on that boat, weren't you?'

'Ye-es,' said Greg, uncertainly.

'And you got blamed for it, didn't you?'

'Well, some people blamed me, yes.'

'There was something very fishy about that whole business,' she said quietly, 'And I can see why you would be taking an interest, now the remains have turned up. So I thought you ought to know that Cyril never did a thing for Mr Heapes.'

'Really?'

'No, not a thing. That bastard Clarmont Brown paid him not to.'

'Paid him not to? Bob Clarmont Brown?'

'Yes,' she said, 'The highly esteemed Sir Robert himself, although he wasn't Sir Robert then, of course.' She paused and, inclining her head to one side, she raised her eyebrows and looked up at Greg intently. 'He paid Cyril to spy on you and that Mrs Vanderling instead.'

'What?' Greg was astonished. 'Spy on us?'

'That's right! Wanted to know everything the two of you got up to.'

'Good Lord! But why? And how do you know this?'

'I typed the reports. And there were photographs of the two of you together, too. Some at her house and others on a boat. Quite suggestive, some of them were, if I remember rightly.'

Greg stared at her, trying to make sense of what she was saying. Why on earth would Clarmont Brown, or anyone else for that matter, have wanted to spy on him and Suzy?

He said, 'What happened to this stuff; the reports ...and photographs, do you know?'

'They all went to Clarmont Brown. And there were no copies kept. I know that because he persuaded me to make sure.'

Greg said, 'You gave all the copies to him?'

'Yes, I did,' she said. She gave a short, harsh laugh. 'I was infatuated with him at the time.'

Greg had an interesting thought. 'Has Clarmont Brown been in contact at all lately?'

'No. No, not lately.' Her answer was almost too quick, Greg thought, especially when, as if to cover herself, she went on, 'Well, not through the office, anyway. Some years since he came through the office. But he has contacted Cyril on his mobile from time to time, that I do know, so he could have. He used Cyril often enough in the old days, certainly, and some of those jobs were decidedly iffy, if you ask me. Cyril always did them by himself. Nobody else, including me, was allowed anywhere near them. But I couldn't help noticing that name, Vanderling, cropping up in phone calls sometimes.'

'I see.' Greg was thinking how Ray Tindall would immediately latch on to that. 'Do you recall any other names perhaps?'

'Such as?'

'Wilson? Or Davis?'

'No, I can't say I do. I expect I only remember Vanderling because it's unusual.'

'Yes, I see,' said Greg. 'But I'm right in thinking you believed Clarmont Brown was getting Mr Ritter involved in something not quite above board, am I?'

'Definitely.'

'It might be interesting to see details of some of those jobs,' he said, more in hope than expectation.

She gave her short bark of a laugh again. 'I'm sure,' she said, 'But what files were kept were about as vague as they could be. No names of people, just Mr A, or Mr B, and no places, just location one, location two, that sort of thing. As I say, they were definitely iffy.'

'Well, I'm grateful to you for telling me all this, Mrs Ritter,' said Greg. 'Thank you. If you should think of anything else that might be of some help to us, please give me a call.' He gave her a rueful smile, 'I had no idea we were spied on all those years ago.'

'Well, you know now,' she said. 'I'd better be getting back. He'll wonder where I've gone. But I wanted you to know what that bastard Clarmont Brown did. He had something to do with that boy's disappearance, I'm sure he did. And it wouldn't surprise me if he was behind your friend the ex-copper getting hurt, either. Anyway, good luck.'

She touched his arm and Greg watched as she went to the bookshop counter, selected a magazine, apparently at random, paid for it and went out.

He wondered how much else she knew.

THIRTYEIGHT

Half an hour later Greg parked his car in Dan's space at Seastone Yacht Club, reciting to himself the various significances of what Molly Ritter had told him. Firstly, Clarmont Brown had paid Cyril Ritter to spy on him and Suzy. Secondly, Clarmont Brown had used Ritter for underhand activities (with which the name Vanderling was linked), over several years - certainly until nineteen ninetyeight, the year Roddy drowned. And thirdly, Molly believed that Clarmont Brown was involved in Nigel's death and probably in the attack on Tindall as well.

The one thing they had in common was Clarmont Brown, and Greg wondered, as he walked across the road to the café, what Ray would make of it all.

Sophie was busy in the café and told him to go on upstairs. Ray was in his den.

Greg sat himself in the visitors' chair as before. He said, 'Cyril Ritter wasn't any more co-operative with me than he was with you, but his wife was helpful.'

He started to tell Ray about their meeting in the bookshop.

Ray was intrigued by the revelation that Clarmont Brown had wanted Greg and Suzy spied upon and he thought he might know a reason why.

'I reckon they were worried she might talk too much, might let slip details of their operations.'

'That's rubbish,' said Greg. 'I can assure you, categorically, that Suzy would not have known anything at all about any of these so-called operations you're so convinced about.'

'But how do you know?'

'Suzy and I were very close for over twenty years, Ray, right up until she died in two thousand and one, and she never gave even the slightest indication of anything untoward … 'Greg stopped in mid-thought. Then he said slowly, 'Not until after Roddy died, anyway.'

'Go on.'

'Well, I know she was never really convinced that Roddy would have just fallen off the jetty at the yacht club and drowned.

He was still a good swimmer, apparently. She told me she asked for a proper post mortem, but it didn't show up anything unusual. But that's not all. When I saw Arthur Heapes on Sunday, he told me Suzy had confided in him at the time.'

Greg gave Ray a full account of what Arthur had told him regarding Suzy's anxieties.

Ray was all attention, making copious notes and asking probing questions as he went along.

'This is good, Greg. See, it's all pointing in the right direction, isn't it?' He smiled happily and sat back in his chair. 'So, getting back to your friend Mrs Ritter, what else did she have to say?'

'Well, nothing specific, but again it's about Clarmont Brown. Mind you, she *is* harbouring a grudge. It seems she fancied him at one time and he took advantage and then let her down.'

'Hell hath no fury, eh? That could come in handy some time.'

'Yes, I got the impression she might be willing to co-operate if the right questions were asked. Anyway, she says that Cyril Ritter used to do a lot of jobs for Clarmont Brown at one time, some of which were what she called "decidedly iffy". I gathered she meant they were not strictly legal.'

'Hmmn. Ritter doesn't figure anywhere in my files,' said Ray. 'And I don't recall his name ever cropping up in connection with anything suspicious, either. Must have been very careful.'

'She said she never saw any details and only rudimentary records were kept, but, you'll be interested to know this, she remembered hearing the name "Vanderling" mentioned in phone calls.'

'Ah ha!'

'And, for what it's worth, she also said she's sure Clarmont Brown had something to do with Nigel's disappearance and with you getting beaten up.'

'OK. Well, your visit paid off, didn't it?' said Ray. 'Alright, apart from the spying bit, which I reckon is worth giving some thought to, the rest of it's only her opinion, but it could well be based on fact and anyway, it shows we're on the right track.' He nodded and smiled in satisfaction.

'So where do we go from here?' said Greg.

'Well, I've started going through the file, looking at contacts for all the prime movers. So let's have a look at Sir Bob.' Ray flicked through the notes on his desk. 'Right. First one's a bit sensitive, I'm afraid, your old mate, Sophie's brother Frank.'

Greg raised his eyebrows. 'Why is he sensitive?'

'A bit too close to home. See, he was apprenticed to Sir Bob and then he worked for him for several years, ended up managing the boatyard. Then, all of a sudden he decided to pack up and go to Australia, and set up on his own. Doing very nicely, too.'

'Yes, Sophie told me about that.'

'But I don't suppose she told you where he got his start-up money from?'

'No.'

'Have a guess.'

'Clarmont Brown?'

'Correct. Sir Bob himself. We only found out about that when we were over there last Christmas. It's a really good set-up he's got there and I'd often wondered how he'd managed it, so I asked him straight out. He told me Clarmont Brown had given him a loan - on very generous terms, it seems. Now then, Sir Bob is not well known for his generosity, and in view of what I knew about his activities, it set me thinking. So, as I say, sensitive.'

'Have you spoken to Sophie about this?' asked Greg.

'Of course. Family thing, isn't it?'

'Right. So when did Frank actually go to Australia?'

'Just after Easter nineteen ninetyeight.'

'Roddy was drowned that Easter.'

Ray nodded and smiled. 'The coincidence has been noted in the file.' He went back to his notes. 'Anyway, as a contact, Frank is a bit too far away to be helpful at the moment, so we'll put him aside. Next is Jeremy Marlow. Know him?'

'He was one of Nigel's cronies.'

'Was he? Well, what we know about him is that he left the army in a hurry about twenty years ago. Rumour was that Captain Marlow could not account for certain bits of MOD equipment he was responsible for. Clarmont Brown gave him a job in the Amusement Arcade and now he's nominally manager of the whole Pier and Arcade business. He's never there, though. It seems he's the main man for dealing with the cash from all the clubs. If the idea of money laundering should occur to you, you would not be far behind me.'

'Really?'

'No proof though, and so far, no access. But a but of

surveillance might pay dividends.' He returned to his notes. 'The next one on the list is the lovely Lady Eleanor, third and current wife.'

'Third?'

'Yes. Josie Wilson was the first. She divorced him. Second one died. Overdose. He married this one about three years ago. English rose type, butter wouldn't melt, etcetera. He met her in Las Vegas. She was head croupier in a big casino. He brought her back to UK and put her in charge of all the croupiers in his Cockaigne clubs.'

'So how many of these clubs are there, do you know?'

'Half a dozen at least. All outside London, incidentally. I know of Portsmouth, Southampton, Liverpool and Manchester. I heard there's one in Bristol and another in the Birmingham area, but I don't know where for certain.'

'Quite a big job for her ladyship, then,' said Greg. 'American, is she?'

'No, no, English public school. Papa was, or is, some sort of landed gentry, so they say. She lives in Clarmont House and runs her side of the business from the Quarterdeck Club. Member of the Yacht Club, but she doesn't sail. Comes in here occasionally for coffee with friends. Signs herself "Elli" without an "e" on the end, but apart from that she seems a pleasant enough woman, always has a little smile and a hello when you see her in the village.'

'You said she lives in Clarmont House as if it meant something,' said Greg.

'Did I? Well, all I meant was she's there more or less all the time. Her husband spends most of his time on the mainland. We don't see much of him in the village.'

'He was at Dan's house on Sunday when I got back from here,' said Greg.

'Oh, yes?'

'I gathered he and Dan had some kind of disagreement, but Dan wouldn't talk about it.'

Ray looked thoughtful. 'Something to do with the Yacht Club, no doubt?'

'No idea.'

Ray didn't pursue the topic. 'Well, anyway,' he said, 'That's her ladyship.' He eyed Greg tentatively. 'Good looking woman.

Must get lonely from time to time, hubby being away so much. Might be useful, cultivating her acquaintance,'

'Oh yes? And just how would one go about doing that, I wonder?' said Greg.

'Well, one could join the Quarterdeck Club, I suppose.'

'I suppose one could,' said Greg.

Sophie came in with a tray of tea and biscuits. Greg cleared a space at the end of Ray's desk so that she could put it down.

'I'm just closing,' she said, turning to Greg. 'Not worth staying open late at this time of the year. In a few weeks time it'll be different though, as I expect you'll remember.'

'Yes, we were always open to eleven in the summer, later sometimes if Sam felt like it.'

'Now then,' she went on, 'Ray tells me you're staying at Dan Vanderling's in Bembridge while he's away.'

'That's right.'

'So rather than go back to an empty house, would you like to stay and have a meal with us this evening? It would be no trouble, and afterwards perhaps we could have a chat.'

'Yes, alright, thanks, that will be nice.'

When they had finished their tea and biscuits, Ray said, 'I fancy a bit of fresh air. Care for a little stroll?'

'You sure you should? You're supposed to be in bed, aren't you?'

Ray's bruises looked worse, if anything, but the swelling on his eye had gone down a little, and although he winced as he stood up, he assured Greg he would feel better for a short spell outside.

They walked slowly along Quay Lane until they came to the Slipway. Ray said he didn't want to go any further and they sat in the late afternoon sun on the bench seat against the wall, almost opposite the entrance to the Quarterdeck Club next to the Quay Hotel at the bottom of the High Street.

Ray launched into a detailed history of the changes in the village since Greg had left, and Greg was happy just to sit and listen. One of the pieces of information that Ray thought should interest him was that his other close friend from his teen years, Pete Grant, was now general manager of G.L.H. (Seastone) Limited.

'And if I told you "G.L.H." stands for Graham and Louise

Holdings,' he said, 'Who would that make you think of?'

'Wilsons,' said Greg.

'Yes. Peter Grant came up through their building company, rose from site foreman through to managing director, and now he's their top man in UK. Must know a thing or two about their business, I would think. Would you fancy a reunion at all?'

Greg laughed. 'I haven't spoken to him for thirtytwo years, Ray.'

'No, but if you were to meet by chance, say, you could get talking over old times, and how things have changed since the old days, etcetera. Just a thought.'

Greg saw Ray's expression change suddenly and he looked across the road as a black Mercedes two seater pulled into a reserved space outside the Quarterdeck Club. The driver's door opened and an elegant pair of legs swivelled into view. The woman who rose gracefully from the car was wearing a charcoal grey business suit, beautifully cut to display her shapely body. She had long, ash-blonde hair, which swung down across her face as she reached back into the car for her briefcase. She turned and walked swiftly into the club entrance.

Ray looked at his watch. 'Five o'clock on the dot.' He stood up and grinned at Greg. 'Regular as clockwork, our Elli,' he said.

oOo

Greg stayed talking with the Tindalls until late in the evening and he arrived back at Dan's house just before midnight. He unlocked the back door and immediately noticed a faint smell, unpleasant, sweetish, chemical.

Stale aftershave.

He took Ray's little gun out of his pocket, clicked the safety catch off, pushed the door open quickly and stepped into the kitchen sideways.

He listened. No sound, and the house was in darkness.

He moved slowly across the room into the passage and stood still.

The door to the sitting room was wide open, and as a car passed by outside, light from its headlamps spilled in through the windows, and Greg could faintly make out the shape of someone standing just inside. He pointed the gun at him. He also sensed someone else sitting on the sofa.

'Light switch is just by that door,' he said.

Nobody moved. They must have heard him come in, but he knew they could not see him.

'I'd rather not start shooting in the dark,' he said, moving forwards carefully.

After a moment the man by the door switched the light on and seeing Greg with the gun, moved further back into the room. He was in his early thirties, tall, with long, light blonde hair, strongly built, and athletic-looking.

Greg moved into the room. The smell was much stronger.

Neither of the two men appeared to be armed.

The man on the sofa spoke. 'You weren't in. We decided to come in and wait for you.'

Greg kept his gun in his hand but pointed at the floor. 'Good way of getting yourself shot.'

'We weren't to know you'd have a gun.' He paused. 'How did you know we were here?'

'Aftershave.'

'You smelled it.'

'I did.'

'I must have used too much, then.'

'You did.'

There was a long pause. The man sitting down was plump with a red face and cropped ginger hair. He wore steel-rimmed glasses with thick lenses and was looking up at Greg through small eyes. He leaned forward, both pudgy hands on his knees.

'We are here on government business,' he said.

'Oh yes?'

'And we would like you to do us a favour.'

'I see.'

'In the interest of security.'

'Right.'

There was another pause.

Red Face said, 'You have been making inquiries about the death of a young man named Nigel Heapes.'

'Correct.'

'We would like you to desist.'

'Why?'

'For reasons of national security.'

'How come?'

'I cannot tell you that.'

'Well, that's a shame.'

The blonde man stepped forward. He stared at Greg as if to intimidate him. Greg was intimidated enough to wave the gun vaguely in his direction. He moved back a pace.

Red Face said, 'It would be in your best interests.'

'Is that so.'

'Because you wouldn't want to cause yourself any unnecessary trouble, would you?'

'Piss off.'

'I should be careful what I said if I was you.'

'Alright,' said Greg, 'How about: please ... leave ... immediately.'

Red Face glanced at the blonde man who was still trying his intimidating stare.

'Think about it. And while you're thinking, bear in mind that we may find reason to investigate you.'

Greg laughed. 'Oh deary, deary me.'

Red Face stood up. He and the blonde looked at each other. Red Face raised his eyebrows. Blonde shrugged.

Greg backed out of the room into the passage, his gun pointing in their general direction.

Red Face moved towards the door. 'You'll be hearing from us again,' he said.

'We won't bother to change the locks, then.'

The blonde joined his partner by the doorway and the two of them stood staring at Greg for a long moment.

Greg pointed down the passage at the front door. 'Out!' he said.

They left.

Greg closed the door behind them, then went into the sitting room and opened the window to get rid of the obnoxious smell of aftershave. He stared out onto the street, and watched the two men get into a silver Toyota parked on the other side of the road and drive away.

THIRTYNINE

Next morning, just after eight o'clock Greg called Nick Southwell and told him about his visit to Ritter's office and then, later in the evening, finding the two men in Dan's house.

'I reckon somebody must have been watching Ray Tindall's place,' he said. 'They saw me arrive yesterday morning and followed me here when I left. Then, when my visit to Ritter upset them, they knew where to come.'

'Well, there's certainly no doubt now you're on to something weird, Greg. Do you think they intended to give you a beating too?'

'Possibly. I didn't give them the chance.'

Southwell said 'But they said they were with the government?'

'Yes. Any ideas?'

'Did they say they what wanted?'

'They wanted me to stop making inquiries into the death of Nigel Heapes.'

'A thirtytwo-year-old mystery.'

'That's right. In the interest of security, they said.'

'Hmmn. Did they show you any identification?'

'No, and I didn't like their attitude so I didn't bother to ask.'

'So they could have been anybody, not necessarily from the government.'

'Yes. But they did imply that if I don't co-operate I might find myself under investigation.'

'Strange. But that may have been just an empty threat, of course.'

'Of course. Anyway, I thought you might know if there was anything, you know, official.'

'Well, look, as I see it from what you've told me, Nigel Heapes was certainly not important in his own right, was he? So it looks more and more as though, whoever your visitors were, somebody is afraid that by looking into his death you may dig up something else.'

'That's what I'm thinking, too.'

'I'll ask a few discreet questions, just in case. Okay?'

'Thanks.'

'And listen, Greg, keep in touch. This could get difficult and you've been out for a few years now so you will have lost your edge. Just remember - you've still got a few favours to call in. Okay?'

'Yes, right.'

'In fact, I've got an idea. D'you remember Hamish Petrie?'

'Well, I've never actually met him, but I've heard about him; he was working out of the Hamworthy office when I first joined. Why?'

'He's just finished a little job in South Africa and he's at a loose end at the moment. He's got a sister on the Island and I expect he'd be glad of the chance to spend a few days over there.'

'Oh, well, I shouldn't think it would come to that, Nick.'

'I'll have a word with him anyway and get him to contact you. He's a good man, you'll like him.' Nick rang off before Greg could reply.

He put his phone down and it rang immediately. A woman's voice said 'Mr Gregory?'

'Yes?'

'Hello. This is Molly Ritter. We spoke yesterday afternoon in the bookshop.'

'Hello Mrs Ritter.'

'I'm sorry to bother you, but you did say to ring you if anything came up.'

'That's right.'

'Well, I don't know if it's anything to do with what you were asking about, only, Cyril, my husband, didn't come home last night. And he hasn't been back here to the office, either.'

'I see.'

'When I got back from the bookshop yesterday he was on the phone. I couldn't hear what he was saying but he sounded very upset. Then a bit later, he went out in a hurry and I haven't seen him since.'

'Have you any idea where he went?'

'No, and that's funny, because if it's business he always tells me how to contact him.'

'Have you tried his mobile phone?'

'I think he must have switched it off. And that's not like him.'

'So when he goes away you always know how to contact him,'

do you?'

'Yes, always. Usually on his mobile.'

'Right, well, I don't know what to say, Mrs Ritter.'

'Well, as I say, I don't know if there's any connection, but ...
' Molly Ritter hesitated. 'You remember me telling you about
Clarmont Brown?'

'Yes.'

'Well, not long after Cyril went out, we had a phone call from
the solicitor we always had to use whenever that bastard wanted
any jobs done. Must be three or four years since we last heard
from him. It seems to me, that's a bit of a coincidence, you know,
me just having told you about him. What do you think?'

'Yes, I agree. It is strange. What did he want, this solicitor?'

'He wanted Cyril to call him as soon as he came in and he
gave me a number for him to ring. It was very urgent, he said.
Anyway, Cyril didn't come back to the office before I locked up.
And I haven't seen or heard from him since.'

'And you're worried about him, obviously.'

'Yes, I am. That's why I came in here early. I don't know what
to think. You see, he was in a bit of a state when he went out.'

'Oh yes? What, angry, or frightened, or what?'

'Angry, I suppose. You know, sort of indignant, really.'

'I see. Did he say anything to you before he left?'

'I've been trying to remember. I know I got the impression he
was very upset, but if he's in a bad mood, I'm afraid I tend not to
take too much notice when he goes on a bit.'

Greg made up his mind. Ray Tindall had been badly beaten
after seeing Ritter, then there was last night's incident warning
him off after seeing Ritter, and now Ritter himself was missing.

'What's the name of this solicitor, Mrs Ritter?'

'Russell, Philip Russell. He was based in Portsmouth.'

Greg asked for more details and after looking in her filing
system she found the address and phone number they had used in
the past.

'I don't know if he'd still be there, though,' she said.

'And what was the phone number your husband was to ring?'

She read it out to him It was the number of a mobile.

'I'll see what I can find out,' said Greg, writing the number
below Russell's details in his notebook. 'Meanwhile, perhaps you
ought to inform the police?'

237

'Oh, Cyril would hate that,' she said. 'I think I'll leave it a bit longer. He may just turn up.'

'And how should I contact you?' he said.

She gave him her office and mobile numbers to add to his notes.

'I'll be in touch then, Mrs Ritter,' he said. 'But please let me know if and when your husband comes back, won't you?'

He rang off, then called the Hamworthy office, identified himself and spoke to Sally.

Sally had been with the firm for ten years now and in that time she had honed her tracking skills to perfection. It seemed that if there was information on any subject available somewhere, online or elsewhere, Sally could retrieve it. Greg's simple request to her this time was the name and location of the subscriber to the mobile phone number.

She rang him back after two minutes. 'It's one of those pay-as-you-go things,' she said, 'Want me to do a recce?'

'Yes please.'

"Doing a recce" meant keying the phone number into Sally's system for tracing the location of telecommunications equipment. If the phone responded Sally would know within less than one hundred metres where it was located.

'Hold the line, then,' she said. After a short interval she came back to him. 'Hello, Greg, it's in Albert Road, Southsea, and it's on voicemail. Ready for the message?'

'Yes, go ahead.'

"'Five o'clock, the esplanade, one-o-two.'"

'Is that it?'

'Yep.'

'OK, thanks, Sally.' Greg rang off.

He thought the message sounded like an instruction to meet at an address, number one hundred and two, The Esplanade, or perhaps at a hotel in room number one hundred and two. He decided to try the Esplanade Hotel first as it would only take him a few minutes to get there.

As he arrived he saw a police car driving off.

At reception, he gave his name and asked to speak to the manager. The receptionist said Mr Howard was very busy just at the moment and perhaps he could help. Playing a hunch, Greg gave him his business card from the agency in Poole.

The young man looked up from the card with a puzzled expression. 'A detective agency? We've just had the police here. Is it about the damage to the room?'

'Room one-o-two, wasn't it?' said Greg.

'Yes, that's right. Mr Howard is there now. If you'd like to go on up, Mr Gregory, it's second on the right at the top of he stairs.'

The door to room one-o-two was open and it was obvious there had been a struggle. A chair had been turned over and a small table had a leg broken off. One of the curtains had been pulled off its rail and the manager was examining a torn strip of wallpaper whilst talking to a woman, presumably a chambermaid, who was using a dustpan and brush to collect small pieces of broken glass on a wet patch of carpet.

Greg introduced himself to Howard and showed his card again, explaining that he was trying to find a missing person, whom he had reason to believe had recently visited this room. The manager's eyebrows rose.

'You wouldn't you happen to know him, I suppose, a local man, Mr Cyril Ritter?'

'Yes,' said Howard. 'I do as a matter of fact. Not well, but he's in your line of business, too, isn't he. And you say he was here in this room?'

'I believe so. Do you mind if I have a quick look around?'

'Help yourself,' said Howard. 'At least you're taking a bit of interest, which is more than the police seem to want to do.'

Greg looked around carefully but could see no signs of bloodshed.

'What was the name of the chap who booked the room?'

'Reeves. Chistopher Reeves.'

Greg smiled at the name. 'More than one of them playing Superman?'

'Eh?'

'Never mind. He's checked out, I suppose?'

'No, but he's gone and he hasn't left anything in here. And his car's gone, too.'

'Any phone calls?'

'Not through our phone system. The police asked that, and if he'd run up any bills, so I looked into it and there was no bar bill, but he had a meal here last night, at least this room number was quoted, a meal for two, but the name on the credit card he paid with was not Reeves.' He took a scrap of paper from his pocket and looked at it. 'Ronald Johnson,' he said, 'Mean anything?'

'Not to me.' Greg made a note of the name. 'What about video? Would you have any pictures of him?'

'Bound to, but I wouldn't know what he looked like. Never saw him.'

'Could I bother you to have a look at the tapes for yesterday afternoon, though?' said Greg. 'See if Cyril Ritter did come here?'

He was guessing that Russell could be some sort of courier. He might not necessarily be aware of the contents of the messages he relayed and he might have contacted Ritter direct on his mobile to pass on the number he had to ring. If so, then perhaps Ritter would have come here to room one-o-two.

'OK,' said Howard. 'The night manager changes the tapes in the early hours when it's quiet, so yesterday's will be handy. Let's go and see.'

He asked the chambermaid to clean the room and make it as tidy as she could. Then he led Greg downstairs to his office where they could play last night's tapes from the hotel's video cameras.

Greg asked for the tape from the camera mounted on the wall behind the desk in reception to be played first, starting from three o'clock.

'There!' said the manager, stopping it at ten minutes past five. 'That's Cyril Ritter, isn't it?'

The tape clearly showed Ritter arriving through the main entrance doors.

'Yes, he's the man I'm looking for. Can we go on? See when he left?'

The tape moved on, showing Ritter hurrying directly to the stairs, as if he knew where he was going. There were no more shots of him after that. Ritter had not left the hotel via the front doors.

Greg then asked to see the tape from the camera above the door leading to the car park, and timed at eleven minutes past nine, the image showed Ritter apparently needing to be supported by a tall man with long blonde hair, whose head was bent down as if to comfort his companion, thus partly obscuring his face. Greg easily recognised him, however. It was Red Face's accomplice.

'Old Cyril looks a bit the worse for wear, doesn't he?' said the manager.

'Hmm. You'll have this Reeves fellow's car registration number, I suppose?' asked Greg.

'Of course.'

'OK. Can we see the tape covering the car park, then? From, say, ten past nine?'

The car park camera picked up the image of two men emerging from the hotel at the appropriate time. The sequence jumped from image to image as the men came towards the camera, and it became obvious that Ritter was unable to stand unsupported. The big blonde man virtually dragged him into a light coloured Toyota folding him into the passenger seat.

There was enough light for Greg to note the registration as the car reversed towards the camera and then moved slowly to the car park entrance and turned right. When they checked the number with the details in reception, it was the same as that recorded for Reeves.

'Well,' said Howard, 'It looks to me very much as though Cyril Ritter might have been involved in whatever happened in room one-o-two. What do you think?'

'Yes,' said Greg, 'We saw him come in and go straight upstairs. Then when he came out with that Reeves, or whoever he is, he was either drunk or hurt.'

'Should I tell the coppers, do you think?'

'You'd better, I suppose, just in case,' said Greg. 'They haven't been told Ritter is missing yet, but they're bound to get involved if he doesn't turn up soon. Do you think you could find some way of leaving out my part in this, though?' Greg watched the manager carefully to see if an inducement would be necessary, then decided that Howard was on his side anyway. 'Perhaps you could say you decided to have a look at the tapes, just to see if there was anything funny,' he added. 'No need to mention me, okay?'

Howard gave him a sidelong look.

'Is there any reason why the police haven't been told Cyril Ritter's missing?'

'His wife wants me to find him if I can. She thinks Cyril would be furious if it turned out he wasn't missing at all, just lying low somewhere. After all, it's one of his main businesses, finding missing persons, isn't it? She thinks he'd look stupid in the eyes of the law if he was reported missing himself.'

'Fair enough, I suppose. And you've still got to find him.'

'Yes, before the police get involved if I can.'

'Well, good luck!'

'Thanks. At least I'm on his trail, thanks to your help. It's much appreciated.' Greg shook Howard's hand and went back to his car where he made another call to Sally in the Hamworthy office.

FORTY

Wednesday lunch time

A little over half an hour later, Greg was back in Ray Tindall's den and had started to bring him up to date with all that had happened since they'd parted the evening before.

Ray's reaction to the news that Greg had been followed after leaving the previous morning, was to suggest that it would be easy for anyone across the road in the Yacht Club to spy on the café. He reminded Greg that the Vanderling File implied a strong link with Seastone Yacht Club

'Could be one of the staff keeping an eye on us,' he said.

'Yes, but I think it would be more likely to be a member, don't you?' said Greg, 'Somebody who could leave immediately and follow me when I left.'

From Greg's description of the two men Ray reckoned that it was probably the same two who had beaten him up on Monday evening.

'One of them was certainly big and had long, blonde hair,' he said. 'And now you come to mention it I remember there was a strong smell of aftershave. Should have thought of that earlier.'

Greg's mobile rang. It was Sally.

'Silver Toyota,' she said, and read the registration number back to him. When he confirmed it, she said, 'The registered keeper is indeed recorded as Ronald Johnson, the name you gave me.' She read out an address in Eastney, Southsea. Greg wrote it down.

'It's not an uncommon name,' added Sally, 'But I checked and we've got nothing on file. Alright?'

'Thanks again, Sally.'

'What I'm here for,' she said and rang off.

'We've got a name and address to play with, Ray' said Greg, 'One of my visitors last night. Do you think your former colleagues would have anything on him?'

He showed Tindall Johnson's name and address.

'He had quite a busy evening.' Greg told him about Molly Ritter's phone call and his subsequent visit to the Esplanade Hotel.

Tindall copied down Johnson's details. 'I've got a mate at

Kingston Crescent,' he said, aware that Greg would know from his time with Safeguard Security how the Portsmouth police force was organised. 'He'll follow it up for me. He owes me a few.'

'OK. Good. And you could ask him what he knows about this solicitor Molly Ritter thinks is involved, Philip Russell, in Albert Road, Southsea.'

'Philip Russell. Right. Name rings a bell.' Tindall made a note. 'You were saying friend Cyril looked as if he'd been hurt?'

'Not sure. More as if he was drunk. Or he could have been doped, of course. The thing is, he arrived at ten past five, had a meal with this Johnson, or at least I assume he did because Johnson paid for two meals on his credit card, and it was gone nine o'clock when they left. It's almost as if they were buddies.'

'So why hasn't Cyril contacted the lovely Molly, then?'

'Perhaps someone wants him to keep out of the way for a while,' suggested Greg. 'Anyway, I promised to let her know any developments so I'll call in and see her again and see if anything else turns up.'

'OK In the meantime I've been looking through my notes, so let me fill you in on what I've got so far' said Ray. 'When we spoke on Saturday I told you we suspected Vanderling and his cronies of smuggling, didn't I?'

'Yes, you did,' said Greg. 'Among other things.'

'Right.' He nodded towards the window, indicating the Yacht Club. 'And we reckoned that's where they were based. Trouble was, we could never find evidence strong enough to bring charges. We did think we were in with a chance at one time though. We had a joint operation with the French. In nineteen ninetyseven it was. Drugs. Very successful outcome, except it wasn't what we expected. See, the French came to us and said they'd had a tip-off from our side, Portsmouth. So, based on the information they supplied we put together an operation and it worked like a charm. We caught the whole gang, but the ringleaders were all in the Dover area and there was no link to Vanderling at all.'

'What made you think there would have been?' said Greg.

'See, their informant was a woman who'd been working in an estate agent's office in Southsea. And guess who the estate agents were? Wilsons, no less.'

'Ah, I see, Wilson being one of your Vanderling associates. But the estate agent's is Louise's business, not Graham's.'

'What's in a name, though, eh?'

'Alright, fair enough. So you thought this woman was shopping your Vanderlings, when in fact she wasn't. Did you find out what she was up to, then?'

'See, in the end what we reckoned happened was our Vanderling lot had done a deal with the Dover gang a few months earlier and pulled out of the drug business, but something must have gone wrong with the deal and this woman went to the French.'

'Why them?'

'She had contacts there, and they promised to look after her. They did, too, as we discovered some time later.'

'So you thought your Vanderling associates were smuggling drugs and it turned out that they were not,' said Greg, still reluctant to accept Roddy's involvement in anything criminal.

'We *know* they'd been bringing in drugs. We just couldn't prove it,' said Ray. 'But, we didn't doubt that they'd stopped because pretty soon, by all accounts, they'd switched over to something just as profitable but less risky – immigrants.'

Greg frowned at him. Despite recent events, it was difficult to reconcile these pictures of criminal activities with sleepy, respectable, little Seastone, and with Roddy in particular.

'You're talking about people trafficking?' he said.

'Yes. But again, no proof. It was all circumstantial or hearsay. This was in ninetyseven, mind. I don't know what the current situation is, of course. As I believe I told you when we first met, I retired four years later and the file had been more or less forgotten by then – we had plenty of more urgent things to deal with - and if it hadn't been for Nigel Heapes's bones being discovered I probably would never have followed it up at all. But that bullet wound made me look at the file again.'

'Yes, and that got you beaten up,' said Greg.

'And proved that I'm on to something!' He grinned at Greg and turned back to his file. 'Anyway, I've been looking at the file notes on that drugs bust in ninetyseven and especially its aftermath, and there's quite a few bits and pieces jotted down more or less piecemeal, about the prime movers I mean, so I started putting them together.'

He took a sheet of paper from the file.

'See, looked at from the people-trafficking point of view, they

245

were very well set up.

'First there's the boats. The yacht club cabin cruiser is capable of carrying a dozen passengers comfortably and a good many more if crammed in tight. Davis, this is Teddy, by the way, not his old man, replaced their old MTB years ago with a big powerful catamaran. And the Quarterdeck Club, jointly owned by Wilsons and Clarmont Brown remember, also had a very nice cruiser, usually moored at the yacht club. All these boats are ocean-going vessels.

'Second, private moorings. Apart from the yacht club, Freddy Davis had one in Bembridge Harbour, Clarmont Brown had one at Yarmouth and another on the Medina.

'Third, GLH, Wilsons' firm, rent out several residential properties in Ryde, Sandown and Cowes, and possibly elsewhere.

'Fourth, GLH also has an agency supplying seasonal labour throughout the Island.

'Now, if you put these things together you can see the feasibility. Boats capable of collecting illegal immigrants and ferrying them long distances, to any one of at least three different moorings. They can accomodate them in houses or flats in various parts of the Island, and last but not least, they've got an agency to use them as cheap labour.'

He sat back at looked expectantly at Greg. 'What do you think? Make sense?'

Greg smiled. 'When we were talking last night, you said something like: "If you're clear-headed and shrewd you can get your teeth into a theory and build it into a believable case even if you have few facts and little evidence", remember? So, in the light of that, alright, yes, it makes sense.'

'Ah, but, I also said, didn't I, "if you're a copper, no matter what you believe, evidence is all that counts," and as far as I'm concerned that still applies. See, we never had hard evidence, but we did make a few French contacts on that drugs bust and we got a bit of feedback from them later.'

'What sort of feedback?'

'Well, they kept in touch with their informant, the estate agent woman, although we didn't know who she actually was so Pompey police were never able to pin anything on her. But the French kept an eye on her, and that was how they were able to tell us about the illegal immigrants coming out of Cherbourg and Le

Havre and so on.'

So what did they do about it then?'

Ray Tindall laughed, 'Greg, where refugees are concerned the French are no different from any other Europeans, they can't wait to get rid of 'em, and if someone wants to move them on, okay, it's that way to the coast, mes amis, bon voyage! And, of course, French fisherman would be quite happy to take money to start them on their way.'

'Is it still going on, do you think?'

'Who knows? Nothing has ever come up that points to Clarmont Brown and friends though, as far as I know, and without evidence of a crime, the police can't do anything.'

Greg said, 'Well, with all due respect, Ray, I can't see how any of this is going to help us find out who shot Nigel.'

'Well, alright, I accept that may be your main priority, but my point is that it all comes back to the Vanderling associates. We just need to find a way of getting to them. See, what I was really looking for in the file was any names we could follow up and the estate agent woman seemed a good bet because of what happened in ninetyseven. Trouble is, I can't find any reference to her name.'

Sophie called upstairs.

'Ray? Do you two want to come down for lunch now, before we get busy?'

'Yes, alright, love.' Tindall winced as he eased himself up from his chair. Greg moved to help him but was brusquely waved away.

He followed Tindall down to the café where about half of the tables were already occupied. Sophie sat them next to the kitchen door. She handed Greg a menu. 'Have whatever you fancy,' she said, 'And if it's not on there I expect I can soon knock it up for you.'

'On the house,' added her husband.

'Oh, well,' said Greg, 'I seem to be always eating at your expense.'

'You've come over here to help Ray,' she said. 'The least we can do is feed you.'

At Ray's enthusiastic recommendation they settled on steak and kidney pie with chips, and while they waited for it to be served, Ray said, 'I'm going to make a few calls this afternoon and see if I can find anyone who can lead us to that woman if she's still around.'

FORTYONE

After the best steak and kidney pie he had ever eaten, Greg drove back to Ritter's office in Ryde and parked in a space behind the video rental shop.

The door to the reception area was half open as before. He tapped and entered.

Molly called from the inner office, 'Who is it?'

'It's me, Gregory.'

'Oh, come on through.'

She was sitting back in a large executive chair behind a desk with her feet propped on one end, munching a sandwich. She was dressed in navy blue, the zip-fronted top half-undone over an open-necked cream silk shirt, a short pleated skirt, and mid-calf high-heeled boots. Given how prominently her legs were displayed, it was impossible for Greg not to notice that they were long and shapely. Her wavy dark hair showed no signs of grey and although Greg knew that she must be at least his own age, she looked years younger than he had supposed when he had first seen her.

She put down her sandwich, took a swig from a bottle of mineral water, swung her legs to the floor and stood up.

'Sorry,' she said. 'Just finishing my lunch. Sit yourself down.' She indicated a comfortable leather armchair, and packed the remains of her sandwich back into its wrapper. 'Can I get you a coffee? Tea?'

'No, I'm fine, thanks.' Greg lowered himself into the armchair. 'Have you heard anything from your husband?'

'Not a whisper.' She sat back down behind the desk. 'Have you got any news for me?'

He told her what he had found out so far.

When he described Ritter's companion, she said, 'That sounds like Ron Johnson. He's a chap who's done jobs for us in the past. Come to think of it, usually through Philip Russell. You say Cyril looked as if he was drunk?'

'Yes, or possibly hurt. Would this Johnson be likely to hurt him, do you think?'

She shook her head. 'I don't see why he should. They've always got on alright.'

She took another drink from her bottle of water, then paused and looked thoughtfully at Greg.

'It's not like Cyril to get drunk, though,' she said. 'And Ron's basically a frightener. That's what he does, so I don't know.' She shrugged.

'You're not worried about him?' Greg asked.

'Oh, well.' She picked up a pencil off the desk and twirled it around in the fingers of both hands. 'Cyril's pretty good at self-preservation. He can usually talk his way out of trouble.'

Greg reminded her that the hotel room did look as if some sort of struggle had taken place.

She said, 'Well, all I can think is perhaps Ron Johnson wanted Cyril to do something and Cyril didn't want to do it. He was pretty mad when he went out, as I think I told you, so maybe Ron tried to persuade him?' She looked up at him, eyebrows raised.

She was clearly not bothered much about her husband's safety, thought Greg, and as she seemed inclined to talk, he decided to see what else she might be willing to tell him while he had her attention.

He said, 'You think there's a possible connection to Clarmont Brown here, don't you?"

'Yes, I do. Because of Philip Russell.'

'And have you any ideas on how we could follow it up?'

'Short of asking Phil Russell directly, you mean?'

'You haven't thought to ask him, then, if your husband did ring him?'

'Well, I rang the number we've got for his office and a woman answered and told me Mr Russell was not available, so I left a message for him to ring me back. Then I tried the mobile number he wanted Cyril to ring, but I drew a blank there, number not known, or something.'

Greg thought the phone had probably been thrown away, having fulfilled its objective.

He said, 'What else have you tried?'

'Well, I was going to leave it for a bit till either Cyril turned up or I heard from you.'

'So what do you suggest?'

She tapped the pencil against her chin and looked knowingly

at him. 'What's the very first thing we all have to learn in our job? The more places you look, the more likely you are to find something. Isn't that right?'

'In *our* job, you said?'

'Yes.' She smiled flirtatiously. 'After you left yesterday, Cyril made a few enquiries, so we know you work for the agency in Poole. I think that's what upset him the most, you know, a big firm like yours asking questions he couldn't answer.'

Greg nodded. He was not going to disillusion her by telling her he was only working on behalf of himself and Ray Tindall.

'It's just the two of you here then, is it, Mrs Ritter?' he said.

'It is nowadays, yes. But we've got one or two regulars that we take on from time to time, to do the odd job for us, you know.'

'Any working for you at the moment, by any chance?' He was thinking not only of the café being watched after Tindall's visit to this office on Monday, but also of Johnson's red-faced companion at Dan's house.

'No. Why?' She looked surprised.

'Just curious,' he said.

'Only, if you needed anyone I could pass some names on to you.'

'Thanks. I'll bear that in mind.'

'Anyway,' She put her pencil down and leant forward, arms folded, elbows on the desk, emphasising her cleavage, 'I was going to say that talking to you has made me think. That name, Vanderling. The last time I remember hearing it in the office must have been at least ten years ago.' She sat up, linking her fingers in front of her and resting her chin on her thumbs. 'I remember because it was just before Easter and it was the last time Bob Clarmont Brown came to the office. Cyril had been working on one of those hush-hush jobs of his and it wasn't going very well. Bob came in and started trying to sweet-talk me as usual, but I'd had enough of him by then – he'd let me down once too often – so I gave him short shrift. Anyway, he and Cyril had their heads together here in this office for what seemed like ages. And they were definitely talking about the Seastone Yacht Club. And that,' she paused for effect, 'Was only a day or two before Commander Vanderling was found drowned there. Coincidence? I wonder.'

Greg regarded her in silence while he thought about what she was implying. She had been quite frank about her hostility to

Clarmont Brown, and that was easy to accept, but was she including her husband in this suggestion that Roddy's drowning may not have been accidental?'

'Did your husband confide in you at all about what they'd been discussing?' he said.

'No,' she said. 'One thing about Cyril is he never, ever breaks a confidence. But after Bob left he did say we wouldn't be getting any more work from him, and he seemed more than happy about the fact. And he was right, too, we never did get any more jobs from him.'

Greg was not learning anything useful. He decided it was time to be more direct.

'So,' he said, 'Reading between the lines, I take it you think that when you overheard Clarmont Brown talking to your husband about Seastone Yacht Club, he was trying to persuade him to help in getting rid of Roddy Vanderling. Is that right, Mrs Ritter?'

She leant back in the big chair and smiled slowly at him in a challenging way.

'They call you Greg, don't they?' she said. 'Call me Molly, Greg. It's more friendly.'

Greg smiled back at her, happy to play her game. 'Alright, Molly,' he said, 'But you didn't answer my question. Is that what you think?'

She grinned at him and nodded rapidly in agreement. 'Yes, that's exactly what I think.'

'Why? What makes you so sure?'

'Because on our way home from the pub a night or two later, Cyril popped into the police station to have a word with someone, and the desk sergeant told us Commander Vanderling had been found drowned at Seastone Yacht Club earlier in the evening. Cyril just nodded and said he'd been living on borrowed time anyway, and the copper said, yes he had a heart problem, didn't he. When we got outside I sort of casually asked Cyril how he knew Mr Vanderling had a heart problem and he just said, "I didn't". "What did you mean about living on borrowed time then," I said. Cyril stopped and looked at me very seriously, and he said "The dirty bastard finally outlived his usefulness, Molly."'

'Did you ever find out what he meant?'

'Oh, I knew what he meant. Bob had been using Vanderling for years and didn't need him any more. I realised then that Cyril must have refused to have anything to do with getting rid of him and that was why Bob wouldn't be giving us any more jobs.'

Greg remembered what Suzy had said to Arthur about Roddy telling her he had done things he shouldn't have, and that he felt threatened. It looked as though Suzy had been right to wonder about the way he died. It was also beginning to look as though Tindall was fully justified in his conviction that Roddy was tied up closely with Clarmont Brown's activities, whatever they were.

But there was still something he didn't understand.

He said, 'OK, so your husband reckoned Clarmont Brown arranged for Roddy Vanderling to be bumped off. But why should he call him a dirty bastard?'

'Oh, well. That's Cyril. I mean, you come across all sorts in this line of work, don't you, and I suppose that can make you, I don't know, a bit cynical perhaps? But there are some things even Cyril draws the line at.'

'Such as?'

She frowned. 'Well, you know what Vanderling was like.'

'I must be missing something here,' said Greg.

Molly raised her eyebrows. 'You mean you didn't know? Only I always thought, you know, you and Mrs Vanderling ... ' She paused, then seeing his puzzled expression, she said, 'Little girls, Greg. That was his thing.'

'Roddy? Are you sure?'

'Oh yes. Quite sure. It was our very first job for Bob Clarmont Brown. We watched Vanderling for several weeks. I did some of the work myself.' She lifted her head and looked straight at him, as if that proved her point. 'He used to take the yacht club boat over to the mainland, Portsmouth and Weymouth, among other places, where he had contacts, ex-navy men like himself, and they'd fix him up.' She sniffed, scornfully. 'He must have thought he was safe, but Bob had sources in the yacht club and we'd get a tip-off when Vanderling was going on a trip. Bob would make a boat available and leave the rest to us.'

'And you got evidence, did you?'

'Yes, we did. More than enough.'

Greg was appalled! All those years Suzy had been married to him and she could not possibly have known!

'And it didn't occur to you to notify the authorities?' he said.

She stared back at him steadily. 'It's always difficult, isn't it?

Your client is paying you for confidential information and you discover a crime is being committed. Should you report the crime and lose your client, or take his money and keep quiet?' She shrugged. 'I don't know. It's a funny old life, sometimes.'

Greg decided that nothing would be gained by being censorious at this late stage.

'So what did Clarmont Brown do?' he said.

'He paid our fee in full.'

'I meant what did he do with the information you gave him.'

'I know you did, Greg. But your guess is as good as mine.'

'My guess is blackmail,' said Greg.

'There you are then.' She gave him a sardonic smile. Then she changed her expression and said, 'I'm pretty sure I know what he did with the information we got from following you, too.'

'Had me beaten up?'

'Yes.'

'But why?'

'To get you out of the way. Think about it, Greg. He's got information proving Vanderling is a paedophile. That information is very valuable to him because Vanderling is a very wealthy man, someone who sees himself as a pillar of society, and, what's more, idolises his wife, sees her as the perfect lady. He'd be scared stiff she'd leave him if she knew about his nasty little games, so he agrees to do whatever Bob wants. But then you come along and complicate things. And Bob thinks if Vanderling was to find out his beautiful wife wasn't so perfect after all, but was having it off with a teenaged boy whenever she could, perhaps the threat to tell her would lose its value.'

'Yes,' said Greg, 'I can see the logic of that.'

He had been angry and bitter for years about that seemingly purposeless beating, but now that at last he had a reason for it, he felt nothing much more than acceptance of a problem solved.

'How much of this did you know about at the time, though, Molly?' he said.

'Oh, none of it actually at the time, but it didn't take long to put two and two together. Which is why I've always thought that other boy's disappearance was something to do with it, too.'

'Nigel Heapes.'

'Yes, him.'

'Which is where I came in,' said Greg.

'Yes. First that ex-copper, and then you, asking about him.'

'Yes,' said Greg. 'Tell me, did you know Nigel had been shot?'

'Not till I read it in the paper yesterday morning.'

'What about your husband?'

'No, I'm sure he didn't either. But you'd found out about it, hadn't you, and that's why you came here, wasn't it?'

'Yes, to see if you had any ideas on who may have shot him.'

'Well, you can guess by now what my ideas would be about that.'

'Without proof though, it's all opinion, isn't it?'

'What we need is something we can tie directly to that bastard Clarmont Brown.'

'OK. And I'm pretty sure you must have thought of places where it might be interesting to look. Any suggestions?' Greg smiled at her encouragingly.

She gave him a sidelong look. 'Do you know the Quarterdeck Club in Seastone?'

'Yes, I know of it, certainly.'

'Bob was a founder member. He got the idea of setting it up at the time when I was going out with him. He got some local bigwigs to back him - Vanderling was one, I remember - and they had a Grand Opening. Bob took me as his special guest. I'd just started working for Cyril, and in fact, that's how Bob came to use Cyril in the first place, through me. Anyway, the point is, I reckon they've always used the club as a base.'

'Interesting,' said Greg. 'I understand his wife is based there these days.'

'Yes, so they say.' She raised one eyebrow. 'But he isn't. Could be worth looking into.'

'OK. But in the meantime what do you want to do about finding your husband?'

'First find Ron Johnson, wouldn't you say?'

'It would be a start, wouldn't it? And perhaps have a word with your Mr Philip Russell.'

'I'd go careful with him, though, Greg,' she said. 'He has some funny friends.'

FORTYTWO

It was a fine afternoon, sunny but cool, and Greg left his car parked behind the video rental shop - Molly had assured him that it would be unlikely to be disturbed there. He took his little gun from the glove pocket, just in case, and walked down through the town to the hovercraft terminal, arriving only a few minutes before the next ferry was due to leave.

Half an hour after leaving Molly, he was in Southsea, an area he knew well, having worked there for more than two years. He set off to walk in the sunshine along the Esplanade, past the Canoe Lake and then up the Eastney Road to Johnson's address in Reginald Road. He found the house about half way along the terrace on the right-hand side and he rang the bell, then knocked several times but got no answer, so he tried next door.

After ringing their bell three times and waiting for what he thought was long enough, he gave the door two hard thumps and was about to give up and try the house on the other side, when it was flung open. An obese teenager with a shaved head, rings in his eyebrows, and wearing a dirty string vest and baggy grey trousers glared at him.

'Whassup?' he said.

Greg said, 'I'm trying to get in touch with Ronald Johnson.'

The fat lad turned his head and yelled, 'Mum! Cummeer!'

A woman, even fatter, grey haired, in her fifties Greg guessed, waddled to the door. Her son moved aside to try to make way for her, but failed and had to step out onto the pavement.

'This guy wants to know about next door.'

Greg smiled at the woman. She smiled back. Her smile was wider than Greg's, but had fewer teeth to display.

'What?' she said.

'There doesn't seem to be anybody in next door.' Greg showed her his agency card.

She glanced at it and gave it back without saying anything.

Greg said, 'I wondered if you might know when they'll be back.'

'I might do.' She raised her eyebrows, still smiling her gap-toothed smile.

Greg said, 'Our standard payment for useful information is ten pounds.'

She nodded. 'Come in.'

He followed her down a dark passage into a kitchen that smelled strongly of stale cigarette smoke and old grease. The table was littered with beer cans, dirty plates and takeaway containers. A large black and white cat was rooting among them.

'Elvis!' the fat woman yelled.

The cat looked at her and padded to the edge of the table, then leaped gracefully onto the sink, where it balanced on the narrow rim.

The fat boy came and leant on the door frame.

'Get you a cuppa tea, or summat?' the woman asked.

'No thanks,' said Greg. There was no knowing what new germs he might become acquainted with in that kitchen.

'So what d'you want to know?' She went over to the sink and started stroking the cat.

'As I told your son, I'm trying to get in touch with Ronald Johnson.'

'Fuckin' poof!' said the fat boy from the doorway.

Greg turned to look at him.

'Now then, Shaun,' said his mother. 'Ronnie don't live there no more, mate. It's his mum's place, see. She's in the QA. Got summat wrong with her legs. What d'you want 'im for?'

Greg couldn't think of any reason why he should tell her the truth.

'Some people on the Isle of Wight want to see him about a job,' he said.

'Oh, right. You tried his 'ouseboat, then?'

'No. I didn't know he had a houseboat.'

'In Bembridge 'arbour,' she said.

'Oh. Any idea what it's called?'

'No, sorry. But if he ain't there he's got a flat somewhere off Somers Road.'

'Do you happen to know the address?'

'Might do.' She smiled her wide, gappy smile again.

Greg looked in his wallet, took out a twenty pound note and put it on the table.

'Shaun, fetch my 'andbag, lovey, would you.' She reached forward and picked up the note.

The boy left them and came back with a large, black plastic handbag

The woman rummaged around in it. 'His mum give me the address when she went in the 'ospital,' she said, eventually finding what she was looking for, an envelope addressed to Ronald Johnson at a Somers Town address.

Greg copied it into his notebook.

'Thanks,' he said. 'What's the best way to get there from here?'

'Why? You going there straightaway?'

'Yes, I might as well. But I haven't got my car with me.'

'Better get a cab, then. 'Ang on, I'll give me mate a ring. Mini-cab. Okay?'

'Yes, thanks.'

The mobile that the woman pulled out of her capacious bag seemed much too small for her sausage-sized fingers, but she coped somehow and five minutes later a sharp rap at the front door announced the arrival of her mate.

'Thankyou very much,' said Greg, 'You've been very helpful, Mrs … ?'

'Lusby, Karen to my friends,' she said, simpering, 'And you're very welcome,' she added, more to the twenty pound note than to him as she tucked it into her purse.

The minicab was a Ford Fiesta with dents in the bodywork but it was clean and comfortable, except for the strong smell of cigarette smoke inside. The driver was a young, good-looking black woman. She told him her name was Sonia and confirmed that she would take him to Somers Town for four quid. As she drove west, picking her way by the most direct route through the maze of terraced streets, Greg complimented her on her knowledge of the area.

'You know Pompey, then?' she said.

'Used to work here.'

'Born and bred here, me,' she told him. 'Lived here all me life. Should know it. Mind you, there's plenty around here that only know their the way to the M27.'

When they arrived outside Johnson's block of flats, Greg said, 'If the chap I want to see isn't in, I'll want to go down Albert Road, and then to the hovercraft terminal afterwards.'

He gave her a five pound note and asked if she would wait.

'OK,' she said with a smile, looking at her watch, 'I'll give you, what, five minutes?'

As it happened, Greg had no more luck at the flat than he'd had in Reginald Road and he was just about to start disturbing the neighbours when a door opened further along the corridor and a little old lady looked out at him.

'You looking for Big Ronnie?' she called. 'He's over on the Island.'

'Oh, staying on his boat, is he?' said Greg, making his way towards her.

'Spec so.'

'You wouldn't happen to know the name of his boat, I suppose?'

'No,' she said, frowning, 'I don't think he ever said, but he give me this number in case he had any callers.'

She handed him a piece of paper and Greg copied down the number of a mobile phone.

'Thanks,' he said, giving back the paper.

'Who shall I say called?' she said.

'Doesn't matter,' said Greg. 'I'm going over to the Island myself, anyway, so I'll arrange to see him over there. Thanks a lot.'

Sonia was waiting for him as promised when he came out. He got back into the Fiesta and asked her to take him to the address in Albert Road that Molly had given him for Philip Russell.

'I just want to see where it is,' he said. 'If you could stop outside for a moment, Sonia.'

The traffic was not very heavy at that time of day and Sonia easily found the place. It was an antique shop with offices above, the name Russell, Solicitor and Commissioner for Oaths displayed in gold letters across the first floor windows. Greg asked her to drive on for a short distance and then turn round and come back and stop on the opposite side of the road for a few moments while he studied the building, memorising the layout and relationship to adjacent properties.

Then he said, 'OK, hovercraft terminal now then.'

When they arrived he said, 'I expect I'll be coming back in the next few days, Sonia, and I might need wheels. Have you got a card, or a number I can reach you on?'

'You can always reach me through Karen,' she said.

'Yes, but I don't have her number either,' said Greg.

She hesitated, then gave him a mobile number.

He wrote it down and smiled. 'This is Karen's number, isn't it?' He had already guessed that Sonia's was not a registered minicab.

She shrugged, then grinned, disarmingly. 'Can't fool you, can we.'

'It's all right, I won't tell anyone. But I might expect you to be discreet as well. Okay?'

She nodded, and after considering for a moment she gave him another phone number.

'Thanks,' he said, writing it down. 'My name's Greg, by the way. What do I owe you?'

'The fiver'l cover it, Greg,' she said. 'I'll look forward to hearing from you some time.'

oOo

Greg rang Molly from the Southsea hovercraft terminal while he waited for the next flight. She still hadn't heard from Cyril.

'And I've had no luck with Johnson,' he said. 'That Eastney address is his mother's. I traced him to his council flat but he wasn't there either. A neighbour said he's on the Island. Apparently, he's got a houseboat in Bembridge Harbour. Did you know that?'

'No. I didn't.'

'Any chance you could find out what it's called?'

'Yeah, Okay, I'll look into it.'

'Good. I've got to go, the hovercraft's just coming in. Keep in touch.'

oOo

Back at the café Greg filled Tindall in on his day so far. They were in Ray's den, drinking tea.

While Greg talked, Ray made careful notes, recording in what he was calling his Vanderling Casefile all relevant points, such as names, locations and phone numbers.

He said, 'Must have come as a bit of shock, hearing that about your friend Roddy.'

'He wasn't my friend, Ray. But yes, it certainly is a shock. And I'm still finding it hard to believe.'

'It was all kept very quiet, wasn't it?' Ray paused as if a thought

259

had come to him. 'Dan couldn't possibly have known, could he?'

'No. No way. I wouldn't want to be the one to tell him either. And if Suzy had ever had any idea she would have left him.'

'But are you a bit more convinced now about the tie-up between him and the others?'

'Yes, I have to admit it doesn't seem so far-fetched any more,' said Greg.

'And what about Molly Ritter's ideas on the Quarterdeck Club as Clarmont Brown's base? Seems to tie in with what I was saying yesterday, doesn't it?'

'Yes. I don't know that she has any proof though.'

'But it's worth looking into.' Ray paused, then he said, 'I believe Dan's a member, by the way. Should help if you wanted to join.'

'You're really keen for me to do that, aren't you? That's the second time you've suggested it. Molly seemed to have the same idea, too.'

Ray nodded and grinned at him. 'Well, there you are then. And you get on so well with the ladies, judging by today's success with Molly, and ... er,' he looked down at his notes, 'Karen and Sonia, it's obvious the sooner you try your luck with Lady Eleanor the better.'

'Alright, alright,' said Greg, 'One of us ought to have a good look at the place. I'll get a meal at the Quay Hotel tonight and ask about membership.'

'Good. So, summing up your day, I think we can say we may not have made any real progress yet but we have confirmed that we're heading in the right direction. Agreed?'

'Yes. And when Molly identifies Johnson's boat – there can't be that many to check on in Bembridge Harbour – we might have a lead to her husband. I'm sure from what she's said he's got evidence linking Clarmont Brown to shadiness of some sort, and that may well tie in with your ideas on the Vanderling Associates. And then there's Johnson himself, of course. I'd like to ask him who told him to break into Dan's house last night.'

Ray said, 'Well, let's hope we hear from her pretty soon.'

'Was your contact in Kingston Crescent able to help with anything on Johnson, or Russell?'

'He's looking into it for me.' He referred to his casefile. 'Johnson's name didn't ring a bell, but Russell's well-known to them. He's one of the city's higher-profile solicitors.'

'Oh, really? His office doesn't look anything special.'

'Well, apparently he specialises in representing the more successful criminals, and I quote: "he makes a very good living out of cleverly argued acquittals, and somehow he always seems to get away with cutting corners in the process of law so that his clients can continue to pursue their successful criminal careers" unquote.'

Ray leant back in his chair. 'I've had an interesting afternoon, too. I rang another of my old pals in the force, the one that told me about the bullet hole in Nigel's skull. I said to him at the time I reckoned there was a connection with the old Vanderling File, and now he tells me he's going to try and get it reopened.'

'Oh yes? Did he say why?'

'Well, there's quite a bit of office politics behind it. See, the intelligence unit of the Hampshire CID is based on the mainland, and they had a call referred to them the other day from an informant over here. What he said made my pal remember what I'd told him, so he asked his boss - he's a Detective Superintendent and his remit covers the Island – he asked him if there was any progress on the Nigel Heapes case.'

'And?'

'Well, we've seen haven't we, the local CID haven't been inclined to spend a lot of time and effort on it. Can't blame them really. Their Government Performance Indicators have been pretty good and their clear-up rate is above average.' Tindall sighed. 'See, like all the other damn-fool government league tables, PIs decide priorities these days. Using valuable resources on a thirtytwo-year-old case wouldn't gain them any Brownie points at all. So, if they've been told to hold off and get on with their normal routine work they won't have seen any reason to argue.'

'OK, but why would they be told to do that?'

'Good question. See, this informant came up with something linked to an influential Island businessman, and the Island CID passed him on to the mainland unit directly. Now, my pal wondered why they did that instead of dealing with it themselves, as they normally would have done.'

He tapped his fingers rhythmically on the edge of the table. It seemed to indicate that all was not right with his world.

'It makes me sick. And it comes down from the very top. The

drop in standards, I mean. And it's got nothing to do with nostalgia, the good old days syndrome. I can see there's no need these days for all coppers to be big and strong and have twenty-twenty vision. And shortening the training period for cadets isn't necessarily a bad thing either, because they can always catch up on courses later on. But it's the quality of new recruits that bothers people like me. Alright, there's a need to get bodies on the street, no question, but they've got to be capable of doing the job when they get there. It just seems to me from what I've seen over the last ten years that these days any idiot can become a copper. And get promoted beyond his ability, more often than not. And to cap it all they bring in these CSOs to fill what they call "the gaps". And what are they, these CSOs? Coppers who couldn't make the grade!'

'You're not saying something I haven't heard before,' said Greg, wondering where this had come from and where it was leading.

Then Ray said. 'But I feel sorry for Tracey Nash.'

'Tracey Nash?' said Greg. 'That's the detective sergeant who came to see me on Saturday.'

'Yes, and if I remember rightly, you said you and Dan both thought she was just going through the motions.'

'Yes, we did.'

'Well, there you are, then. See, she's the informant's usual contact, but she was told to give him the brush-off. That's why he rang the mainland. I can imagine how she feels, a potentially tasty little morsel she could get her teeth into, taken right out of her hands.'

'What was the informant offering, then?' asked Greg, hoping to get him to the point

Tindall raised his eyebrows and gave Greg a meaningful look.

'Information on a Mister Grant, your old pal Peter Grant who runs a business called GLH.'

'Ah yes, the Wilsons' firm, Graham and Louise Holdings.'

'And I told you we were looking into GLH at one time, didn't I, and that's why my pal wants the file reopened. See, the informant knows someone, HGV driver, drive anything, go anywhere, who's done a lot of jobs for GLH over the years. Well, it appears this chap had a hell of a row with Grant about a month ago, beat the shit out of him, informant says. Couple of days later he had to collect a container from Manchester, left on the first ferry, never got to Manchester, hasn't been seen since.'

'So?'

'The informant said the fellow was really pissed off after his row with Grant. He said he had enough on GLH to put Grant away for years.'

'Such as?'

'Asylum seekers for one. He reckons Grant has got them packed away all over the Island, in properties GLH owns, and he gets them work through GLH's employment agency, low-end labour, mostly seasonal, on the land or tourist type work. Then at the end of the summer season when the jobs on the Island peter out, GLH ships them over to the mainland, in matey's vehicle, apparently.'

'But matey's gone missing.'

'So it seems.'

'About a month ago, you said. And presumably the informant himself has not come forward with any hard evidence?'

'Presumably not, or else my pal would have said.'

'I can't see why you're sympathising with Sergeant Nash, then. I mean, what is she missing?'

'See, obviously, the informant must be serious or else he would have given up after she sent him packing. Mainland doesn't want to know, though, so I'm going to see if I can get her to pass him over to us.'

'You know Sergeant Nash, then, do you?'

'She was on the team when I did one of the cold cases I told you about. Pretty good, too. She was a DC then, and very keen.'

'OK. But the informant won't want to give his information away for nothing, will he? He'll want to be paid for his trouble, surely.'

'Well, that goes without saying. I'm quite happy to pay him. See, this is like a hobby to me and hobbies have to be paid for, don't they?'

'Ye-es,' said Greg, 'But this is a bit too hit-and-miss for me. Okay?'

Ray looked at him in dismay. 'Oh, well, look Greg,' he said, 'I don't expect you to have to pay for anything. See, I should have made it clear from the start I'll to cover all your expenses. Sorry. How much are you out so far?' He reached for a pencil and notepad.

'No, no, don't worry about that. My boss reckons it's about time I got properly involved in some sort of investigation, and I'm sure he'll cover any costs if necessary. And in any case, I'm curious to get to the bottom of this business as well.'

'OK then, if you're sure. But I don't want you to be too much out of pocket, mind.'

Greg said, 'So you'll be getting in touch with Sergeant Nash, then?'

'Already have. She's coming to see me this evening – she heard about me being thumped and said she'd call in, bring me a bunch of grapes.' He smiled. 'I think she wants to keep tabs on us, in case we actually turn up anything.'

'And take it over before you pass on it to your pals on the mainland? Makes sense.' Greg grinned and stood up. 'It's coming up to six o'clock. I think I'll toddle along to the Pier Hotel and see if there's any news on old Arthur. And then I'll come back and take a look at the Quarterdeck Club. See you in the morning.'

FORTYTHREE

Wednesday evening.

Greg left his car in Dan's parking space at the yacht club and set out to walk along the sea wall path to the Pier Hotel. The weather had changed during the afternoon; it was now dull and overcast and the light breeze coming off the sea was chilly.

At the reception desk he rang the bell and Jason appeared almost immediately.

Greg said, 'Hello Jason, I've just called in to ask if you've any news of your grandfather.'

'Hello Greg.' Jason smiled, pleased to see him. 'Yes,' he said, 'He's fine. Dad saw him this afternoon and he said he can probably come home from hospital tomorrow.'

'Great. That's good news. No ill effects?'

'No, I don't think so. Anyway, come on through and Dad can tell you himself.'

He led the way to the family sitting room at the back of the hotel, where Simon was watching the local news on television.

'Dad, here's Greg come to see us. I'll leave you to tell him about Grandad. See you later, Greg.'

Simon stood up as Greg entered the room.

'Hey, Greg! Good to see you.'

'Just popped in to see how Arthur is,' said Greg. 'I gather he's coming home tomorrow?'

'Yes, if all's well,' said Simon, switching off the TV. 'Can I get you a drink, or something?'

'No, I'm fine, thanks.'

'Well, come and sit down for a minute.'

When they were settled, Simon said, 'Sorry about that phone call yesterday morning. I was upset about Dad.'

'That's alright. Quite understandable. But he's going to be OK now?'

'Well, they say there won't be any lasting damage. They've told him they're putting him on some pills to thin his blood. He said it was the same stuff we use as rat poison!'

'Warfarin?'

'Yes, that's it.' Simon leant back in his chair and gave Greg an inquisitve look. 'What's brought you back to the Island so soon, though?'

Greg explained how Ray Tindall believed that Nigel's death was linked to a criminal organisation which he had unsuccessfully pursued during his CID career, and that this organisation still existed.

'I mentioned this to Arthur on Sunday,' continued Greg, 'And he gave me the name of a detective he used to try and find Nigel. I told Ray and he went to see this chap on Monday. A few hours later Ray was beaten up.'

'Good Lord! Is he all right?'

'Badly bruised. But in good spirits because he thinks his beating proves he's onto something. He rang me because he thought I was closely involved at the time and knew all the background, and I might be willing to help him, now that we know how Nigel died.'

'Yes, I've been wanting to ask Dad about that. I mean, why the hell would any one have wanted to shoot Nigel?'

'Why indeed? Anyway, I've agreed to do what I can.'

'A bit of private inquiry work, eh?'

'Yes. Well, I've had a bit of experience, and I haven't got much on at the moment, so ...'

'Where are you staying? We could put you up here.'

'Thanks, but Dan has offered the use of his place while he's away. But thanks anyway.'

'But you'll stay and have dinner with us this evening. Unless you have other plans?'

'Ah, well,' Greg felt awkward about suggesting he had planned to eat at the Quay Hotel, a rival establishment in the village. 'I'm not committed to anything,' he said, 'But I was thinking I might go along to the Quarterdeck Club this evening. Do you know anything about it?'

'No, not really. Not my scene. They're pretty tight on security, I believe, and you won't get in unless you're with a member.' He paused, thinking for a moment. 'Hang on, Jason's been there once or twice, as a guest. Let's ask him.'

Simon left the room and came back after a minute or two with Jason.

'You were asking about the Quarterdeck Club, Greg?' he said.

'Is it to do with your enquiries?' said Simon. 'Greg's looking into Nigel's death,' he explained.

'It might be,' said Greg, cautiously, not wanting to involve either of them in any way. 'It's been suggested that it could be a useful place to meet people who might be able to help. I gather Dan's a member and I'm sure he'd be happy to sign me in, but as he's away at the moment I was wondering what might be best to do.'

'I know some people who are members,' said Jason. 'I could see if one of them could sign you in, if you like?'

'Would you? That would be great.'

Jason took out his mobile phone and called a number.

'Hi Jonty, it's Jason … yes, and the same to you.' He laughed. 'OK. Look, you wouldn't happen to be going to the Quarterdeck Club this evening, would you? … No, what it is, I've got a cousin on a visit to the Island,' he winked at Greg, 'And he was asking about the club. Any chance you could do me a favour and sign him in? … Okay, good.' He put his hand over the phone and asked Greg what time he wanted to go to the club.

Greg looked at Simon, 'After dinner?'

'Say nine thirty?' said Simon.

Greg nodded.

Jason spoke into the phone again, 'Would nine thirty be all right, Jonty?… Okay … His name? Yes it's William Gregory… All right, thanks Jonty… Yes, fair enough.' He rang off and said to Greg. 'If you go to the door at half past nine and ask for Jonty Grant, he'll sign you in.'

'Thanks Jason. Did you say Jonty Grant?'

'That's right, Jonathan Grant. He's a nice guy. Works for the council. He's three or four years older than me and he's good fun. You'll like him.'

Greg wondered if this Jonathan might be related to his old friend, Peter Grant, now of GLH. He would be the right age for a son. Before meeting him he'd better ring Ray and see if he knew.

'You'd better be getting back, Jason,' said Simon, 'And I must stir my stumps, too. Greg, we usually eat at about eight o'clock. You could stay here or wait in the residents' bar if you like.'

'I think I'd like to take a stroll along the old pier first, Simon, thank you. I haven't been on it for years.'

'OK, well, see you later then.'

Greg left the hotel by the front entrance and went across the esplanade, past the amusement arcade and on to the pier.

A woman walking a dog came towards him and he thought of Rocky and Zillah, remembering guiltily that he had said he would phone. At this time of day Zillah would be busy with her livestock, though. He resolved to phone her when he returned to Bembridge, if it was not too late. The only other people on the pier, spaced out at about thirty feet intervals on the leeward side, were lone anglers, sitting bent over uncomfortably, it seemed, on low stools, and muffled against the damp air.

Greg walked along almost to the pontoon at the end and stood, leaning forward, both hands on the rail, looking out over the bay, the salt breeze cold on his face. Out beyond the rocks, to the east, there was nothing at all upon the sea. Somewhere there should be a horizon, but the water and the sky were the same metallic grey and he could not see where they merged. It felt as if he was looking into eternity.

He stood for a while ruminating on the events of the day so far. It had been a busy day: Molly Ritter telling him Cyril was missing, the tracing of Cyril to the hotel and the identification of Johnson, the tracing of Johnson to Southsea and the possible location of a houseboat at Bembridge, Molly's revelations about Roddy Vanderling, and Ray's conviction that Sergeant Nash's informant would reveal links to the activities of the Vanderling Associates.

He took out his phone and rang Ray's number to report progress and ask him about Jonathan Grant. Ray confirmed that Peter Grant did have a son of that name and age. They agreed that Greg should use the opportunity that meeting the young man presented, to arrange a reunion with his father.

As he rang off the sound of a powerful engine made him turn to look the other way. A speedboat was coming in from the west, travelling fast, the bow smacking the water as it crossed the waves. He watched it heel around the end of the pier, stern down, engine howling, three men in the cockpit. Close in, the man in yellow at the wheel throttled back and the craft died in the water, sputtering as it rose on a wave and fell into a trough, until with a final brief snarl it turned broadside on to meet the pontoon, just below where he stood.

One man stepped out with a line and tied the boat at the bow, then caught another line thrown casually and secured the stern.

The man in yellow looked up and across at him, stared for a moment, then without turning his head, said something to the others. They both turned and looked up at Greg too. Then the man in yellow nodded a greeting. It was Teddy Davis.

As Greg nodded a reply, his mobile rang. He turned out of the wind to answer it. 'Gregory.'

A voice with a soft Scottish accent said, 'Hi. Hamish Petrie here. Nick Southwell gave me your number.'

'Oh, hello. Yes, Nick said he was going to get you to contact me.'

'I'm staying with my sister in Shanklin for a wee while. Nick told me to arrange a meeting while I'm here.'

'Okay, but did he tell you I'm not actually working for the office?'

'No. All he actually said was "Greg's a good bloke, you'll like him."'

Greg laughed. 'That's what he said about you, too.'

'Nick's not a bad judge of character,' said Hamish, 'As a rule. When do you want to meet?'

'Tomorrow. O Nine hundred hours.' Greg gave him the address in Bembridge, knowing nothing else was needed.

Hamish repeated time and place and rang off.

Greg turned back to face the pontoon, but Teddy Davis and his companions had gone.

FORTYFOUR

After dinner at the Pier Hotel with Simon and his family, Greg walked back along the sea wall path and presented himself at the entrance to the Quarterdeck Club at exactly nine thirty.

The club occupied the lower end of a terrace of three-storey Victorian houses at the bottom of the hill where the High Street met Quay Lane. The whole terrace had been acquired by the Wilsons in the early nineteen seventies with the intention of converting it all into the Quay Hotel, but Clarmont Brown, who owned premises next door in Quay Lane from where he ran his boat hire business, had noted that under the recent nineteen seventyone legislation the village fell into one of the permitted areas for gaming clubs. With the support of Roddy Vanderling, whose idea the name was, he had soon persuaded the Wilsons to set up the Quarterdeck Club, and he was now co-owner with the Wilson's, having bought Roddy's original shares from Suzy after Roddy died in nineteen ninetyeight.

According to Ray Tindall, though, Clarmont Brown rarely came to the village these days, so he was unlikely to be there this evening.

When Greg gave his name to the uniformed attendant at the reception desk, a plump young man with rosy cheeks, and thick, dark hair slicked back and heavily gelled came forward and introduced himself with a wide smile.

'Jonty Grant. Jason said you were his cousin?' he said, as if wondering if it were true.

Greg realised he had been expecting somebody much younger.

'Distant cousin,' he said, 'More his father's generation.'

Jonty laughed and Greg thought he could see a resemblance to his boyhood friend, Peter.

'Ah, yes, Jason's found cousins everywhere since he got involved in his family history.' He took a sheet of paper from a tray on the desk and handed it to Greg with a pen. 'Bit of paperwork, I'm afraid. You have to fill in your full name and address, please, and sign that you are over eighteen. Not that you could come in at all if you weren't. Club rules.'

Greg filled in the required information, ignoring the invitation to enter his home, work and mobile phone numbers and his email address. Jonty also signed the form, then passed it to the attendant who promptly entered the details onto a computer screen.

Greg raised his eyebrows at this and Jonty said, 'Credit check. If you are going to gamble here, the management likes to be sure of your creditworthiness. And by the way, it's cash, cheque or debit card, no credit cards.'

Greg nodded.

'Was there any particular game you were interested in, Mr Gregory?'

'Call me Greg, if you will. No, I really just wanted to have a look around, see what goes on before deciding about membership, if you see what I mean.'

'Alright. Let's go on through into the lounge and get a drink, shall we, and then I'll show you around, if you like.'

'Thanks, but I don't want to interfere in your evening, so please feel free to join your usual friends. I shall be quite alright on my own.'

'Don't worry about that.' Jonty ushered him into the sun lounge. 'I'm sure my friends would be pleased to have you join us as well.'

While Jonty was ordering the drinks at the bar, Greg gazed around the room. It was furnished like a large formal conservatory, with upholstered cane chairs and glass topped tables among potted plants. The outer walls were floor-to-ceiling glass giving panoramic views in daylight to the north and east. At this time in the evening the lights of the Spinnaker Tower and Southsea seafront were bright across the water. Several tables were occupied but apart from themselves the only men in sight were the two barmen, and passing his eyes from one group of women to another, comparing them, Greg decided they could all have had access to the same set of machinery to blonde and tan them, burn off and suck away their fat, lift their faces and inflate their lips. He was not at all impressed by the results, though.

Jonty passed him a whiskey.

'Thanks,' he said. 'I don't see any men here, Jonty.'

'They'll all be upstairs, or playing billiards or something in the games room. Your health.' He raised his glass. 'Actually, I think a lot of these women,' he indicated them with a nod of his head, 'Just like to come in here for a gossip. And of course, it's the place to be for some of them. Here and the Yacht Club.'

'Cheers,' said Greg, 'And thanks for signing me in. To be honest, strictly speaking, I could have waited till the end of the week. I've got a friend who's a member, but he's away until Friday. Only, when I happened to mention it to Jason, he said he'd speak to you.'

'Well, it's no trouble. What's your friend's name.'

'Dan Vanderling.'

'Oh, I know Dan! Used to see him a lot when I first joined. We don't see him in here very often these days though.'

'Have you been a member long?'

'Eight years. Eighteenth birthday present from my Dad.' Jonty grinned. 'Dad's usually here too, most evenings.'

'What about your mother? Does she join the other ladies?' Greg indicated the groups of women at the tables.

Jonty shook his head, his expression blank. 'No. She left us years ago. It's just Dad and me. And my gran.'

'Oh, I'm sorry, I didn't mean ...'

'That's all right. You weren't to know. What about about you, then, Greg? What brings you to Seastone? Holiday? Business? Or what?'

Greg sipped his whiskey and thought for a long moment. He decided to take a chance. 'It's a long story, Jonty, but first I have to ask you something. Your father, is his name Peter, perhaps?'

Surprise showed on Jonty's face. 'Yes, it is. How did you know?'

'I lived here in Seastone when I was a boy and one of my friends was called Peter Grant. You look a bit like him, too.'

'Wow!' exclaimed Jonty, 'Look, Dad's lived here all his life. It must be him! He's here somewhere, in the card room I expect. I bet he'd be pleased to see you. How long since you last met?'

'Thirtytwo years.'

'Wow!' Jonty looked delighted at the unexpected turn of events. 'Well, what do you think, shall we go and find him?'

'Yes, why not.'

'He'd never let me forget it otherwise,' laughed Jonty. 'Come on. Bring your drink with you.'

Greg followed him across the room and through the open door into a corridor.

'We'll try the games room first,' said Jonty. 'He might be in

272

there.'

He was. Greg recognised the strongly built, ruddy-faced, balding man of average height, standing by one of the two snooker tables and leaning on his cue watching his opponent trying to find a way out of a snooker.

'Dad!'

Peter Grant looked up and smiled at his son, 'Hello nipper. Alright?'

'I've found an old friend of yours!'

He turned his head and noticed Greg. A puzzled expression gradually changed to a faint smile as recognition dawned. 'Greg?'

'Hello Pete.' Greg stepped forward and held out his hand.

Pete put his cue aside and took Greg's hand tentatively at first then grasped it and shook it firmly. 'Well, I'll be damned!'

The two men grinned at each other. Greg noted that Pete's face bore marks of fairly recent cuts which had required stitching. It seemed that Tindall's story about a fight could be true.

Jonty said, 'Jason asked me if I'd sign Greg in, and we were just having a drink before showing him around, chatting, you know, and Greg said when he used to live here he knew a Peter Grant, so here we are!'

'Well, Greg it's what, more than thirty years?'

'Yes.'

Pete said, 'I heard you'd been seen in the village. You had to see the police or something, about Nigel Heapes turning up at last?'

'That's right.'

'Shot in the head, eh? Weird.'

'Yes, weird's the word for it.'

Jonty was looking from one to the other in puzzlement.

Pete said 'Are you on your own then, Greg, not meeting anyone here?'

'No, no. I just came in to have a look at the place.'

'Great.' Pete turned to his playing companion with apologies, conceding the game and explaining that Greg was an old friend who had turned up unexpectedly.

'Now, shall we find somewhere to sit down? Let's go in the old saloon, it'll be quiet in there. I see you've got a drink. Get me a Scotch, Jonty, will you?'

'Take mine, Dad. I'll get myself one. Leave you two to

reminisce.'

Greg followed Pete across the games room and through a door into a small, dark, wood-panelled room that smelled of wax polish, ancient tobacco smoke and alcohol. It was furnished with comfortable armchairs surrounding low tables and Pete indicated a corner table with two of the chairs drawn up close to it. They sat down.

'Cheers then, Greg' said Pete, raising his glass. 'Here's to old times!'

'Old times,' echoed Greg.

'So, how long are you back for?'

'Well, I don't really know at the moment.'

'My mother-in-law told me she'd seen you. On Saturday. You remember Barbara Black. She said she rather got the impression you wouldn't be staying around for long.'

'Hmmn. Yes, I can see how she would think that. I wasn't too happy at the time. About coming back here I mean, and having all that business brought up again. I'm afraid I may have been a bit short with her.'

'Yes, she said you weren't very friendly.'

'I didn't recognise her at first. She's aged a lot.'

'Crippled with arthritis, poor old thing. She thinks the world of Jonty.' Pete paused and looked off into the middle distance. 'I don't know what I'd have done without her. Maureen left us when Jonty was a baby. Barbara came to live with us and took over. Been with us ever since.' He looked back at Greg, smiled and took a drink from his glass. 'Anyway, what have you been up to all these years?'

'Well, I did twenty years in the army, invalided out with a pension and now I work part-time for a security firm. How about you?'

'Is that it? In one sentence? What about family, wife? Kids?'

'Never married. And still living on my own.'

'No significant other?'

'Well, yes, I've got a very good relationship with my next door neighbour, and that suits me fine. What about you? Is there anyone special?'

Pete smiled. 'I haven't remained celibate all these years. Maureen left us twentyfive years ago and I suppose I hoped it might all resolve itself at first, but I got a divorce eventually. I've been wary about settling down with anyone again though. Once bitten, you know. But there is someone, except she isn't free. We meet when we can, discreetly.' He raised his eyebrows and gave an exaggerated shrug. 'Nobody said life has to be easy.'

They were quiet for a moment. Then Greg said, 'You were an apprentice brickie, weren't you. I remember you had a notion to set up your own building firm. How did that go?'

'It didn't. But I haven't done so bad. When I finished the apprenticeship and got all my papers and so on, Graham Wilson, (you'll remember him, your girlfriend's dad), he was just setting up his own building firm to convert his buildings at Manor Farm into houses and flats. He took me on as his brickie. The firm grew and I grew with it, from site foreman right up to general manager. He was a good boss. Then he retired. He sold the building company and put me in charge of the organisation that controls all the properties he's acquired through the years. And that's where I am now.' He shrugged in exactly the same way as before, as if to say again that nobody said life has to be easy.

This made Greg think that perhaps Pete was not entirely happy in his job and he was about to see if he could draw him out by commenting on the scars on his face, when a young woman came into the room and spoke his name.

'Yes, I'm Gregory,' he said.

'I have a message from Lady Eleanor,' she said. 'She asks if you would like to join her for a drink in the manager's office.'

Greg looked at Pete, not knowing what to make of this.

Pete said, 'Lady Eleanor Clarmont Brown. She's the club manager.'

Greg already knew this, of course.

'But why would she invite me for a drink?' he said. 'I mean, I've never met the lady.'

'Well, now's your chance.' Pete smiled. 'When you came in you filled in a form, didn't you? She will have seen your details and more than likely just wants to check you over.'

'Does she check every potential new member then?'

'No idea. Don't look so worried, she's very pleasant and really quite harmless!'

'Well, alright, probably won't take long. Will you still be around?'

'Yes, sure. I'll be in the games room, where we met.'

FORTYFIVE

Greg followed the young woman out of the old saloon and along a corridor. The girl stopped by a plain door and pressed a button. The door slid to one side. It was a lift. She waved him inside.

'It takes you direct to Lady Eleanor's room,' she said, and pressed the button again.

The door closed and the lift rose two floors and stopped. The door opened and the woman Greg had seen entering the club at five o'clock the previous evening was waiting for him.

Elli Clarmont Brown was wearing a charcoal grey business suit, the tailored jacket open over a man's snowy-white shirt, unbuttoned at the top to reveal a plain gold chain at her throat. Seen close to, she was a strikingly good-looking woman. He guessed she must be about forty years old and she looked very fit and healthy. She had large, clear, green eyes, a wide mouth and her flawless skin owed little to cosmetics. Her long blonde hair hung slightly over one side of her face as she moved forward, holding out her hand. 'Welcome to the Quarterdeck Club, Mr Gregory.'

'Thank you, Lady Eleanor.' He took her hand. She had a surprisingly firm grip.

'Come and sit down.' She indicated a visitor's armchair facing her desk, which was almost bare except for a few items of stationery, a laptop computer, and a separate keyboard arrangement with a telephone handset attached.

There were several closed circuit television screens fixed to the wall facing the desk, each showing a colour picture of a different room. Some rooms appeared to have no activity. Greg noticed Pete playing darts in the games room. Elli could keep an eye on the whole club, it seemed, without having to get up from her desk.

She had moved to a drinks cabinet in the corner of the room. 'What will you have to drink?'

'A small whiskey would be nice, thanks.'

'Anything in it?'

'A little water, please.'

She used tongs to drop two ice cubes each into two small glasses, then half-filled them with Scotch. Greg got a whiff of it, strong and smoky, as she poured, a single malt he did not recognise. She passed one of the glasses to him and went to sit in the executive chair behind her desk.

She raised her glass and smiled. 'Your good health.'

'And yours.'

They each took a sip of whiskey.

She said, 'Well, have you seen enough of the club yet to think you will want to join us?'

'I've seen the sun-lounge, the games room and the old saloon,' he said. 'And I've met an old friend.'

'Yes, so Jonty Grant has been telling everybody. He was highly amused, it seems.' She smiled at him in a friendly way. 'Perhaps I should have given you more time to have a look around. I like to ask new members how they think we might compare to other gambling clubs, you see, but you won't have had the chance to judge yet, will you?'

'No, I'm afraid not.'

'What would you expect to get from us though? I mean, what type of gaming particularly interests you?'

Greg could see he was going to have to keep his wits about him. He had not expected he would have to show a valid reason for joining the club and mentally he chided himself for not giving enough thought to this visit.

'Well, to be frank,' he said, 'I generally tend to avoid those games which give a built-in advantage to the House. I would be unlikely to play roulette, for example. But what type of gaming are you able to offer, Lady Eleanor?'

'Please call me Elli; everybody does.' She took another sip of whiskey and gave him a considering look over the rim of her glass. 'Let me give you some background. In this club we have always made two types of gambling available to our members: "bankers" games, where as I'm sure you know, the money staked (the "bank") is held by us (the "house") and the odds paid are allowed to be slightly in our favour. We can usually provide any of the more common games, Roulette, Blackjack, Craps, Baccarat, Casino Stud Poker, Chemin de Fer, and Three Card Poker, for instance. But we also provide a separate card room where members of the club and their guests can play amongst themselves. We make a charge for this room, but otherwise we make no profit from the gambling. Your friend Peter Grant plays there quite often. Perhaps it could be the sort of thing that might suit you too?'

Greg nodded, 'Yes, I believe it could be. Tell me, um Elli, is membership open to anyone?'

'We'll take anyone whose credit is good.' She smiled at him again. 'You, for example, could join immediately, Mr Gregory.'

'My credit is good, then?'

'Yes, of course, or we would not be having this conversation. But,' she went on, 'There used to be a statutory membership requirement and a rule that a new member had to wait for twentyfour hours before joining a gambling club like ours. The new Gambling Act has abolished that, but we want to remain a private club and we don't intend to open our doors to everyone, so this change in the law makes no difference to the way we operate.' She paused for a moment, looking into her half-empty glass. Then she said, looking directly at him, 'In any case, as you may well be aware, there's a rule in the new Act, (I believe it is meant to control money laundering), that requires all our visitors to be positively identified. So it's six of one and half a dozen of the other as far as we're concerned and we will continue to choose the people we deal with. So, positive vetting, Mr Gregory.'

'If I'm to call you Elli, you must call me Greg,' he said.

'All right, Greg. Can I refresh your drink?'

'No, thanks. This is my second whiskey and I shall have to drive home.'

'You are not staying in the village, then?'

'No.'

She looked at the computer screen. 'I see your home address is in the New Forest. Are you intending to move to the Island?'

'No, I have no plans to do that.'

'Then you won't be able to be a very active member, if you do join, will you?'

'Probably not, but I have family here and I shall visit from time to time.'

'You have family in the village?'

'I'm related to the Heapes family.'

'But you are not staying with them at the Pier Hotel.'

'No,' he said, 'I'm not.' He smiled at her and raised his

eyebrows. 'This is beginning to feel like an interrogation, Elli.'

She finished her drink with one swallow, put the glass down on the desk and leant back in her chair with her hands loosely clasped at her waist.

'Cards on the table, Greg,' she said. 'I recognised your name as soon as I saw it come up on this screen as Jonty Grant's guest, and I really didn't think you would be here just for the gambling. So I thought I'd see if we could get along. I believe we can.'

'I'm not sure I'm with you, Elli.'

She leant forward, elbows on the desk, fingers linked under her chin. 'You see,' she said, fixing him with her large, green eyes, 'I know you were implicated in the disappearance of the man whose bones were discovered recently. And I know you have been asking questions about what happened at the time. What I would very much like to know is why my husband is so concerned that such questions should be stopped.'

'Your husband.'

'Yes. I believe you are well acquainted with him.'

'I knew him many years ago,' said Greg, wondering where this was leading.

'Then you will know what he is like – I am told he has not changed a great deal. The point is, when he was told that the retired policeman, Tindall, had been making enquiries of a certain private detective in Ryde, he became rather upset. He has become very much more so since he has learnt that you, too, have been asking questions, Greg. I would like to know why.'

'I would like to know that, too.'

'Then, perhaps we may, between us, be able to contrive a means of finding out?'

Everything he had seen at Quarterdeck Club so far this evening had indicated to Greg that Elli was very much in charge there, and what she was now suggesting seemed to be at variance with Molly Ritter's idea that Clarmont Brown was using the club as a base for his criminal activities.

'May I ask what your concern is in this, Elli?' he said.

'Suffice it to say that I have my reasons for wanting to know, but now is not the time to discuss them. If you are free tomorrow, though, would you care to come to lunch with me at Clarmont House? It will be just the two of us. Say twelve thirty?'

'Yes, alright, thank you.'

Elli stood. 'Now I must let you get back to your friend. I'm sure you'll have a lot of catching up to do.' She pressed a number on the keyboard on her desk. A voice said, 'Yes, Lady Eleanor?'

'Would you meet Mr Gregory at the lift and take him back to the games room, please, Ann?'

'Yes, Lady Eleanor.'

'Thank you.'

Greg stood up and offered his hand. 'Thanks for the whiskey, Elli, and the chat. I'll see you tomorrow at twelve thirty, then.'

They shook hands.

'I'll look forward to it,' said Elli as the door to the lift opened.

Greg and Pete spent the next half-hour or so in the games room, playing darts and reminiscing. At eleven o'clock, Pete said it was time to go home and they parted outside the club with agreement to meet again soon.

Greg had not made any comment about the fading marks of violence on Pete's face, nor had Pete volunteered any information. He had not asked Greg about his talk with Elli either, and as he walked along Quay Lane to his car at the Yacht Club, Greg realised that apart from his initial query about how long he was staying, Pete had shown no curiosity about his return to the village. He wondered why and it bothered him all the way back to Bembridge.

It had become his usual course of action in recent years whenever he felt uneasy, to talk to Zillah, and as he had intended to ring her anyway, he did so as soon as he was back at Dan's house.

She assured him that everything was fine at her end, and that Rocky was his usual well-behaved self. Then she asked him how he was getting on and Greg gave her a summary of his progress so far.

She expressed concern about the visit of the two men to Dan's house, and relief that Nick had seen fit to send assistance in the form of Hamish. 'I gather from what you've told me,' she said, 'This Clarmont Brown must be running an organisation with rather more resources than you and a retired policeman can command. It's good you have back-up from Nick.'

When he came to his unexpected meeting with Elli and his uneasiness about Peter Grant's apparent disinterest, bearing in mind his senior position in the GLH organisation, she said, 'I think Peter Grant probably knows all about your investigation, and also why her ladyship wanted to meet you, but he was playing safe, not wanting to draw attention to himself.' She paused. 'You know, all this sounds quite fascinating from here, kidnapped private eye, the Commander's guilty secret, people trafficking, gambling clubs, and so on, but these people you're asking questions about are quite capable of causing you grief. Make sure you keep taking care, I don't want to have to adopt a German Shepherd dog just yet. Ring me again soon. 'Bye.'

Greg said goodbye and hung up. He felt better, more complete, as he always felt after speaking with Zillah.

FORTYSIX

Thursday morning

Hamish Petrie arrived on his trials bike exactly on time.

He was a good-looking man in his mid-thirties, with long, wavy, dark hair, sharp features, the nose very slightly crooked, and deepset brown eyes. The same height as Greg but slimmer, dressed in black motor cycling leathers, he had a wiry leanness suggesting coiled energy.

They shook hands, looked each other in the eye and smiled a greeting, acknowledging immediately the relaxed, casual rapport of skilled professionals who have been there, done it, and are ready to go again.

Greg had coffee already prepared and he poured while Hamish was finding a place for his helmet and gauntlets.

They sat at Dan's kitchen table and Greg started to explain the situation to Hamish.

When he came to the point where he had found the two men in Dan's house, Hamish said, 'They told you they were on government business, acting in the interests of national security?

'Right.'

'And there was no sign of a break-in?'

'No. They knew what they were doing.'

'Makes you wonder.'

'That's why I spoke to Nick. He said he'd ask a few questions. In fact, that's when he suggested getting in touch with you.'

'Well, I'm glad to lend a hand if needed,' said Hamish. 'So what's the current position?'

Greg had just about brought Hamish up to date when Dan's phone rang.

'Is that Gregory?' said a voice.

'Yes.'

'I know something about the Heapes shooting.' The voice sounded strange, as if somebody was speaking into a bucket.

'Really?'

'You want to know?'

'Who's speaking?'

'You want to know who killed Heapes?'

'Yes, I certainly do.'

'Right. You know Parkhurst Forest?'

'Well, I know where it is.'

'Okay. Turn left off the Newport to Cowes road and park on the left-hand side near the end of the forest. We'll find you.'

Greg noted the "we".'When?' he said.

'When can you get there?'

Greg thought they must be amateurs, or stupid, or both. 'Say, half-past ten?' he said.

'Half ten, right,' said the voice and hung up.

Greg turned to Hamish. 'Job for you already.' he said. 'Okay?' Hamish smiled. 'Where?'

'Parkhurst Forest. You'll need to be in position well before ten thirty.'

'Equipment?'

'Yes.'

'Okay. What's it about?'

Greg told him.

Hamish said, 'Doesn't sound like the same lot that broke in the other night. Strange. Let's have a look at the map.'

They quickly found the place. It looked straightforward enough.

'Okay,' said Hamish, 'Here's what we do: I'll find somewhere handy to leave the bike and then I'll take the footpath into the woods from this little lane here where it's called Marks Corner. I'll phone you when I've found the right place to wait. You ring me when you leave the Newport road.'

At ten fifteen Greg had turned onto the forest road. He pulled in and called Hamish.

'Nothing doing yet,' said Hamish, 'Keep the phone on and come along slowly and I'll tell you when to stop.'

Greg drove in silence for a minute or so, then he heard Hamish say, 'Slow right down and stop by that big oak. See it?'

Greg pulled over to the edge of the road. 'Here?'

'Perfect.'

'Where are you?'

'I'm right above you, up the tree.'

'Great. I'm getting out and I'll stand by the driver's door. I'll leave it to you to decide whether to show yourself.'

283

'Okay. Phones off.'

Greg took Ray's little toy-like gun out of the glove compartment and put it up his sleeve. He got out of the car and leaned back on the door. It was very quiet and still. Nothing moved in the forest or on the road. A blackbird started singing some distance away and a cow mooed mournfully.

After a few minutes a dark BMW came slowly along from the other direction and stopped almost opposite. The driver, a young, thin-faced man with dark, curly hair looked out of the open window at the number plate on Greg's car and said, 'You're Gregory?'

'Yes'

'Good.'.He switched off the engine and got out. He was small and slim, wearing a cream open-necked shirt and chocolate brown trousers. Greg thought he looked effeminate. A heavily-built man with a shaven skull and wearing camouflage jacket and trousers and heavy boots got out of the passenger side and came across the road, peered into Greg's car and nodded to his companion. They stopped in front of Greg, too close for comfort.

The thin-faced man said, 'You're keen to find out about Heapes.'

'That's right.'

'Who's paying you, then?'

'Should somebody pay me?'

'Well, surely somebody should pay you, at least enough to make it worth your while getting hurt, don't you think?'

'Who's going to hurt me?'

'I am,' said the big man.

Greg stepped rapidly back towards the front of the car, the little gun appearing in his hand.

The thin-faced man giggled, 'Oh, what a sweet little gun.'

'It has sweet little bullets, too,' said Greg, 'Enough to make either of you go pop at this range.'

The big man hesitated. Greg could see he was not quite sure whether to take the risk that the gun really was a toy.

'Alright,' said Thin Face, with a smile, 'So what do we do now?'

'You said you'd tell me who shot Nigel Heapes.'

'So I did.'

'So, who was it?'

284

'You going to shoot us both if I don't tell you?'

'He won't have to,' Hamish said from above. He jumped lightly down behind them, chopping the edge of his hand at the back of the big man's neck as he landed.

'Whaaaah!' squealed Thin Face, stumbling back.

'Stand still!' ordered Greg.

The big man collapsed in a camouflaged heap.

'Awright! Awright!' Thin Face, scared now, held up his hands, palms facing outwards.

'So,' said Greg, pointing the little gun at him. 'It seems I shall only have to shoot you. What's your name?'

'Kilroy, Ray Kilroy.'

'Huh! We all know where you've been,' said Hamish.

'And him?' Greg indicated the unconscious heap on the ground.

'Brewster.'

'Who killed Nigel Heapes, then?'

'I don't know! I don't know anything about it! Honest!'

'No, I didn't think you would. But you do know who sent you to hurt me.'

'All I know, a guy came to see me.'

'Name?'

'Didn't tell me.'

'Surprise, surprise. And why did he come to you, especially?'

'He said he'd heard I was someone who could organise things.'

'Who would have told him that, then?'

'I don't know.'

Hamish took one step forward, smacking one leather-gauntleted hand onto the other.

Thin Face cowered away. 'Ooh. Um It could have been somebody I know in Southsea.'

'And who would that be?' said Greg.

'A guy called Russell, Philip Russell.'

'Really. And what does he do for a living?'

'He's a solicitor.'

'So this nameless one who wants you to hurt me came recommended by a solicitor called Philip Russell who practises in Southsea. Give me his business address and phone number.'

'Well, I only have a phone number. It's in my briefcase.'

'In the car?' said Hamish.

'Yes.'

'Stay where you are.' Hamish said, moving across the road to the BMW. 'I'll get it.'

It was still peaceful. No cars had passed since Kilroy and Brewster had arrived. The blackbird was still singing but the cow had settled down.

Hamish came back with the briefcase, opened it and checked inside.

'Be sure you tell us the truth, now,' he said, passing it to Kilroy.

'Kilroy wouldn't lie to us, would you Kilroy?' said Greg, putting the gun in his pocket.

'No, no. Here's Phil's phone number.'

Hamish took a business card out of his pocket and wrote the number on the back.

'And how do we get in touch with you?' said Greg.

'I've got an office in Newport, Trafalgar Road. I work from home.'

Hamish turned the business card round and held it up. 'In your briefcase,' he said.

The card read *Raymond.Kilroy Logistics* with an address in Mill Hill Road, Cowes.

Kilroy looked at Greg. 'Well, alright, for goodness sake! I didn't want Rambo here coming to find me, did I?'

Greg shook his head in sorrow. 'You are way out of your depth, aren't you Raymond. I've got your name, I've got the number plate of your car, did you think I wouldn't check up on you?'

Kilroy looked sheepish. 'Didn't think,' he said.

'You haven't been thinking from the very start. Now listen, I'm going to carry on looking into Nigel Heapes's death. If anybody tries to put me off again I will come looking for you – with Rambo here. Is that clear?'

'But I can't stop anybody ... ' Kilroy began.

'I don't care. Rambo doesn't care, do you Rambo?'

'Anything happens to him,' said Hamish 'You're dead.' He opened his jacket wide enough for Kilroy to see the Sig Sauer in its holster.

'Now clear off, and take your litter with you,' said Greg.

Brewster was trying to sit up. Hamish bent down and grabbed his jacket, hauled him to his feet, and swung him round, shoving him staggering in the direction of the BMW. Kilroy gripped his arm and guided him onto the back seat of the car.

Greg and Hamish watched as they drove off.

'I'll take you back to your bike,' said Greg.

Hamish had a pained expression on his face. 'Rambo?' he said. He moved to the passenger side of Greg's car and opened the door nodding his head in the direction it was facing. 'Bike's about half a mile up there.'

As they drove off he said, 'Hopeless, weren't they. Not in the same league as those two you saw on Tuesday, from what you said.'

'That's right. It's almost as if someone else sent them. But at least they're tied back to this fellow Russell, that Molly Ritter told me about.'

'Perhaps we ought to go and see him,' said Hamish.

'Yes, or at least have a bit of a poke around in his office some time soon.'

Hamish looked across at him and grinned. 'Surely you're not suggesting…?'

'We'll have a word with Ray Tindall first, I think. He may be able to find a way.'

'The ex-CID chap, runs a café?'

'That's right. Follow me back to Seastone and I'll introduce you. I told him Nick was sending someone to give us a hand.'

'Do a good lunch, do they? I'm starving.'

Greg smiled. 'If steak and kidney pie's on the menu, go for it. Sophie makes a steak and kidney pie to die for. Can't stay for it myself though, I'm due at Clarmont House at twelve thirty, so I'll have to give Ray a quick sitrep and then leave you with him for an hour or so. He'll probably bend your ear on his Vanderling file theory, and I'll be interested to see what you make of it.'

FORTYSEVEN

Greg, Ray and Hamish were sharing the table next to the kitchen door. They were all drinking coffee. Hamish had impressed the other two by the efficacy with which he had dispatched two platefuls of steak and kidney pudding in the time it took Greg to bring Ray up to date.

Ray was making a record of all that Greg was telling him. He looked up from his notes and said, 'It seems to me that this morning's bully boys and those two the other night may not have been sent by the same people. So who knows you've been asking about the shooting?'

'Whoever Ritter may have told, and I presume that would be Russell, and perhaps whoever Russell's working for, Clarmont Brown, if Molly's to be believed.'

'Do you think she is?'

'Yes, I'm pretty sure she is. But in any case, Elli Clarmont Brown made it clear last night that she and Bob are both well aware of what I've been up to. And,' he added, 'I can't help thinking Pete Grant is, too.'

Ray smiled knowingly. 'I would expect him to be. But Russell is linked to both lots of bully boys, isn't he? This morning's through Kilroy and the others through Johnson, who also seems to have spirited Ritter away. Looks as if Russell ought to be looked into, doesn't it?'

Greg nodded to Hamish, 'Just what we were saying earlier, wasn't it.'

'OK. In the meantime, I've been making a little headway, too. See, Tracey Nash came to see me last night.' Ray turned to Hamish. 'That's the Detective Sergeant involved in the case when the bones were originally found.'

Hamish nodded. 'Greg's told me. She interviewed him last weekend.'

'Right. Well, she's been in touch with her informant and he gave her the name of the chap who beat up Grant. He's still missing, by the way. He's called Spencer Davis. Ring any bells?'

Greg and Hamish shook their heads.

'Sixties pop singer. Teddy Davis must have been a fan,' said Ray.

'Teddy's son, eh?' said Greg. 'I saw Teddy last night. He was bringing a boat in to the pier just as Hamish was ringing me. He had two other chaps with him, both young enough to be his son.'

'Interesting. Now, something else turned up too, last night. My mate in Kingston Crescent still hasn't come up with anything we don't know about the Johnson character. But, - remember I told you about the joint op we had with the French in nineteen ninetyseven, and the woman in Wilson's estate agents who gave the Frenchies the tip-off? Well, it turns out her name was Russell.'

'Must be a connection,' said Greg.

'Married to our friend the bent solicitor at the time, but not any more. It's a long time ago, but she ought to be worth talking to, eh? Trouble is, she moved out of the area after the divorce and we don't know where she went.'

Hamish said, 'Job for Sally, Greg?'

'Do we have her full name and last known address, Ray?' said Greg.

'I'll see what I can do.'

Greg stood up. 'I'd better be getting a move on. Don't want to be late for lunch with her ladyship. In the meantime, can you two give some thought to what we can do about Russell?'

Greg decided to leave his car parked outside the Yacht Club. It was only about a five-minute walk from the café to Clarmont House.

As he set out along Seastone Terrace towards the Square he wondered what Elli Clarmont Brown really wanted. He was curious to see her house, too. He tried to recall the two days he had worked with old Henry Niton all those years ago in the grounds of Chiverton's Place, as it had been called then. He pictured in his mind's eye a large, brooding house covered in ivy and moss, with the downstairs windows boarded up, a long, winding gravel drive overgrown with rhododendrons, and an area of cracked and weed-choked paving around the house itself. And he remembered clearing a path from the derelict kitchen garden through to the lane that ran along the rear of the property, and afterwards sitting in the potting shed with Henry while they waited for the rain to stop.

He walked through the Square and turned right into the upper end of Salterns Road. Facing him all across the lower end of the road was a high wall, cream coloured stucco, a grafitti artist's delight, he thought, anywhere else but Seastone. In the centre, recessed well back, was a pair of solid wooden gates flanked by tall pillars beneath a wrought iron arch. When he came closer he noticed the security camera high up in the arch.

On the right hand side in the recess, a narrow pedestrian gate was locked. Next to it was a wide letter box and a keypad set into the wall at car window height. He pressed the button marked "pedestrians" and after a few moments Elli's voice was clear and crisp on the entry-phone, inviting him to come in as the gate swung open silently.

Inside, it was like a public park: close-cut lawns interrupted by serpentine tarmac paths, beds of flowers carefully tended, specimen trees scattered here and there, and all along the inner wall, various climbers and fan-trained shrubs with colourful ground cover plants beneath. The gravel drive bordered by low box hedges curved gracefully for fifty metres or so to a wide area along the austere front of the big house, then continuing on to a block of garages where the old stables had been.

The solid black front door opened and a fat, yellow labrador leaped from the top of the four broad stone steps and bounded up to Greg, barking enthusiastically before inspecting his shoes and legs for smells of interest.

Elli Clarmont Brown walked more sedately towards him, offering her hand and welcoming him with a smile that softened the handsome, patrician lines of her face. She was dressed in faded jeans with a tooled leather belt and a crisp white blouse tucked in, white trainers on her feet, and her fair hair in a ponytail held in a white ribbon.

'This is Deuce,' she said. 'She thinks she's a guard dog.'

'Hello Deuce.' He bent down to greet the dog, who was wagging her tail furiously. Then he looked up at Elli. 'This place is a lot different from when I last saw it.'

'Oh? When was that?'

'Oh, more than thirty years ago. It was coming up for auction at the time. It had been empty for years and all this,' he indicated the immaculate grounds around them, 'Was like a wilderness. I spent a couple of days helping clear the worst of it along the drive and around the house.'

'It would soon become a wilderness again, I'm sure,' she said, 'But for the very conscientious couple who take care of it - and the house - for me. It's their day off today so we won't be disturbed.'

Deuce hurtled in ahead of them and disappeared into the interior.

'Please come in,' said Elli, leading the way. 'I thought we'd eat in the kitchen,'

Greg smelled brewing coffee. He followed, across a marble-floored foyer into a wide passage that led past several doors to a large, bright and airy kitchen, fully fitted with modern equipment. Two large windows overlooked the recently cut lawn, the stripes running directly away in perfect parallels. A radio was playing softly somewhere in the room, Classic FM. A refectory table in the centre of the room was spread with cold meats and salad. Elli indicated a chair.

Greg sat.

Elli moved to a cafetiere on the counter. 'Coffee?'

'Thanks, black, no sugar, please.'

Deuce reappeared with a ball which she dropped at his chair, then snatched up again and ran out as an elderly red setter ambled into the room, stared at Greg, then came and nudged his hand.

'Do the dogs bother you?' asked Elli.

'Not a bit.' Greg stroked the red setter's head. 'I'm used to dogs. I've got a German Shepherd.'

'That's Ace. He's fourteen years old and from America. My oldest friend. Or at least,' she smiled, looking across at him, 'The one I've had the longest. He seems to like you.'

She brought two mugs of coffee and sat opposite him. 'Help yourself to everything,' she said, passing him a plate of thinly sliced beef.

Ace walked in a small circle three times before curling himself up and settling down on the floor next to Greg's chair.

They ate in near silence for a while, Classic FM in the background, Greg quite happy to wait for Elli to say what she needed to say. Besides, the food was excellent, varied and plentiful.

Eventually Elli said, looking down at her half-empty plate. 'I married Bob three years ago. I'd been a widow for four years. I adored my first husband and Bob was very much like him. On the outside, that is. He swept me off my feet.' She looked up at Greg. 'But Jack, my first husband, was a good man, a kind man. An honest man.'

Greg waited.

Elli said, 'I don't know how much you know about Bob's business interests?'

'Very little. When I lived in the village he had his own small boat-building firm. He had a little business hiring out boats to visitors too, and he took fishing parties out in his launch as another sideline. But of course, I'm aware that he has expanded his interests since then.'

'Yes,' she said. 'He has. When I met him he told me he owned a chain of gambling clubs in the UK. I was head croupier in a big casino in Las Vegas at the time. He said he needed someone he could trust to oversee the handling of cash in the clubs and offered me the job of controlling all the croupiers. I wasn't sure I was ready to come back to England and I liked the job I had, but Bob has a certain charisma and he turned on the charm. I fell for it.'

She pushed some shreds of lettuce around her plate with her fork. 'In fact, at first the job of controlling all the croupiers seemed quite promising. There are seven establishments in various cities, and they are all called Cockaigne. They are basically gambling clubs, but members can take advantage of other facilities as well, such as escort services, currency exchange and loans, or travel and accomodation. No expense is spared to provide the highest quality service. In every respect, that is. The Cockaigne Club is very exclusive, you see, and only the very wealthy can afford to be members. I have to admit I was impressed when I saw the membership list.' She gave a wry smile and glanced up at him. 'I was brought up to be a snob, Greg, and however hard one tries, one never quite outgrows one's early conditioning.'

Greg helped himself to more potato salad. 'So the Quarterdeck Club is not part of the same set-up, then,' he said, raising his eyebrows and smiling at her quizzically. 'I mean, you were quite prepared to accept me, so it can't be.'

'Yes, it's quite separate,' she said, seriously. 'Bear with me, will you. I'm coming to that.' She continued toying with her food, not making eye-contact. Eventually she went on, 'The first thing Bob wanted me to do was to visit each of the clubs, vet every one of the croupiers and set performance levels. I did this. A few of the existing staff were definitely not up to scratch and he fired them, leaving it to me to find replacements and ensure continuity of service. So far, so good.' She paused.

'One thing I learnt in the United States,' she said, looking up at him, 'Was that in the gambling industry it always makes more sense to stay within the law rather than try to find ways around it. I believe the same applies here, too, even though the authorities here don't always seem to be as competent as their American counterparts.

'Bearing in mind that Bob had said originally that he wanted someone he could trust to oversee the handling of cash, he had appointed me Chief Cashier. In effect this meant that I was the one in the Cockaigne organisation legally responsible for the cash itself and all records of it. Naturally enough I started to look into how the takings were controlled.'

Greg could see conflict in her face, and he assumed she was wondering whether she should trust him and if so, how much she should reveal.

Presumably having decided, she continued. 'There was a system, which was supposed to be the same for all the clubs, with security staff physically collecting the cash, and it looked all right on paper, but after I had been to three clubs I began to get the feeling that the actual sums banked and the amounts recorded by the croupiers did not match. I went back to check the records in detail, and my suspicions were confirmed. Considerably more was being banked than the recorded takings. Very soon after that I discovered that my dear husband really only wanted me as a figurehead, because the only person he can actually trust to oversee the handling of his cash is himself.'

She put her fork down and leant back in her chair.

'As you can imagine there was a row. He had taken me for a fool. I resigned, of course, and threatened to expose him. His threats in return were more sinister, and I came to realise how ruthless he could be and that my life could be in danger. I'm serious, Greg, I believe it could be. I tried offering him a compromise: I would keep quiet and stay away from Cockaigne and all his other enterprises if he gave me the Quarterdeck Club and Clarmont House. Rather to my surprise, he agreed and it was settled. This was a year ago.' She paused. 'But I think I know him well enough now to believe that this situation can change at any time when it suits him.'

'So,' she said, leaning forward and staring fixedly at Greg. 'In the meantime, I have to do whatever I can to protect myself, and I'm prepared to use any help I can get.'

'Alright,' said Greg.

'I believe Bob is so anxious to prevent questions being asked about the death of that young man all those years ago because there is something about it that makes him vulnerable.'

'It would certainly seem so,' said Greg.

She said. 'I intend to use it if I can find out what it is. Have you any ideas?'

Greg smiled at her. He saw that she could possibly be a useful ally, but so far, all she had told him, whilst interesting, had merely tended to confirm opinions he and Ray Tindall had already formed. He wondered if she would really have access to hard evidence of any kind, and if so, would she be prepared to share it?

'Ideas?' he said. 'Yes, I have. But first let me explain my position here, Elli.'

He gave her a brief summary of the events that had brought back him to the Island, emphasising that, having had his whole life affected by what happened to Nigel Heapes, it was the revelation that Nigel had been shot which had motivated him to try for retribution and led to him agree to help Ray Tindall in his investigations.

He told her about the two attempts to warn him off, and that Cyril Ritter had disappeared, but made no mention of Johnson or Russell. He did not tell her anything about Hamish, nor of Nick's support. He did give her Ray's ideas about the Vanderling Associates in some detail, and included everything that Molly Ritter had told him about Bob Clarmont Brown's apparent hold over Roddy Vanderling, and her suspicion that he could have been responsible for Roddy's death.

'From what I've been told it seems likely that it was your husband who had me beaten up at the time, too,' he added

He finished by telling her what he and Ray had surmised about the way Nigel was killed.

Elli was quiet for a long moment. Then she said, 'Suppose Bob was the one who fired the shot that killed Nigel and that's why he's so worried?'

'Do you think he could be?'

'Yes, I'm quite sure he's capable of it.'

'Well, if he was it would be impossible to prove,' said Greg. 'If Nigel was shot by whoever it was I saw out on the rocks, nobody else would have seen him, and I could not have idenitied him at the time, let alone all these years later.'

'That can't be what frightens him, then. But I'm convinced there is something that he believes will link him directly with the killing.'

'Yes. Ray Tindall thinks it could be the mysterious parcel Nigel thought I had. But there's no evidence such a parcel ever existed.'

They both sat quietly with their own thoughts.

Greg finished his meal and put his knife and fork together on his empty plate.

'That was very nice, Elli. Thankyou.'

Elli stood up. 'Can I get you anything else? Some fruit? More coffee?'

'Coffee please,' he said.

Ace looked up as Elli left the table. He stood, shook himself and in a lazy manner, put his paws out in front and did a stretch, backside higher than his head, straightened up and yawned, a tongue like a rasher of back bacon lolling from his mouth. Then he turned and gently laid his head on Greg's lap.

Greg was stroking his head as Elli returned with his mug of coffee.

She looked down at the dog, and raised her eyebrows. 'He's usually quite shy with strangers,' she said. 'I was surprised when he went to sit next to you because normally he's protective and he'll stay close to me when somebody new comes. Perhaps it's his way of saying we are all on the same side. What do you think?'

Greg smiled. 'Yes, I think that probably is what he's saying.'

She was silent for a moment as if wondering how to go on. Then she said, looking directly at him, 'I think I have made it clear to you why I want my husband's activities stopped. It's time somebody did something about him. He has the moral sense of Saddam Hussein,' She paused, 'Or maybe Robert Mugabe.'

Greg remained silent, merely nodding in acquiescence, while waiting to see what she really wanted from him.

'I think we should be able to work together,' she continued. 'You must want to square your account with him too, after discovering what you have about him.'

'Alright,' he said, 'But have you any thoughts about what you would be able to do? I mean, you are estranged from him, are you not, and you no longer have access to his business activities, do you, so what do you have in mind?'

'I never expect to get something for nothing, Greg,' she said reprovingly. 'I'm talking about co-operating. I have a contact, a friend, in fact, who is head croupier at the Southampton Cockaigne. She was helping me when I found the discrepancies between her cash takings and the bank records, and when she heard about what had happened to me she got in touch and offered to help if she could.'

'Why would she do that?'

'Because she is one of Bob's cast-offs, although I didn't know that at the time. Anyway, she feels she owes him no favours. The point is, she is in a position to get copies of the current records, and if I asked her to do that I'm sure she would be more than willing if she knew we would use the information.'

Greg made up his mind. Possession of such material, no matter how it had been obtained, would be a step forward in their investigations and could only improve Ray's chances of persuading his ex-colleagues to re-open the Vanderling File, so, although he had been reluctant to take seriously the idea of working with Clarmont Brown's wife, he now accepted that she was sincere in her need to enroll his help against her husband.

He said, 'That is just the kind of evidence we need to help build a case against him. How soon would you be able get it, do you think?'

'I'll speak to her this afternoon,' said Elli.

'Great.' Greg moved Ace's head to one side as he prepared to stand up.

Elli raised a hand to stay him. 'There is something else,' she said. 'Peter Grant will be with us as well.'

'Oh yes?' Greg settled back again. The dog padded slowly out of the room.

'Yes,' said Elli. 'He has confided in me that there are some aspects of his job that he is worried about. In fact, he would have got around to mentioning his concerns to you when you were talking in the club last night but I jumped the gun by inviting you to my office, and then, afterwards we agreed that I should speak to you today and see how the land lies.'

This could explain Pete's apparent lack of interest which Greg had mentioned when he spoke to Zillah on the phone. Another thought occurred to him too: Pete had mentioned a lady friend whom he had to meet discreetly because she wasn't free. Could this be Elli, he wondered?

'This is tied up with your husband's businesses as well, is it, Elli?' he said.

'Yes. But it will be best if he speaks to you about it himself. What do you think?'

'Alright.'

'Can you see him this evening?'

'Yes,' said Greg. 'At the club?'

'It would be better to meet privately somewhere, I think. Peter suggested you might call at his house in Springvale. Shall I ask him to call you?'

'Alright.' Greg gave her his mobile number, then pushed back his chair and stood up. 'Thank you for the lunch, Elli,' he said, with a smile. 'And the interesting conversation.'

Elli stood as well. 'Thank you for agreeing to come and talk,' she said. She led him back through the house to the front door where she offered him her hand.

'I can understand that you would be cautious about discussing my husband's affairs with me,' she said. 'But I believe now you can see that we are of one mind in this.'

FORTYEIGHT

Thursday afternoon

On his way back to the café, Greg stopped in the Square to phone Molly, taking the opportunity while waiting for her to answer to check for anyone following him. There was no sign of a tail, nor had he seen anyone earlier on his way to Clarmont House, and he assumed that the watcher, whoever he, or she, was, who had followed him from the café to Dan's house on Tuesday, was not aware of the rear exit into Rope Walk.

When Molly eventually did answer she still had not heard anything from her husband.

'I haven't managed to find out the name of Johnson's houseboat yet, either,' she said. 'But I'm working on it.'

'Do you think Johnson would have taken your husband there?'

'No idea. It's possible, of course. I've been thinking and I reckon Ron Johnson's been told to keep Cyril out of the way for a while, so he might have taken him over to the mainland by now.'

'So what do you want to do?'

'I'll call you when I get the name of the houseboat, then we could see if he is there. If not, I'll have to report him missing, I suppose. Don't really want to do that, though.'

'You don't seem worried about him.'

'No, I'm not really. Cyril's pretty good at looking after himself. He'll be okay.'

'Right. Now, tell me something, Molly. I met a character called Raymond Kilroy this morning. Does the name ring a bell?'

'Well, I know of a Ray Kilroy who they say gives a good price for things that fall off the back of a lorry. He's got a removals van and a warehouse in Cowes, and he'll do house or office removals, small jobs at short notice. And he has some pretty rough fellows working for him.'

'He had one called Brewster with him this morning.'

'Oh, Brewster, the Bruiser, he's out again then, is he? Did he give you any trouble?'

'Nothing too difficult to handle.'

She laughed, 'Good for you. What was it all about, then?'

298

'Our friend Russell wanted them to stop me asking questions.'

'Well, well. Russell again.'

'Yes, and while we're talking about him, would you happen to know anything about his ex-wife who used to work for Wilson's estate agents in Southsea?'

'Ah. Well, what I can say is Cyril reckoned it was Bob who was the cause of the marriage break-up. He certainly took up with her soon after. He set her up in his gambling club in Southampton, apparently, and there was talk of him marrying her at one point.'

'Really?' Greg immediately thought of what Elli had just been telling him about a friend in Southampton. 'Is she still there do you know?'

'No, I don't. It was several years ago.'

'Okay, thanks, Molly. Well, I'll wait to hear from you about Johnson's boat, then. Bye-bye.'

Back at the café Greg told the others about his lunch with Elli.

Ray was delighted at the apparent progress. 'What did I say? Told you she would be worth cultivating, didn't I! And Peter Grant wants to get in on the act as well, eh? That could be interesting, getting a bit of insight into GLH. Let's have a look at the file.'

Ray's 'Vanderling File' consisted of four volumes, one for each of what he called 'Main Villains', so that there was a slim one for Roddy Vanderling, another for Freddy Davis, a bigger one for Clarmont Brown, and the biggest for the Wilsons. This had a separate section headed GLH, and Ray opened it up.

'Peter Grant first appears in the file eighteen months ago when he took over as General Manager of GLH,' he said. 'Up until then he'd been in charge of Seastone Construction Limited, which Graham Wilson set up thirty-odd years ago. As far as anyone knows, this was a perfectly legitimate building company and it must have been quite successful because Wilson got a good price for it when he sold it.' Ray turned a page. 'GLH is the holding company for a large number of separate little firms, mostly guest houses and boat charter businesses on the Island and along the South Coast of the mainland, but it also includes properties in Spain and Freddy Davis's business in Seastone. It used to include Wilsons Estate Agents, too, when it used them for all Seastone Construction sales. Nowadays, though, Wilsons Estate Agents is a separate business, but GLH still uses them for all its various lettings.'

'Speaking of Wilsons,' said Greg, 'You said the woman who informed the French on that joint op in nineteen ninetyseven, worked for them and was married to our friend Russell at the time, right?'

'Yes, that's right.' Ray referred to his file again. 'According to my mate at Kingston Crescent, Mrs Jill Russell was the manager from nineteen ninetyfive until nineteen ninetynine. Hamish passed her details on to your people in Poole and they've come up with a match, a Jill Russell, telephone number and address in Southampton, Ocean Village. Moved there from an address in Southsea in nineteen ninetynine. Been there ever since. In two thousand and one she was age thirtyeight, marital status divorced. And what do you think her occupation was?'

'Croupier.'

'Yeah. How did you guess?'

'Well, I spoke to Molly Ritter just now,' said Greg. 'No news of her husband, but she did tell me that Russell's ex-wife was involved with Clarmont Brown at the time of the divorce, and he set her up with a job in the Southampton Cockaigne. So from what you just said I'm thinking she must be the friend Elli was talking about.'

Ray smiled. 'Bit of luck if she is.'

'So do we go and see her?' said Hamish

'We might not have to. Let's see what Elli comes up with first.'

Hamish passed a sheet of paper to Greg. 'Things we might need for Russell's office. We've ticked the things we've already got. Cast your eye over it, see if you think we've missed anything.'

It was a list of burglars' tools, everything needed to get past obstacles, and it started with a ticked item, picklocks, two sets of three: tension spike, hook and thin, flat tumbler pick.

Greg raised an eyebrow at Ray. 'Picklocks?'

'I've got a little collection of souvenirs.'

Greg read on: 'Tool belt and tools: large screwdriver, set of small screwdrivers, a hammer, wire cutters, pliers, mole wrench, files, hacksaw blades, Stanley knife and blades, baling wire, bungee cords, putty, quick drying wax. Latex gloves, backpack, poly bags, digital camera, penlight, rechargeable flashlight, rechargeable drill, alarm decoder. Alarm decoder?'

Ray said, 'See, my mate at Kingston Crescent says the office is alarmed and once it's set off you've got about twenty seconds to switch it off before it trips a buzzer in the local nick. Hamish reckons he can get a decoder.'

Hamish nodded. 'Sally's sending it by courier.'

'How does it work?'

'It's a wee gizmo like a car key remote and when the alarm goes off it reads the sonic pitch and decodes it. Takes about three seconds max. When a little red light comes on, you point it at where the noise is coming from, and bingo, off it goes.'

'Marvellous.' Greg passed the list back to Hamish. 'I think you must have covered everything. I wouldn't have thought of half of it.'

'Ray's the expert, and he's already got most of the stuff. So, when are we going, then?'

'The sooner the better. I thought we'd go over this evening after I've seen Pete. I'll give Sonia the minicab a ring and get her to pick us up.'

'All night job is it?'

'Want to put your toothbrush in the backpack just in case?' said Greg.

Ray said, 'You're thinking of borrowing Dan's little runabout.'

'Right.' Greg smiled at Hamish. 'Then we won't be bothered for time. And we might as well have a look at Johnson's pad too, while we're over there.'

'Do we know what we're going to be looking for?'

Greg shrugged. 'Something useful is bound to turn up. But basically, anything connected with Clarmont Brown, the Cockaigne Club, Cyril Ritter, Seastone Yacht Club, or in fact anything we've come across so far.'

Greg's mobile rang. 'Hello.'

'Hi, Greg. It's Pete. I've just been talking to Elli. Are you free to come to my place this evening, say, eight o'clock?'

'Yes, sure.'

'Good. You know the Vale House Hotel?'

'Yes.'

'My place is the house on the left of the entrance in Shore Lane, The Old Lodge, can't miss it.'

'Okay.'

'Uh, would you mind parking in the hotel car park? I've got a side gate that opens onto the hotel drive. Come in there if you would. I don't want it known that we're meeting. Okay?'

'Alright, Pete. Eight o'clock, then. Cheers.'

Greg rang off and told the others what he had arranged. 'I don't want to spend too much time there,' he said. 'But Elli said he's worried about something to do with his job, and that he wants to help us. I'm not too sure what that means, but from what you've told us about GLH, Ray, we ought to hear what he's got to say.'

'Oh, yes. Definitely.'

Hamish said, 'Trust him, do you? I mean, he's being awful secretive, isn't he?'

'Elli suggested he might be nervous about us meeting in public. She seems to think we're being watched. Anyway, I'll leave the car at the Yacht Club and walk along the shore. It's not far and I'll be able to see if anyone follows. I'll get there early, too, just in case. Then, if one of you can pick me up at eight thirty, okay? In the hotel carpark.'

Hamish said, 'My sister's expecting me back for dinner this evening.'

Ray said, 'I'll pick you up.'

'Good, thanks. I'll want to leave from the Yacht Club by half ten if I can, Hamish, so we'll meet here at ten o'clock. Okay?'

'Aye, sure.'

FORTYNINE

Thursday evening

Greg arrived at the side gate to The Old Lodge at five minutes to eight. He had left his car in the Yacht Club carpark and walked unhurriedly along the sea wall path and then down onto the beach, stopping every so often to gaze around. There were few people about and he would easily have seen if anybody was following him. Nobody was.

He went through the gate and followed a path to the back door of the big, rather ugly pile of a house, which seemed to him to have been put together piecemeal without regard to its overall appearance. He rang the bell and immediately a dog started barking. He realised it must be Barbara's, the one he had thrown the ball for by the pier on Saturday morning. The barking stopped as Barbara opened the door.

'Hello, Greg. Come in. Peter is in his study. This way.'

He followed her through the house to a room at the front. Pete was sitting in front of a computer. He stood up when he saw Greg and stepped toward him, smiling, hand outstretched.

'Thanks for coming, Greg,' he said. They shook hands. Pete's palm was clammy, but his grip was tight. 'Take a pew. Drink?'

'No thanks.' Greg sat in a small easy chair by the desk.

Pete swivelled his executive-type chair around to face him and sat so that they were about two metres apart. His smile of greeting faded and he leaned forward, head down, hands on knees.

'This is not easy, Greg.'

Greg said nothing.

'I've worked for Graham Wilson all my working life. He's been very good to me, and it feels, well, disloyal to be telling tales about the firm.' He sighed and looked up. 'Elli is the only one I've talked to about it, and she thinks you might be able to help.'

'Alright.' Greg waited.

'Obviously I wouldn't want Graham to think I'm pointing a finger at him.'

'I understand,' said Greg.

'So what I've got to say must remain in confidence.'

303

'No,' said Greg.

'What?' Pete frowned at him.

'No. I can't accept confidences, Pete. I'm helping Ray Tindall investigate an organisation that we believe murdered Nigel Heapes. That organisation includes your boss.'

'But Elli said you were after Bob Clarmont Brown for that.'

'Yes, and Elli's got her own agenda, hasn't she. But it's a bit more complicated than that.'

Pete stared at him, then sat back in his chair, eyes closed, hands clasped behind his head.

There was a long silence.

Greg sat patiently, recognising that Pete must have a conflict of loyalties here. On the one hand he would feel indebted to the man he saw as his benefactor, Graham Wilson, and on the other, if, as Ray believed, illegal activities were being carried out within Wilson's firm, he would be anxious about his own responsibilities as its head.

Eventually Pete took a deep breath, opened his eyes and sat forward.

'I was General Manager of Graham's building firm, Seastone Construction,' he said. 'And when he told me he was going to retire it didn't come as a surprise. He was well past retirement age and he hadn't been around much in recent years anyway. Since his wife retired from their Estate Agency they've been spending most of their time at their place in Barbados.

'He told me he was going to sell Seastone Construction and he gave me a choice. I could take a lump sum, shake hands and say goodbye, but he would much rather I considered taking over the management of the company that controlled all his other businesses, GLH. He said GLH ran like a well-oiled clock and I'd find it easy after running Seastone Construction.'

Pete gave a wry smile. 'It's partly my own fault, really. There'd been a few dodgy decisions made in Seastone Construction, and I'd turned a blind eye, knowing which side my bread was buttered. I'm talking about planning permissions, building regs, that sort of thing, and I must have given Graham the impression I'd go on doing the same in GLH. But its one thing to look the other way when you see the odd brown envelope change hands, it's a bit different when you know serious offences are being committed and you're the one in line to take the rap.'

'You say serious offences, but what, specifically, are we talking about?'

'What it comes down to is people trafficking, Greg. That, to me, is serious.'

'Alright. And you think Graham Wilson is behind it, do you?'

'He must know about it at least. As I said, he's not been around much in the last few years, but I reckon it's been going on for quite a while.' Pete paused, frowning and said, 'You don't seem to be surprised about the people trafficking. Did you know something already then?'

'I've seen the police file on GLH, Pete.'

'Jesus! Police file?' He turned in his chair and looked out of the window. After a moment he said, 'I had no idea. This is worse than I thought. How much do you know?'

'We don't actually *know* anything, Pete. And, in all fairness, the file does date from the late nineteen nineties and there's nothing in it that directly incriminates you, so rest assured on that. We do have a lot of circumstantial stuff, but no hard evidence. That's why I told Elli I'd listen to what you had to say.'

'You want evidence.'

'That's right.'

'A few weeks ago I could have got you hard evidence all right, but … ' He rubbed his hand over his forehead. 'Never mind. You don't need to know about that.'

'What do I need to know about, Pete?'

There was another long pause, then Pete sighed heavily. 'Okay. It's more or less what I wanted to tell you anyway, but let's start with a little bit of history.

'I started work for Graham Wilson in nineteen seventyeight as a carpenter in his original building firm, Manor Farm Construction Limited, that he set up to convert his farm buildings into holiday apartments. By the time I joined them they were building the Manor Farm Estate on his land all along Manor Farm Road. He'd also set up Wilsons Estate Agents for his wife Louise, and they ran the two companies side by side. By the end of the nineteen eighties they had acquired quite a number of different properties and they decided to form a group. They called the parent company GLH, Graham and Louise Holdings. Seastone Construction was formed and I was made Sites Manager which meant in effect I was site foreman on all new developments. Then in nineteen ninetynine, Graham withdrew from the building work and made me General Manager, reporting directly to him.'

Pete looked across at Greg, an open expression on his face. 'I suppose what I'm really trying to do here, Greg, is justify myself,' he said. 'You see, up to eighteen months ago I'd never had anything to do with GLH, well, not directly, and I assumed I'd go on reporting to Graham like I always had. So that's what I did at first, mostly by phone and email because he was hardly ever around.

'But the job turned out to be a doddle, just as he'd said it would be. GLH being a holding company is not expected to produce anything itself. Its only purpose should be to own and control all the other businesses. It's really only a couple of offices, one called Maintenance and the other Finance, both of them run by managers who've been there ages. I very soon found they resented any interference by me and in fact there was nothing much for me to do at all. But when I told Graham I couldn't see the point of my job, he just said he thought I'd earned a bit of a rest and should take it easy while I could.

'Anyway, after a few months - it would have been about a year ago - Elli rang me up one day. I didn't know her then, except I'd seen her around and I knew she was Bob Clarmont Brown's wife. She had a query about the transfer of Clarmont House and the Quarterdeck Club from GLH into her possession. It was the first I'd heard of any transfer so I checked with Graham and he told me it had all been arranged and all I had to do was sign the relevant documents. That seemed peculiar to me. I mean, I was supposed to be in charge and nobody had told me about the disposal of two substantial business assets. But I sorted out Elli's query for her through GLH's solicitor and the transfers went through without a hitch.

'Afterwards, when she had taken the club over, Elli invited me up to her office for a drink to say thanks and we got chatting. She told me she'd left the Cockaigne job but she didn't say why, just that it was not right for her. She wanted to know about GLH, what actual businesses it controls, and I realised then how little I really knew. I told her what I could, and as I was leaving she said to me, "A word of warning: don't get caught like I nearly was." She wouldn't say any more at the time but I decided to look into what GLH actually does control.'

Greg said, 'And you found out about people trafficking.'

Pete nodded, 'Yes, among other things.'

'And that's why you wanted to talk this evening.'

'Yes.'

'But you suggested just now that you can't supply any evidence. Is that why you haven't got in touch with the police?'

Pete sat back in his chair, with his elbows on the arm-rests, hands together, fingers interlinked across his waistline and tapped his thumbs together. He stared pensively at Greg, then looked away across the room, gazing at the ceiling.

'How much have you had to do with the local police?' he said at last.

'Very little. I gave a statement to a detective sergeant, but otherwise nothing.'

Pete turned back to face Greg. 'And they haven't taken a great deal of interest in finding out what happened to Nigel Heapes, have they?' he said. 'But you and Ray Tindall obviously think it's worth making an effort, so haven't you wondered why they don't?'

'Well,' said Greg, 'Ray seems to think there is very little credit to be gained for them from spending time on a thirtytwo-year-old case.'

'And I daresay he's right,' said Pete. 'But there may be a better reason. Somebody may have asked them not to look too closely.'

'And you have that someone in mind,' said Greg with a smile, guessing who it would be.

'Bob Clarmont Brown.'

Greg's smile broadened. 'You've been listening to Elli.'

'Yes, alright, but that's not all. I didn't only look into what GLH controls. I found out who controls GLH, too. Yes, that's right, you guessed it, Sir Bob. Okay? He is the major shareholder with fifty per cent of the shares so he only ever needs the support of one other shareholder to get what he wants. The other shareholders are Graham and Louise Wilson, Freddy and Teddy Davis, Jeremy Marlow, Marlow's daughter Fiona Threlfall, who owns Wilsons Estate Agents now, and her husband Joshua Threlfall who is joint proprietor with Sir Bob in the Cockaigne organisation. A nice tight little group, easy for him to control.'

'Alright, that more or less confirms what Ray has believed to be the case for some time. But what's it got to do with not telling the police what you know?'

'I did tell them,' said Pete. 'About a month ago. I rang up and said I had evidence that illegal immigrants had been brought into the country. They put me on to CID and I spoke to an Inspector Cresswell. He came here that evening and he sat in that chair and I showed him what I'd found out and he was very impressed. When he left he took all the evidence I'd put together and said he'd need me to come to Ryde police station in the morning to make a formal statement. Charming fellow. You may have met him. It so happens he's in charge of the Heapes enquiry now.'

Greg was puzzled. 'So what's happening about the illegal immigrants?'

'See this?' Pete pointed to the marks on his face. 'When I got to my office first thing the next morning somebody was waiting for me. Teddy Davis's son, Spencer. Have you met him? He's a big guy and he had a cosh with him. I didn't stand a chance. When I came round he'd gone, but Jeremy Marlow was there. He's the Finance director and his office is next to mine. He tidied me up a bit and took me home. On the way he explained to me that I was mistaken about illegal immigrants so there was really no need for me to go to Ryde to make a statement. Or for any other reason. He suggested I should take a few days off work and when I came back I should try to take it easy and not do too much research into the company's records in case I came to any more wrong conclusions. Then he showed me a picture of Jonty that had been on my desk. It was torn in half. I got the message.'

It was Greg's turn to sit and stare.

'When I'd recovered enough to think,' continued Pete, 'I realised the inspector must have gone straight to somebody in GLH with what I'd given him, and that scared me.'

'You hadn't told anybody else?'

'Only Elli, and I knew I could trust her. Besides, Ryde police never did ask why I hadn't turned up to give the statement, so that proved to me that Cresswell hadn't reported it.'

'Yes,' Greg considered for a moment and then nodded slowly. 'And after what happened to you, I can see how the warning about Jonty would be enough to make you think twice about taking it further. You must have been fretting over this for some time then, Pete.'

'Yes, I have,' Pete agreed. 'Then the bones they found were

identified as Nigel Heapes and Elli realised that her husband was really worried about what you and Ray Tindall are doing, so she thought we ought to sound you out about digging into GLH and Cockaigne as well.'

'But what makes you think Ray and I can do anything?'

'Elli says Bob has never had to face any real inquiries into any of his businesses before, and she's convinced that if you follow up on what I was doing you might well make him do something to give himself away.'

Greg pursed his lips and frowned. 'I don't know,' he said. 'She may be right, but so far the attempts to put us off have been pretty feeble.' He shrugged, 'Admittedly we have not dug as deep as you did yet. Anyway, tell me about these illegals.'

Pete turned back to his desk. 'I was just going to print this lot off when you came in.' He started his printer and while they waited he said, 'I've put together what I can from the notes I had left. There's a list of addresses where I know illegals have been boarded in the past. There's names of places where GLH gets work. Anyway, you'll see.'

'How does it work?' asked Greg. 'I mean, how does GLH get in touch with the illegals, or vice versa?'

'There's no trouble picking them up. GLH has contacts in France, and Teddy Davis meets the French boats a few miles off the back of the Island, transfers them to his launch and drops them off at various moorings – he's got one in Bembridge Harbour, and GLH has two more, one in Yarmouth and another on the Medina.' He waved a hand at the printer. 'I've included their locations. One place they don't come to is Seastone.'

'So after they're dropped off, where do they go from there?'

'GLH has properties in Sandown, Ryde and Cowes where they can be tucked away three or four to a room. The GLH employment agency finds them work, mostly seasonal, hotels, holiday camps, fruit picking, etc, so they have total control over them from the start – the agency deducts their rent from their earnings, so GLH gets most of what they do earn.'

'What happens at the end of the season?'

'Teddy's son, Spencer, runs them over to the mainland, a dozen or so at a time in his van, takes them to Southampton, Bristol, Liverpool or Birmingham, and other places where Clarmont Brown has businessess. He employs some of the men in his security business, nightwatchman sort of thing, or passes them on to gang-masters. Some of the women may get jobs in the Cockaigne escort agency. But whatever happens, you can be sure he takes his cut.'

'And nobody has looked into this at all?' said Greg.

'Well, I told you what happened to me. For all I know there may have been others before me, but Clarmont Brown appears to have covered the police end of it, so who knows?'

Pete passed the sheets of printout to Greg, who stood up, ready to leave.

'He's doing quite well out of the reconstruction in Iraq, too,' said Pete as they walked through the house to the back door.

'In what way?'

'He supplies private defence contractors with staff from his security companies in UK.'

'To do what?'

'You name it – protect the Green Zone, act as bodyguards, chauffeurs, escorts for local dignitaries, check houses, offices, cars for booby traps, intervene in riot situations … '

'In other words he supplies mercenaries.'

'Well, whatever, it's all above board, sanctioned by the government.' Pete paused and turned to Greg with a guarded expression. He put his hand on Greg's forearm.

'Bob Clarmont Brown has been running all his various shady businesses successfully for a good many years now,' he said, 'And Elli reckons he's likely to have covered his tracks pretty thoroughly, so it will take something special to catch him out. He really does seem to be worried about the Nigel Heapes affair though, and perhaps he sees that as his weak link. So far, from what you've said, he doesn't seem to have taken you too seriously, but make no mistake, this is a very powerful man and he must have very influential friends and we reckon if you push him too hard he'll throw everything at you. Okay? Just take care, mate.'

FIFTY

Greg, Hamish and Ray left Seastone Yacht Club in Dan's motorboat just before ten thirty. Ray had persuaded Greg that there were two good reasons why he should go with them.

'See,' he had said, 'Somebody ought to guard the boat while you two are busy, didn't they. And, if by chance something might happen that upsets the local force, I might know who to talk to.'

Recognising that Ray needed to feel part of the action, Greg had agreed.

During the afternoon he had told Ray all about his meeting with Pete, and then while Ray was writing up his notes, he and Hamish had spent time thoroughly checking the boat and getting it fueled and ready for the trip. Later, Greg had phoned Dan to tell him what he was planning to do and Dan had suggested they left the boat at the Wight Diver's berth by the Hayling Island ferry.

'Shouldn't be any problem,' he'd said, 'They know me there and it should be alright anyway at that time of night, especially if Ray stays with it.'

Then Greg had rung Sonia and arranged that she would pick them up in her unofficial minicab and take them around as necessary.

The trip across was uneventful and as they approached Fort Cumberland Greg rang Sonia again to tell her where they would be coming in. By the time they arrived she had parked the Fiesta on the shingle by the boarding pontoon and was leaning against it smoking a cigarette. She nipped the end off and put the butt back in the packet as Greg approached with Hamish, and she eyed Hamish appreciatively as Greg introduced him.

Greg asked her to drive them to Albert Road and let them out in a quiet place not far from the antique shop she had taken him to before.

She found a suitable spot in a side street just past the shop on the opposite side of the road. Greg gave her a twenty pound note and asked her to stand by for a phone call to pick them up.

'We shouldn't be much more than twenty minutes or so,' he

said as they stood on the pavement. 'Pick us up here. And then we'll want to go somewhere else.'

'Okay,' she said. She had shown no curiosity at all about the purpose of their visit. 'I won't be very far away, in case you need me in a hurry.'

Hamish grinned down at her. 'Sounds like you've had experience as a getaway driver, Sonia.'

She grinned back. 'Not yet I haven't,' she said, 'But there's a first time for everything, isn't there!' She wound up her window and pulled away.

Greg and Hamish walked back into Albert Road and along to the antique shop. Greg had the alarm decoder and a small torch in his pocket and he noted as they crossed the road just before the antique shop that the solicitor's window blinds were closed. Hamish was wearing the backpack. The picklocks and a pencil light were in his pockets. The occasional car went by and there were a few stray pedestrians about, but it was unlikely anybody was taking any notice of them.

The door to Russell's office was to the right of the shop entrance.

Greg watched the street while Hamish picked the lock. It took him about half a minute. Greg followed him inside, alarm decoder at the ready. They saw in the light from the streetlamps that a carpeted flight of stairs led up to a small landing. Greg pointed to a small dark object inserted into the door jamb at floor level on the hinge side. He recognised it as an alarm which would be set off emitting an ear-splitting noise as it was squeezed after the door had been opened and then closed.

Hamish nodded and indicated the backpack. Greg found the pliers and screwdriver and while Hamish held the penlight, he bent down and gently eased the little disc out.

Holding it firmly he unscrewed and removed the casing, snipped the conductor and ground wires, pruned the insulation and wound the two together. Then he replaced the casing, crossed his fingers, and pressed. Silence. He smiled and put the device back in place.

'They'll probably never know,' said Hamish.

Greg closed and locked the door behind him.

Hamish switched on his penlight and they went up the stairs. On the landing facing them was a glass door with "Russell,

Solicitor and Commissioner for Oaths" in gold letters across the centre. They noted a security camera above it. Hamish went to work on the lock. Again it took only about half a minute. They went through into an austere reception area. Greg closed the door behind him and immediately an alarm went off.

He pointed the decoder at the light in the box blinking above the entrance, pressed the button in the centre and counted: one-thousand-and-one, one-thousand-and-two, one-thousand-and-three.

A red light appeared at the front of the decoder. Greg pressed the button again and the ear-splitting racket stopped. 'It works,' he said.

They stood still, waiting for a couple of minutes in case anyone nearby might come to investigate the alarm. They checked for other obvious alarms but did not see any.

They looked around. Everything, the walls, doors and window frame, even the carpet tiles appeared to be pale beige in the dim light. Facing them was a desk, bare except for a telephone console and a computer monitor and keyboard. A typist's swivel chair and two hard straight-backed chairs were arranged around the desk. There were no tables with magazines, no pictures on the wall and no plants.

Greg went to the window. It looked out onto a yard almost filled by several single-storey flat-roofed outbuildings which he assumed belonged to the antique shop. There seemed to be a central path leading through them to a narrow gate which he guessed would open into an alley along the back of the shops. The door next to the window was locked but did not appear to be alarmed.

Hamish took off the backpack and went to the desk. The drawers were not locked but the contents were only spare stationery items, a couple of magazines and an appointments book. He tried the handle of the door to the left of the desk. The room it opened into was quite dark, the blinds effectively cutting out the light from Albert Road, and he took out the flashlight.

Greg joined him. 'The other door's locked,' he said.

'Okay. Let's have a quick look in here though,' said Hamish.

It was a comfortably furnished small office, presumably Philip Russell's own. The two end walls were lined with books on law, and against the inner wall were a drinks cupboard and two wooden filing cabinets, and above them, framed pictures and certificates. A polished wooden desk with a large, leather executive chair was positioned diagonally to the right. All that was on it was a telephone, empty in and out trays and a stainless steel executive toy. Hamish tried the desk drawers first. They were unlocked. Greg held the torch while he lifted out suspension files and hunted through folders without finding anything useful. They checked the two wooden filing cabinets and drew a blank there too.

'Let's have a wee look at that other door.'

This was a more difficult lock to pick and after five minutes Hamish decided to remove the screws from the cover plate of door handle, which he did as carefully as possible so that no obvious marks were left. He popped the lock washer off the bolt axle, pulled out the bolt switch using pliers and used a screwdriver to turn the bolt so that it slid free. The door came open and Greg went in.

This was a typical office area with functional desks and work areas, office equipment and filing cabinets. A large safe with a combination lock stood against one wall. Next to the window overlooking the yard was an emergency escape door. Greg had a close look at it. He could see from the window that it would open onto a spiral fire escape.

'We could go out this way,' he said.

Hamish came to see. 'Aye, we could. I'll put yon lock back together again from this side then.'

Greg indicated the safe.

'What do you think?'

Hamish inspected it. He shook his head.

'Take too long,' he said. 'I knew we wouldnae think of everything and Ray cannae have had any Semtex amongst his souvenirs.'

'What do you think about the computers?' said Greg.

'Need Sally for that. Wouldna hurt to check through the bins though, eh?'

By the time Greg had finished carefully sorting through the contents of the waste bins, Hamish had locked them into the room.

'Any luck?'

'Not a thing,' said Greg. 'We'll have to go through the files.'

The filing cabinets against the left-hand wall were labelled alphabetically. Greg went to a desk standing next to an old-fashioned Rolodex System where he found an Active Files Index, and there under the letter C was reference C03, Clarmont Brown.

'Here's something!' he said. 'Under the Cs, Clarmont Brown is C03, and there's a record 07429 with today's date on it.'

Hamish busied himself at the filing cabinet and soon found the relevant file. He took it out and opened it.

'C03-07429. It's a printout of emails, to clarmont@clarmontbrowngroup.com,' he said, 'Subject: Heapes. Let's see. The first one was on Monday morning and the latest this morning. There's no replies shown. Listen.

Hi Bob   Cyril Ritter in Ryde reports ex-copper CID asking questions.   Have you any instructions?

Best regards   Phil.

Next is Tuesday afternoon, 16:15:38

Bob,   CR again. WJ Gregory now asking questions. CR is unsteady. Instructions please,

Best regards   Phil

Then Wednesday 9:11:22

Bob,   i) RJ has CR safe and quiet. ii) WJG still active Regards, Phil.

And here's the latest. It's timed at eleven fiftyfive this morning so Kilroy must have reported back pretty quickly.

Bob,   Action taken is per instruction. WJG still active and now has a partner.

Please note, this office will take no further instruction in this matter, Phil

It sounds as though Phil's a bit pissed off, doesn't it?'

'Yes,' said Greg, 'But it confirms the tie-up between Clarmont Brown and Russell. Copy it, will you, and see what else there is. I'll have a look for GLH.'

He went back to the Active Files Index and had just identified a reference to GLH when Hamish hissed, 'Quiet!' and his torch went out.

Greg immediately switched his off and they listened in the dark.

Hamish went to the front window and lifted a corner of the blind just far enough to see out to the street.

'There's a vehicle parked outside,' he murmured.

A strip of light appeared at the bottom of the door they had come through.

'Let's go,' said Greg.

Hamish picked up the backpack and had a quick look around, then joined Greg at the door

It was a standard emergency exit with a central bar which when pushed, opened the door outwards. They had no way of telling if they would be heard but they made as little noise as possible opening it and pushing it closed. They felt their way carefully down the fire escape and had reached the gate into the alley when a light went on in the window of the room they had just left.

The gate was padlocked on the inside. Hamish made a stirrup with his hands and hoisted Greg up, passed him the backpack and then as he hauled himself over he looked back.

'Nobody following just yet,' he said.

Greg speed-dialled Sonia as they hurried along the alley in the direction back to where she had left them.

'Quick as you can,' he said. 'We're on our way.'

'I've just arrived,' she said. 'You said twenty minutes.'

'So I did. Thanks.' He rang off.

'Sonia's ready and waiting for us,' he told Hamish. 'It would have been nice to have had a bit more time, though. Still, at least we got some confirmation.'

Hamish said, 'The office will have to know about that decoder. It stopped the noise all right but obviously didn't block the phone call like it's meant to.'

The alley led to a side road which joined Albert Road almost opposite the one in which Sonia was waiting. As they started to cross Hamish indicated the large car parked outside Russell's door less than a hundred yards away. There was someone leaning against it, smoking a cigarette and looking in their direction. They continued casually on their way, resisting the impulse to look back.

'I think we might as well go and have a look at Johnson's place,' said Greg. 'If he's there we'll ask him what he did with Cyril Ritter. If he's not we might find some reference to his houseboat.'

The Fiesta's lights came on as they approached.

They got in. Greg sat in front and Hamish in the back. Sonia said, 'Where to now?'

'That block of flats in Somers Town, please, where you took

316

me yesterday,' said Greg.

Sonia set off, turned into Albert Road and accelerated steadily away.

Hamish was looking out of the back window at the car parked outside Russell's. When they had travelled about a couple of hundred metres, it did a U-turn and started moving in their direction.

'We might have company,' he said.

Greg turned and watched the big car quickly make up the distance between them, then slow to stay a few car-lengths behind.

He said, 'We don't want anyone following us, Sonia. Go on up to Winston Churchill Avenue, will you, and go right around the roundabout and come back down to Albert Road again. Just take it steady and let's see if they stay with us.'

The big car fell back slightly after the roundabout but kept following.

Greg said, 'Listen, Sonia. These people following us could be very nasty. We don't want to get you into any trouble on our account, so perhaps you'd better pull over and let us out.'

'Well, okay, if you say so,' she said, 'But they'd have to catch us first, wouldn't they? Besides, if I drop you off you've got a long walk back to your boat.'

'Do you think you could lose them then?' said Hamish.

She grinned over her shoulder at him. 'Not if you want to end up in Somers Town, I couldn't. But I reckon I could in Eastney or Milton. Lots of little corners to tuck in round there. Want me to give it a go?'

'Well, alright, if you're sure,' said Greg.

'Great!' she said.

She drove steadily all along Albert Road until it ran into Highland Road. Then after a short distance she did a sudden left turn and accelerated rapidly to the next junction where she turned right and then shortly left again, repeating this procedure at high speed several times in the maze of streets bounded by Goldsmith Avenue, Eastney Road and Highland Road. In many of these narrow streets cars were parked on both sides of the road at this time of night, leaving barely enough room in the centre, but Sonia assured her passengers that having lived in the area all her life she knew every bit of it.

Hamish was keeping a lookout from the back of the Fiesta

317

and after a while he said, 'I think you've lost them, Sonia.'

She said, 'Good. There's a place just down here I can pull in behind some sheds if you're sure they're not still following. They'll never find us there.'

A short distance later she eased the Fiesta between two parked cars and up a pot-holed gravel track between two buildings, and turned right at the end.

The headlights revealed a ramshackle collection of workshops, a vehicle body repair shop, a paintshop, an electrical appliance serviceman, a flat roofing business, and various other trades, grouped around an area of cracked concrete. It was a kind of private industrial estate.

Sonia backed the Fiesta into the space between two battered cars outside the vehicle repair shop and switched off her lights.

'How's that?' She smiled happily round at Hamish.

'Bloody marvellous!' he said. 'I can't believe you've never done this before.'

'Honest!' she said. 'But, you know, you wonder what it would be like, don't you, to be followed like that and have to lose them. It was great! So what do we do now, Greg? Do you still want to go to Somers Town?'

'No, I think we'll forget that.'

'Only I could borrow my mate's Peugeot if you like, you know, in case they're still looking for this, I mean. It's only just round the corner from here. Cost you another twenty though.'

'That's not a bad idea, Sonia. Not to go to Somers Town, but if they are still looking for us it would be the best way of getting back to the boat.'

'Okay.' She punched a number into her mobile and waited until eventually it was answered. 'Yeah, I know, sorry,' she said, 'Only I really need to borrow your wheels ... yeah, right now ... I'll tell you later, okay? ... Yeah, usual terms ... Thanks, you're a real mate ... Key in the usual place is it? ... Okay, go on back to sleep ... See you.' She rang off. 'Right. I'll go and get the Peugeot and meet you out at the end of the track where we came in. Only mind the pot-holes in the dark.'

She waited while they got out of the car, then locked it and set off into the darkness and disappeared between a pair of sheds.

Greg switched on his flashlight and they made their way back out towards the road.

Hamish said, 'Where did you find her? She's great.'

Greg grinned at him. 'You've got to know where to look, haven't you?' he said.

They only had to wait a few minutes before Sonia came to pick them up.

It was little more than two miles to the Wight Diver's berth where they had left Ray with Dan's boat. When they arrived, Greg called out to the boat to reassure Ray, realising he would not recognise the Peugeot.

Ray said, 'I wasn't expecting you back so soon. What happened? Trouble?'

'Yes. Nothing serious, but we haven't had much success I'm afraid.'

Greg gave Sonia the extra twenty pounds. 'I reckon you've earned this,' he said.

'Thanks,' she said, tucking the note into the pocket of her jeans. 'It's been interesting. When are you coming back?'

Greg laughed, 'I don't know about that,' he said, 'But we'll certainly give you a call the next time we need a getaway driver.'

FIFTYONE

Friday morning

Greg was swabbing the floor of the kitchen in the Pier Hotel while he waited for the big dish-washing machine to finish its cycle. He was supposed to be meeting Suzy and he was going to be late so he turned the dial on the machine to 'fast spin' and laughed at the rhythmic clashing of the plates and dishes as they whirled around inside. Then, suddenly he knew this was wrong and he reached forward to switch the machine off. But the noise would not stop and he woke to the sound of his mobile ringing on the table beside his bed. Next to it the clock showed eight twenty. Less than four hours sleep. He grabbed the phone.

'Yes?' he snarled.

A pleasant voice said, 'Good morning, Greg.'

'Oh. Hi, Zillah.'

'You sound half-asleep. Did I wake you?

'Yes, you did. I was having a weird dream.'

'Late night?'

'Very. Got to bed at four thirty.'

Zillah said, 'Ah well, never mind. But are you making any headway?'

'Not much, but we'll keep digging till we find something.'

'I see,' she said. There was a pause. 'So you won't be coming home just yet, then?'

'Why? Rocky's alright, is he?'

'Rocky is fine. And in case you might wonder, I'm fine too.'

'Oh. Good. Only, if Rocky's in the way I can always come and get him.'

'Rocky is not in the way. Quite the opposite in fact. One of the reasons I'm ringing is to tell you he has just flushed a muntjac out of my vegetable garden. I'd heard they had been seen lately in this part of the Forest. Little devils are small enough to get through the slightest gap. Rocky chased it out through that hole in the hedge you were going to fix.'

'Ah. So that's why you want me to come home, is it?'

'Greg, I am not asking you to come home.'

'Oh. Alright.'

'But if, from time to time you can spare a moment or two for Rocky and me, we will both be pleased to see you.'

'Right. What was the other reason?'

'What?'

'For ringing.'

'We are allowed to miss you, aren't we?'

'Sorry.'

'Quite so. Now perhaps you'd like to go back to sleep so that when you wake up again you'll be more ready to face the rigours of your day.'

Greg laughed. 'I love it when you get all bossy,' he said, and he told her all that had happened on the previous day.

When he had finished she said, 'As you say, you have not made much real progress so far. Do you have anything in particular planned for today?'

'We're hoping to get something useful from Elli's friend in Southampton, and we want to get to Ronald Johnson if we can. With any luck Molly Ritter will have found out the name of his houseboat and that might help us find her husband.'

'Well,' said Zillah, 'Good luck, but it does seem to me that you'll need a great deal more manpower if you are going to have any chance of finding anything to incriminate this Clarmont Brown character, especially if the local police are co-operating with him. But I'm glad you've got some good back-up in Hamish.'

'Yes, he's a good man and we got on pretty well I think. At least, when we parted last night he told me he'd had an amusing day. We're all meeting for coffee at Ray's this morning.'

'I'd better let you get on, then. I just thought you'd be glad to hear that Rocky is earning his keep.'

'Yes, and I'll see how it goes today and I'll ring you this evening to let you know if I can get home for the weekend.'

'Fine. Take care.'

Greg got out of bed and went downstairs While he waited for the kettle to boil for his morning coffee he went through his usual morning exercise routine in Dan's kitchen and found himself looking forward to a good long run with Rocky when he went home eventually.

After coffee he showered and dressed and went into Dan's study to check for any messages. There were two. The first was timed at six thirtynine pm Thursday.

321

"Mr Gregory, it's Raymond Kilroy, you know, we met this morning at Parkhurst Forest. Umm, I think I'm in trouble, Mr Gregory, After what happened, I mean. Well, I know I am. I really need to talk to somebody. Can you meet me in the Pilot Boat? Soon as possible? Well, now if you can. I'll wait for you."

The second was also from Kilroy, timed at eleven thirteen. He sounded depressed. Or drunk.

"Mr Gregory, you didn't get my message. I came to your house but you weren't there. Can you give me a ring on 615322, please. It's my mum's number in Cowes. Thankyou."

Greg wondered how Kilroy would know where he was living, but then realised he must have been told the address as well as the telephone number when he'd rung the previous morning.

He rang the Cowes number and a woman's voice said 'Hello?'

Greg said, 'Can I speak to Mr Raymond Kilroy, please?'

'No, sorry, he's not here at the moment.'

'Is that Mrs Kilroy?'

'Yes, that's right.'

'My name is William Gregory, Mrs Kilroy. Mr Kilroy left a message on my answer phone last night asking me to ring him on this number. Do you know when he will be in?'

'No I don't, I'm afraid.'

'Actually, he rang me to ask me to meet him last night but I wasn't at home so I didn't get the message, so he left another one for me to ring him on this number.'

'What did you say your name was?'

'Gregory, William Gregory.'

'Oh, I don't think I've heard him mention you.'

'No, we only met yesterday.'

'Oh, you wouldn't be the gentleman from Bembridge by any chance?'

'Yes, that's where I'm calling from.'

'Only he told me he was going to Bembridge to meet somebody last night. That must have been you, then.'

'Yes, it must have been.'

'And you didn't see him?'

'No. That's why I'm ringing.'

'Yes. I see.' There was a pause, and then she said, 'Only Raymond didn't come home last night and I haven't heard from him and that's not like him at all. He always lets me know if he's going to be late or if he's staying with a friend. He's very considerate like that.'

'Well, when you do hear from him, would you tell him I shall be out all day and ask him to ring me, William Gregory, on my mobile, please?'

She assured him she would, and Greg gave her his phone number and rang off.

After breakfast he drove to Seastone and just as he was parking as usual in Dan's space at the Yacht Club, his mobile rang. It was Dan himself, calling to say he was on his way home and would meet Greg at the Yacht Club at lunchtime.

Greg crossed the road to the café and found Ray and Hamish seated at one of the tables, drinking coffee with Sophie.

She got up as he came in and went to the counter to fetch a cup for him. 'You were so late getting back last night,' she said, 'There wasn't much point Hamish going all the way back to Shanklin and disturbing his sister so he stayed in the spare room. I let them sleep on, Greg, and that's why they've only just finished breakfast.'

Ray indicated his file on the table in front of him. He said, 'I'm just bringing it up to date. Not that we achieved a lot last night, but it's all relevant.'

Greg didn't know what he meant by relevant, but said, 'Well, here's something else for you to record. Raymond Kilroy tried to get in touch yesterday evening.'

He told them about the messages on Dan's answer phone.

'I spoke to his mother,' he said, 'And she told me he didn't go home last night. I gave her my mobile number for him to ring when he comes in.'

'What do you think he wants?' said Hamish.

'He sounded scared, as if he'd upset his bosses. Maybe he wants some sort of protection in return for information he thinks we might be glad of.' Greg turned to Ray, 'Hamish threatened him with dire consequences if anything untoward happened to me.'

Hamish grinned. 'The wee puttock called me "Rambo",' he said.

'Yes, but if he's been unwise enough to pass your threat on to whoever debriefed him,' said Greg, 'He may be worried about consequences from there as well.'

'Anyway, it's another potential source,' said Ray. 'Now then Greg, with regard to what Peter Grant told you about a certain CID inspector, I'm going to give Tracey Nash a ring, see if she'd like to talk to me about illegal immigrants. Tracey's straight, I'd bet my pension on that, and I think she trusts me too. It will be interesting to hear what she has to say, if anything. In any case it won't hurt to get her fully on side if we can. But I'd better see her on my own, I think. She might want to see you later, of course. Okay?'

'Yes, no problem.'

Hamish stood up. 'If you've no pressing need for my presence Greg, I'm away to my sister now. But you've got my number and I'll come when called.'

'Thanks, Hamish,' said Greg. 'I daresay we'll be grateful for back-up again before this is over.'

Hamish thanked Ray and Sophie for their hospitality and went through to the back of the premiss where he'd left his motor bike.

Greg also prepared to leave. He said, 'I'm going to call in at the Pier Hotel to see how Arthur is getting on, Ray. And Dan's on his way back. I'm meeting him for lunch across the road, then I expect we'll go back to Bembridge. I'm hoping Molly Ritter will come up with the name of Johnson's houseboat and we'll get a lead on her husband's whereabouts, but if nothing crops up before tomorrow morning, I'll be spending the weekend at home.'

'What about the info Elli is supposed to be getting from her friend in Southampton?'

'Well, we won't be able to act on that before the weekend anyway, will we,' said Greg.

'And your friend Kilroy?'

'He'll have my mobile number so if he rings I'll take it from there. I'll be back on Monday in any case, but let me know how you get on with Sergeant Nash, won't you.'

Greg was about halfway along the sea wall path when his mobile rang. It was Mrs Kilroy.

'Hello, Mr Gregory. You said to ring you if I thought of anything.'

'That's right, Mrs Kilroy.'

'Well, I've been worrying about Raymond, and going over everything in my mind since you rang, and I rang his number at work and they haven't heard from him today either, but I remembered him using the phone just before he went out yesterday, so I went to have a look at the little notepad I keep by it and there's two numbers he must have written down. Anyway, I rang both of them but one was just a machine and the other one said they'd never heard of Raymond,'

'I see. Did you recognise the numbers Mrs Kilroy?'

'No, I didn't.'

'Alright, well, let me have the numbers and I'll look into it at once.'

Greg recognised both numbers. One was Dan's, the other was Seastone Yacht Club.

'Does Raymond live with you all the time, Mrs Kilroy?' he asked.

'Not all the time, no, but he's been staying here for the last six weeks.'

'So we could expect him to get in touch some time today, then. But I'll look into it anyway, Mrs Kilroy. Thanks for ringing.'

Greg rang Sally at Hamworthy, and asked her to trace any numbers used from Mrs Kilroy's phone number during the last six weeks. Sally said she would ring him back in about half an hour.

At the Pier Hotel Greg was pleased to find Arthur much recovered and in good spirits. He and Simon were still highly indignant at being kept in the dark by the police about the cause of Nigel's death, and they declared they they were completely baffled as to why anyone would have wanted to shoot him. Greg made sympathetic comments and told them that he was continuing to help Ray Tindall investigate the killing and would certainly let them know as soon as he had anything definite to tell them.

He left after about half an hour and as he was on his way back to the Yacht Club, Sally rang back with a list of the telephone numbers to which calls had been made from Mrs Kilroy's phone during the last six weeks. Five were of land lines, all with local names and addresses. The others were of mobiles, amongst which she had identified Philip Russell, Teddy Davis, Spencer Davis and Jeremy Marlow. Clearly, Kilroy had had considerable contact with the GLH organisation.

FIFTYTWO

Friday lunchtime

Dan had just got back to the Yacht Club and was leaning into the Range Rover to retrieve his brief case when Greg arrived. They greeted each other and went into the club together.

'Did you have a good trip?' said `Greg.

'Oh, well, business-wise I got the problem with the decking sorted and I fixed up a couple more things while I was there too, so it was worth the trip just for that. And it was good to spend a few days with my old school chum. We had a lot of fun. He really looked after me. How about you? How's Ray Tindall's investigation going?'

Greg started with the break-in by the two men on Tuesday.

'How did they know you were at my place?' said Dan.

'I must have been followed there from the café in the morning,' said Greg. 'We reckon somebody could have been watching from here, saw me arrive and waited till I left.'

'Watching from here?' Dan stopped and looked sharply at him. 'Yes,' he said, thinking about it. 'From the Members lounge upstairs, possibly. Did you see how they got in?'

'No. If they picked the lock it was a very neat job, but no damage was done.'

Greg was telling him about Nick sending help in the form of Hamish as they reached Dan's office. Dan opened his briefcase, took out some papers and put them on the desk and then started going through the stack of mail in his in-tray. He paused, picked out an unopened envelope and passed it to Greg. 'One for you.'

It was marked, *"Private and Confidential"*

Mr Gregory c/o Mr D. Vanderling, Seastone Yacht Club.

Greg opened it. Inside was a letter dated Thursday 19th. He read:

I can't trust phones or CID, ex- or otherwise, but I'll talk to you

IF YOU COME ALONE!

I'm on a houseboat in Bembridge harbour for the next couple of days.

I'll put a sign you'll recognise on the boat.

There was no signature. Puzzled, Greg stared at the writing, then handed it to Dan.

Dan read it. 'Who's it from? Any idea?' he asked. He passed it back.

Greg frowned. 'I think it must be from Cyril Ritter, the private eye,' he said. 'He's been missing since Tuesday afternoon. I'm sure his wife would have let me know if he'd turned up or if he'd been in touch. It's strange, though. We were told about a houseboat at Bembridge, and we've been trying to locate it, thinking he might be on it.'

'What are you going to do?'

Greg thought for a moment. 'It's dated yesterday,' he said, 'So whoever it is will still be there for the rest of today presumably. I think I'll have a word with Ray and maybe we'll pop along later. After lunch though, I'm starving.'

'Yes, me too,' said Dan. 'Come on then. You can tell me all about it as we eat.'

Over lunch, stressing that what he was saying was in confidence, Greg gave Dan an outline of the investigation's progress. He deliberately omitted any reference to Roddy and he emphasised that although they believed that their suspicions of Clarmont Brown and GLH were fully justified, they had no real evidence as yet. He finished by telling Dan about Elli and Peter Grant and their offer to help.

'Well, well, Elli and Peter Grant, eh?' said Dan. 'They've kept that very quiet.'

'Yes, and that's the way it has to stay,' said Greg. 'At least for the foreseeable future.'

'Well, I'm off again in the morning anyway, so I'm not likely to see them for a while. And,' he added, as he signed the bill for their lunch, 'I've got nearly a week's work to catch up on before I go, so I expect I'll be home pretty late this evening. Will you be in, or what?'

'Not sure. Depends what happens this afternoon.'

'Alright. See you when I see you then.'

Greg left him and went across the road to the café. Ray was in his den.

'You're not going on your own,' he said when Greg had shown him the letter. 'I'm coming with you. See, I agree with you it does seem to be from Ritter, and bearing in mind who you last

327

saw him with, we'll go along together.'

Greg smiled. 'Yes. Good. If you are up to it. How are the bruises?

Ray stood up from his chair. 'Look worse than they feel. Back to normal,' he said.

They went downstairs. Ray picked up a pair of binoculars and waved them at Greg.

'Well known as a good place for bird-watching, Bembridge Harbour,' he said, 'And if I'm going to be hanging around at all these will give me a good excuse.'

They looked in at the café on their way out so that Ray could tell Sophie he was going out for an hour or so. Then, as they got into Ray's car, he said. 'I presume we're talking about the houseboats along Embankment Road.'

Greg said, 'Well, yes. I don't know of any others.'

'Right, so how do you want to do it?'

Greg said, 'I thought perhaps we could drive slowly by and if we don't see the sign I'll get out and go back on foot while you stand by from the car.'

'Alright. What do you think this sign is that you're supposed to recognise?'

'Presumably something he knows would give me a clue and wouldn't mean anything to anyone else.'

'Such as?'

'No idea. But I expect I'll recognise it when I see it.'

Ray made a face and said, 'Oh. Well, best of luck to us, then!'

They did not speak for a while. Then Greg said, 'I heard from Mrs Kilroy. Her son wasn't at work this morning and nobody has heard from him. That's two people gone missing now. Anyway, she gave me a couple of phone numbers he's called lately, one was Dan's - must have been when he called me last night - the other was the Yacht Club. I got Sally at Hamworthy to run a check on her phone number and it showed a definite link between Kilroy and the Vanderling Associates.'

'Ah! At last!' Ray grinned at him. 'You've accepted my name for them!'

'Well, it's as good a name as any,' admitted Greg. Then, changing the subject, 'Have you managed to speak to Sergeant Nash about Pete's story yet?'

'No. She was out when I rang. I left a message asking her to ring me when she could. Didn't say what it was about, of course, but she knows me well enough, so she'll get in touch when she's got a moment.'

'What do you think she'll say when you tell her one of her guvnors is bent?'

'She'll want proof. Which means we'll have to get your friend Grant to speak to her himself.'

'I can't see him doing that at the moment.'

They came down the hill out of St Helens onto the embankment and Ray slowed down as they approached the houseboats beside the road.

Greg looked carefully as they eased past, then he saw it. At the end of one of the gangplanks a weathered piece of marine ply had the one word 'SUZY' written in capitals in black marker pen.

'Got it,' he said. 'Go on around the bend and drop me off.'

'That was quick,' said Ray. 'What was the sign?'

Greg told him.

'Yes, clever,' Ray nodded. 'It would be significant to you and nobody else would notice it.'

He stopped the car a short way past the last houseboat. 'I'll turn round and park on the corner, by the entrance to Harbour Farm. I'll be able to see from there. Be careful Greg. There may be nobody there, but in any case try not to leave any sign that you've been there. You never know.'

Greg got out and walked casually back. He saw that the boat with the notice was called 'Solent Breezes'. Those on either side appeared to be unoccupied. He walked up the gangplank and onto the deck. With a handkerchief wrapped around his hand he tried the main cabin door. It opened.

He called 'Hello?' There was no reply. He peered into the main cabin. It was quite large and well-furnished and it looked neat and clean. He had half-expected it to smell damp and musty but it had the pleasant lived in atmosphere of a normal occupied room. He called again, but again there was no answer. He went on into the cabin and down some steps, through a galley and into a smaller room beyond. The air in here was stale and unpleasant and the blinds were closed on the windows. He raised the nearest one and glanced around. It was a bedroom with two single bunks, bedding neatly squared on one and on the other a large tarpaulin had been roughly bundled up. He turned to go out, then looked back at the tarpaulin which seemed out of keeping with the general neatness on the boat.

He lifted a loose corner that was hanging down at one end of the bunk and saw a man's shoe. His heart jumped. He prodded the bundle and then realised it was a man lying on the bunk, fully dressed but loosely covered by a piece of tarpaulin. When he looked closer he saw that it was Raymond Kilroy and he was dead. A quick check showed he had been strangled.

Greg's immediate thought was that he had been set up and that he had been intended to find the body. But that made no sense because the note had been sent the day before and Kilroy had called him very late in the evening.

There was no point in staying on the boat though, and so, thankful that he had heeded Ray's warning and had not touched anything except the tarpaulin, he went back up to the main cabin. Ray was waiting for him in the doorway.

'Nobody here then,' he said.

Greg said, 'Only Kilroy and he's dead.'

Ray pursed his lips and drew in a breath with a sucking noise. 'Oh dear. We had better make ourselves scarce then, I think.'

Ray had parked the car a little way further on towards St Helens. On their way to it he said, 'As responsible citizens we ought to call in and report the death, of course.'

'Yes,' said Greg, 'I agree but anonymously, eh?'

They stopped in St Helens to use a public phone box. Ray dialled the emergency number to make the report, being careful to give the name and location of the boat.

FIFTYTHREE

Friday afternoon

When they got back to the café Greg took out his mobile and called Molly.

'Hello, Molly, it's Greg. Any news from your husband?'

'Hi, Greg. Yes, I was just going to ring you. He sent me a text just now to say he's alright but he's got to lie low for a few days and he'll be in touch again soon.'

'Did he say where he was?'

'No, that's all he said, except if anyone asks for him, he's on holiday.'

'Well, look Molly, I want your opinion on something. I've had an anonymous letter asking me to go to a houseboat in Bembridge Harbour. Listen.' He read the letter. 'What do you think? Could it be from him?'

'Could be. I don't know. Would that be the same boat as we're looking for, I wonder?'

'Seems likely, eh? Any luck in that area?'

'No. There doesn't seem to be any boat registered in Johnson's name anywhere on the Island. And I've got a list of all the boats in Bembridge Harbour and none of them are his.'

'Right. Okay, good. Could you have a look at that list for me and see if there's a boat called Solent Breezes on it?'

'Hang on.' Greg heard a click as the phone was put down. After a few seconds she was back. 'Hello, Greg. Solent Breezes, registered to Edwin Davis, The Post Office Stores, Seastone.'

'Teddy Davis, eh? Perhaps Johnson rents it from him.'

'Whatever. Now, listen Greg, I've got a feeling Cyril's still on the Island.'

'So the letter could be from him and he could be using that houseboat. Is that what you think?'

'Well, I don't know about that, but after he left that text I started thinking who he could be staying with and I reckon he'll most likely be with one of his old drinking mates, an ex-copper called Ernie Attrill. Lives in Cowes now. Want his phone number?'

'You haven't tried ringing yourself?'

'No. Cyril would go bananas if he thought I was trying to

331

trace him.'

'Okay, give me the number then.'

She did so and he thanked her and rang off.

'Cyril Ritter's been in touch,' he said to Ray. 'He didn't say where he was but Molly thinks he may be in Cowes with an old pal, an ex-copper called Attrill. Do you know him at all?'

'Ernie Attrill? Yes, he was my station sergeant when I first started,' said Ray. 'Pretty steady sort of chap. Sergeant at Ryde he was, when he retired. That was years ago. He must be getting on a bit now.'

'And she says the houseboat is registered to Teddy Davis.'

'So I gathered. Might be interesting to have a word with him to see if he knows Kilroy's body's on board. Before Tracey and her boys get to him, I mean, which they will when they check who owns the boat.'

Greg said, 'That's an idea. If he knows about Kilroy he'll wonder how much we know when we ask questions about the houseboat, and if he doesn't already know then he'll certainly think we're on to something after the police have been to see him. Teddy never had much of a backbone and he might well panic and let something slip. Let me just call this number Molly gave me first, though.'

He keyed in the number and the phone was picked up almost immediately.

'Mr Attrill?'

'Speaking.'

'My name is Willam Gregory. I'd like to speak to Mr Ritter if he is with you, please.'

'Oh, right, yes, he's here. One moment.'

Greg heard him say, 'Cyril! I've got your Mr Gregory on the phone.'

There was a pause and then Ritter said, 'Hello Mr Gregory, I might have known you wouldn't take long to find me. Did you get my note?'

'Yes, I did.'

'Didn't work too well though, did it? Sorry about that.'

'Sorry! Look, what's going on?'

'I don't really know, to be honest. Did you manage to find the houseboat?'

'Yes, I found it.'

'Saw my sign?'

'Suzy, yes.'

'When was this?'

'About an hour ago. Why?'

'Well, at lunchtime I went in to St Helens for some fags and on my way back I saw a car I recognised parked by the gangplank so I didn't go back.'

'Whose car was it?

'The chap who owns the houseboat.'

'Teddy Davis.'

'No. Ron Johnson.'

'The boat's registered in the name of Edwin Davis.'

'Really? I always thought it was Big Ronnie's. You've been busy.'

'Yes, I have, too busy to be buggered about, Mr Ritter.'

'Look, I'm sorry, as I said, but I couldn't go back to the boat because Johnson was after me. Was he still there when you got there?'

'No, he wasn't. Somebody else was, though. Does the name Raymond Kilroy mean anything to you?'

'Ye-es,' said Ritter hesitantly.

'What do you know about him?'

'Bit of a shady character. He's got a van and a warehouse, sort of a storage place in Cowes. He does small removal jobs, among other things. What was he doing on the boat?'

'Nothing. He's dead.'

There was a short silence. Then Ritter said, 'Dead? What did he die of?'

'From what I could see it looked as though he'd been strangled.'

'Jesus!' Greg heard Ritter call out. 'Ernie? Remember Ray Kilroy? He's dead!' Attrill must have said something and Ritter replied, 'Strangled apparently. On Johnson's boat.' He came back on the line to Greg. 'Look, Mr Gregory, I didn't set you up, if that's what you're thinking.'

'I'm not, as it happens.'

'Oh ... Good ... So what happened? What did you do?'

'I got out immediately, of course. Then called the police and told them about the body.'

'Anonymously.'

'Of course.'

'Yes … Good … Did you tell anyone you were going to the boat?'

'Only Ray Tindall, but Dan Vanderling saw your note. Why?'

'Because the coppers will find my prints all over the place, won't they, and they'll come looking for me. They won't find me straightaway though, unless somebody tells them where I am, if you get my meaning.'

Greg glanced across at Tindall. 'Yes, alright, but we're not likely to tell the police where you are, are we, Mr Ritter?' he said.

Ritter was quiet for a long moment, then he said, 'Ray Kilroy wouldn't have come to see me, Mr Gregory. Nobody knew I was there. I thought the last place they'd look for me would be on Big Ronnie's boat.'

'Who are *they*, Mr Ritter, and why are you hiding from them?'

'They want me out of the way in case you and that ex-copper ask too many questions.'

'*Who* wants you out of the way?'

There was another silence on the other end of the line. Greg waited. Ritter, after all, was the one who had sent the note saying he wanted to talk.

Eventually Ritter said, 'Listen, I've got something you'll find useful. That was what I wanted to see you about on the boat, but I want a guarantee that you'll look after me.'

'I can't guarantee anything.'

'Well, what I mean is I shall want proper recognition for what I've got and you're going to have to make sure I'm safe until this is all over.'

'Until what is all over, Mr Ritter?'

'Oh, come on! You and that ex-copper want to know what happened to that chap Heapes, don't you, and you're not going to give up until you've found out, are you?'

Greg said, 'So are you going to tell us what did happen then, Mr Ritter?'

'Oh, I can tell you that all right, if you haven't already worked it out for yourselves. The great, high-and-mighty Sir Robert Clarmont Brown shot the poor sod, that's what happened. Trouble is, there's no way anybody can prove it after all this time.'

'So what is it you think we'll be interested in?' said Greg, patiently.

'He's always been bloody clever at covering his tracks and letting other suckers take any flak that's going, but even he can't get lucky all the time. He just happened to turn up while I was doing a little surveillance job for somebody not so long ago, and I took the opportunity of keeping the camera going. You'd be interested in the video, I'm sure.'

'Alright.'

'Only, it's worth quite a bit to me, Mr Gregory.'

Greg said, 'If you're thinking of trying to sell me something, Mr Ritter, you can forget it.'

'No, no, it's not that. It's just that it's like a kind of insurance to me and I wouldn't want to waste it.'

'I see. Well, perhaps I'd better have a look at it then. How do I get to you?'

'You don't.'

Greg took a deep breath. 'Okay,' he said, thinking that if Ritter made such hard work of passing on information to his clients, it was small wonder his business had not prospered much over the years.

'Well, obviously,' Ritter continued, 'It's not safe for me here. It didn't take you long to find me, did it, so anyone else could too. I'll be moving on as soon as we're off the phone.'

Greg realised that Ritter had no idea that he and Molly had been in contact.

'What do you suggest then?' he said.

'I haven't got the video with me anyway,' said Ritter. 'What I thought was, I'll ring my wife and tell her where it is, then she could get it and ring you. What's your phone number?'

Greg told him his mobile number.

Ritter repeated it. 'I'll ring you when you've had a chance to see the video and you can let me know what you think,' he said and rang off.

'Well,' said Greg, 'That was interesting. Ritter did send that letter. He says he has a video we would be interested in. Concerning Clarmont Brown.' He told Ray what Ritter had said.

Ray said, 'He didn't say what it was he was watching when Clarmont Brown turned up?'

'No, and I didn't think to ask him.'

'Well, we'll find out soon enough and it's probably not relevant anyway,' said Ray, getting to his feet. 'Let's go and see Teddy now then, shall we?'

As they walked up the High Street, Greg said, 'I've been thinking about what happened to Kilroy and wondering why. I reckon when those two broke into Dan's place on Tuesday they must have bugged his phone. I could kick myself for not checking.'

Ray paused, looking sideways at him.'So when he rang you last night, they'll have heard the messages he left.'

'Exactly.'

Ray nodded. 'And got rid of Kilroy pretty damn quick. It begins to look as though somebody is running scared, Greg.'

'It does, doesn't it.'

'Have you used Dan's phone for anything else since Tuesday?'

'No. And I only checked the messages in case there was something urgent for Dan.'

'Good.'

'But I'd better warn him not to use his phone until I can locate the bug.'

'No, don't do that. Or rather, warn him by all means, but it might pay to leave the bug there, if there is one.'

'Ah. You mean, don't let them know we know about it.'

'That's right.'

'Yes, okay. And we might find a use for it, too.'

They continued on their way.

'Speaking of messages,' Ray went on, 'What about Kilroy's mum? You left your mobile number with her, didn't you, asking her to get him to ring you?'

'Yes … Oh, I see what you're getting at. She'll tell the police I've been enquiring about him, and they'll want to talk to me. Shit.'

'What did the messages actually say?'

'He was in trouble over what happened in Parkhurst Forest and he needed to talk to someone, so would I meet him in the Pilot Boat.'

'First thing to do then, is erase the messages from Dan's tape, because they'll want to listen to them. Less said about Parkhurst and the Pilot Boat, etcetera, the better.'

'Right. But Mrs Kilroy said he told her he was going to Bembridge to meet someone and she'll tell the police she and I agreed it must have been me.'

336

'Plead ignorance, Greg. You never met him and have no idea why he wanted to see you.'

'Alright, so if I'm asked about the messages?'

Ray considered for a moment. 'Tell them he said he was given your name as someone who was interested in the Nigel Heapes case. See, it usually helps to stay close to the truth.'

Greg smiled. 'Right, yes. So who gave him my name?'

'A Portsmouth solicitor called Russell?'

Greg laughed aloud. 'You are a bloody devious so-and-so, aren't you. Leading the cops on to make the connections you want them to make.' He thought for a moment. 'Supposing the other fellow, Brewster, gets involved though?

'Not very likely. See, Brewster's just a low-life anyway. Your word against his.'

'Yes. Well, I'll just have to play it by ear,' said Greg.

'It will be interesting to see who'll be in charge of the investigation, though,' said Ray, 'See, Cresswell is the DI running the Heapes case at the moment and if he really is as involved with GLH as Peter Grant says he is, I reckon he'll try and get that case put firmly on the back-burner so he can take this one on. Wouldn't that be great.'

They came to the Post Office Stores.

Ray said, 'Let me handle this, Greg.' He opened the door and walked directly to the checkout desk where Teddy was dealing with a customer.

Greg followed and stood a pace or two behind him. Close up he saw that the years had not been kind to Teddy. Never particularly stalwart he was now round-shouldered and pot-bellied and he had the bloated features and rheumy eyes of a heavy drinker.

The customer left and Ray said, 'Afternoon Teddy.' He took his wallet from his jacket pocket. 'I was passing by and thought I might as well come in and settle up my paper bill. How much do I owe you?'

'Hello Ray,' said Teddy. 'Let's have a look.' He reached under the counter, pulled out a big ledger and started to thumb through its pages.

Ray said, 'Are you still renting out that houseboat of yours? What's it called? Solent Breezes?'

Teddy looked up, his expression showing slight puzzlement.

'Ye-es,' he said. 'Why?"

'Got any vacancies, have you?'

'Oh, no. No I haven't. It's leased out to someone. Long-term let, sort of thing.'

'Oh, Ronnie Johnson's still renting it then, is he?'

Teddy's eyes opened wide in surprise, then flicked to the side as he noticed Greg.

Greg nodded and gave him an encouraging smile.

Teddy looked back at Ray. 'You know Ronnie, do you?' he said

'Know of him. Greg's met him though, haven't you Greg?'

'Yes,' said Greg, moving forward. 'He came to see me the other night. With another chap whose name I didn't catch. Fat fellow, red face.'

Teddy smiled politely.

'I don't know if you've heard,' said Ray, 'But now they've identified those bones as Nigel Heapes, Greg and I have been taking an interest in finding out how he died.'

'Yes, I did hear something about that,' said Teddy, still smiling.

'Oh, you did, did you?' said Ray, aggressively. 'Who told you, then?'

'Oh, well, I, um, I dunno, I suppose I heard it somewhere, that's all.'

'Alright. Only it happens to be true, Teddy, and when your friend Johnson called on Greg he told him to stop asking questions about it, didn't he Greg?'

'Yes, he did. And, he said he'd come to see me on government business,' said Greg.

Ray put his hands on the counter and leant across, his face inches from Teddy's. 'You wouldn't happen to know what government department he works for, by any chance, would you Teddy?' he said, slowly.

'No. No, I mean, well, he's not exactly a friend of mine.' Teddy backed away. 'I don't know anything about what he does or who he works for. I mean to say,' he laughed nervously, 'As long as he's regular with his rent, it's none of my business really, is it?'

'Hmmn,' Ray pushed himself off the counter and stood upright 'What about your lad, though?' he said. 'Spencer? Would he know Johnson?'.

'No. No, I wouldn't think so,' Teddy said hurriedly. He glanced aside at Greg, then looked down into his ledger.

'Haven't seen him about lately, your lad,' said Ray. 'What's he getting up to these days, then?'

'Oh, well, you know, he's still got the van. Mostly travelling about, collections and deliveries, sort of thing.' Teddy looked up. 'That's nine pound ninety, then, please, Ray, right up to date.'

Ray handed him a ten pound note. 'Talking of collections and deliveries,' he said. 'Where are you keeping that big catamaran of yours these days?'

Teddy put the note in his till and took out a ten pence piece. He turned back, frowning, his eyes darting from Ray to Greg and back several times.

Eventually he said, 'What's that supposed to mean?' He placed the coin firmly on the counter in front of Ray. 'You didn't come in here just to pay your bill, did you?' He looked accusingly at Greg. 'What's going on?'

Greg stared back at him in silence.

Ray said, 'We think the tenant of your houseboat, Solent Breezes, knows who killed Nigel.'

Teddy started to put on an indignant expression but before he could say anything, Greg said, 'And we think you might know as well, so if anything should happen that might make you feel like sharing that knowledge with us, this is my mobile number.' He gave him one of the agency cards.

Teddy took it wordlessly, his whole demeanour showing that he understood.

Ray picked up his ten pence change and dropped it into the RNLI charity box by Teddy's elbow, smiling at him as he did so. 'Bye for now.'

FIFTYFOUR

Friday afternoon

'Teddy wouldn't win too many Oscars, would he?' said Ray as they walked back down to the café. 'When you said you thought he might know who killed Nigel, he nearly peed in his pants. He definitely knows something, eh? But he obviously doesn't know about Kilroy yet.'

'No. Wonder how he'll react when they come and tell him.'

'We'll have another word with him later, shall we?'

Greg's mobile rang. It was Molly, telling him she had a package for him if he wanted to come and collect it. He said he would go at once.

Then he and Ray speculated on what the video might contain. They wondered what Ritter's surveillance job could have been if Clarmont Brown was involved, but they had come to no convincing conclusions by the time they parted at the café. Greg crossed the road to the Yacht Club car park, saying he would come straight back with the tape.

Ten minutes later he slid his car into the space he'd used before at the rear of the video rental shop beneath Ritter's office.

Molly was coming down the stairs as he entered the building.

'That was quick,' she said. She had a sealed Jiffy bag in her hand and waved it towards the back entrance of the rental shop. 'If you want to see if this is worth bothering with, I thought we could ask Barry if we could use one of his machines.'

Greg grinned at her. 'Nice try, Molly.'

She stared at him, all wide-eyed innocence.

'Well done,' he said, taking the package from her. 'You've guessed that's what's in here. And of course you're dying to know what's so secret that your husband had to keep it hidden away. But he told you to hand it straight over to me, didn't he?'

She frowned at him and made a little-girl face, pouting. 'I thought we were friends, working together. Why can't I be allowed to see it?'

'I don't know,' said Greg. 'But I'm sure your husband has a good reason for hiding it. Perhaps he thought it wouldn't be safe for you to know.'

'I'll bet it's something to do with that bastard Brown!' she said.

340

'Yes, it is, but as I haven't seen it yet I can't say any more than that, I'm afraid. Sorry.'

She shrugged, then looked up at him with a smug little smile, 'Anyway, Cyril's got no idea how you found him. He doesn't know I've been helping you, does he?'

'No.'

'That's one up to me, then.' She laughed at herself and gave her chest a pat. 'And what about that letter you got? Was it him that sent it?'

'Yes, it was.'

She put her hand on his sleeve. 'But I found him for you anyway.'

'Right,' said Greg. He did not tell her that Cyril would almost certainly have moved on by now, and as for the letter, there was no way he was going to say anything more to her about the houseboat. Cyril Ritter had demonstrated that he did not have total confidence in his wife's discretion, and, casting his memory back to their first meeting when she had dodged out to meet him in the bookshop, Greg could easily see why.

He gently disengaged her hand.

'I must go,' he said. He brandished the package. 'Thanks for this. I'll be in touch.'

When he got back to the café, Ray was waiting in his den.

Greg handed the jiffy bag to him and sat down.

Ray used a sharp knife to open it. He took out the DVD, put it in the player and pressed play.

A still picture appeared on the screen together with the date and time, 4.13.2007, 18.17.43.

'Last Friday evening,' said Ray. 'Digital camera, I reckon. Pretty clear image, isn't it?'

Ritter's voice in a flat monotone said, 'Quay Rocks guest house, Upton Road, Shanklin. Subject has been followed here directly from Ryde police station and has just entered the building.'

The time changed to 18.23.26 as a large, white van drew to a halt in front of the guest house.

Ritter said, 'Vauxhall Movano van, HG56 SDD, registered owner, Spencer Davis of 16 Elfin Lane, Seastone.'

The door on the van's passenger side opened and a big, fair-haired man got out. As he walked to the rear of the vehicle, Ritter said, 'Ronald Johnson of Reginald Road, Eastney, Portsmouth.'

Johnson opened the doors and another large man stepped out. Ritter said, 'Lee Brewster, current address unkown, lately of Wormword Scrubs.'

Brewster was followed by several young black men.

Greg said, 'Illegals?'

Ray said, 'Looks like it. Six of them.'

They watched Johnson and Brewster usher the six black men around the other side of the van and out of sight, but the camera zoomed in and their heads could just be seen beyond the van as they passed along a passageway to the side of the guest house. The white van moved away and the picture froze again until the time showed 19.03.33, when a silver Toyota with tinted windows arrived and stopped where the van had stood.

Nobody left the Toyota but the camera continued recording, zooming in to the car at first but the tinted windows did not permit a view of the occupants. The time was seen to be passing on the screen and at just after 19.07 a man came out of the guest house and approached the car.

Ritter said, 'Subject has left the building and is approaching a silver Toyota, registration number believed to be HK 56 XKY and registered to Edwin Davis of The Post Office Stores, Seastone.'

Ray leaned forward. 'That's Colin Cresswell,' he said 'The DI Peter Grant told about the illegals. Looks as though there is a connection.'

Greg said, 'But what's Ritter doing snooping on him?'

'Very curious,' said Ray.

The passenger window of the car was lowered as Cresswell came up to it. The camera immediately zoomed in again and Ritter said, 'The passenger in the front seat of the Toyota is identified as Sir Robert Clarmont Brown, formerly of Clarmont House, Seastone.'

Cresswell stood by the side of the Toyota. He appeared to be remonstrating with Clarmont Brown. Then he stood back, spread his hands downwards and outwards and turned away, shoving both hands in his coat pockets and staring past the rear of the car. He was clearly very unhappy.

Clarmont Brown's arm came out of the window. There was an envelope in his hand and he tapped it gently against the side of the car.

Eventually Cresswell turned around and said something.

Clarmont Brown raised his arm and held up the envelope. Cresswell bent down to take it.

The camera focussed on the envelope as Cresswell moved away from the car to stand on the pavement in front of the guest house. He tore the envelope open. It contained banknotes and Cresswell counted them slowly and carefully. Then he waved the notes at Clarmont Brown and turned away, stuffing them in his pocket as he strode off.

Clarmont Brown got out of the Toyota and hurried after him. He was wearing the same light brown safari suit that Greg had seen him in at Dan's on the following Sunday.

The two men stood arguing forcefully.

Meanwhile, the Toyota's driver got out of the car and Ritter's voice announced, 'The driver of the Toyota is confirmed as Edwin Davis of The Post Office Stores, Seastone.'

Teddy was standing back, waiting, between the two men and the Toyota. After several minutes Clarmont Brown put a hand on Cresswell's shoulder and appeared to be conceding a point. He offered Cresswell his hand and they shook, then they each turned away, raising a hand in farewell.

The camera traversed between the two of them as they drew apart until Clarmont Brown and Teddy got back into the Toyota, then it followed Cresswell to a car parked further down the road.

As Cresswell drove off, Ritter said, 'It is unsafe to follow Subject at the present time,' and the camera returned to the Toyota.

Clarmont Brown and Teddy both got out of the car again and went around the side of the guest house, following the route that Johnson, Brewster and the black men had taken earlier.

Ritter said, 'The intention will be to keep the Toyota under observation for as long as necessary.' The time was now showing 19.18 and the picture froze again.

At 19.26 Clarmont Brown and Teddy returned to the car. Teddy did a three-point turn and the camera followed its departure back in the direction it had arrived from. The screen went blank and when a picture came back it was showing the rear of the Toyota parked at the kerbside. Teddy was getting into it. The time was 19.47. Ritter said, 'The location is number twenty, Pier Road, Seastone, the residence of Mr and Mrs Jeremy Marlow. Clarmont Brown has entered. He has been followed here directly from Quay

343

Rocks guest house, Shanklin. End of session.'

Ray said, 'Well, that was very interesting. No good on its own in a court of law, of course, but it could be useful evidence of collusion.' He got up to remove the DVD. 'We don't need to run it again, do we?'

'No,' said Greg. 'What puzzles me, though, is why Ritter was following Cresswell in the first place. Who would want to employ a private investigator to follow a CID inspector?'

'Yes, that's peculiar all right. But he made a pretty good job of it, didn't he? Wonder where he had hidden himself?' Ray stood up and removed the DVD. 'You'll be going back to Dan's for dinner, I suppose?'

'I hadn't really thought,' said Greg. 'Dan said he'll be working late, so we left it vague.'

'Stop and eat with us, then.' Without waiting for an answer, he went to the door of his den and called downstairs.

Sophie's voice came from some distance away, 'What is it?'

'Greg's staying for dinner.'

She came to the foot of the stairs. 'Chicken and mushroom pie or plaice and chips, Greg?'

'Oh, pie, please!'

'Be about half an hour.'

'Thanks.'

Ray came back in and sat himself down again. He said, 'Ritter must have been following Cresswell because his client was aware of the connection with the illegals and wanted proof. Well, he got it. But, you know what I think?' He leaned forward. 'I reckon Ritter gave the original to his client and what we've just seen is a copy he made to give him some bargaining power over Clarmont Brown.' He looked at Greg expectantly.

Greg nodded in agreement. 'And then Johnson came after him and he found himself in trouble, but managed to get away. I wonder how he did that? He doesn't look much, does he, but he's pretty resourceful. Molly said he could look after himself.'

'Yes,' said Ray, 'And now he's using us while he's lying low himself. But we don't need to concern ourselves with him. Or Cresswell, for that matter. No, what we've got to do is make good use of what can be implied from what we saw on the DVD.'

Greg said, 'How do you mean, implied?'

'See, we know he has always been very careful to cover his

tracks in the past, but now here he is handing over money to a police officer in broad daylight. Why? I mean, Teddy was in the car, for heaven's sake, he must have seen it! And we know how steady Teddy is, don't we?'

'Perhaps Cresswell has been leaning on him.'

'No, it's more than that.' Ray sounded impatient. 'See, right from the start, when I first went to see Ritter on Monday, there's been what I reckon is panicky reaction.' He ticked off his fingers, one by one, as he continued. 'Number one, they beat me up. Two, they sent a couple of goons to Dan's to put you off, then they kidnapped Ritter, then they went after you again at Parkhurst Forest, and now they've bumped off Kilroy, apparently to stop him talking to you.' he paused. 'I reckon Sir Bob's losing control. Elli's right. What did she tell you? He's scared stiff something will link him back to Nigel Heapes because any whiff of scandal will cost him his chance of a peerage.'

'So what are you suggesting we should do?'

Ray leaned back in his chair again. 'Well, first of all it won't hurt if we remind ourselves what we're trying to do here. For my part it's pretty clear,' he reached out and picked up one of the binders of his Vanderling Casefile. 'What I want is to write on the last page of this file, "Case Completed". As I've said before, it's been niggling at me for years. I know it's no longer any of my business, I freely admit that, but now that they're reopening the original file, I want us to do what we can, whenever we can, to move things along and Ritter's DVD has given us a chance.' He paused. 'But what about you? I got you involved because I thought you'd want to put the record straight over the blame for Nigel's death. Now, all the rest of it - GLH, illegal immigrants, money laundering and so on, must have changed the focus a bit for you.'

Greg smiled ruefully. 'I can't say I had any clear picture of what we were trying to do when I agreed to help. I mean, you and all my friends expected me to show a keen interest in finding out who killed Nigel. But in fact I realised I'd got my life into a rut and this was a way of doing something interesting and, well, worthwhile I suppose. But I was soon made to feel personally involved, so like you, I won't be happy until everyone concerned has been arrested and charged. And I now know I owe Clarmont Brown something, so if we find out it was him who shot Nigel so much the better.'

'Good, so we are on the same track.' He sat forward in his chair. 'Now then, in my experience, quite often it's not just clever detection work, or the painstaking collection of bits of evidence that catches the villains - it's the mistakes they make themselves. Take this DVD for a start. Cresswell and Sir Bob are in cahoots, so they should never have let themselves be seen together anywhere in public, should they, but they did and got caught on camera. We can use that and maybe nudge them into making more mistakes.'

'What do you have in mind?'

'For a start, when the coppers have been to see Teddy, he'll realise we already knew about Kilroy's body on his houseboat, so while he's still flapping about that, we'll ask him about his son Spencer and Johnson and Clarmont Brown and the black men in that guest house in Shanklin. Ten to one he'll crack and let something out.'

'Or he'll go running to Sir Bob,' said Greg.

Ray shrugged. 'Either way we'll be forcing the issue. And, when Tracey Nash gets around to returning my call, we'll show her this DVD. In private. She needn't know where it came from. And we must get Peter Grant to talk to her too, if we can. Let her take care of Cresswell.' He smiled. 'Should be interesting.'

'Will she be on the Kilroy case, do you think?' said Greg.

'Yes, probably, and talking of which, it might be an idea to switch your mobile off unless you want to talk to the cops tonight.'

'I can always ignore them. And they know Dan's landline number anyway. Which reminds me, I'd better warn him it might be bugged.'

Ray stood up. 'I'd better see if Sophie needs a hand. I'll leave you to it.' He went to the top of the stairs. 'Come on down when you're ready.'

Greg rang Dan at the Yacht Club and told him about the probable bug on his phone.

Dan was unconcerned. 'I won't be home tonight anyway,' he said. 'I'm going straight to Lucy's from here and then we'll just call in first thing in the morning for me to pack before we set off for the Med. No doubt you'll arrange to get it sorted out while I'm away?'

'Yes, of course. See you in the morning then.'

Greg rang off and checked his watch before putting his phone away. It was too early to ring Zillah.

He went downstairs and found Sophie in their private dining room, setting the table for dinner. Ray was in the empty café, putting the closed sign on the door. Greg helped him clear the tables and stack the chairs on them in readiness for the cleaner in the morning. By the time they had finished, Sophie was about to serve their meal.

As they ate, Ray summarised for Sophie what they had learned that day.

When he had brought her up-to-date, she said, 'I've known Bob Clarmont Brown a long time and one thing about him is he's always hated being beaten. At anything. He's always got to be best. What you need is to find some way to really provoke him. And I think you're right about Teddy Davis. He is a weak link and it would be worth pushing him a bit. Funny, his dad and his son are both quite tough, but it seems to have by-passed Teddy.'

After dinner, Greg stayed for a while chatting with Ray and Sophie, but when Ray began to show that he was feeling the effects of the previous night's activities, Greg thanked them for their hospitality yet again and made his way back to Dan's house.

As a precaution, he parked his car some distance away and watched carefully before approaching the house on foot, but there was no indication that anybody had been there since he'd left in the morning.

As soon as he got inside he went straight to Dan's phone to erase Kilroy's messages. There was one more message, however. Detective Sergeant Tracey Nash, wanted him to ring her at Ryde police station in the morning.

Just before getting ready for bed he rang Zillah to tell her he would not in fact be home for the weekend. As soon as she answered he asked how she was and then enquired about Rocky. She laughed and said he had now a much better sense of priorities at the end of the day than he'd had at its beginning. They gave each other a brief account of their day, then she told him he should get a good night's sleep and they said goodnight.

He felt pleasantly tired as he stretched out in bed, thinking of what Sophie had said about Clarmont Brown and an idea came into his head as he was drifting into sleep.

It seemed that he had just dozed off when his mobile phone rang. He glanced at his watch. It was five minutes to midnight.

He groped for the phone and said 'Hello?'

There was a brief silence, then he heard a deep breath and a man's voice, 'Is that Greg?'

'Yes.'

'It's Teddy here, Teddy Davis.'

'Hello Teddy. What's wrong?'

'I know why you were asking about my houseboat. I've had the coppers here all evening.'

Teddy sounded as though he'd had a lot to drink.

Greg said, 'Oh yes?'

'Yeah. They've just left. You knew about it, didn't you? The dead bloke.'

Greg ignored the question. 'So who was it who came to see you? Your friend Detective Inspector Colin Cresswell, was it?'

'Eh?'

'We know you are well acquainted with him, Teddy.'

'How do you mean?'

'Did he tell you to ring me?'

'No he didn't. And when I told him you and Ray Tindall were in here earlier asking about the houseboat and Ronnie Johnson, he was not happy.'

'No, I don't suppose he was,' said Greg. 'But what are you ringing me for at this time of night, then? What do you want?'

'Um ... I've been thinking about what you said and I reckon we ought to have a chat.'

'It's a bit late, Teddy. Can't it wait until the morning?'

'No. Listen, you want to know about Nigel, right? Why he copped it?'

'You know we do,' said Greg.

'How much do you actually know?' said Teddy.

Greg had had a long day and he was too tired to bicker on the phone with Teddy. He said, 'Listen, Teddy, it's late and I'm too tired to play silly buggers. If you really want to help, ring me in the morning and we'll make arrangements to meet somewhere private. Okay?'

Greg switched his phone off and yawned. He settled back onto the pillow thinking he'd had quite enough of Friday. He closed his eyes for a moment. When he opened them again, it was Saturday morning.

FIFTYFIVE

Saturday morning

Greg was washing up his breakfast plates when Dan let himself into the kitchen, saying, 'Here he is. I told you he was domesticated. Morning, Greg. This is Lucy.'

Greg turned to the doorway and saw a tall, slim brunette. Her face was lightly sun-tanned, a little longer than the perfect oval, with wide-set brown eyes, a small cleft in her chin, above a long, smooth neck. Her hair was shoulder length and wavy. Dimples showed as she smiled, 'Hello Greg.' She came towards him and held out her hand.

Greg hurriedly wiped his on the tea towel before taking it.

'Hello Lucy.'

They stood smiling at each other. Then Dan said, 'We'll let you get on. We haven't got a lot of time so we'd better go straight up and pack.'

Lucy raised her eyebrows and pouted her lips in mock dismay, then shrugged as Dan ushered her out of the room.

Dan said, 'Put the kettle on, will you, and we'll have a cup of coffee with you before we go.'

Greg smiled to himself as he tidied the kitchen, thinking that Dan seemed unusually self-conscious about introducing him to the new lady in his life. But it was true that they did have very little time this morning to get properly acquainted. She was certainly very attractive. Lovely face, and he'd admired the roll-and-sway of her walk as she crossed the room. He wondered wistfully what Suzy would have made of her.

He had coffee ready for them when they returned.

Dan lugged a couple of holdalls to the kitchen door. 'All ready to go,' he said, plonking himself down at the kitchen table. Lucy sat demurely opposite him.

Greg poured coffee and brought cups to them, then fetched one for himself.

As he joined them, Lucy said, 'Greg, before we go, there's something Dan has to tell you.'

She looked expectantly across the table. Dan avoided her gaze. He looked down at his his coffee cup, picked it up and sipped.

Then he put it down and stared at it for a long moment before taking a deep breath and letting it out in a sigh.

'It's about Bob Clarmont Brown,' he said. 'You remember he was here when you came back from Seastone last Sunday?'

'Yes, I thought you'd been having a row or something, but you didn't want to talk about it.'

'No, I didn't. But I should have done.' Dan laughed humourlessly. 'I realised that after what you told me over lunch yesterday.'

'Oh, yes?'

'He's been badgering me for ages to sell him the Yacht Club, but there's no way I'd want to do that. Then on Sunday he turned up out of the blue, saying he had to have at least a half-share in the marina development. He was perfectly happy to pay a good price, money was not a problem. I told him I was definitely not selling, but he'd obviously expected that and he'd come prepared. He said he'd rather avoid unpleasantness if he could, but … ' He looked up at Greg. 'If I valued my father's good name, it would be in my best interest to co-operate.'

Greg's heart gave a lurch. He thought he could guess what was coming, but he had to ask. 'What did he mean by that?'

Dan stood up abruptly and went and stood with his back to them, gazing out of the window. 'He showed me a photograph. It was an old polaroid. The colours were a bit faded, but it quite clearly showed Dad, stark naked and obviously aroused. He was fondling a little girl, also naked. It made me feel sick.'

It was confirmation of what Molly had told Greg and he did not know what to say. He knew what a shock it must have been to Dan and wished he'd been able to comfort him at the time. But of course, he himself hadn't known that about Roddy then.

Lucy was watching him. When he remained silent, she said, 'This has not come as a surprise to you, has it, Greg, this thing about Dan's father?'

Dan turned his head to look at him.

Greg said, 'It was certainly a surprise, and a shock, when I first heard of it a few days ago. I was hoping you'd never need to know, Dan. I'm very sorry.'

Dan said, 'But what about my mother, Greg? You knew her as well as anybody did. She couldn't have known, surely?'

'No. Your mother never showed the slightest sign that she had any idea,' said Greg.

Dan shook his head in bafflement. 'Christ! He must have been bloody mad!'

'But I do remember her saying some years ago,' said Greg, 'That Roddy had told her once he had done something very wrong and he hoped she would be able to forgive him if she ever found out. Perhaps that was it.'

Dan came back to the table and sat. Lucy reached across the table and took his hand in hers.

He said, 'Clarmont Brown told me he had more pictures like that one. He said they'd come from Nigel Heapes, and he had proof that Roddy had killed Nigel to stop him blackmailing him.'

Greg almost laughed aloud. That's ridiculous!' he said. 'So what did you say to him?'

'I didn't have to say anything to him because you arrived at that point and he left.'

'Right. But has he contacted you since about it?'

'No, not yet, But I've thought about it since and when he does I'll tell him he can go to hell.'

'Good. That's just what I was going to say. Roddy's been gone over ten years, and in any case there's no way anyone can prove he shot Nigel. On the other hand, I can prove that Clarmont Brown himself commissioned those photos, because it was the person who took them who told me about them. But he need not know that.'

Dan picked up his coffee cup again. He said, 'I've had a week to take it in, and to be honest, I feel more disgusted with Clarmont Brown now than with Dad, although, God knows it's hard to accept that your father was a paedophile. Anyway, I'm glad I've told you. Lucy said you'd agree I should call his bluff.'

Lucy said, 'It shows what a pathetic character Clarmont Brown must be though, don't you agree, Greg? All those businesses, all the money he must have and yet he has to stoop so low.'

Greg was agreeing with her when his mobile rang on the kitchen windowsill. He got up and crossed the room to answer it.

A woman's voice said, 'Mr Gregory?'

'Speaking.'

'Good morning. Detective Sergeant Nash here, sir. We met last Saturday, if you remember, at Mr Vanderling's house in Bembridge.'

'Yes. Good morning, Sergeant,' he said, brightly. He waved apologetically to the others and went out into the dining room. 'I got your message. Sorry, I haven't had time to get back to you yet. Busy morning, Mr Vanderling's just off on holiday.'

'I'll be as brief as I can then, sir. Firstly, in case you're wondering how I got the number of your mobile, I obtained it from Mrs Grace Kilroy.'

'Who? Oh, yes, that's right, I left it with her, didn't I? Mr Kilroy wanted to speak to me about something apparently, but he wasn't at home yesterday morning when I rang.'

'Would that be Mr Raymond Kilroy, sir?'

Greg said, 'Yes, that's what he said his name was.'

'You don't know Mr Kilroy well then, sir?'

'Don't know him at all, Sergeant. But Mr Vanderling has been away and I've been checking his phone for messages when I come in at night. On Thursday, Mr Kilroy had left a phone number for me to ring but I was rather late so I left it until the morning.'

'Did Mr Kilroy say what he wanted to talk to you about?'

'Well, actually he said he was given my name as somebody who was interested in knowing who killed Nigel Heapes.'

'I see. And is that all he said?'

'Well, yes, apart from leaving his phone number. I haven't heard from him yet, though.'

There was a slight pause. Then she said, in a much more friendly tone of voice, 'I've just had an interesting conversation with Ray Tindall and we agreed it would be helpful if we could all get together this morning at his place. The sooner the better, really. Would that be all right with you?'

'Yes, certainly. I was going to see him this morning anyway. I could be there by nine thirty?'

'Good. I'll see you there then, sir.' She rang off.

Dan and Lucy were ready to leave and waiting to say goodbye. Greg was glad that Dan had not had time to bring up the subject of the anonymous message. The fewer people who knew he had been to the houseboat, the better. He went out with them to the Range Rover.

Dan said. 'By the time we come back I expect you will have sorted it all out and we can spend a few quiet days together. What do you think?'

'Yes, if all's well. That'll be good.'

'Great. I want Lucy to get to know you properly. We'll see you in a fortnight, then.'

Greg wished them a happy holiday, relieved as he watched them drive off, that Dan was not showing too close an interest in the investigations.

He went back indoors, washed up the coffee things and collected his coat and car keys. Then he locked the house and had just got into his car to go to Seastone when his phone rang again.

It was Teddy Davis.

'What is it, Teddy?'

'You said to ring you this morning.'

'Yes, if you're really serious about helping, that is.'

'Yes, I am. I'm not messing about, Greg. Honest. I really do want to help. But you said we could meet somewhere private. I mean, I don't want to end up like Kilroy. Know what I mean?'

'Of course. Alright, let me think.' Greg thought rapidly. Ray believed Teddy could help them so if Teddy was willing to meet them, it was too good a chance to miss. But where in the village could they talk to him and be sure not to be seen? The café was out, as was the Yacht Club. Pete wouldn't welcome them at his house. Elli? Yes, there was a possibility.

'How about the Quarterdeck Club, Teddy? If I arrange for a private room?'

Teddy hesitated. 'I dunno,' he said.

'There won't be anybody there during the day, will there?' said Greg. 'Look, I'm going to be busy for most of the morning, but what about, say, eleven o'clock? Would that be alright?'

'Well, alright. I suppose I could say I was calling in about the account if anyone asked.'

'Yes, good idea. I'll see you there then.'

Then he rang Clarmont House, hoping Elli would be there. She was.

'Greg here, Elli,' he said, 'And I need you to help, urgently, if you will.'

'Yes, of course, Greg. What is it?'

'Is there somewhere in the Quarterdeck Club we can use as a temporary interview room?'

'Oh. When?'

'Today. This morning.'

She laughed, 'Yes, you did say urgently. Let me see. The baccarat room will not be in use until this evening. It has tables and chairs and can be made quite private. Would that do?'

'Yes, I'm sure it will. We'd like to use it from eleven o'clock if possible.'

'Gosh, well, yes, I had better go and make arrangements, then.'

Greg said, 'Thanks. I'll have Ray Tindall with me, I expect. Can you let us in a bit before eleven, and, um, make yourself scarce so that our visitor doesn't see you?'

She laughed. 'Cloak and dagger stuff, is it? But yes, of course. And I have something for you, too. I was intending to call you this morning, to tell you that my friend in Southampton Cockaigne has excelled herself. She has sent me a complete copy of all last year's transactions. I'll bring it with me.'

'That's great! See you later then, and thanks again, Elli.'

Greg rang Ray next and left a message, confirming that he was on his way.

FIFTYSIX

Saturday morning

It was one minute before half-past nine when Greg walked across to the café from the Yacht Club car park.

Sophie saw him coming and opened the door for him. She removed the "Closed" sign and left the door open. It was a fine, sunny morning.

'They're upstairs waiting for you,' she said. 'D'you want a cup of coffee to take up with you?"

'No thanks. Sergeant Nash is already here then, is she?'

'Came about ten minutes ago.'

'Damn. I wanted a quick word with Ray before she got here. Could you get him to come down for a minute? Say you need his help or something? Don't say I'm here, though.'

Sophie smiled. 'Secrets from the CID, eh?'

She went out of the café and Greg heard her call to Ray.

When Ray came in a moment or two later, Greg was sitting at a table in the corner. Ray came and sat opposite him. He nodded his approval as Greg told him about the arrangement to see Teddy at the Quarterdeck Club.

'Elli says she has the Cockaigne accounts, too,' Greg added.

'Hey, that's good work! Did she say what it shows?'

'No, but she wouldn't have mentioned it if it was no use.'

'No, I suppose not.'

Greg said, 'I don't think Sergeant Nash needs to know any of this yet though, do you?'

'No, not yet. Let's see what we can get out of Teddy first.' Ray looked thoughtfully at Greg. 'We might need her co-operation afterwards though, so we ought to get her on our side if we can. See, she might come across as a bit stodgy, but she's no fool and she gets results.'

'Okay. But when she rang me, she said she'd just had an interesting conversation with you. What was that all about?'

'She was returning my call. See, obviously she knows I'm interested in connecting the Heapes case to the old Vanderling File, and I told her I had information about illegal immigrants and GLH. She said she'd call in and see me about it. Then she asked me if I knew you at all. I said you were helping me follow up some leads and she said she'd spoken to you last week and wanted another word with you. I suggested perhaps we could get together here and she agreed.'

'Did she tell you it was Kilroy she wanted to talk to me about?'

'No, but I guessed that's what it would be. When she arrived just now though, all she said was she'd spoken to you and you said you'd be here at half past nine. Didn't mention Kilroy. But then, she wouldn't expect me to know anything about that, would she? What did you tell her?'

'What we agreed - Kilroy said he'd been told I was interested in Nigel's death and he left a number for me to ring.'

'Good. Anyway, I've just been telling her about what Peter Grant told you. She wondered if you could get him to join us, sort of informally, and repeat it to her. What do you think?'

'I could ask him, but he'll want a guarantee anything he says won't get back to him.'

'That goes without saying, but he did say he wanted to help. Give him a ring, will you?'

'I haven't got his number. He'll be in the book I suppose?'

'Probably.' Ray stood up. 'Come on through and let's have a look.'

They found Peter Grant's home number.

Ray said, 'Come on up when you've finished.'

Greg rang and Pete answered immediately. He was understandably reluctant at first to talk to another member of the police, but Greg assured him that both Ray Tindall and himself were convinced it was the best thing to do.

'Ray has worked with Detective Sergeant Nash,' he said, 'And he believes she is absolutely straight and the right person to deal with that rotten bastard you spoke to. And what you say will be off the record. There won't be any notes taken and you won't have to sign anything. Look, just come into the café and Sophie Tindall will invite you into her living room and we'll take it from there. What do you say?'

Greg heard him take a deep breath.

'Yes, alright then,' he said. 'It's got to be sorted out somehow, hasn't it? I just don't want anything getting back to them that puts Jonty at risk, that's all.'

'Sure. We understand that, Pete. See you in a minute then.'

Greg rang off and went to ask Sophie to look out for Pete and bring him to join them when he arrived.

Upstairs, Ray had positioned Tracey Nash in front of the screen. He was sitting to her left and Greg took the vacant chair Ray had set for him on her other side.

He said, 'Peter Grant has agreed to come and tell you what happened after he spoke to your Inspector Cresswell, Sergeant. He'll be along shortly.'

She smiled at him. 'Thankyou,' she said. 'Can we get on now, Ray?'

Ray started the DVD.

Greg watched Tracey Nash and was intrigued at her reaction as the picture of the guest house appeared on the screen. She stiffened and a red flush gradually spread from her neck to cover her face, then slowly faded, leaving her looking very pale, with a thin film of perspiration on her brow.

They watched in silence to the end. Then she said, 'Very interesting. Would you mind telling me how this came into your possession?'

Ray looked at Greg. Greg shrugged. 'It was given to us by somebody who knows we are interested in finding out who killed Nigel Heapes, Sergeant,' he said.

Tracey looked at him solemnly. 'Name?' she said.

Ray removed the DVD from the machine. He said, 'Cyril Ritter. He's a private investigator.'

Tracey frowned. 'Yes, I know who he is. He had no right.' She looked from one to the other of them, still frowning. Then she said, almost as if talking to herself. 'This is very awkward. He must have made a copy. I was a fool to trust him.'

Ray stared at her in amazement. He said, 'Was it you then, Tracey? It was, wasn't it! You commissioned him to spy on your own guvnor. You're taking a hell of a risk, aren't you?'

Tracey gave a short, barking laugh. 'How much did you pay him for it?'

'He didn't want to be paid,' said Greg. 'He said he made the DVD as a kind of insurance. He just wanted to make sure it was used.'

Tracey gave him a puzzled look. 'Insurance?' she said. 'And why would he give it to you? I don't get it.'

Ray said, 'It's not your guvnor he's worried about, Tracey.

357

It's the people your guvnor's involved with. For a start he's scared of Ron Johnson, and he's got a long-standing grudge against Clarmont Brown.'

She thought about that for a long moment. Then she said slowly, 'Sir Robert Clarmont Brown is in your old Vanderling file, I know, but what about Ronald Johnson? Is he in it, too?'

'He is a recent addition,' said Ray.

'I see. And why would Cyril Ritter be afraid of him?'

Greg said, 'As you know Ray went to see Mr Ritter on Monday and that evening he was beaten up. I went to see him on Tuesday afternoon and his wife, Molly, rang me the next morning to say he'd gone missing. I traced him to the Esplanade Hotel where their cctv showed him either drunk or drugged and being hustled into a car by Johnson. He must have got away somehow because later Molly gave me a phone number where I managed to speak to him. That was when he arranged for us to get that DVD.'

She pushed her chair back and turned towards Greg.

'You know Ronald Johnson then, do you, Mr Gregory?'

'I first came across him on Tuesday evening when he broke into Dan Vanderling's house with another man and threatened me about continuing to enquire into Nigel's death.'

She raised her eyebrows, and that made her pale blue eyes look even more protuberant.

'Broke into Mr Vanderling's house? And threatened you? Why have you not reported this, Mr Gregory?'

'They did no damage and they left peacefully,' he said.

She continued to stare at him for a while, then she said, 'From what we know of Ronald Johnson, he does not usually make idle threats. You must have been very persuasive.'

Greg shrugged.

After giving him another long stare, Tracey sat back in her chair, linked her hands across her broad waistline and turned to face Ray. 'It seems to me that you must have been digging quite deeply into this matter, Ray. But you of all people know what we think about civilians poking about in matters which are best left to us.'

'Yes, ordinary, every day civilians. Not experts like us, though,' he said with a broad smile.

'But what makes you think you'd know more about it than the police?'

Greg said, 'Well, we've no way of telling what the police do know. Not from the lack of interest you appear to be taking in Nigel or the Vanderling File, anyway.'

'And,' added Ray, 'Investigating crimes is one of the things I've been trained to do.'

'OK, I take your point, but officially I'm bound to tell you to leave it alone, aren't I? Just be careful, that's all. Even ex-policemen and ex-Special Servicemen don't live for ever, you know.'

'Is that right? Well, thanks for letting us know,' said Ray. 'It won't be such a nasty surprise to us now when we don't, will it, Greg?'

'In the meantime,' said Tracey, 'I'd like to have a good look at your Vanderling File.'

'You're more than welcome. But I don't want you to take it away. We'll go through together, if you like.'

There was a knock on the door, and Sophie opened it, saying, 'Peter Grant is downstairs in the sitting room. Shall I send him up?'

Ray looked at Tracey.

'Yes, please,' she said.

A minute or so later, Pete came in looking very uncertain. Greg introduced him to Tracey while Ray went out to fetch a chair for him.

Tracey soon put Pete at ease and he went through the story that he had told Greg on Thursday evening. Ray and Greg remained quiet until he had finished.

Tracey thanked him. She warned him that if the decision was made to investigate GLH, it was probable that he would be investigated as well, and he would be expected to co-operate fully with the police at that time. The matter might well eventually involve the arrest of members of GLH and at the very least he should expect to be called upon to give evidence in court.

Pete accepted this.

'If that's all then, we won't keep you any longer, Mr Grant,' she said. 'But please bear in mind that I may want to speak to you again fairly soon, and it will be in an official capacity.'

Pete stood up looking relieved. Greg escorted him back downstairs.

When they reached Ray's sitting room, Pete said, 'There's

one other thing. Greg. I don't know if it means anything, but last Friday morning, I had a phone call from Graham Wilson. He told me Freddy Davis had to come home urgently and he said Teddy was away for a few days so would I go and collect him from Gatwick.'

Greg said, 'On Friday? Teddy wasn't far away. He was in Shanklin chauffeuring Clarmont Brown around.'

'Well, I wouldn't know. When I picked Freddy up he wanted me to take him straight to his bank in Ryde because he had to get something from his safe deposit. When we got there he said he'd only be a couple of minutes so I waited outside on a double-yellow. Sure enough he was out in no time at all. He had two small brown paper parcels with him. Then I drove him to Teddy's place, but, on Saturday afternoon, Teddy told me he'd gone back to Spain, so I thought if he came home just for that it must have been important.'

'Yes, I see. You think the packages were what was in his safe deposit.'

'Well, seems likely, eh?'

'How big were they?'

'One was a biggish envelope and the other was about the size of a video cassette. In fact, he dropped it on the floor of the car as he got out and I picked it up for him. That's what it felt like, too.'

'Hmmn ... Well, that could be interesting. Thanks.'

'Well, I just thought you ought to know.' Pete went through into the café and as he was leaving he said, 'Do you think Sergeant Nash will get anywhere with what I told her?'

'Ray seems to think quite highly of her. I reckon she'll give it her best shot.'

Pete said, 'Let's hope so anyway. See you around, then.'

'Okay. And thanks for coming, Pete.'

Back in Ray's den Tracey looked up as Greg came in.

She said, 'Mr Grant's account of the attack on him is different from the version I heard.'

'You already knew about it?' said Greg.

She turned to Ray. 'You remember I told you I had to pass one of my sources over to the mainland?'

'Yes.'

'One of the things he reported was one of GLH's drivers having a fight with Mr Grant. The driver's name was Spencer Davis.

And the informant's name,' she added, looking hard at Greg, 'Was Raymond Kilroy.'

Greg look of surprise was not entirely false.

'That's the fellow you rang me about, who wanted to get in touch with me,' he said.

'That's right.'

'And he's a police informer, is he?'

'Let's just say he has been willing to pass bits of information to the police.'

Greg nodded. 'For a price, I imagine.' He pretended to consider for a moment. 'He said he'd heard I was interested in finding out who killed Nigel Heapes. Do you think he might genuinely have information about the Heapes killing?'

'Who knows?' She leaned forward in her chair, maintaining eye-contact with Greg. 'But I was wondering, how did he know you would be at Mr Vanderling's house?'

Ray said, 'Perhaps there's a connection with those two who broke in on Tuesday.'

'Yes, that's a point,' said Greg, taking his cue from Ray. 'And talking of connections, Sergeant, you never did say why you rang me about him.'

'No, I didn't, did I.' She sat back and looked from one to the other. 'Raymond Kilroy was found dead yesterday afternoon. He'd been murdered.'

Greg said, 'Ah. And when, um, Mrs Kilroy gave you my mobile number you thought maybe I might know something about it.' He nodded as if in understanding. 'Yes, I can see where you're coming from.'

'Who's heading the investigation, Tracey?' asked Ray.

'DI Cresswell. He's handed the Nigel Heapes case over to me. He reckons at the inquest next week the verdict will allow us to tie up the loose ends and close the file. Well, we'll see about that, won't we.'

FIFTYSEVEN

The Quarterdeck Club's main entrance was unlocked and Greg and Ray let themselves in.

It was quiet except for the sound of a vacuum cleaner somewhere on the ground floor. They went in through the reception area and along the corridor and took the lift to Elli's office.

She was seated at her desk and smiled a greeting as they entered. She indicated one of the cctv screens showing a view of a room containing two large oval tables with chairs set around them.

'I thought the baccarat room would be the most suitable,' she said. 'It's lockable if you should need privacy.'

'Sounds good,' said Ray. He was admiring the comprehensive display.

'Fine,' said Elli. 'So what's the plan of action?'

Greg said, 'Teddy Davis says he has something to tell us and I've asked him to come here at eleven o'clock.' He checked his watch. 'It's just after a quarter to now. Ray's the experienced interviewer and he knows how people like Teddy should be handled, so we thought it would be best if he meets Teddy at the front door and takes him along to the room. You and I can watch and take notes from up here, if that's alright?'

'Yes, of course,' said Elli. 'But it can all be recorded if you like, to save taking notes.'

Ray was still studying the screens. 'Your cameras record everything then, do they?'

'Yes,' she said. 'It all goes through a central processor.' She indicated a blank screen in the centre of the display. 'I can replay the last twentyfour hours on that screen from any camera or in fact from up to any four cameras simultaneously. When Bob bought the club from the Wilsons he updated their old system with what was then state-of-the-art equipment. I'm sure he had his reasons. I have no reason to bother as a rule,' She smiled at Greg. 'But I confess that after we met on Wednesday evening I did replay your conversation with Peter in the old saloon, just in case there was something I needed to be careful about when you came to lunch the next day.'

'Playing safe,' said Ray.

'In my position I have to.'

She opened a drawer in her desk, took out a CD and brandished it. 'Now, this is very interesting. It contains a copy of the last set of audited annual accounts for Southampton Cockaigne Club on which tax returns to HM Revenue and Customs were based. It also contains complete details with weekly summaries of all transactions that actually went through the Southampton site for that period. Believe me, you don't have to be an accounting genius to see the discrepancies. You can have this. I've made my own copy.'

Ray was nearest and he took it from her. 'Thanks. We can certainly make use of it.'

'Good.' She stood up. 'Let me show you how to get to the baccarat room from the main entrance. And we can pick up the key on the way if you think you may need it '

'Might be useful,' said Ray.

They all went down in the lift and Elli gave Ray, who had not been inside the club before, a brief explanation of the layout. Then she and Greg returned to her office, leaving Ray in the reception area to wait for Teddy.

They watched the screens in silence for a few minutes. Teddy was late but eventually came into view, approaching the entrance with his usual slouching walk.

They followed his progress to the baccarat room and watched as he and Ray entered and settled themselves at one of the two oval tables. Elli tuned in the volume and zoomed in on Teddy They could hear him breathe in and out noisily as Ray waited quietly. Then, after a few more noisy in and outs, Teddy took one very deep breath and snorted it out.

'Right,' he said.

'So, what do you want to tell us?' said Ray.

'How much do you actually know?' said Teddy.

Ray ignored the question. 'Who was involved? How many of you?'

'Involved in what?'

Ray propped his elbows on the table and rested his mouth on the knuckles of his folded hands. He remained staring across at

Teddy for almost a full minute. Teddy stared back.

Then Ray repeated, 'How many of you were involved?'

'In what?' Teddy asked again, with the kind of smirk a child would make when they ask a question they think would irritate an adult.

Ray stood up and left the room without saying anything.

Greg and Elli watched as Teddy waited for Ray to return. When he did not, Teddy went to follow him but couldn't open the door. By this time Ray had joined them in the office.

'I locked him in,' he said. 'That was good thinking about the key, Elli.'

Teddy shook the door and shouted, but eventually turned away, circled the room once, then returned to his chair and slumped down.

Ray picked up his file and started writing in it.

'I'll let him stew for a few minutes, then I'll throw everything at him,' he said.

'What are you going to do?' asked Elli.

'See, I've come across quite a few people like Teddy, weak characters who think they're brighter than they really are. They thrive in the shadow of a strong man all the time they believe he'll protect them. They think it makes them tough, too. But show them their strong man is vulnerable and they'll crumble. I'm going make up a little story for him, using a bit of what we know so far, and see what he can tell us.'

Ray wrote steadily for about five minutes, by which time they could see that Teddy had become fidgety and obviously irritated.

'Right, that should do it,' Ray said. He went back down to the baccarat room.

'Looks as if you've left it too late, I'm afraid, Teddy,' he said as he entered. 'I had hoped not to have to throw too much at you, make out you just let them use your boat from time to time, didn't have any idea what was really going on.'

He put the file on the table between them and sat down. 'Bob's the one I've been targeting. It was all his doing in the first place, wasn't it, and now it's him who's screwed the whole thing up. So it seemed only fair that he should take the rap.'

Teddy looked puzzled. 'Bob?'

'Clarmont Brown. He's come forward and given a voluntary statement to the police.'

Teddy eyed him warily. 'What about?'

'GLH and how Kilroy and Ronnie Johnson got involved in the first place. But I expect you know all about that. Bob would have claimed he'd covered everything, right? But in the end he went just a bit too far. Anyway, he's decided to pass the buck.'

'Hang on, what do you mean, pass the buck? What for?'

Ray made a show of opening the file and finding his place. He leant back in his chair. 'Listen, this is his statement. He's dropped you right in it, I'm afraid. What's really damaging is where he says: ...' He traced his finger down the page. 'Here we are. He says, "Teddy Davis told me that Raymond Kilroy had asked him for several thousand pounds or he would tell the police on the mainland that his son Spencer Davis was smuggling illegal immigrants in his boat from the Island to various towns on the mainland. I knew that there could be no truth in this allegation, of course, and I told Teddy to ignore the threat. But Teddy said that if the police were to investigate, certain dodgy trips to France to collect cheap cigarettes and booze, etcetera, might come to light, and then he would be in trouble and he asked me to use my influence to keep Kilroy quiet."'

Teddy's face showed shock.

'What the hell's he on about?' he yelled indignantly. 'I don't believe this! Raymond Kilroy? I only ever met the bloke a couple of times and that was months ago!'

Ray shrugged. 'Your word against his, Teddy. Anyway, that's not all. He goes on, "Teddy said that he had heard that Kilroy was meeting a contact at the Pilot Boat Inn in Bembridge later in the evening and would I go there and sort it out for him. I told him it was all nonsense and not to worry. I said there was nothing I could do myself and I suggested he took legal advice. I gave him the name of a solicitor that I thought could help him. But he was still very upset and said he would go there himself if I would come with him, so in the end I agreed. When I got there, Teddy had brought along some very rough-looking characters and I decided not to go in. Actually, I'd already had a bit too much to drink and I was feeling rather sick, so I left them there. I just wanted to get home to bed,"'

Ray looked up. 'Well?'

Teddy was smiling in disbelief. 'It's a load of bollocks! He's made it all up!'

'Really? It sounds pretty convincing. And Kilroy's body was found on your boat, wasn't it?'

'You don't believe this, do you? This … this! He's lying! The bastard!'

'He's talking, that's the main thing, Teddy. Look,' Ray leaned forward encouragingly. 'We know you know something about what happened to Nigel Heapes. Okay? We fancy Clarmont Brown for it, to be honest, and if we can pass him on to the police for the Kilroy job that gives us a good bit of leverage, see? But if you won't talk and he's willing to cooperate, there's not much I can do.'

Teddy squirmed in his chair. He stared past Ray towards the window. Then his shoulders slumped and he looked down at the table with his hands covering his face. He sighed shakily.

'It all started when I found those bloody pictures,' he mumbled. There was a long pause.

Ray waited patiently, knowing it was best now to let Teddy tell it in his own time.

At last Teddy looked up with a twisted smile. 'If Nigel hadn't been so bloody hasty … ' He shook his head, then took a deep, shuddering breath. 'What happened was, on the Saturday morning my Dad sent me down here to the Quarterdeck Club, only it wasn't like this then. The Wilsons were running it and I had to give something to Louise Wilson. There wasn't anybody in her office. I waited for ages and I got fed up and I sort of started looking around. Then I see this envelope on the desk with the corner of a photo poking out so I goes and has a look. I couldn't believe it! It was a picture of the Commander with a young girl with no clothes on. I mean really young, like about ten years old? No tits or anything? It was horrible, I mean, you know.' He made a vague gesture of disgust. 'And the envelope was full of pictures like that.' He shook his head and looked up at Ray. 'I mean. The Commander, of all people, you know?' He shook his head again. 'Anyway, I slipped the envelope in my pocket and got out of there pdq.'

He paused as if wondering how to continue.

'I was going to show them to my Dad, see, but when I gets back to the shop, Nigel's there and I shows them to him. He laughs and gets all excited, says we can make a fortune out of them. But I reckoned I ought to see what my Dad said first. Nigel got mad and went off in a temper. Anyway, I did show the photos to my Dad and he said I was right to give them to him and he'd take care of it.

'So then, late that night, Dad brings me down here, to the Quarterdeck Club, and Bob's there with the Wilsons and he tells me they know I must have pinched the pictures and showed them to Nigel because Nigel had upset the Commander. They were all very, very pissed off. Louise Wilson said I wasn't to be trusted, and I could see my Dad was scared for me. But he'd brought the pictures with him and he handed them over, and he said he'd make sure I'd keep my mouth shut, but they'd have to do something about Nigel. Bob told me to ring Nigel there and then and tell him I reckoned he was right about the photos, so I did. Then Bob asked my Dad where his dinghy was and Dad said Foreland, so Bob said I had to go and see Nigel in the morning and tell him I'd put the photos in our dinghy last night, but now my Dad had lent it to someone and they were going to leave it at Foreland about tea time. Bob said he'd deal with it from there.'

Teddy looked up at Ray. 'And that's all I know really. I mean, you know, about when Nigel disappeared.'

'Except you must have told him what time Greg was sailing the dinghy back to Seastone that Sunday evening?'

'Well, yeah, okay. That's what my Dad told me to tell him.'

'And that the photos were still on board.'

'Yeah. Wrapped up in a parcel in the stern by the tiller.'

'So when Nigel was shot, you must have guessed what had happened.'

'I didn't know he was shot, for Christ's sake!'

'Alright, but whatever happened to him you must have guessed it was Bob Clarmont Brown's doing.'

Teddy mumbled something.

'What?'

'I didn't know anything. I mean, he just disappeared, didn't he!'

'Yes, and when he didn't turn up you were happy to let Greg take the blame for it.'

'Hang on! How was I to know he wasn't in on it as well?'

'Okay. Yes, fair enough.' Ray nodded as if accepting that Teddy had a point. 'What we want now though, is the copies your father made of those pictures, and the video tape that he tucked away with them.'

Teddy's face was a picture of amazement.

Above in Elli's office, Greg murmured, 'Good one, Ray.' To Elli he said, 'Your friend Pete told us just now that Teddy's father came home last week and collected what looked like a video cassette from his bank in Ryde. Ray has played a hunch and it seems to have paid off.'

Teddy, meanwhile, sat staring at Ray. 'How the hell did you find out about that?'

'You don't need to worry about that, Teddy What really matters is who else knows about it.'

Teddy shook his head, looking at Ray in disbelief. 'Dad said nobody knows about it except him and the Wilsons,' he said. 'I knew Dad'd copied the pictures, but I didn't know about the tape until Dad told me last Saturday.'

'So what does he want you to do with the tape and the pictures now, then?'

Teddy frowned and wriggled uncomfortably. 'You wouldn't happen to have a fag on you, would you? I'm supposed to be giving it up, but I'm dying for one.'

'Sorry. Anyway, you can't smoke in here.' Ray put his hand in his jacket pocket. 'I've got some Polo mints, if that's any use?'

He offered the pack to Teddy, who reached across and took it.

'Ta,' he said. He spent a little while unwrapping a mint and sucking on it, and then he said, 'Look we never knew what happened to Nigel, see? We all knew Bob must have done something. But Dad and me, we didn't know what. Didn't want to. It was never spoken of. But when we got the news about Nigel's bones being found with a bullet hole in his head, Dad got worried.' He looked up at Ray. 'You weren't here when the Commander died, were you?'

'No.'

'No. Well, that's when Dad got out.'

Ray knew better than to ask him to explain.

'He'd had enough, and he was past pension age anyway and he'd always fancied retiring to Spain so that's what he did.'

There was another long pause while Teddy stared down into the green baize of the table top. Eventually he nodded to himself and when he looked up at Ray his normal furtive expression had gone. It seemed he had decided there was no point in trying to hide anything any more.

'Look, Ray,' he said earnestly, leaning forward and looking Ray in the eye, 'I don't know nothing about what happened to that bloke Kilroy. Okay, he was found on my boat, but I didn't have nothing to do with it and I'm not going to be set up for it. That's why I'm here. I reckon enough's enough. So I'll tell you what I know about what happened to Nigel. Okay?'

Ray nodded encouragingly. 'Alright, Teddy.'

'When Dad came home last week, he told me how it all started and what all the fuss was about when I found them photos.'

He sat back in his chair and looked across the table at Ray as if glad to be telling the story.

'See, my Dad had an old MTB in those days, and he said Bob got him to use it for trips abroad to pick up stuff. They were doing alright and Bob got the Wilsons to come in with them. But Bob reckoned to really get on they needed more cash. Then Louise Wilson found that out about the Commander, you know, the little girls, so Bob had him followed and that's how they got the photos. The Commander was a very rich man, see, and he wanted his nasty little ways kept secret, so Bob thought his cash problem was over. But then I found the photos and showed them to Nigel and the silly sod went to the Commander himself. 'Course, that put the cat amongst the pigeons, 'cos the more people knew about the little girls, the less hold Bob had over the Commander. They all agreed on that, so, you know, . . .' Teddy raised his eyebrows and shrugged.

Ray said, 'So Nigel had to be taken care of.'

'Well, Dad said they couldn't see any other way round it. He said he let Bob know he'd made copies of the pictures and if anything ever happened to me he'd give the game away. Anyway, I kept my mouth shut and Nigel was never found, so it all worked out alright. At least, up to when the Commander died.'

'What happened then?'

'Dad said Bob thought he was going to be able to buy the Yacht Club and carry on as before. But the Vanderlings didn't want to sell it. That buggered things up a bit and Graham Wilson had a row with him. Here, in the club. What Bob didn't know was Louise Wilson had it all on tape. Graham showed Dad the video, and that was what made Dad make up his mind to retire out of it. So then Graham gave him the video and asked him to look after it in case they should ever need it.'

'And that's why your dad came and got it,' said Ray. 'Because Graham Wilson thinks they may need it now.'

'Yeah. Dad says Graham reckons Bob really got the wind up when the bones were identified because he'd just heard he was in with a chance of a peerage. Any whiff of a scandal would put paid to that, wouldn't it, and being the sort of bloke he is he'd pretty soon pass the buck. So Graham was going to warn him, see, remind him of the row they had over getting rid of the Commander and tell him he's got a video of it.'

Ray nodded wisely. 'Well, I don't know about you, but it seems to me that video's a pretty hot property. What do you reckon, could it be used in evidence, d'you think?'

Teddy thought for a moment or two. 'Well, I dunno,' he said. 'See, Bob never says he actually did anything himself. Graham's mad at him 'cos they'd all agreed it was too risky but Bob had gone ahead anyway. Then Bob says something like "Roddy got scared after his heart attack and he was going to tell Suzy everything, so somebody had to do something." And then Graham calls him a bloody fool and Bob hits him and then Jerry Marlow comes in and parts them. But I reckon it looks bad for him, don't you?'

'Yes, I do and it sounds to me as though you ought to let us look after that video tape, Teddy. We can make better use of it than your Dad and Graham Wilson ever could. I'm sure it would go a long way towards getting you off the hook, too. What do you say?'

Teddy hesitated, staring down at his hands on the green baize. 'Well, my Dad wants me to hang on to it till Graham Wilson comes for it. Still, I reckon you're right.' He looked up again. 'Bob's had it, hasn't he?'

Ray nodded. 'I believe his days of glory may be numbered, Teddy.' He stood up and moved to open the door. 'I think it would be best, you know, if you could go and get that video and the photos and bring them down to the café straightaway.' He put his hand on Teddy's shoulder as he ushered him out of the room. 'You've convinced me you had nothing to do with the Kilroy business, so I can put a word in there for you.'

Upstairs, as they watched Ray escort Teddy to the front door, Elli said. 'I almost feel sorry for Teddy. I don't suppose there is anything in what he said that the police could act on, though, do you?'

'Probably not. But it's convinced me it's enough for us.'

She turned from the screens to face him. 'What do you mean?'

'Ray and I have believed for some time that the only way we'll get to Bob is to provoke him into coming to us. We just need to find a way of letting him know how much we've found out and wait for him to take the bait.'

Elli put her hand on Greg's arm. 'I'd like to make a suggestion.'

'Go ahead.'

'I happen to know that Bob is coming to the Island today. Would you like me to see if I can arrange a meeting?'

'Could you do that?'

'I'm sure I could persuade him to meet me here in the office. Would that be any good?'

Greg grinned. 'Then I could be here instead of you. It would be perfect.'

The lift door opened and Ray stepped into the room.

'Well, that went alright, didn't it?' he said with a satisfied smile.

'You were brilliant,' said Elli.

Greg said, 'I think we've got enough now to chuck at Bob Clarmont Brown, don't you?'

'Oh yes. We just need to find a way of letting him know.'

'Elli says he'll be on the Island today and she's going to try and get him to come here on the pretext of meeting her. But it will be me waiting for him.'

'When?'

Elli said, 'That will be depend on him, but I can let you know in good time I'm sure.'

Ray hesitated, the ex-policeman in him making him cautious. 'On your own?' he said to Greg.

'Well, yes.'

'Hmmn.' Ray stroked his chin thoughtfully. 'See, I'm going to have a word with Tracey, tell her what we've found out from Teddy and what we're going to do. We might need her co-operation if anything goes wrong.' He looked meaningfully at Greg. 'And you should give Hamish a ring. No harm in having back-up.'

'Okay,' said Greg. 'But I'll meet Bob on my own.'

FIFTYEIGHT

Just before four o'clock that afternoon Greg was leaning his hips on the front of Elli's desk, watching the cctv screens. Clarmont Brown's black Mercedes SUV pulled into the parking area in front of the Quarterdeck Club. Greg watched while he locked the car and came through the club entrance and along the corridor to the lift. After a minute or so the lift door opened and Clarmont Brown stepped into the office.

He had taken two steps into the room before he registered Greg's presence.

'What are you doing here?' he said, as the lift door closed behind him.

'And good afternoon to you, too, Bob,' said Greg.

'Where's Elli? My wife, Lady Eleanor?'

Greg didn't answer.

'I arranged to meet her here.'

Greg stayed silent.

Clarmont Brown looked around the small room, his eyes darting from side to side, then quickly scanning the bank of screens.

'Well?' he said, turning back to Greg.

Greg still said nothing.

'To hell with this. I haven't got time to play silly buggers with you.'

He started to turn back to the lift.

Greg straightened up and moved towards him. 'Just a minute, Bob.'

Clarmont Brown turned round to face him and Greg hit him as hard as he could with a left hook to the belly, and a smashing right to the mouth as he doubled forward. He yelled, staggered back against the wall by the lift door and sank to a sitting position, his hands fluttering weakly on the carpet, his eyes unfocussed, as blood gushed from his nose.

Greg stepped back and leaned his hips on the desk again, folded his arms and waited.

Gradually Clarmont Brown's eyes began to refocus. He tried

once to push himself upright but failed. He sat back and stared in amazement at Greg, his eyes, smarting from the effect of the blow, glittered like those of a snake about to strike.

Greg said, 'That was payment of the first instalment of a long-outstanding debt.' He paused for effect and then added slowly, 'Further payments may take a different form, but they *will* be made. Until the debt is paid in full.'

The reptilian gaze began to waver as Clarmont Brown became aware of the pain in his mouth and of the blood still running down his chin and all over the front of his immaculate cream suit.

'Just so that you understand,' continued Greg ' ... Are you listening? ... I have videos of you with known criminals, and with groups of aliens later proven to be illegal immigrants. I have copies of ledgers and other documents from Cockaigne clubs which HM Revenue and Customs would find useful, I have a video of a row between you and Graham Wilson which incriminates you in the death of Roddy Vanderling and I have the photographs of Roddy with little girls with which you blackmailed him, and for which you shot Nigel Heapes for finding out about. You might like to give some thought to the value I might put on all of this to settle that outstanding debt.'

Clarmont Brown managed to find a handkerchief to hold to his face while he slowly got his feet under himself and slid upright against the wall.

'Does Elli know about this?' he mumbled through the handkerchief.

'Let me know by this time tomorrow what you propose. You know where to find me.'

'I want to know if my wife is part of this, this ... outrageous attack on me.'

'I don't care what you want,' said Greg. 'You have until this time tomorrow.'

Clarmont Brown gathered himself and straightened up. He pressed the button to open the lift door, glaring venomously at Greg until the door opened, then he turned and entered the lift.

As soon as the lift started down, Hamish came in from the corridor outside Elli's office and leaned gracefully against the door frame, looking like a magazine advertisement for casual menswear.

'It sounded pretty good from out there,' he said. 'Outrageous, eh?'

Greg rubbed the knuckles of his right hand, which were beginning to show a slight swelling.

'You wouldn't believe how much satisfaction I got out of that,' he said.

Together they watched the screens until Clarmont Brown drove off in his Mercedes.

'What do you think he'll do?' said Hamish.

'He might make a date to agree terms, but I doubt it. I knocked him down. Hurt him. I don't suppose anybody has ever tried that before, so his pride has been badly damaged and he'll want to get his own back. No, he'll send his heavy gang.'

'Perhaps he'll come with them and you'll get another go at him.'

'No,' said Greg. 'He won't do that. Anyway, as far as I'm concerned I'll be happy for the law to do the rest.'

'You've passed everything on to Sergeant Nash.'

'I have, but it would be good if we can back up what she has.'

Hamish thought about that for a moment. 'You didn't hit him just to get even, did you?'

'Well, that *was* a big part of it.'

Hamish smiled at him, appreciatively. 'No,' he said. 'You deliberately provoked him, didn't you, knowing he'd send some of his goons after you, so we can catch one of them and make him talk.'

'Right,' said Greg. 'And we know he doesn't like to waste any time. He soon got Johnson and his red-faced buddy into action, didn't he? And he got hold of Brewster and Kilroy, pretty quickly too. I think he'll send some of his heavies, probably tonight. All we have to do is be ready for them and be sure to grab at least one to pass on to Tracey.'

'Just you and me?'

Greg grinned. 'Who else would we need? But Ray won't want to be left out, and he'll make a good spare man, I reckon.'

'Aye,' said Hamish. 'He's alright, he's steady, and he owes them one, too.' Then he looked thoughtful for a moment. 'What about Elli? Brown will have a go at her as well, won't he?'

'Oh yes. Most definitely. She'll have to be severely punished for what she did. That was unforgivable and he'll want to see to her himself.'

'So what's she going to do?'

'Well, she says he's unlikely to come here, to the club, and I agree. We think he'll go to Clarmont House to catch her when she comes home from work at about two o'clock. So she'll leave here early and go home with Pete. He doesn't know about Pete. And just in case he does call in here, Pete's going to be here all evening with Jonty and half of Jonty's rugby team.'

Hamish said, 'But what if he sends another gang. I mean, he's got plenty of resources, hasn't he? What about his security firms? He's not short of hard men, after all.'

'No, he'll want to sort Elli out himself. She and I have talked about this and we're certain he'll want as few people involved as possible. He's kept it pretty low-key so far, hasn't he - Kilroy excepted, of course - and this is mainly because he has to avoid publicity. That's why Elli and I agreed that we had to set him up and hit him where it hurts most - his self-pride - so he has to retaliate.'

Hamish smiled. 'So he'll be waiting at Clarmont House about the same time as we expect his goons to call on us at Dan's then, eh?'

'Almost certainly.'

'So that's where we'll find him when we've dealt with the goons.'

'Well, I hope it's where Tracey's chaps will find him,' said Greg, 'But we'll see.'

'Well, we'll be ready.'

'Of course.'

FIFTYNINE

Sunday 2 am

At twenty to two Greg's mobile vibrated in his hip pocket. He took it out, listened.

Hamish whispered, 'They're here. Four of them, just got out of a silver Toyota across the road, just past the street light about three doors down ... They're in a bit of a huddle ... Now they're heading this way ... Don't see any weapons yet.'

'Let Ray know. Leave phones on now.'

Greg was in the big rhododendron about ten feet to the right of the front door. He had Sam's old .38 semi-automatic in his pocket and a New York Police Department nightstick, provided by Ray from his "souvenirs". He crouched down, waiting.

Hamish was on the roof of the garage with a knife and a rope, and Ray was indoors at the top of the stairs facing the front door and covering the hall with Dan's shotgun.

Greg peered through a small gap in the foliage. He could dimly make out the front gate, and suddenly there was movement as it opened. Two men headed straight down the drive towards the back of the house. They would have to pass Hamish. Two others approached the front door. Greg waited. The first man came to the door and tried a key in the lock. Greg and Dan had agreed not to bother with changing the locks after the first intrusion, so the man's key still fitted. He said something in a low voice to his companion, and the door started to open.

Immediately, Greg came out of his crouch, swiftly crossing the ten feet or so to bring the nightstick down on the back of the second man's head as he went to follow his partner inside. The man grunted as he fell, and Ray's voice sounded loud and clear, 'Police! Stay where you are! We are armed! Drop your weapons and stay where you are!'

The hall light came on. The man inside whirled around and ran into Greg. It was Red Face. They fell together over the fallen man and Greg lost his hold on the stick.

Red Face was on his feet first and turned to run, but Greg grabbed his foot and brought him down. They came upright again together and Red Face took two steps towards him with his fists held high. He kicked savagely at Greg's groin but he was nowhere near quick enough. Greg took one fast step forwards diagonally to the right, and hit him very hard with a straight left, breaking his nose and shocking him into trying to cover his face with his hands, while Greg forced him backwards with a flurry of savage rights and lefts.

Then, moving quickly in, Greg gripped his shoulders, turned him through one hundred and eighty degrees and put his foot in the small of his back. One hard shove propelled him towards the wall of the house and his head came back. On impact it shot forward again, and the ruins of his nose drew a dark line down the wall as he slid slowly to the ground, out cold.

The man Greg had coshed was now on his feet and coming at him. It was Brewster the big bruiser. He swung a great, clubbing punch which caught Greg on the shoulder, knocking him down to his knees. Before he could get up again, Brewster aimed a full-blooded kick at his head. Greg just managed to dodge the boot, and catching the heel in his hand, he gripped it tight, propped it on his shoulder and stood up quickly. Brewster's head hit the ground hard and he didn't get up.

Greg pulled the two of them together and leaned them back to back. They were both still unconscious. Red Face's nose was bleeding heavily and he was breathing noisily through his mouth. There was blood on the back of Brewster's shaven head. Greg undid Brewster's belt and took it off, passing it around his throat and crossing it over between the backs of their necks into a figure of eight before buckling it in the lowest hole in front of Red Face. Then he slid it round so that he could shove the buckled ends between their shoulder blades. He checked there was just enough slackness for them to breathe. It should keep them out of the way for a while. Then he searched both of them thoroughly and relieved them of their weapons. Red Face had a small silenced automatic in his waistband and a can of Mace in his jacket. He also had a mobile phone which Greg took as well. Brewster had a flick-knife and a knuckle-duster.

Greg's phone squawked. He put it to his ear.

Hamish said, 'I've got two. How are you doing?'

'Same.'

'One of mine is very poorly,' said Hamish. 'Might be a wee problem.'

'Serious?'

'Aye, he'll no' be getting better. Big blond chappie, could be your Johnson. Want to come and see?'

'Okay.'

A flashlight shone from the doorway and Ray said, 'Alright, Greg?'

'I'm fine, but Hamish has a problem. Better come and have a look, we might need your advice. These two will keep for now.'

Ray shone his torch on the two thugs. 'Oh dear,' he said. 'I think they might be in need of medical attention.'

'Probably,' said Greg.

They went around towards the back of the house and found Hamish by the side door to the garage, two bodies at his feet, a large knife in his hand.

He nudged one with his foot. 'This one had a gun with a silencer. Missed me, but I couldn't let him have a second go.'

Ray shone his torch and Greg said, 'Yes, that's Ronald Johnson.'

His head was twisted unnaturally to one side.

Ray bent down for a closer look, felt for a pulse, then stood up. 'I see what you mean about a problem. From the colour of his hair, I'd say this was one of the bastards that beat me up.' That was the only other comment he made.

'He'll no' be doing any more o' that,' said Hamish.

'Okay,' said Greg, 'What about the other one?'

Ray swung the beam of the torch revealing a heavily built young man, with a shaved head, silver rings in his eyebrows, and a thin red line across his Adam's Apple slowly oozing blood. He was trussed hands to feet and his pale, blue eyes were wide open with fear.

'Spencer Davis,' said Ray. 'We wondered when you'd turn up.'

Hamish said, pointing with his knife, 'He's keeping very quiet because I asked him to, but I expect he'll want to talk to us in a wee while, won't you, laddie?'

Davis nodded vigorously. He had come out tonight expecting to have some fun, but it had all gone wrong for him and he was clearly terrified.

Ray said to Hamish, 'Did you see which one was driving?'

Hamish indicated Johnson, 'Him, I think.'

'I took these from the other two,' said Greg, handing the weapons to Ray. 'But they didn't have car keys.' He bent down to go through Johnson's pockets, found some keys and held them up.

'Good. Now then, this is what we do,' said Ray, moving away so that Spencer Davis would not hear. 'We'll make the other two secure and put them with Johnson in their car, taking due care about fingerprints, etcetera, and leave them somewhere suitable - let's see, the car ferry terminal at Fishbourne should do. You and I can do that, Hamish. See, when their car is found, all their weapons will be in the boot. Johnson's gun has been fired, which will complicate matters nicely. The other two villains will have a hard enough job explaining what happened to them, let alone how Johnson came to break his neck. Tracey will eventually put two and two together, I'm sure, but she'll know there'll be no proof that any of us was involved, and meanwhile she's got a chance of a breakthrough in a number of outstanding cases.' He smiled in satisfaction.

Greg said, 'But what about Clarmont Brown? We'd have heard if he's been to the club after Elli, and he hasn't come with this lot, so I reckon he will have gone to Clarmont House. If he has, we have to make sure he stays there long enough for Tracey's chaps to pick him up.'

Ray checked his watch. 'It's only five to two. If he did go there he won't have left yet. But you're right, he won't wait all night for Elli to turn up. Do what you can to keep him there, but don't try anything drastic, okay? We want him in one piece, ideally. You too.'

'Right' said Greg, 'Before we go, though, we'd better make sure there's no trace of our visitors - one of them has left a lot of his DNA on Dan's wall.'

Hamish said, 'We'll see to that. You get on.'

'We'll be with you as soon as we can,' said Ray. 'Oh, you'd better chuck young Spencer in the back of your car and take him with you. I'll give Tracey a call. Tell her our little scheme is working so far, and she can pick Spencer up at Clarmont House. Whatever else happens she should get something useful out of him.'

'Okay, good. I'll leave him in the car by the back gate in Pond Lane. I remembered there used to be a fieldgate there so I asked Elli. There's a security gate there now, but Elli gave me her card to open it. I'll leave it open.'

SIXTY

Sunday 2.15 a.m.

With Spencer Davis trussed and gagged on the back seat, Greg drove along Pond Lane with his lights off. It was dark under the trees, just enough light for him to make out the gateway. He parked on the verge just past the gates.

He took his pocket torch out of the glove pocket and opened the car door. The interior light came on. He checked that his prisoner was secure, then closed the door quietly. Before going to open the gates it occurred to him that Clarmont Brown might also have come this way, so he walked a few paces further along the lane and switched on his torch for a quick look. There was no vehicle parked nearby and he made his way back to the gateway. Shielding the light from the torch with his hand, he located the slot for Elli's card in the right-hand gatepost and slipped it in and left it there. The big double gates swung open slowly and silently.

It was a clear night, with no moon, and as his eyes adjusted, he saw that the narrow tarmac drive led away at an angle that would take it around where the old, walled, kitchen garden had been as he remembered it, and sure enough, after about thirty paces, he was able to make out the wall over to his left. He headed across the grass towards where he guessed the door would have been. There was still a door there and it opened easily.

The light spilling across the lawn from two of the ground floor windows in the back of the house about fifty yards away was just enough for him to see that there was now a large swimming pool with a wide paved surround where the kitchen garden had been. He stood absolutely still by the door, watching for several minutes. It was so quiet the silence seemed to close in on him. Had Elli left the lights on when she went out, or did it mean that Clarmont Brown was in the house?

At last, keeping close to the wall, he moved around the pool towards the brick lean-to where he had sheltered from the rain with old Henry Niton all those years ago. This, he now saw, housed the pump and filtration equipment for the pool and he stopped there in a patch of shadow, trying to locate security lights and cameras; if Clarmont Brown had gone to all that trouble when

380

he'd acquired the Quarterdeck Club, he was bound to have done at least as much at his home, as it then was, and it seemed unlikely that Elli would have changed it since.

He spotted what looked like a floodlight high up on the right-hand corner of the building as he faced it. This would cover an approach from the drive. He was still not close enough to identify anything more though, and trying to visualise the layout of the house, he realised that the lighted windows were those of the kitchen where he'd had lunch with Elli. It seemed longer than a couple of days ago.

There was no sign of movement within the house. He decided to take a chance and ran quickly across the lawn, arriving apparently undetected to the left of the lighted windows. Crouching down he eased along to the nearest window and cautiously peered in. There was nobody in the kitchen, but an interior door was open and he made out a faint light against the wall at the end of the passage, suggesting that lights were on in another room. He tried the kitchen door. It was locked.

To avoid the risk of setting off the floodlight, he made his way quietly in the other direction, keeping to the paving stones all the way. He passed some french windows, also locked. Around the corner, in the middle of the side wall of the house there was a small enclosed porch. He carefully tried this door too. A path led away from it across the grass towards a high wooden fence which linked up with the garage block where the original stables had been. This building was bigger than he would have expected and he realised it must include the living quarters of the couple who looked after the house and garden for Elli.

Reaching the end of the main house he checked for lights and cameras again. There was a floodlight fitted high up on the corner above his head. From where he stood, he could see there was no car parked anywhere near the house; if Clarmont Brown was here he was not advertising the fact. Greg wondered if he had parked by the garages and started to go to check.

As he stepped onto the gravel it crunched noisily under his foot and after a few more paces, a dog started barking from the flat behind the garages and then another joined in. Ace and Deuce, he thought. Elli must have left them with the couple, not trusting them to her husband's tender mercies if he found them in the house. He moved quickly off the drive onto the grass and ran

381

back to crouch low behind a bush in the angle of the house wall and the little porch.

The driveway was suddenly brightly illuminated as a security light above the garages came on. From his position behind the bush he could see the garage doors were closed and there was no car parked outside. Perhaps Clarmont Brown had not come, or if he had, he'd left his car elsewhere, not wanting Elli to know he was there when she arrived home. Greg stayed where he was. He wondered what to do now. He'd come with no specific plan, just the general notion of keeping Clarmont Brown here by some means, such as disabling his car, until the police arrived, but clearly that was not an option.

He heard a man's voice from the direction of the old stable block. The dogs stopped barking, and Greg hoped they would not be let loose and betray his presence. He remained completely still, listening intently. A moving light appeared behind the fence. Somebody carrying a flashlight. The door in the fence opened and the man said something and directed his light towards the main house. The two dogs came out, and one of them, barking frantically, raced diagonally across in front of Greg and disappeared around the corner towards the front of the house. The other padded slowly along the path towards Greg, paused for a moment then came behind the bush and gave his face a lick. It was the elderly red setter, Ace, who had made friends with him at lunch on Thursday.

The man stood uncertainly by the fence door, exploring the grounds haphazardly with the beam of his torch without detecting Greg. The other dog, the labrador Deuce, re-appeared, still travelling at speed but no longer barking. Having circled the house and found no sign of her mistress, she had lost interest and hurtled back through the door beside the man. He whistled and Ace turned his head, gave Greg a final sideways look, and then trotted back.

As the man and dog were going back behind the fence, the edge of the venetian blind in the downstairs window less than two metres from where Greg crouched, was pushed aside. The silhouette of part of a man's face appeared in the light reflected from the drive. He was looking away from Greg towards the garage block and there was no mistaking Clarmont Brown. Greg found himself holding his breath until the head withdrew and the blind returned to normal

So Bob was inside the house. How to keep him there though?

Greg was still trying to think of a strategy, when he heard the inner door of the porch being unlocked. He immediately came to his feet and moved to stand ready at the end next to the outer door. By good fortune this opened outwards towards him, hiding him from view. Clarmont Brown also had a flashlight, the beam of which he was directing towards the rear of the house, before setting off, apparently on his own investigation.

Greg peered around the door and watched until Clarmont Brown turned the corner of the building. Then, without further thought, he slipped through the porch, which opened straight into the room Clarmont Brown had looked out of. It was a small room with windows on either side of the doorway. To his left there were open shelves of towels, white linen, table cloths and napkins, and a partly open door with a faint light coming through, and on the other side a wooden table, two tall metal cabinets, a fireplace and a narrow flight of stairs.

The light above the garages went off and he was left in the dark.

He felt Sam's old .38 automatic weighing heavily in his pocket and he toyed with the idea of holding Bob at gunpoint until Tracey's men arrived, but although he had cleaned the gun and checked it over thoroughly he was very reluctant to put much trust in it and he doubted if Bob would give in quietly, anyway. Still, he accepted that, as a last resort, that was what it might come to.

Light reflected off the open outer door of the porch. Bob was coming back.

Greg moved to his right, found the stairs and went up them to a small landing, where he knelt down, peering around the newel post in time see Clarmont Brown come in, close the doors without bothering to re-lock them and go on through into the house, muttering to himself. At least, thought Greg, I know he is still here, but how long will it be before he gets tired of waiting for Elli? He looked at his watch: just after half-past two. Bob will have expected her to be home by now and it won't be long before he starts to wonder if she's coming home at all tonight.

He went quietly down the stairs and across to the door that Bob had gone through. The faint light he'd seen earlier was coming from a room at the end of a passage. Thinking about the layout of the house, he reckoned it would be the room to the right of the front door as you came in and was possibly Elli's sitting room, where Bob would be waiting for her. Very slowly, and without making the slightest sound, he crept along the passage until he could look through the partly open door.

A soft, warm glow came from a lamp on a small table next to heavy drapes hung from floor to ceiling against the far wall. He couldn't see Bob but he could hear him, still muttering, apparently waiting on his mobile phone for someone to answer. Greg guessed he was trying to contact Johnson.

There was a telephone on the table and it gave Greg an idea.

He withdrew cautiously and went back up to the place on the landing. Using the little penlight on his key-chain he found the number for Clarmont House on his own phone and keyed it in. After several rings Clarmont Brown picked up.

'Hello Bob,' said Greg, quietly.

'What? Who's this?'

'It's no good trying to get in touch with Big Ronnie, I'm afraid,' said Greg. 'He won't be able to hear you. And none of the others you sent to Bembridge with him can help you, either.'

There was a long pause. Then he heard Clarmont Brown take a deep breath, hissing between his teeth. 'You!' He snarled the word.

'And just to round things off nicely, you've been wasting your time here too, because Elli isn't coming home tonight.'

Again there was a long pause and Greg said, deliberately provoking him, 'It's all falling apart now, isn't it, Bob. If only you'd left Ray Tindall alone after he called on your old friend Ritter. But you panicked, didn't you, and bang went the peerage. Dear, oh dear. What was it going to be? Lord Clarmont of Seastone? No, wait a minute, that wouldn't do you justice at all, would it? Lord Vectis! Yes, I can just see you fancying that.'

'Where are you?' Clarmont Brown was losing control, his voice high-pitched, trembling with fury. 'You're here, aren't you, you bastard! Yes! That was you earlier, setting the dogs off!'

Greg stayed silent.

'Right!' Clarmont Brown screeched. 'This time I'm going to settle you once and for all!'

The line went dead and Greg heard rapid footsteps coming along the passage towards him. He crouched down and peered around the newel post again and saw Bob snap the light on and stride across the room to the steel cabinets near the foot of the stairs. He had a set of keys in his hand and he unlocked one of the cabinets, swung the doors open and reached inside. Greg couldn't see what he was doing because Bob's back and the cabinet door masked his view, but after a few clicks and thumps and the rattling sound of a chain being released, Bob took a pace backwards. He had a shotgun in his hand. He broke it open, loaded both barrels, slammed it closed and rushed from the room.

Greg was shocked. He had not anticipated this. His immediate thought was that Tracey's men might well be arriving soon. They'd have to be warned.

He listened. He could hear Clarmont Brown somewhere in the house and he felt exposed on the landing. He had the choice of continuing up another flight of narrow stairs, which he supposed led to where the former servants' quarters would have been, or moving into the passage that led off it. He decided against the stairs and felt his way along the wall until he came to a door on his right. He opened it and stood just inside.

He keyed in Ray's number on his mobile. After a couple of rings it was answered.

Ray said, 'Hi Greg, You okay?'

From the background noise Greg guessed Ray was in his car. He said, keeping his voice low, 'Alright so far, but we've got to get a message to Tracey a.s.a.p. We were right, Bob did come here to wait for Elli. I tried to make sure he stayed here, but I'm afraid I've pushed him a bit too far and now he's looking for me with a loaded shotgun.'

'Bloody hell, Greg! What did you do, for God's sake?'

'Never mind that. Can you get on to Tracey and let her know? I think he's flipped and he's likely to shoot anything that moves.'

'Yeah, yeah, sure, okay. I'll get on to her straightaway. Look, we're just leaving Fishbourne so we can be with you in, what, about fifteen minutes? Try and keep out of his way and we'll meet you at the front gate, alright?'

'I don't know. I'm inside the house at the moment and I don't know where Bob is so I'll have to find him first.'

Ray groaned. 'You just keep out of his way till we get there, d'you hear me?'

'Yes, alright.' Greg rang off and listened before stepping back through the door. He couldn't hear anything but as he waited the passage was suddenly illuminated from a window at the end and he realised Bob had switched on the outside security lights. He moved to the window and looked out. He was in the back of the house, facing the lawn and swimming pool. The whole area was brightly lit. He watched and listened again. There was no sign nor sound of Bob.

To his left was another door and he opened it and went in.

It was a bathroom with an open door leading into an obviously spare bedroom, bare mattresses on twin beds. A faint strip of light was shining along the bottom edge of a door on the far side. He crept over to it. Feeling for the knob, his hand encountered a key in the old-fashioned lock. He turned the knob and opened the door very carefully. He was at one corner of a wide landing and the light was coming from downstairs.

He moved slowly along the landing keeping close to the wall, and saw that the stairs led down to the marble-floored foyer at the front of the house. A cool draught hit his face suggesting that the front door had been left open. Bob was outside, then.

Greg took the gun out of his pocket and held it by his side as he moved towards the head of the stairs, but he stopped by the end baluster as he heard a noise from beyond the front door. Clarmont Brown rushed in, holding the shotgun at the ready, looking rapidly from left to right.

Greg called out, 'Drop the gun, Bob!'

Clarmont Brown swung around, bringing the shotgun up in one smooth movement, and fired.

The solid baluster took most of the blast, but Greg was knocked backward as pellets ripped into his left side, and chunks of wood flew about his head and shoulders. He dropped to the floor and fired back just as Clarmont Brown was starting up the stairs to finish him off. A grunt followed by a humming sound told him Bob had been hit and was hurting.

Greg's left hip felt as if it was on fire with sparks flying down his leg and up into his side. He stumbled, half crawling back into the spare bedroom and turned the key in the lock, then made his way back as quickly as he could through the en suite bathroom towards the passage, intending to get well out of Bob's way. He could hear him yelling incoherently on the landing, then trying the locked door and screaming obscenities as he thumped at it,

386

presumably with the stock of the shotgun. It was solid wood, however, and would not yield. Then, as Greg entered the passage from the bathroom, closing the door behind him, Clarmont Brown discharged the other barrel at the lock.

Greg reached the little landing and paused before starting to go down the narrow stairs. He could feel a numbness spreading along his left side, but the heat in his hip was still intense, and as he wondered vaguely how pain and nothing could exist together, he became aware of a throbbing pain in his head and a cold, clammy, sick sensation began to overwhelm him. He realised he was passing out.

He put out his hand to steady himself but his wounded leg gave way and he toppled down the stairs, crashing into the metal cabinet at the bottom. He tried to stand up but waves of nausea kept sweeping over him and he fell on hands and knees. The left side of his face was burning with pain. He was tasting blood, his mouth was swollen, and his left eye was closing. His left hand was useless, the arm broken below the elbow in the fall. There was a dull ache now in his left side and all down his left leg, and his trousers were soaked with blood.

He tried to concentrate but it was hard. He seemed to be passing in and out of consciousness and just wanted to find a quiet place to lie down and recover but too much time was passing and he didn't know whether Bob had taken any extra cartridges with him or would have to come back here to reload. He knew he had to stop him somehow. He held his breath for a moment, listening, but all was now quiet. Where the hell was the man?

He made another effort to stand up and suddenly Bob was there, standing straight above him, staring at him in astonishment. He was using the shotgun as a prop, holding it in one hand by its barrel. He brought the other hand over and started to swing it with both hands like a club. Greg launched himself upward on his good leg, making a wedge shape with the fingers of his right hand, and driving forward with every last scrap of strength left to him. He connected where he wanted to, impaling the side of Clarmont Brown's neck just below his ear and he felt something snap against his fingers. Clarmont Brown made a weird howling sound and the shotgun fell out of his hands, clattering down between them. He folded up and fell heavily. His legs twitched a few times then became still. He tried to say something, his chest heaving for breath and his eyes fixed on Greg, but he could make only a guttural grunting sound.

Greg took the shotgun and wedging it under his left arm he broke it open with his right hand. It was empty. He threw it away, then dragged himself to Clarmont Brown and searched him thoroughly for weapons, finding nothing. He took out his mobile, and suddenly feeling completely spent, he flopped back against the wall into a sitting position. He put the phone on the floor and after several attempts with his one good hand he managed to key in Ray's number before darkness folded around him.

EPILOGUE

Brackenslade Two weeks later

It was the morning of Greg's second day out of hospital.

Zillah had collected him from St Mary's and brought him back to convalesce with the other wounded creatures of which she always had at least one in care.

He was well on the way to full recovery now. His left arm was still in plaster, and walking was still difficult, the shotgun blast having badly damaged the muscles and ligaments of his left thigh and hip, but although several pellets and slivers of wood from the baluster had been dug out of his side and shoulder, he'd been fortunate to suffer no other serious injury.

Hamish had found him, unconscious and bleeding, and had applied a tourniquet to his leg to stem the flow of blood from ruptured vessels in his thigh. He and Ray had arrived at Clarmont House a few minutes before the police and Hamish had scouted the whole area before, having found nothing, they both went into the house.

Tracey had called for an ambulance on receiving Ray's phone call about Clarmont Brown's shotgun, and it arrived shortly after she and her men did. Paramedics quickly dealt with Greg, but apart from noting the deep graze along Clarmont Brown's ribcage where Greg had shot him, they could not make out what was wrong with him, and although he was conscious he was unable to speak to them. Later, at St Mary's, it was discovered that blood vessels in his neck had burst and he'd suffered a severe stroke.

This Saturday morning, Greg was returning from a gentle stroll on the heath, Rocky in close attendance by his side, and as he made his way carefully down the long slope, a car came up the lane and stopped outside Zillah's gate. A man got out. It was Nick Southwell. He saw Greg coming and walked to meet him. Rocky immediately placed himself between them until Greg called him to heel.

The two men met with a smile and shook hands.

Nick said, 'I heard you were up and about again so I thought I'd come and see for myself. How are you feeling?'

'Fine thanks. Still a bit slow on my feet, but otherwise alright.'

'That's good to hear. And you couldn't have a better nurse than Zillah.'

'That's true.'

They walked on down towards the gate. Greg said, 'I never thanked you for your support, sending Hamish and letting us use Sally and so on. Ray and I couldn't have got far on our own. It's much appreciated. Thanks.'

Nick said, 'Ah, well, I have to confess it was not entirely altruistic, although I expect I couldn't have refused anyway. But, as I'd hoped it would, it's paid dividends.' He paused as they reached the gate. 'I'll explain in a minute. But first, before we go in, do you have any idea how long it'll be before you can get back to work?'

Greg gave him a sharp look. 'Well, I could start today if you don't need me to run anywhere.'

Nick shook his head. 'No, no running, I need you in the office to take over from Big Al for a few weeks. Sally will show you the ropes. And she'll ferry you back and forth until your plaster comes off. What d'you say? Could you start on Monday?'

'Yes, sure.'

'Good man.' Nick looked hard at Greg, eyebrows raised. 'Zillah won't argue?'

'You know Zillah. She'll trust my judgement on this.'

'Yes.' Nick smiled. 'Of course. It shouldn't be for more than a month. I hope not anyway because I've put Hamish on a rather tricky job and he'll need back-up. Think you'll be fit enough in a month's time?'

'Sooner than that I hope.' Afterwards, recalling that he'd agreed to this 'tricky job' without thinking about it, Greg realised that he was at last free of the self-doubt and depression that had plagued him since the explosion in which Luke had died.

He pushed open the gate. Rocky decided Nick could be trusted with Greg and rushed in ahead of them to find Zillah. He had become used to following her around during her morning routines on the smallholding while Greg had been away.

As it happened she was just coming back up the path from the stables and she smiled with pleasure at seeing Nick with Greg.

'My two favourite men,' she said, giving Nick a big hug.

He stepped back, holding her at arm's length. 'You're looking as good as ever,' he said.

'Oh,' she said. 'Well, thankyou, but I would have preferred "better than".'

Nick and Greg laughed and putting her arms around them both she ushered them towards the kitchen. 'Coffee time,' she said.

When they were all seated around the kitchen table with their coffee, Greg told her what he'd arranged with Nick about going back to work.

She raised her eyebrows, then said, 'Nick, you always were a hard bastard.'

'True,' he said, 'But otherwise a gentleman, I hope.'

She didn't reply but shook her head and took a sip of coffee.

After a short silence Nick said, 'I don't know how much you know about what's been happening to Clarmont Brown's empire, Greg?'

'Well, Ray's been keeping me up to date about events on his patch. I gather Teddy Davis has been a great help to the police and so has his son, Spencer, and the other two we caught at Dan's, and GLH is being taken apart. As we expected they found clear evidence of people trafficking. The Marlows have been arrested, among others, Freddy Davis has had a heart attack so he's still in Spain, and they're still trying to find the Wilsons. Ray's delighted, of course. He's going to be able to close his Vanderling File at last.'

'And what about you? Debt repaid?'

Greg thought for a moment. Then he said, 'I'd have been content with seeing Bob sent to jail. I'm sure in my own mind he shot Nigel, and I think he killed Roddy too. Those are the two things I blame him for that affected my life directly. But it could never have been proved. I was glad to help Ray try to bring him to justice for his other crimes. But the way it's turned out he's got a different kind of life sentence.' He paused and looked at them both. 'I can't regret what happened to him, though.'

Nick gave him a steady look. 'It was you or him, wasn't it, in that room?'

Greg just nodded.

They were quiet for a while, sipping their coffee. Then Nick said, 'When I offered to send Hamish to help you on the Island, it wasn't just out of the goodness of my heart. You see, there's quite a bit of competition in the security market, internationally I mean, and Clarmont Brown's security firms were regularly undercutting me and getting contracts I thought I had in my pocket.'

Greg said, 'I remember Pete Grant telling me Bob had his own security companies, I think he said something about supplying private defence contractors abroad with staff from his security companies in UK.'

'That's right. And now, as a result of what you and Ray Tindall have done, with help from Hamish, Brown's empire is being dismantled. I want to pick up some of the pieces. That's why I want you to take over from Big Al in the office for a few weeks. I need his expertise where it really counts.'

Nick glanced at his watch and stood up. 'Now I must love you and leave you. Parting is such sweet sorrow and all that. Lovely to see you, Zillah. Thanks for the coffee. I'll see myself out.' He moved to the door and the others stood up. 'Sally will pick you up on Monday morning, then, Greg. Oh, and look, I know you've given statements to the police but if they need to interview you again, see if you can get them to come to you at the office, alright? Bye now.' And he was gone.

Zillah collected their coffee cups and took them to the sink to wash. She said, 'He doesn't change, does he? But he's been a good friend for a long time now.'

'Yes,' said Greg. He knew she would make no further comment about him going back to work so soon.

She threw him a tea towel. 'Here, make yourself useful. You've got some more visitors coming in a minute. Dan phoned just after you went out.'

'Oh, yes, of course, they were due back today.'

'Yes. He said they were expecting to find you still at his house, but when you weren't and there was not even a message from you, he rang Ray Tindall. Ray told him what had happened and that you were here. He was worried about you but I think I reassured him. Anyway, he said they'll be here as soon as they can.'

'They're both coming? That's a good sign.' Greg explained that the holiday together was partly a kind of trial for Dan and Lucy to see how compatible they were, and when they arrived at Zillah's house about an hour later, they were so obviously enthralled with each other that Greg's first words to them were: 'So when is the happy day?'

Dan grinned. 'It will be some time in early September, after the Regatta.'

'Wow! That's great!'

'But how are you, Greg, really?' said Dan.

'Pretty good. I'm fine. Superficial stuff, soon get over it.'

'Plus,' said Zillah, 'He's really, really brave and of course, he never complains.'

They laughed.

'So tell us all about it, Greg,' said Dan. 'Ray gave me a general idea on the phone, but what actually happened?'

So Greg gave them a summary of the events that had taken place after they left him on that Saturday morning two weeks earlier.

When he'd finished, Lucy said, hugging Dan's arm with both hands, 'Write it all down, Greg, will you? For Dan and me? For your grandchildren?'

'Grandchildren?' Greg, startled, looked from one to the other.

They were both smiling broadly.

Dan said, 'Well, you know, there may well be some in the not too distant future.'